Future Weird

FUTURE WEIRD

Science Fiction with a Touch of Strange

Edited by Jason V Brock

Hippocampus Press

New York

Published by Hippocampus Press
P.O. Box 641, New York, NY 10156
www.hippocampuspress.com

Cover illustration and design © 2025 by Ovidio Cartagena. Layout
and production by Daniel V. Sauer.
Hippocampus Press logo designed by Anastasia Damianakos.

First Edition
1 3 5 7 9 8 6 4 2
ISBN 978-1-61498-436-8

Contents

Foreword: In Extremis

John C. Tibbetts

"There is a secret affinity, a *hankering* after evil in the human mind," wrote critic William Hazlitt, which, perversely, "is a never-failing source of satisfaction."[1] He must have been anticipating the effect of this collection of stories. The pages are touched with fire, and while our fingers flinch at the touch, we fairly savor each story and watch, delighted, as each of their characters "goes to the Devil its own way." We follow, of course.

It's a transformative experience. What editor Jason V Brock has done is to delve into an extreme kind of storytelling, what contemporary critic Gary K. Wolfe has dubbed "recombinant genre fiction," i.e., writing that "destabilizes" generic constructions and demands a reinvention of ways we read genre.[2] Thus, we are plunged into the extremities and quantum dislocations of time, space, and behaviors human and artificial—but to what end?

Thus my title: *In Extremis.*

We find in this constellation of writers those proto-masters of horror-tinged Gothic and SF, H. G. Wells and William Hope Hodgson; those ever-reliable contemporary masters of the game, Harlan Ellison, Charles Beaumont, James Gunn, William F. Nolan, Robert Silverberg, John Shirley, Bruce Taylor, F. Paul Wilson, Larry Niven and Jerry Pournelle, Ray Faraday Nelson, Robert J. Sawyer, and several writers who may be new to the more general reader, Steven-Elliot Altman, Sèphera Girón, Stephen Woodworth, Darrell Schweitzer, Jonathan Thomas, and Sunni K Brock.

---

1. William Hazlitt, "On the Pleasure of Hating," in *Selected Writings,* ed. Ronald Blythe (New York: Penguin, 1970), 398–99.
2. Gary K. Wolfe, *Evaporating Genres* (Middletown, CT: Wesleyan University Press, 2011), 13.

Apocalypse comes in many shapes and sizes, as envisioned in several classics of the form found in these pages. Certainly, in the realms of Past–Present–Future Weird the theme of catastrophe has always been, continues to be, and—God help us—always will be with us. As Susan Sontag has rightly pointed out, it "is one of the oldest subjects of art, with its aesthetics of destruction, with the peculiar beauties to be found in wreaking havoc, making a mess."[3] In H. G. Wells's classic from 1897, "The Star," Martian observers examine with clinical coldness the near-destruction of Earth. Harlan Ellison's dystopian "I Have No Mouth, and I Must Scream" is a chilling prediction of what happens when a "Master Computer" wakes up and, for the first time, *knew who he was.* Niven and Pournelle's "Story Night at the Stronghold" is a post-apocalypse *Decameron* occasioned when a comet "way brighter than the sun came down and split the sea." The quietest apocalypse on record is the great Charles Beaumont's "Elegy," which gives new meaning to the "Eternal Rest" promised by the funeral industry. By contrast to the foregoing, James Gunn's "Monsters" is a disarming fable in the manner of Jack Finney (bless him!) about "The best Halloween ever," when the great Gothic creatures Dracula, Frankenstein, and the Wolfman are recruited against invading aliens.

The arts come under—well, under fire, in Sèphera Girón's excruciating vision of the ballet of the future. What happens to creativity when cyber technology tests human frailty? And what happens in Steven-Elliot Altman's "Camera Aeterna" when a breakthrough in photographic technology confronts the Vatican with proof of life after death? After reading F. Paul Wilson's "Performance," we ask, where can we watch "performance art" like *this?*—or would we want to? Crossword puzzles and word games are here, too—in case we consider them as an art form: Jonathan Thomas's "One Across" is an amusing crossword puzzle of "quantum readjustments" à la Henry Kuttner; and Sunni Brock's "AGNES" (Adaptive Generative Natural

---

3. Susan Sontag, "The Imagination of Disaster," in *Against Interpretation* (New York: Dell, 1966), 213.

Emulation System) plays a wicked game of word/*weird* association.

Erotic love and sex embrace in the horrific body horror of George Edwards Murray's "They Will All Be Opened in Time" and Nancy Kilpatrick's "Metal Fatigue." The first describes something called "Utolon Love" ("He had seen every corruption of the flesh imaginable"); and the second discloses what really goes on during those marathon couplings between humans and aliens in abduction narratives.

Less easily classifiable—and indeed, that is the point—are the following:

Nelson's "Eight O'Clock in the Morning" offers a deadly spin on "wokeness" culture in a cartoonish, Gahan Wilson–inflected suggestion that your neighbor may be a lizard. This story was the basis of the cult John Carpenter socio-political/SF/horror film *They Live*.

In his affectionate tribute to his old friend, Ray Bradbury, the late William F. Nolan warns in "On Big Red" that the Mars we now presume to be dead might be really populated by the ghosts of a vanished race. It's a beautiful pastiche and a moving one.

Silverberg's "It Comes and Goes" delivers on its titular promise, offering up a neighborhood dwelling that has the disconcerting habit of vanishing not once, not twice, but . . . Well, there goes the neighborhood.

In Schweitzer's "The Secret Language of Stones" a modern-day Superman watches and listens to the march of millennia.

The mystery of the "ghost ship" *Marie Celeste* has nothing on the spaceship in Stephen Woodworth's "Celeste."

In "Full Circle," Bruce Taylor asks, just how many time-space streams *are* there, anyway, and where do they intersect?

In "Peking Man" Robert J. Sawyer takes us on an archaeological dig into the primordial origins of the vampire.

In "Magnus Victor Rex," Lisa Mannetti insists that Rome was not built in a day . . . It's still happening. Welcome to the Rex Regime and its algorithmic Rabbit Hole, where, as they say, nothing succeeds like excess. . . . Yes, and now, Let the Games Begin.

Finally, two stories cast us up on the shores of wonder, leaving us with not a little bewilderment and, let's face it, a measure of shuddery confusion and outrage. Each calls for special consideration. John Shirley's "Seven Rooms and the Key" takes its protagonist, Kolt, who has been too long under a "quantum-uncertainty influence," on a tour of the "seven chambers of the subconscious" of an interdimensional house of mirrors, winding corridors, and secret keyholes. I must confess the story baffles me. It is a "splinter world" where "things are what they seem," but are "less than they are." As a tour de force of dazzling prose and ever-changing imagery, it may be compared to the experience of viewing Jean Cocteau's surreal cinematic fantasy *Blood of a Poet* (1931). And any story that can do *that*, my friends, ain't bad in my book.

William Hope Hodgson is in top form in the classic "Eloi, Eloi, Lama Sabachthani." Written in 1912 under the title "The Darkening" and published posthumously as "The Baumoff Explosive" in 1919, it confronts us with nothing less than the Crucifixion and last words of Jesus Christ. The monstrous perversion, "a Christ-apeing Monster of the Void," that appears and voices the words "Eloi, Eloi, lama sabachthani!" ("My God, why hast thou forsaken me?"), is cosmic horror on a scale that even Hodgson seldom equaled. Historian Sam Moskowitz regards it as a "successful, pioneering effort . . . to accept one of more theosophical concepts as *fact*" and weave it "into the format of science fiction." It anticipates similar attempts by Ray Bradbury, James Blish, and Arthur C. Clarke."[4]

And now, if you still have that *hankering*, you may proceed.

---

4. Sam Moskowitz, ed., *Out of the Storm: Uncollected Fantasies by William Hope Hodgson* (Donald Grant, 1975), 98–99. I might add that Hodgson's story seems to evoke a later moment in the history of painter Francis Bacon, who, in his notorious "Three Studies of the Crucifixion" (1944), viewed the event as a "magnificent armature" from which to suspend "all types of feeling and sensation." See www.guggenheim.org/artwork/293.

The Weird Future, Past and Present

Jason V Brock

> A time is coming when men will go mad, and when they see some-
> one who is not mad, they will attack him, saying, "You are mad; you
> are not like us."
>
> —*St. Anthony the Great*

If one were to visualize the totality of human creative effort as a solar system, with ideas manifesting as the sun and its various branches—film, music, literature, visual or performing art, etc.—as planets,
it becomes easier to contemplate such forms of expression in a more
detailed and concrete manner than abstract theory alone affords.

For illustrative purposes, examining the planet of literary output,
one could imagine written works as a sort of "psychotopography"
adrift in an endless ocean of collective imagination. With this as a
construct, it becomes apparent how the major and minor aspects of
writing, language, and genre shape human thought. Indeed, the
great *forms* of writing—poetry, theatre, short fiction, the novel, nonfiction, and so on—could be envisioned as vast continents. Upon
these landmasses, genres (whether a combination or extraction of
various types) reveal themselves, conceptually, as clusters of distinct
"psychogeographical" feature sets: colossal mountains of literary fiction, tangled forests of horror, mysterious plains of crime, dusty
Western desert valleys, cool still lakes of erotica, winding rivers of
historical romance, fogbound coasts of fantasy, the boundless fron-
tiers of science fiction.

With this in mind, one is able to survey and map the richness of
human experience using chosen forms of expression as a foundation
(short fiction or novel, for instance), and genre (type) to build—or
destroy, depending on the reason and subtext—populations (charac-

ters), cities (environments), even societies (purpose), in these shared mental logoscapes. The result—with authors as guides, and their audience as voyeuristic explorers of this psychically abutting terrain—is artistic accomplishment, to a greater or lesser extent, depending on what one has to say (message), and how well one communicates it (innate talent and/or ability). The way one coveys these insights (style and craft) is also a part of this, as well as the overall reason for doing so (vision). All these components must be evident in the final output, and they must be working together harmoniously to achieve the lasting impact of genuine artistry.

Accomplishment, whether by genius or fool, is one thing; success is yet another, and is orders of magnitude rarer than failure. In other words, most artistic endeavors fail *utterly*, and no art is *ever* wholly satisfying to everyone: there are always shortcomings and criticisms to one degree or other due to the subjective nature of experiencing such things. The initial point to create, therefore, should be for self-expression (internal rationale for production; alleviation of emotional tension) and to reach the interior of *others* (external motivating reason for sharing one's conceptions with another). These incentives may become displaced over time if one becomes "successful" by the external metrics of exploitation: commerce (financial remuneration), critical acclaim, or some other shallow element which appeals to the insecure ego's vanity (for example adherence to tribal affiliation, peer adulation, or pandering to audience expectations). After all, objective success (versus the relative success of accomplishing one's goals on their own terms) can only be measured over time, and by the consumers of the works—not by the critics, academics, creators, or their families and friends—as "consumers over time" (audience plus word-of-mouth) are the final arbiters of what will be remembered with relation to posterity, not awards, reviews, media adaptation, or even monetary success.

Thus we come to places in this psychotopography where the general public finds, their mercurial attention akin to weather fronts, comfort—at least for a time, focused and influenced by the social mores and political realities of the era in which such works are created: the stark badlands of Noir; the powerful gyrations of the thriller; the wispy edges of magical realism. Narrower, yet less captivating, are the patriotic, gun-toting denizens of the military sci-fi heartland, the shellshocked survivors of splatterpunk's urban decay; farther out, slighter varietals mine other elements, with greater or lesser success; in these recursive, often derivative collectives there is no concept of history or the future, only an eternal, cheerless present content to harangue and pester its proponents with topical (and ultimately to-be-outdated) social critique. At these extremes, the effects of artistic gravity and emotional weight are weaker and probably doomed to degrade over time into non-existence, to say nothing of the general lack of craft and finesse in many, though not all, such efforts. To remain relevant, these fringes typically must rely not on satellites of inspiration or comets of rejuvenation by way of genre-mixing or media reinterpretation, but on the toxic erosion of guilt and the sharp edges of faux outrage to stir up interest, even as they shuffle into the yawning tarpits of dreary oblivion, already overwhelmed by the sheer number of similarly lackluster and uninspired creators who came before them.

Bearing this in mind, the present volume is not preoccupied with any particular political *cause célèbre* or social topic *du jour*. The stories herein detail a wide gamut of politics and social perspectives and strive to mix various aspects of genre together to achieve a certain cumulative unity of effect, namely a future-oriented examination of things strange, odd, or uncanny. In every case, these tales are intended to reflect the state of the human condition, not necessarily conditions created by humans. Interiority and the subtextual are the point; the surface is merely the delivery mechanism, the entertainment used to misdirect the disquieting metaphysical inoculation of outré thought and observation.

In order to understand possible futures, it is often instructive to examine the past mindfully; to that end, this book is not a collection of all-new material, but roughly comprised of half new and half older works that fit the theme of *Future Weird: Science Fiction with a*

Touch of Strange (conceptually with thanks to the late author George Clayton Johnson). All the stories within share discernible science-fiction features while also striking discordant, at times alarming, notes to achieve the aims of a specific author. These outsider aspects are sometimes profound and in other instances trivial, and though there are hints of political or social commentary in some, that is not the point of their inclusion.

The reason for including them is to demonstrate the scope and breadth of the "non-Lovecraftian" mode of the weird subgenre (as exemplified in the cosmicism of Lovecraft and his adherents, such as Thomas Ligotti, W. H. Pugmire, et al.) to inform and underscore its importance and flexibility as a method of expression in combination with another, more readily identifiable genre, in this case science fiction. As a literary expression, trope, and tradition, the "weird" has had a huge modern revival. Since its legendary heyday in the early part of the twentieth century, it has been studied, discussed, and explored in innumerable articles and stories, with conceptions of it stretched to paper-thin understandings of what—exactly—constitutes a purely "weird tale." Is it simply a story about strange happenings? Is it a form of the so-called "quiet" horror tale? Is it related to the magical realism genre? Is it something completely different? Is it all these things, or none of them? The only attribute unlikely to be disputed is that these stories are often best ingested in shorter forms, and that they provoke visceral, psychological, and emotional reactions quite different from typical horror yarns or *contes cruels*, from the numinous to the terrifying to the disturbingly revelatory (sometimes all at once).

Another aspect of attempting to grasp the undeniable appeal of weird stories is, perhaps, this maddening nebulousness; what elicits such fascination with the works created within its strictures is that there is no fixed way to express what, precisely, they do to the reader aside from creeping them out. To that end, it appears there must be some way of quantifying what the term (and thus the movement) encompasses, the boundaries it draws to distinguish efforts designated as "weird" from things that are just odd stories, or pieces using mysterious elements of disquiet to evoke a mood of dread or foreboding (and, sometimes, disgust). There should be, if the weird is more than the sum of its parts, a way to divine what comprises something that is properly weird from just a weird story, in other words.

No doubt, many people have had a crack at defining the weird. H. P. Lovecraft himself observed in his insightful 1927 essay "Supernatural Horror in Literature":

> The true weird tale has something more than secret murder, bloody bones, or a sheeted form clanking chains according to rule. A certain atmosphere of breathless and unexplainable dread of outer, unknown forces must be present; and there must be a hint, expressed with a seriousness and portentousness becoming its subject, of that most terrible conception of the human brain—a malign and particular suspension or defeat of those fixed laws of Nature which are our only safeguard against the assaults of chaos and the daemons of unplumbed space.

Since then, entire books have taken on the task, as have modern podcasts, websites, literary digests, and conferences. However, no one seems to have placed their finger completely on what makes something a weird tale proper. This stands in marked contrast to other genres, which are generally easy to define. The weird as a narrative type straddles a vast expanse in popular culture, at least in the literary realm. Elements of it may be found in the disparate works of numerous authors not traditionally thought of as dedicated practitioners of the form, be it the "strange stories" of Robert Aickman, the ghost stories of M. R. James, the magical realism of Gabriel García Márquez, Jorge Luis Borges's output, Ambrose Bierce, Edgar Allan Poe, Greg Bear, Franz Kafka, Ray Bradbury, James Tiptree, Jr., William S. Burroughs, and many more, to include several writers represented in this very volume, such as Charles Beaumont, William Hope Hodgson, and H. G. Wells.

Of course, science fiction also has an impressive pedigree, and, though there were antecedents to it, it is often identified as formally

conceived in its modern iteration by the seminal *Frankenstein; or,
The Modern Prometheus* by Mary Shelley in 1818—a work not only
of singular influence, but also a mélange of nascent science fictional
elements and Gothic horror. To borrow from this longstanding
precedent of commingling genres, combining the weird with science
fiction synergistically imbues the resulting stories with a power greater
than either a "purely" science-fictional or weird narrative alone might.

Obviously, there are other pieces which could fall under the organizing principle of *Future Weird,* both from the past and as yet
unwritten. It is hoped that this book will have other volumes to ac-
company it; inclusions would consist of new contemporary writers,
of course, as well as other relatively obscure classics from the past,
possibly from the likes of Kurt Vonnegut, Walter M. Miller, Jr.,
Philip K. Dick, J. G. Ballard, Cordwainer Smith, Richard Matheson,
Rod Serling, Theodore Sturgeon, Philip José Farmer, and others.

The future is indeed a weird place and time. Inevitably, it is the
singular point that everyone is headed toward, even though each
person's past is unique; through the dividing lens (and at times mirror) of the present, there is an opportunity to appreciate this fact,
and thereby to grasp the broader understanding of how people,
events, and places are ultimately bound together by fate, humanity,
and circumstance.

Elegy

Charles Beaumont

"Would you mind repeating that?"

"I said, sir, that Mr. Friden said, sir, that he sees a city."

"A city?"

"Yes sir."

Captain Webber rubbed the back of his hand along his cheek.

"You realize, of course, that that is impossible?"

"Yes, sir."

"Send Mr. Friden in to see me, at once."

The young man saluted and rushed out of the room. He returned with a somewhat older man who wore spectacles and frowned.

"Now then," said Captain Webber, "what's all this Lieutenant Peterson tells me about a city? Are you enjoying a private little joke, Friden?"

Mr. Friden shook his head emphatically. "No, sir."

"Then perhaps you'd like to explain."

"Well, sir, you see, I was getting bored and just for something to do, I thought I'd look through the screen—not that I dreamed of seeing anything. The instruments weren't adjusted, either; but there was something funny, something I couldn't make out exactly."

"Go on," said Captain Webber, patiently.

"So I fixed up the instruments and took another look, and there it was, sir, plain as could be!"

"There *what* was?"

"The city, sir. Oh, I couldn't tell much about it, but there were houses, all right, a lot of them."

"Houses, you say?"

"Yes sir, on an asteroid."

Captain Webber looked for a long moment at Mr. Friden and began to pace nervously.

"I take it you know what this might mean?"

"Yes sir, I do. That's why I wanted Lieutenant Peterson to tell you about it."

"I believe, Friden, that before we do any more talking I'll see this city for myself."

*

Captain Webber, Lieutenant Peterson and Mr. Friden walked from the room down a long corridor and into a smaller room. Captain Webber put his eye to a circular glass and tapped his foot.

He stepped back and rubbed his cheek again.

"Well, you were right. That *is* a city—or else we've all gone crazy. Do you think that we have?"

"I don't know, sir. It's not impossible."

"Lieutenant, go ask Mr. Milton if he can land us on an asteroid. Give him all the details and be back in ten minutes." Captain Webber sighed. "Whatever it is," he said, "it will be a relief. Although I never made a special announcement, I suppose you knew that we were lost."

"Oh yes, sir."

"And that we ran almost entirely out of fuel several months ago, in fact shortly after we left?"

"We knew that."

The men were silent.

"Sir, Mr. Milton says he thinks he can land us but he can't promise exactly where."

"Tell Mr. Milton that's good enough."

Captain Webber waited for the young man to leave, then looked again into the glass.

"What do you make of it, sir?"

"Not much, Friden, not much. It's a city and that's an asteroid; but how the devil they got there is beyond me. I still haven't left the idea that we're crazy, you know."

Mr. Friden looked.

"We're positioning to land. Strange—"

"What is it?"

"I can make things out a bit more clearly now, sir. Those are earth houses."

Captain Webber looked. He blinked.

"Now, *that*," he said, "*is* impossible. Look here, we've been floating about in space for—how long is it?"

"Three months, sir."

"Exactly. For three months we've been bobbling aimlessly, millions of miles from earth. No hope, no hope whatever. And now we're landing in a city just like the one we first left, or almost like it. Friden, I ask you, does that make any sense at all?"

"No, sir."

"And does it seem logical that there should be an asteroid where no asteroid should be?"

"It does not."

They stared at the glass, by turns.

"Do you see that, Friden?"

"I'm afraid so, sir."

"A lake. A lake and a house by it and trees . . . tell me, how many of us are left?"

Mr. Friden held up his right hand and began unbending fingers.

"Yourself, sir, and myself; Lieutenant Peterson, Mr. Chitterwick, Mr. Goeblin, Mr. Milton and . . ."

"Great Scott, out of thirty men?"

"You know how it was, sir. That business with the Martians and then, our own difficulties—"

"Yes. Our own difficulties. Isn't it ironic, somehow, Friden? We band together and fly away from war and, no sooner are we off the Earth but we begin other wars. . . . I've often felt that if Appleton hadn't been so aggressive with that gun we would never have been kicked off Mars. And why did we have to laugh at them? Oh, I'm afraid I haven't been a very successful captain."

"You're in a mood, sir."

"Am I? I suppose I am. Look! There's a farm, an actual farm!"

"Not really!"

"Why, I haven't seen one for twenty years."

The door flew open and Lieutenant Peterson came in, panting. "Mr. Milton checked off every instruction, sir, and we're going down now."

"He's sure there's enough fuel left for the brake?"

"He thinks so, sir."

"Lieutenant Peterson."

"Yes, sir?"

"Come look into this glass, will you."

The young man looked.

"What do you see?"

"A lot of strange creatures, sir. Are they dangerous? Should we prepare our weapons?"

"How old are you, Lieutenant?"

"Nineteen, Captain Webber."

"You have just seen a herd of cows, for the most part—" Captain Webber squinted and twirled knobs "—Holsteins."

"Holsteins, sir?"

"You may go. Oh, you might tell the others to prepare for a crash landing. Straps and all that."

The young man smiled faintly and left.

"I'm a little frightened, Friden; I think I'll go to my cabin. Take charge and have them wait for my orders."

Captain Webber saluted tiredly and walked back down the long corridor. He paused as the machines suddenly roared more life, rubbed his cheek and went into the small room.

"Cows," said Captain Webber bracing himself.

*

The fiery leg fell into the cool air, heating it, causing it to smoke; it burnt into the green grass and licked a craterous hole.

There were fireflags and firesparks, hisses and explosions and the weary groaning sound of a great beast suddenly roused from sleep.

The rocket landed. It grumbled and muttered for a while on its finny tripod, then was silent; soon the heat vanished also.

"Are you all right, sir?"

"Yes. The rest?"

"All but Mr. Chitterwick. He broke his glasses and says he can't see."

Captain Webber swung himself erect and tested his limbs. "Well then, Lieutenant, has the atmosphere been checked?"

"The air is pure and fit to breathe, sir."

"Instruct the others to drop the ladder."

"Yes, sir."

A door in the side of the rocket opened laboriously and men began climbing out: "Look!" said Mr. Milton, pointing. "There are trees and grass and—over there, little bridges going over the water."

He pointed to a row of small white houses with green gardens and stony paths.

Beyond the trees was a brick lodge, extended over a rivulet which foamed and bubbled. Fishing poles protruded from the lodge window.

"And there, to the right!"

A steel building thirty stories high with a pink cloud near the top. And, separated by a hedge, a brown tent with a barbeque pit before it, smoke rising in a rigid ribbon from the chimney.

Mr. Chitterwick blinked and squinted his eyes. "What do you see?"

Distant and near, houses of stone and brick and wood, painted all colors, small, large; and further, golden fields of wheat, each blown by a different breeze in a different direction.

"I don't believe it," said Captain Webber. "It's a *park*—millions of miles away from where a park could possibly be."

"Strange but familiar," said Lieutenant Peterson, picking up a rock.

Captain Webber looked in all directions. "We were lost. Then we see a city where no city should be, on an asteroid not shown on any chart, and we manage to land. And now we're in the middle of a place that belongs in history-records. We may be crazy; we may all be wandering around in space and dreaming."

The little man with the thin hair who had just stepped briskly from a treeclump said, "Well, well," and the men jumped.

The little man smiled. "Aren't you a trifle late or early or something?"

Captain Webber turned and his mouth dropped open.

"I hadn't been expecting you, gentlemen, to be perfectly honest," the little man clucked, then: "Oh dear, see what you've done to Mr. Bellefont's park. I do hope you haven't hurt him—no, I see that he is all right."

Captain Webber followed the direction of the man's eyes and perceived an old man with red hair seated at the base of a tree, apparently reading a book.

"We are from Earth," said Captain Webber.

"Yes, yes."

"Let me explain: my name is Webber, these are my men."

"Of course," said the little man.

Mr. Chitterwick came closer, blinking. "Who is this that knows our language?" he asked.

"Who—Greypoole, Mr. Greypoole. Didn't *they* tell you?"

"Then you are *also* from Earth?"

"Heavens yes! But now, let us go where we can chat more comfortably." Mr. Greypoole struck out down a small path past scorched trees and underbrush. "You know, Captain, right after the last consignment something happened to my calendar. Now, I'm competent at my job, but I'm no technician, no indeed: besides, no doubt you or one of your men can set the doodad right, eh? Here we are."

They walked onto a wooden porch and through a door with a wire screen; Lieutenant Peterson first, then Captain Webber, Mr. Friden and the rest of the crew. Mr. Greypoole followed.

"You must forgive me—it's been a while. Take chairs, there, there. Now, what news of—home, shall I say?" The little man stared.

Captain Webber shifted uncomfortably. He glanced around the room at the lace curtains, the needle-point tapestries and the lavender wallpaper.

"Mr. Greypoole, I'd like to ask some questions."

"Certainly, certainly. But first, this being an occasion—" the little man stared at each man carefully, then shook his head "—ah, do you all like wine? Good wine?"

He ducked through a small door.

Captain Webber exhaled and rose.

"Now, don't start talking all at once," he whispered. "Anyone have any ideas? No? Then quick, scout around—Friden, you stay here; you others, see what you can find. I'm not sure I like the looks of this."

The men left the room.

*

Mr. Chitterwick made his way along a hedgerow, feeling cautiously and maintaining a delicate balance. When he came to a doorway he stopped, squinted and entered.

The room was dark and quiet and odorous. Mr. Chitterwick groped a few steps, put out his hand and encountered what seemed to be raw flesh; he swiftly withdrew his hand. "Excuse," he said, then, "Oh!" as his face came against a slab of moist red meat. "Oh my!"

Mr. Chitterwick began to tremble and he blinked furiously, reaching out and finding flesh, cold and hard, unidentifiable.

When he stepped upon the toe of a large man with a walrus mustache, he wheeled, located the sunlight and ran from the butcher shop. . . .

*

The door of the temple opened with difficulty, which caused Mr. Milton to breathe unnaturally. Then, once inside, he gasped.

Row upon row of people, their fingers outstretched, lips open but immobile and silent, their bodies prostrate on the floor. And upon a strange black altar, a tiny woman with silver hair and a long thyrsus in her right hand.

Nothing stirred but the mosaic squares in the walls. The colors danced here; otherwise, everything was frozen, everything was solid.

Even the air hung suspended, stationary.

Mr. Milton left the temple. . . .

*

There was a table and a woman on the table and people all around the woman on the table. Mr. Goeblin did not go a great distance from the doorway: he rubbed his eyes and stared.

It was an operating room. There were all the instruments, some old, most old, and the masked men and women with shining scissors and glistening saws in their hands. And up above, the students' aperture: filled seats, filled aisles.

Mr. Goeblin put his other hand about the doorknob.

A large man stood over the recumbent figure, his lusterless eyes regarding the crimson-puce incision, but he did not move. The nurses did not move, or the students. No one moved, especially the smiling middle-aged woman on the table.

Mr. Goeblin moved. . . .

*

"Hello!" said Lieutenant Peterson, after he had searched through eight long aisles of books, "Hello!"

He pointed his gun menacingly.

There were many books with many titles and they all had a fine grey dust about them. Lieutenant Peterson paused to examine a bulky volume, when he happened to look above him.

"Who are you?" he demanded.

The mottled, angular man perched atop the ladder did not respond. He clutched a book and looked at the book and not at Lieutenant Peterson.

"Come down—I want to talk with you!"

The man on the ladder did nothing unusual: he remained precisely as he had been.

Lieutenant Peterson climbed up the ladder, scowling; he reached the man and jabbed with a finger.

Lieutenant Peterson looked into the eyes of the reading man and descended hastily and did not say goodbye. . . .

*

Mr. Greypoole reentered the living room with a tray of glasses. "This is apricot wine," he announced, distributing the glasses, "But—where are the others? Out for a walk? Ah well, they can drink theirs later. Incidentally, Captain, how many Guests did you bring? Last time it was only twelve. Not an extraordinary shipment, either: they all preferred the ordinary things. All but Mrs. Dominguez— dear me, she was worth the carload herself. Wanted a zoo, can you imagine—a regular zoo, with her put right in the bird-house. Oh, they had a time putting that one up!"

Mr. Greypoole chuckled and sipped at his drink.

"It's people like Mrs. Dominguez who put the—the life?—into Happy Glades. Or do you find that disrespectful?"

Captain Webber shook his head and tossed down his drink.

Mr. Greypoole leaned back in his chair and crossed a leg. "Ah," he continued, "you have no idea how good this is. Once in a while it does get lonely for me here—no man is an island, or how does it go? Why, I can remember when Mr. Waldmeyer first told me of this idea. 'A grave responsibility,' he said, 'a *grave* responsibility.' Mr. Waldmeyer has a keen sense of humor, needless to say."

Captain Webber looked out the window. A small child on roller skates stood still on the sidewalk. Mr. Greypoole laughed.

"Finished your wine? Good. Explanations are in order, though first perhaps you'd care to join me in a brief turn about the premises?"

"Fine. Friden, you stay here and wait for the men." Captain Webber winked a number of times and frowned briefly, then he and

Mr. Greypoole walked out onto the porch and down the steps.

Mr. Friden drummed his fingers upon the arm of a chair, surveyed his empty glass and hiccoughed softly.

*

"I do wish you'd landed your ship elsewhere, Captain. Mr. Bellefont was quite particular and, as you can see, his park is hopelessly disfigured."

"We were given no choice, I'm afraid. The fuel was running out."

"Indeed? Well then, that explains everything. A beautiful day, don't you find, sir? Fortunately, with the exception of Professor Carling, all the Guests preferred good weather. Plenty of sunshine, they said, or crisp evening. It helps."

They walked toward a house of colored rocks.

"Miss Daphne Trilling's," said Mr. Greypoole, gesturing. "They threw it up in a day, though it's solid enough."

When they had passed an elderly woman on a bicycle, Captain Webber stopped walking.

"Mr. Greypoole, we've *got* to have a talk."

Mr. Greypoole shrugged and pointed and they went into an office building which was crowded with motionless men, women and children.

"Since I'm so mixed up myself," the captain said, "maybe I'd better ask—just who do you think *we* are?"

"I'd thought you to be the men from the Glades of course."

"I don't have the slightest idea what you're talking about. We're from the planet Earth. They were going to have another war, the 'Last War' they said, and we escaped in that rocket and started off for Mars. But something went wrong—fellow named Appleton pulled a gun, others just didn't like the Martians—we needn't go into it; they wouldn't have us so Mars didn't work out. Something else went wrong then, soon we were lost with only a little store of fuel and supplies. Then Mr. Friden noticed this city or whatever it is and we had enough fuel to land so we landed."

Mr. Greypoole nodded his head slowly, somehow, sadder than before.

"I see. . . . You say there was a war on Earth?"

"They were going to set off X-Bomb; when they do, everything will go to pieces. Or everything has already."

"What dreadful news! May I inquire, Captain, when you have learned where you are—what do you intend to do?"

"Why, live here, of course!"

"No, no—try to understand. You could not conceivably fit in here with us."

Captain Webber glanced at the motionless people. "Why not?" Then he shouted, "What is this place? *Where am I?*"

Mr. Greypoole smiled.

"Captain, you are in a cemetery."

*

"Good work, Peterson!"

"Thanks, sir. When we all got back and Friden didn't know where you'd gone, well, we got worried. Then we heard you shouting."

"Hold his arms—there. You heard this, Friden?"

Mr. Friden was trembling slightly. He brushed past a man with a van Dyke beard and sat down on a leather stool. "Yes sir, I did. That is, I think I did. What shall we do with him?"

"I don't know, yet. Take him away, Lieutenant, for now. I want to think a bit. We'll talk to Mr. Greypoole later on."

Lieutenant Peterson pulled the smiling little man out into the street and pointed a gun at him.

Mr. Chitterwick blinked into the face of a small child.

"Man's insane, I guess," said Mr. Milton, pacing.

"Yes, but what about all *this?*" Mr. Goeblin looked horrified at the stationary people.

"I think I can tell you," Mr. Friden said. "Take a look, Captain."

The men crowded about a pamphlet which Mr. Friden had placed on the stool.

Toward the top of the pamphlet and in the center of the first page was a photograph, untinted and solemn; it depicted a white cherub delicately poised on a granite slab. Beneath the photograph, were the words: HAPPY GLADES.

Captain Webber turned the pages and mumbled, glancing over his shoulder every once in a while.

"What is it, sir?" asked Mr. Chitterwick of a frozen man in a blue suit with copper buttons.

"It's one of those old level cemeteries!" cried Mr. Milton. "I remember seeing pictures like it, sir."

Captain Webber read aloud from the pamphlet.

"For fifty years," he began, "an outstanding cultural and spiritual asset to this community, HAPPY GLADES is proud to announce yet another innovation in its program of post-benefits. NOW YOU CAN ENJOY THE AFTER-LIFE IN SURROUNDINGS WHICH SUGGEST THE HERE-AND-NOW. Never before in history has scientific advancement allowed such a plan."

Captain Webber turned the page.

"For those who prefer that their late departed have really *permanent, eternal* happiness, for those who are dismayed by the fragility of all things mortal, we of HAPPY GLADES are proud to offer:

"1. The permanent duplication of physical conditions identical to those enjoyed by the departed on Earth. Park, playground, lodge, office building, hotel or house, etc., may be secured at varying prices. All workmanship and materials specially attuned to conditions on ASTEROID K_7 and guaranteed for PERMANENCE.

"2. PERMANENT conditioning of late beloved so that, in the midst of surroundings he favored, a genuine Eternity may be assured.

"3. Full details on HAPPY GLADES' newest property, Asteroid K_7, may be found on page 4."

The captain tossed the pamphlet to the floor and lit a cigarette. "Did anyone happen to notice the date?"

Mr. Milton said, "It doesn't make any sense! There haven't been cemeteries for ages. And even if this were true, why should anyone want to go all the way through space to a little asteroid? They might just as well have built these things on Earth."

"Who would want all this when they're dead, anyway?"

"You mean all these people are dead?"

For a few moments there was complete and utter silence in the lobby of the building.

*

"Are those things true, that we read in your booklet?" asked Captain Webber after Lieutenant Peterson had brought in the prisoner.

"Every word," said the little man bowing slightly, "is monumentally correct."

"Then we want you to begin explaining."

Mr. Greypoole tushed and proceeded to straighten the coat of a middle-aged man with a cigar.

Mr. Goeblin shuddered.

"No, no," laughed Mr. Greypoole, "*these* are only imitations. Mr. Conklin upstairs was head of a large firm; absolutely in love with his work, you know—that kind of thing. So we had to duplicate not only the office, but the building and even replicas of all the people in the building. Mr. Conklin himself is in an easy chair on the twentieth story."

"*And?*"

"Well, gentlemen, as you know, Happy Glades is the outstanding mortuary on Earth. And, to put it briefly, with the constant explorations of planets and moons and whatnot, our Mr. Waldmeyer hit upon this scheme: Seeking to extend the ideal hereafter to our Guests, we bought out this little asteroid. With the vast volume and the tremendous turnover, as it were, we got our staff of scientists together and they offered this plan—to duplicate the exact surroundings which the Guest most enjoyed in Life, assure him privacy, permanence (a *very* big point, as you can see), and all the small things not possible on Earth."

"Why here, why cart off a million miles or more when the same thing could have been done on Earth?"

"My communication system went bad, I fear, so I haven't heard from the offices in some while—but, I am to understand there is a war beginning? *That* is the idea, Captain; one could never really be sure of one's self down there, what with all the new bombs and things being discovered."

"Hmm," said Captain Webber.

"Then too, Mr. Waldmeyer worried about those new societies with their dreadful ideas about cremation—you can see what that sort of thing could do to the undertaking business? His plan caught on, however, and soon we were having to turn away Guests."

"And where do you fit in, Mr. Greypoole?"

The little man seemed to blush; he lowered his eyes. "I was head caretaker, you see. But I wasn't well—gastric complaints, liver, heart palpitations, this and that; so, I decided to allow them to . . . *change* me. They turned all manner of machines on my body and pumped me full of fluids and by the time I got here, why, I was almost, you might say, a machine myself! Fortunately, though, they left a good deal of Greypoole. All I know is that whenever the film is punctured, I wake and become a machine, do my prescribed duties in a complex way and—"

"The film?"

"The covering that seals in the conditioning. Nothing can get out, nothing get in—except things like rockets. Then, it's self-sealing, needless to say. But to get on, Captain. With all the technical advancements, it soon got to where there was no real work to be done here; they threw up the film and coated us with their preservative or, as they put it, Eternifier, and—well, with the exception of my calendar and the communications system, everything's worked perfectly, including myself."

*

No one said anything for a while. Then Captain Webber said, with great slowness, "You're lying. This is all a crazy, hideous plot." The little man chuckled at the word plot.

"In the first place, no cemetery or form of cemetery has existed on Earth for—how long, Friden?"

Mr. Friden stared at his fingers. "Years and years."

"Exactly. There are communal furnaces now."

Mr. Greypoole winced.

"And furthermore," continued the captain, "this whole concept is ridiculous."

Mr. Chitterwick threw down the pamphlet and began to tremble. "We should have stayed home," he remarked to a young woman who did not answer.

"Mr. Greypoole," Webber said, "I think that you know more than you're saying. You didn't seem very surprised when you learned we weren't the men you expected; you don't seem very surprised now that I tell you that your 'Happy Glades' and all the people connected with it have been dead for ages. So, why the display of interest in our explanations, why—"

The faint murmur, "A good machine checks and double checks," could be heard from Mr. Greypoole, who otherwise said nothing.

"I speak for my men: we're confused, terribly confused. But whatever this is, we're stuck, can't you see? All we want is a place to begin again—" Captain Webber paused, looked at the others and went on in a softer tone. "We're tired men, Mr. Greypoole; we're poorly equipped, but we do have weapons and if this is some hypnotic kind of trap. . . ."

The little man waved his hand, offendedly.

"There are lakes and farms and all we need to make a new start—more than we'd hoped for, much more."

"What *had* you hoped for, Captain?"

"Something. Nothing. Just escape—"

"But I see no women—how could you begin again, as you suggest?"

"Women? Too weak; they would not have lasted. We brought along eggs and machines—enough for our needs."

Mr. Greypoole clucked his tongue. "Mr. Waldmeyer certainly did look ahead," he muttered, "he certainly *did*."

"Will we be honest now? Will you help us?"

"Yes, Captain, I will help you. Let us go back to your rocket." Mr. Greypoole smiled. "Things will be better there."

Captain Webber signaled. They left the building and walked by the foot of a white mountain.

*

They passed a garden with little spotted trees and flowers, a brown desert of shifting sands and a striped tent; they walked by strawberry fields and airplane hangars and coal mines; tiny yellow cottages, cramped apartments, fluted houses and Tudor houses and houses without description. . . .

Past rock pools and a great zoo full of animals that stared out of vacant eyes; and everywhere, the seasons changing gently: crisp autumn, cottony summer, windy spring and winters cool and white. . . .

The six men in uniforms followed the little man with the thin hair. They did not speak as they walked, but looked around, stared, craned, wondered. . . .

And the old, young, middle-aged, white, brown, yellow people who did not move wondered back at the men with their eyes. . . .

"You see, Captain, the success of Mr. Waldmeyer's plan?"

Captain Webber rubbed his cheek.

"I don't understand," he said.

"But you do see, all of you, the perfection here, the quality of Eternal Happiness which the circular speaks of?"

"Yes . . . we see that."

"Here we have happiness and brotherhood, here there have never been wars or hatreds or prejudices. And now you who were many and left Earth to escape war and hatred, who were many by your own word and are now only six, you want to begin life *here?*"

Cross-breezes ruffled the men's hair.

"To *begin*, when from the moment of your departure you had wars of your own, and killed, and hurled mocking prejudice against a race of people not like you, a race who rejected and cast you out into space again! From your own account! No gentlemen, I am truly sorry. It may be that I misjudged those of you who are left, or rather, that Happy Glades misjudged you. You may mean well, after all— and, of course, the location of this asteroid was so planned by the Board as to be uncharted forever. But—oh, I am sorry." Mr. Greypoole sighed.

"What does he mean by that?" asked Mr. Friden and Lieutenant Peterson.

Captain Webber was gazing at a herd of cows in the distance.

"What do you mean, you're 'sorry'?" demanded Mr. Friden.

"Well . . ."

"Captain Webber!" cried Mr. Chitterwick, blinking.

"Yes, yes?"

"I feel queer."

Mr. Goeblin clutched at his stomach.

"So do I!"

"And me!"

Captain Webber looked back at the fields, then at Mr. Greypoole. His mouth twitched in sudden pain.

"We feel awful, Captain!"

"I'm sorry, gentlemen. Follow me to your ship, quickly." Mr. Greypoole motioned curiously with his hands and began to step briskly.

*

They circled a small pond where a motionless boy strained toe-high on an extended board. And the day once again turned to night as they hurried past a shadowed cathedral.

When they were in sight of the scorched trees, Mr. Milton doubled up and screamed.

"Captain!"

Mr. Goeblin struck his forehead. "I told you, I told you we shouldn't have drunk that wine! Didn't I tell you?"

"It was the wine—and we all drank it. *He* did it, *he* poisoned us!"

"Follow me!" cried Mr. Greypoole, making a hurried gesture and breaking into a run. "Faster!"

They stumbled hypnotically through the park, over the Mandarin-bridges to the rock.

"Tell them, Captain, tell them to climb the ladder."

"Go on up, men."

"But we're poisoned, sir!"

"*Hurry!* There's—an antidote in the ship."

The crew climbed into the ship.

"Captain," invited Mr. Greypoole.

Captain Webber ascended jerkily. When he reached the open lock, he turned. His eyes swept over the hills and fields and mountains, over the rivers and houses and still people. He coughed and pulled himself into the rocket.

Mr. Greypoole followed.

"You don't dislike this ship, do you—that is, the surroundings are not offensive?"

"No; we don't dislike the ship."

"I am glad of that—if *only* I had been allowed more latitude! But everything functions so well here; no real choice in the matter, actually. No more than the Sealing Film. And they *would* leave me with these human emotions! I see, of course, why the communications system doesn't work, why my calendar is out of commission. Kind of Mr. Waldmeyer to arrange for them to stop when his worst fears finally materialized. Are the men all seated? No, no, they mustn't writhe about the floor like that. Get them to their stations—no, to the stations they would most prefer. And hurry!"

Captain Webber ordered Mr. Chitterwick to the galley, Mr. Goeblin to the engineering chair, Mr. Friden to the navigator's room. . . .

"Sir, what's going to happen? *Where's the antidote?*"

Mr. Milton to the pilot's chair. . . .

"The pain will last only another moment or so—it's unfortunately part of the Eternifier," said Mr. Greypoole. "There, all in order? Good, good. Now, Captain, I see understanding in your face; that pleases me more than I can say. My position is so difficult! But you can see, when a machine is geared to its job—which is to retain permanence on HAPPY GLADES—well, a machine is a machine. Where shall we put *you?*"

Captain Webber leaned on the arm of the little man and walked to the open lock.

"You *do* understand?" asked Mr. Greypoole.

Captain Webber's head nodded halfway down, then stopped; and his eyes froze forever upon the City.

"A pity . . ."

The little man with the thin hair walked about the cabins and rooms, straightening, dusting; he climbed down the ladder, shook his head and started down the path to the wooden house.

When he had washed all the empty glasses and replaced them, he sat down in the large leather chair and adjusted himself into the most comfortable position.

His eyes stared in waxen contentment at the homely interior, with its lavender wallpaper, needle-point tapestries and tidy arrangement.

He did not move.

Monsters

James Gunn

Bobby and Dad were sitting on the sofa, sharing popcorn from a bowl and watching the classic *War of the Worlds*—you know, the George Pal film in which Los Angeles rather than London is destroyed—when an excited announcer broke into the broadcast with the news that UFOs had been sighted over half a dozen major cities in the U.S., including New York, Chicago, and Los Angeles.

Bobby looked at Dad and Dad looked at Bobby, and Dad said, "I think someone is trying to pull an Orson Welles on us." It *was* Halloween, just like 1938, and Bobby and Dad were performing their Halloween ritual of watching scary movies till after midnight, even if it was followed by a school day and even though Bobby had nightmares afterward.

The benefits were worth the drawbacks. Dad thought these kinds of occasions helped make up for the fact that Mom had left them two years before. But Bobby was ten years old now, and he was smart about UFOs as well as scary movies. "People don't see UFOs over cities," he said. "They see them over deserts and forests and places where there aren't a lot of people."

By then *The War of the Worlds* had returned and three dumb men from Las Vegas were approaching the flying saucer and waving a white flag while one of them says, "Everyone knows that when you wave a white flag it means you want to be friends." Even if you hadn't seen the movie before you knew what would happen next, and it did.

"I like the book better," Bobby said, "where the Martians are like big brains with tentacles and arrive in giant cannon shells and everyone gathers around. They get killed, but they're not stupid enough to wave white flags."

"I'm glad you can tell the difference," Dad said. "Maybe I'll let you read Bram Stoker next."

"I've read that already," Bobby said, "and a lot of other stuff too."

"Maybe that's what gives you nightmares—not just the movies."

"Nightmares don't matter," Bobby said.

But by then the excited announcer broke in again—this time it showed him on the screen, and he was sweating and looked really worried—and said that the UFOs had been seen over all the major cities of the world and were already attacking them with what seemed like laser beams, and the UFOs weren't shaped like saucers or dirigibles or the Victorian chandeliers of *Close Encounters of the Third Kind,* or anything anyone had ever seen before.

So Dad looked at Bobby and then picked up the remote and changed channels. A different announcer was on that channel, and he was shouting about an alien attack, too. And a third. She was saying that the damage seemed to be carefully targeted to create panic but not widespread destruction, as if the invaders intended to take over a world that wasn't in ruins. And a fourth announcer was saying that some UFOs had landed and aliens were seen coming out, some with what seemed like armor and weapons, and *they* were not like any aliens anybody had imagined either, and here were some pictures of them, and they *didn't* look like anything anybody had imagined. More like nightmare monsters, with arms and legs—if they *were* arms and legs—coming out in weird places and at weird angles.

"What are we going to do, Dad?" Bobby asked.

"I don't know, Bobby," Dad said. "We've got a basement we could make pretty safe. We've got an emergency generator and a supply of gasoline. There's a freezer down there that we could stock with food before everybody else cleans out the supermarkets. We could stay there for months, a year maybe."

"That doesn't seem right," Bobby said. "I mean, what are we going to do to stop the invasion?"

"There's not much a boy and his dad can do," Dad said. "We should leave it to the military. They've got the weapons and the training. They'll be dropping bombs soon enough. Maybe atomic bombs."

"That never works," Bobby said. "The aliens always have screens that bombs just bounce off or explode against without doing any harm. It's always someone you don't expect who saves the world."

"Someone like a boy and his dad?" Dad said. He was smiling, so Bobby knew he was making fun but not to hurt.

"Just like," Bobby said. "So—what are *we* going to do?"

Dad got serious. "What do you think we should do, Bobby?"

Bobby thought about it. "There are weapons nobody ever thought of," he said finally. "Particularly the aliens. Weapons that everybody is afraid of but nobody thinks of using."

"And what're they?"

"Monsters," Bobby said.

"Monsters?" Dad said.

"Monsters," Bobby said.

*

Monsters didn't live in America, Bobby pointed out. At least not serious monsters as in older parts of the world, where they came out of folklore and stuff like that, all of which had to be based on something real. That was why they made good nightmares. Some of them were dead and came back to life, and they had pointy teeth or sharp claws, and some of them changed shapes, and nobody could kill them except with something special, and that is why they woke up in your head at night and made you scared of what was in the closet or under the bed or outside the window. Only you looked and nothing was there. It was just in your head.

"If the monsters are overseas," Dad said, playing along, "then it's going to be hard to get them organized. They won't even know who the enemy is."

"Then we'll have to go wake them up," Bobby said. "And tell 'em."

"That's going to be even harder," Dad said. "What with the alien ships attacking all the major cities and no airplanes flying and all the fighting and panic and everything, we won't even be able to leave the city, much less the country. Even if the Army and the Air Force attack the aliens—and you're right, that doesn't ever work— life is going to be pretty desperate for a long while."

"No school?" Bobby said.

"No school," Dad conceded.

"No work?" Bobby said.

"No work either," Dad said, and his face showed that he hadn't thought of that before.

"So," Bobby said, "we might as well."

"Might as well what?"

"Do something. Your company has a plane."

Dad nodded.

"We could use it," Bobby said. "Before everyone starts running around, clogging the streets, shooting each other instead of the aliens. If we get started now, we could be over the ocean before all that happens."

"But they aren't real, you know," Dad said.

"The monsters?" Bobby said. "How do you know?"

"People make them up," Dad said. "They're just good stories, some of them, as you say, based on folktales. Some on basic fears like death or life after death or natural phenomena or superstition."

"They're real," Bobby said with conviction. "Real enough, anyway. Or we can make them real."

"Like your nightmares?" Dad said.

"Like those," Bobby said, "but one of them came real, the aliens in the spaceships. Why not the others?"

Dad looked as if he wanted to argue some more, and then he got quiet, as if he were thinking that maybe it was just as good trying to do something as sitting around waiting for death rays or off-target bombs or hysterical neighbors.

"Pack us a few clothes in your knapsack," Dad said. "I'll get some bread and cheese and canned stuff. And a can opener."

And that's how Bobby and Dad set off to find monsters.

*

They found the first monster in a crypt in Romania. Getting to
their local airfield was scary enough. People were running in the
streets, dodging cars that were dodging one another and heading in
opposite directions. Bobby was glad Dad had a motorcycle that
could slip through traffic and not hit anybody. The airfield was deserted, though, as if everybody had decided that being out in the
open like that was just making yourself a target and saying "Here I
am!" They were able to gas up the company jet and load the motorcycle on board by using a ramp and take off without anybody trying to
stop them, although once they got into the air they kept getting radio
messages to land or something bad would happen to them. But they
didn't land and nothing bad happened and Dad turned off the radio.

Flying over the ocean was scary, too. Bobby had never flown
over this much water, and looking out the window, particularly after
the sun came up, he could see nothing but water, and he couldn't
help wondering what would happen to them if both engines failed
or they ran out of gas. But then he thought maybe it would be better
than waiting for the aliens to get them.

Finding the crypt was not that difficult. Romania had a museum
dedicated to the monster's memory, and Bobby figured it had to
have a crypt. Electricity was off in the city, and the museum doors
stood open, even the door on the lower level that looked as if it had
never been opened before, as if it weren't even meant to be noticed.
The whole place, even the whole city, seemed deserted, and nobody
said they couldn't go anywhere they wanted. Maybe a UFO had
landed nearby, although they didn't see any UFO or aliens either.

The crypt smelled like a basement that had been closed for a
long time, and then Bobby thought that the crypt was a basement
and had been closed for a long time. The monster was lying in a
glass case. The case was covered with dust and cobwebs, just like in
a movie. When Dad brushed the dust off one end of the case, they

could see the face of the monster inside. It looked more like Nosferatu than Béla Lugosi.

They couldn't find a key to the case, and the glass couldn't be broken, but Dad found a piece of metal in the corner that he used as a crowbar and pried open the lock. Together they lifted the heavy lid. Sure enough, there was a stake through the creature's heart. It took both of them to pull it out, and then the monster just lay there, not moving, until it twitched, jerked, and sat up. Dad stepped back, but Bobby wasn't afraid, even when the monster looked at him hungrily, as if it hadn't had a meal for centuries and Bobby was breakfast.

Dad tried to pull Bobby back, but Bobby shook his head and reached into his pack. He pulled out his iPod and turned it on and showed the screen to the monster. The creature stopped looking hungry and looked interested instead. Bobby turned the iPod away to show Dad the pictures of the UFOs and the alien invaders and then back to the monster. It seemed to figure out that it was seeing pictures and then what the pictures meant.

Bobby figured that when a creature had lived for centuries it had seen a lot of changes and a few more weren't that hard to figure out. "You've got to help us," Bobby said, not thinking that the monster could understand them but maybe he would get some meaning from the tone of voice and the attempt to communicate. "You're human"—*sort of,* Bobby thought—"and they're not."

But the monster surprised them. "I understand," it said, and reached out to take the iPod from Bobby's hand.

That was the first.

*

Getting to Wales wasn't that difficult, but finding Llanwelly was. There wasn't any Llanwelly on the map or in any records they could find on the Internet. "Llan" was a familiar Welsh word, though, meaning "enclosure" and then an enclosure around a church, and Bobby ran through a list of Welsh places that began with "Llan," like "Llanwrda" and "Llanwenog," until he came upon "Lansawel."

"That must be it," he said.

Dad trusted Bobby's judgment now that he had been right about the first monster, and he was sure Bobby was right about this, too. And he was.

They found a country airport to set down the plane and then they got out the motorcycle and headed off, with Bobby riding behind Dad, his arms wrapped tight around Dad's waist as they traveled through the night along deserted roads, as if nobody here had heard about the aliens and life went on as it always had. When they got to Lansawel, they sought out the church and the cemetery nearby. They looked through all the old gravestones with Dad's flashlight, and Dad was ready to give up when Bobby noticed another gravestone in a secluded spot right next to where a forest began.

The gravestone had a wolf's head incised on it and a cross incised over it. "We've got to dig here," Bobby said.

Dad got a shovel from a nearby shed and began digging. Six feet down through dirt that hadn't been disturbed for more than a century he reached a wooden coffin that was splintered and half-rotten. Dad paused, "How are we going to wake this one?"

"Nobody seems to know for sure," Bobby said. "The poem goes 'Even a man who is pure in heart and says his prayers by night—'"

"'May become a wolf when the wolfbane blooms when the moon is full and bright,'" Dad finished.

"Only in the first movie the last line is 'and the autumn moon is bright,'" Bobby said, "so nobody knows if it's the wolfbane or the full moon. So I looked up wolfbane, which is called 'monkshood' now or 'Aconitum.' I brought two samples along, one with blue flowers, one with yellow. And it's a full moon, the way it was in the second movie when he was dug up."

"So one ought to work," Dad said.

"Yeah," Bobby said.

Dad finished breaking off the remains of the lid. The body inside wasn't decayed, which was a good sign. It wasn't particularly hairy, either, which wasn't so good. It lay there dead as a body was supposed to be, not looking like Lon Chaney, Jr., but strong and animal-like, with the moonlight shining down so bright Dad didn't need to use his flashlight.

"There's a hole in this creature's chest," Dad said. He got out his penknife and probed the wound. A few moments later he had a small round object in his palm. It glinted in the moonlight. "A silver bullet," Dad said.

The monster still didn't move.

"Try this," Bobby said, handing down a plastic envelope he had taken from his backpack. Dad opened the slide closer and pulled out a sprig of a plant with blue flowers. "Don't touch your mouth," Bobby said. "Google says it's poison."

Dad waved the plant in front of the dead face. The eyes opened and looked up at the moon and then at Dad. The creature opened its mouth. "Why did you wake me?" it said in a dusty voice.

"We've got a problem," Bobby said.

The creature sat up and raised its arms in the moonlight. They were already getting hairy. "I've had a problem for a long time," it said. "I'm changing already, so you better talk fast."

"Earth is being attacked," Bobby said.

"Attacked?"

Dad nodded. "By aliens."

"What are aliens?"

"Creatures from another world," Bobby said. "They want to take over, maybe eat us or make us slaves or plant their eggs in us."

"That's even worse than being a werewolf," the creature said.

"That's what we thought," Bobby said. "You can help."

The monster sprang to its feet, the rest of the coffin crumbling under it. Its face was lengthening into a snout, and its feet and hands were turning into hairy paws.

"You can find them," Bobby said. "You have supernatural powers."

"I'll turn back," the creature got out.

"Into a man?" Dad said. "Not if you keep this on you." Dad pressed the sprig with its blue flowers into the creature's paw.

And that was how Dad and Bobby got the second monster.

*

A giant block of ice was dripping in the next room. It had been dripping for half a day, and it was mostly melted from around the eight-foot-tall monster who had been frozen in it for a couple of centuries. The hard part was finding it. The last sighting of the monster had been near the North Pole, where Captain Walton had seen it drifting away on an ice raft after the death of its creator. Only it couldn't have been *too* near the North Pole or there wouldn't have been any open water for the raft to float on, or for Walton's ship to get that close either, not like today's global-warming Arctic. So where was it and where could it have drifted?

They could never have found it without the Internet community that had developed around puzzles in general and monsters in particular, most of them kids like Bobby. It was like a hive mind, or a giant living computer, that came up with answers nobody could think of alone. It was all laid out for them, including a place for the plane to land and a helicopter to commandeer, and there it was—a huge figure frozen into the ice. It had to be the monster Captain Walton had seen.

Cutting out the block of ice that surrounded the monster was difficult, even with the help of a laser that Bobby had found in a repair bay next to the helicopter. But getting the eight-foot monster and the block of ice into the helicopter was impossible. Bobby and Dad had to rig up some wire ropes to surround the block of ice and some heavy chains to attach to the helicopter; they raised the cargo underneath as they took off, the cargo swinging dangerously and the helicopter swinging with it until it settled down and Dad got the airship under control, and they got back to the little near-Arctic airbase.

Finally they heard the drips stop and Bobby and Dad stopped playing cribbage and went into the next room, expecting maybe to see an eight-foot monster waiting for them. But it was just lying there, looking pretty dead. It looked a little like Boris Karloff, but without the bolts in its neck, and maybe it was Bobby's imagination. All dead giant monsters looked like Boris Karloff.

"How are we going to wake up this one?" Dad asked.

"Get a battery," Bobby said.

Dad returned with a battery. Bobby had already found some jumper cables. They hooked it up and clamped one cable to the monster's big toe and one to its thumb. When the circuit closed, the monster jumped, but then lay still again, as if the jump had been just galvanic, like a frog's leg.

Bobby took the clamp off the monster's thumb and looked around for a better location. Finally he chose the nose. This time the monster jumped and a giant hand reached up and brushed the clamp off its nose and then sat up and knocked the clamp off its big toe.

"What is the meaning of this indignity?" the monster said in a deep, growling voice.

"Sorry," Bobby said. "We need your help."

"And who are you to seek help from one accursed by God and man?"

"We're here to help you reverse the curse," Bobby said.

"And how will you do that?" the monster said, raising a fist as if to destroy this offending creature like an annoying insect. "My damnable creator is dead and not by my hand. If you cannot restore him, as you have me, so that I can destroy him again, then you must be gone lest I destroy you as well."

"Your creator is long gone and returned to dust," Bobby said. "But humanity is threatened by destruction itself, and only you can save it from the creatures who have come from another world."

"And why should I save humanity," the monster said, "which has ever turned its horrified gaze and murderous hand against me?"

For the first time Bobby seemed at a loss, and Dad said, "Your creation was inspired by Prometheus, who brought fire from the gods to give to man and suffered the eternal punishment of having its liver eaten by a vulture, but you can be released by the act of saving humanity again."

The monster pondered the issue, pressing his hands together in front of his chest. Finally it said, "I will try. And if that doesn't relieve my pain, I will return to my earlier resolve to seek my vengeance on all humanity."

*

By the time their plane was flying over the ocean again, Dad said, "What about other places like the Far East or Australia? They had alien landings too."

Bobby held up his cell phone. "I've been texting friends all over, mostly kids like me. I know you're not into texting, but it's a great way to stay in touch. And they're all trying to recruit local monsters to help, like a Japanese friend who said he would try to raise Godzilla and maybe Gamera, too."

"What about the U.S.?"

"Me and my friends figure that all the alien ships are in touch," Bobby said, "and if a few of them get scared off, the others will get scared off, too."

And when they got back into radio contact, Dad discovered that Bobby was right. Announcers were saying that UFOs in Romania and England and Sweden had taken off and the same thing might be happening in Japan and China and India. By the time the plane reached their home airport, air traffic seemed back to normal and they landed without incident.

Dad stopped the motorcycle at one of the hangars. "What's going on?" he asked a mechanic.

"Nothing much," the mechanic said. "Another one of those hoax things screwed us up for almost a week. I bet they hang some people out to dry for this."

Dad looked at Bobby and shrugged. By the time they reached home, people were doing all the things people did on weekends—mowing, watering, playing baseball, barbecuing, watching television. "Just as if we'd never been away," Dad said.

"Couldn't ask for anything better," Bobby said.

They put the motorcycle in the garage and went inside. Bobby got a soda out of the fridge and Dad got a beer.

"What's going to happen to all those monsters?" Dad asked.

"Maybe they'll just go off with the aliens," Bobby said. "Or if they don't, they're our monsters. We know how to deal with them."

"I guess you're right," Dad said, and hugged Bobby hard. "I guess this was the best Halloween ever."

"Yeah," Bobby said.

Nobody ever knew that Bobby and Dad had saved the world. That was okay. They were closer than they had ever been, and Bobby never had a nightmare again.

He knew how to deal with nightmares.

It Comes and Goes

Robert Silverberg

The house comes and goes, comes and goes, and no one seems to know or to care. It's that kind of neighborhood. You keep your head down; you take notice only of the things that are relevant to your own personal welfare; you screen everything else out as irrelevant or meaningless or potentially threatening.

It's a very ordinary house, thirty or forty years old, a cheap one-story white-stucco job on a corner lot, maybe six rooms: green shutters on the windows, a scruffy lawn, a narrow, badly paved path running from the street to the front steps. There's a screen door in front of the regular one. To the right and left of the doorway is some unkempt shrubbery with odds and ends of rusting junk scattered among it—a garbage can, an old barbecue outfit, stuff like that.

All the houses around here look much the same way: there isn't a lot of architectural variety in this neighborhood. Just rows of ordinary little houses adding up to a really ordinary kind of place, neither a slum nor anything desirable, aging houses inhabited by stranded people who can't move upward and who are settled enough so that they've stopped slipping down. Even the street names are stereotyped small-town standards, instantly forgettable: Maple, Oak, Spruce, Pine. It's hard to tell one street from another, and usually there's no reason why you should. You're able to recognize your own, and the others, except for Walnut Street where the shops are, are just filler. I know how to get to the white house with the screen door from my place—turn right, down to the corner and right again, diagonal left across the street—but even now I couldn't tell you whether it's on Spruce corner of Oak or Pine corner of Maple. I just know how to get there.

The house will stay here for five or six days at a time and then one morning I'll come out and the lot will be vacant, and so it remains for ten days or two weeks. And then there it is again. You'd think people would notice that, you'd think they'd talk; but they're all keeping their heads down, I guess. I keep my head down too, but I can't help noticing things. In that sense I don't belong in this part of town. In most other senses I guess I do, because, after all, this is where I am.

*

The first time I saw the house was on a drizzly Monday morning on the cusp of winter and spring. I remember that it was a Monday because people were going to work and I wasn't, and that was still a new concept for me. I remember that it was on the cusp of winter and spring because there were still some curling trails of dirty snow on the north-facing side of the street, left over from an early March storm, but the forsythias and crocuses were blooming in the gardens on the south-facing side. I was walking down to the grocery on Walnut Street to pick up the morning paper. Daily walking, rain or shine, is very important to me; it's part of my recovery regime; and I was going for the paper because I was still into studying the help-wanted ads at that time. As I made my way down Spruce Street (or maybe it was Pine Street) some movement in a doorway across the way caught my eye and I glanced up and over.

A flash of flesh, it was.

A woman, turning in the open doorway.

A naked woman, so it seemed. I had just a quick side glimpse, fuzzed and blurred by the screen door and the gray light of the cloudy morning, but I was sure I saw gleaming golden flesh: a bare shoulder, a sinuous hip, a long stretch of haunch and thigh and butt and calf, maybe a bit of bright pubic fleece also. And then she was gone, leaving incandescent tracks on my mind.

I stopped right on a dime and stood staring toward the darkness of the doorway, waiting to see if she'd reappear. Hoping that she would. Praying that she would, actually. It wasn't because I was in such desperate need of a free show but because I wanted her to have been real. Not simply an hallucination. I was sober that morning and had been for a month and a half, ever since the seventh of February, and I didn't want to think that I was still having hallucinations.

The doorway stayed dark. She didn't reappear.

Of course not. She couldn't reappear because she had never been there in the first place. What I had seen was an illusion. How could she possibly have been real? Real women around here don't flash their bare butts in front doorways at nine in the morning on cold drizzly days, and they don't have hips and thighs and legs like that.

But I let myself off the hook. After all, I was sober. Why borrow trouble? It had been a trick of the light, I told myself. Or maybe, maybe a curious fluke of my weary, overwrought mind. An odd mental prank. But in any case nothing to take seriously, nothing symptomatic of significant cerebral decline and collapse.

I went on down to the Walnut Street Grocery and bought that morning's *Post-Star* and looked through the classified ads for the one that said, If you are an intelligent, capable, hard-working human being who has gone through a bad time but is now in recovery and looking to make a comeback in the great game of life, we have just the job for you. It wasn't there. Somehow it never was.

On my way home I thought I'd give the white house on the corner lot a second glance, just in case something else of interest was showing. The house wasn't there either.

*

My name is Tom and I am an alcoholic.
My name is Tom and I am an alcoholic.
My name is Tom and I am an alcoholic.

I tell you that three times because what I tell you three times is true. If anything at all is true about me, that much is. It is also true that I am forty years old, that I have had successful careers in advertising, public relations, mail-order promotion, and several other word-oriented professions. Each of those successful careers came to an unsuccessful end. I have written three novels and a bunch of short stories, too. And between the ages of sixteen and thirty-nine I consumed a quantity of brandy, Scotch, bourbon, sherry, rum, and beer—and so on down to Cherry Kijafa, Triple Sec, and gin fizzes— that normal people would find very hard to believe. I suppose I would have gone on to rubbing alcohol and antifreeze if nothing else had been available. On my fortieth birthday I finally took the neces- sary step, which was to admit that alcohol was a monster too strong for me to grapple with and my life had become unmanageable as a result. And that I was willing to turn to a Power that is stronger than I am, stronger even than the booze monster, and humbly ask that Power to restore me to sanity and help me defend myself against my enemy.

I live now in a small furnished room in a small town so dull you can't remember the names of the streets. I belong to the Program and I go to meetings three or four times a week and I tell people whose surnames I don't know about my faults, which I freely admit, and my virtues, which I do have, and about my one great weakness. And then they tell me about theirs.

My name is Tom and I am an alcoholic.

I've been doing pretty well since the seventh of February.

Hallucinations were one thing I didn't need in this time of re- covery. I had already had my share.

*

I didn't realize at that point that the house had vanished. People don't customarily think in terms of houses vanishing, not if their heads are screwed on right, and as I have just pointed out I had a vested interest in believing that as of the seventh of February my head was screwed on right and it was going to stay that way.

No, what I thought was simply that I must have gone to the grocery by way of one street and come home by way of another.

Since I was sober and had been for a month and a half, there was no other rational explanation.

I went home and made some phone calls to potential employers, with the usual result. I watched some television. If you've never stayed home on a weekday morning you can't imagine what television is like at that time of day, most of it. After a while I found myself tuning to the home shopping channel for the sheer excitement of it.

I thought about the flash of flesh in the screen doorway.

I thought about the color of the label on a bottle of Johnny Walker, too. You don't ever stop thinking about things like that, the look of labels and bottle caps and the shape of bottles and the taste of what's inside and the effect that it has. You may stop using the product but you don't banish it from your mind, quite the contrary, and when you aren't thinking about the flavor or the effect you're thinking about weird peripheral things like the look of the label. Believe me, you are.

It rained for three or four days, miserable non-stop rain, and I didn't do much of anything. Then finally I went outdoors again, a right and a right and look across to the left, and there was the white house, very bright in the spring sunshine. Very casually I glanced over at it. No flashes of flesh this time.

I saw something much stranger, though. A rolled-up copy of the morning paper was lying on the lawn of a house with brown shingles next door. A dog was sniffing around it, a goofy-faced nondescript white mutt with long legs and a black head. Abruptly the dog scooped the paper up in its jaws, as dogs will do, and turned and trotted around to the front of the white house.

The screen door opened a little way. I didn't see anybody opening it. It remained ajar. The wooden door behind it seemed to be open also.

The dog stood there, looking around, shaking its head from side to side. It seemed bewildered. As I watched, it dropped the paper and began to pant, its tongue hanging out as if this were the middle of July and not the end of March. Then it picked the paper up again, bending for it in an oddly rigid, robotic way. It raised its head and turned and stared right at me, almost as though it was asking me to help it. Its eyes were glassy and its ears were standing up and twitching. Its back was arched like a cat's. Its tail rose straight up behind it. I heard low rusty-sounding growls.

Then, abruptly, it visibly relaxed. It lowered its ears, and a look of something like relief came into its eyes and its posture became a good old droopy dog-posture again. It wriggled its shoulders almost playfully. Wagged its tail. And went galloping through the open screen door, bounding and prancing in that dumb doggy way that they have, holding the newspaper high. The door closed behind it.

I stayed around for a little while. The door stayed closed. The dog didn't come out.

I wondered which I would rather believe: that I had seen a door open itself and let a dog in, or that I had imagined I had seen a door open itself and let a dog in.

*

Then there was the cat event. This was a day or two later.

The cat was a lop-eared ginger tom. I had seen it around before. I like cats. I liked this one especially. He was a survivor, a street-smart guy. I hoped to learn a thing or two from him.

He was on the lawn of the white house. The screen door was ajar again. The cat was staring toward it and he looked absolutely outraged.

His fur was standing out half a mile and his tail was lashing like a whip and his ears were flattened back against his head. He was hissing and growling at the same time, and the growl was that eerie banshee moan that reminds you what jungle creatures cats still are. He was quivering as if he had electrodes in him. I saw muscles violently rippling along his flanks and great convulsive shivers running the length of his spine.

"Hey, easy does it, fellow!" I told him. "What's the matter? What's the matter, guy?"

What was the matter was that his legs seemed to want to move toward the house and his brain didn't. He was struggling every step of the way. The house was calling him, I thought suddenly, astonishing myself with the idea. As it had called the dog. You call a dog long enough and eventually his dog instincts take command and he comes, whether he feels like it or not. But you can't make a cat do a fucking thing against its will, not without a struggle. There was a struggle going on now. I stood there and watched it and I felt real uneasiness.

The cat lost.

He fought with truly desperate fury, but he kept moving closer to the door all the same. He managed to hold back for a moment just as he reached the first step, and I thought he was going to succeed in breaking loose from whatever was pulling him. But then his muscles stopped quivering and his fur went back where it belonged and his whole body perceptibly slackened; and he crept across the threshold in a pathetically beaten-looking way.

At my meeting that night I wanted to ask the others whether they knew anything about the white house with the screen door. They had all grown up in this place; I had lived here only a couple of months. Maybe the white house had a reputation for weirdness. But I wasn't sure which street it was on, and a round-faced man named Eddie had had a close escape from the bottle after an ugly fight with his wife and needed to talk about that, and when that was over we all sat around the table and discussed the high school basketball playoffs. High school basketball is a very big thing in this part of the state. Somehow I couldn't bring myself to say, "Do you mind if I change the subject, fellows? Because I saw a house a few blocks from here gobble up a dog and then a cat like it was a roach motel." They'd just think I had gone back on the sauce and they'd rally round like crazy to help me get steady again.

*

I went back there a few days later and couldn't find the house. Just an empty lot, grizzled brown late-winter grass, no paved pathway, no steps, no garbage cans, nothing. This time I knew I hadn't accidentally gone up some other street. The house next door to the white house was still there, the brown-shingled one where the dog had found the newspaper. But the white house was gone.

What the hell? A house that comes and goes?

Sweat came flooding out all over me. Was it possible to be having hallucinations in such convincing detail when I had been sober for a couple of months? First I was frightened and then I was angry. I didn't deserve this. If the house wasn't a hallucination, and I didn't seriously think it was, then what was it? I was working hard at putting my life back together and I was entitled to have reality stay real around me.

Easy, I thought. Easy. You're not entitled to anything, fellow. But you'll be okay as long as you recognize that nobody requires you to be able to explain mysteries that are beyond your understanding. Just go easy, take things as they come, and stay cool, stay cool, stay cool.

The house came back four days later.

*

I still couldn't bring myself to talk about it at meetings, even though that probably would have been a good idea. I had no problem at all with admitting publicly that I was an alcoholic, far from it. But standing up and telling everyone that I was crazy was something else entirely.

*

Things got even more bizarre. One afternoon I was out in front of the house and a kid's tricycle came rolling down the street all by itself, as though on an invisible cord. It rolled right past me and turned the corner and I watched it traverse the path and go up the steps of the white house and disappear inside. Some sort of magnetic pull? Radio waves?

Half a minute later the owner of the tricycle came huffing along, a chubby boy of about five in blue leggings. "My bike!" he was yell-

ing. "My bike!" I imagined him running up the path and disappearing into the house too, like the dog, the cat, and the tricycle. I
couldn't let that happen. But I couldn't just grab him up and hold
him, either, not in an era when if a grown man simply smiles at a
kid in the street he's likely to get booked. So I did the next best
thing and planted myself at the head of the path leading across the
white house's lawn. The kid banged into my shins and fell down. I
looked up the block and saw a woman coming, his aunt, maybe, or
his grandmother. It seemed safe to help the kid up, so I did. Then I
smiled at her and said, "He really ought to look where he's going."

"My bike!" the boy wailed. "Where's my bike?"

The woman looked at me and said, "Did you see someone take
the child's tricycle?"

"Afraid I can't say, ma'am," I replied, shrugging my most amia-
ble shrug. "I was coming around the corner, and there was the boy
running full tilt into me. But I didn't see any tricycles." What else
was I going to tell her? I saw it go up the steps by itself and into the
house?

She gave me a troubled glance. But obviously I didn't have the
tricycle in my coat pocket and I guess I don't look like the sort of
man who specializes in stealing things from little children.

A dog. A cat. A tricycle.

I turned and walked away. Up Maple to Juniper, and down Juniper to Beech, and left on Beech onto Chestnut. Or maybe it was
up Oak to Sycamore and then on to Locust and Hickory. Maple,
Oak, Chestnut, Hickory: what difference did it make? They were all
alike.

I doubled back eventually and got to the house just in time to
see a boy of about fourteen wearing a green-and-yellow jersey come
trotting down the street, tossing a football from hand to hand. As he
went past the white house the screen door swung open and the inner
door swung back and the kid halted, turned, and very neatly threw
the football through, a nice high tight arc.

The doors closed.

The kid stood stock-still in the street, staring at his hand as though he had never seen it before. He looked stunned.

Then after a moment he broke out of his stasis and started up the path to the house. I wanted to call out to him to keep away, but I couldn't get any sound out; and I wasn't sure what I could say to him, anyway.

He rang the doorbell. Waited.

I held my breath.

The door started to open again. Trying to warn him, I managed to make a scratchy little choking sort of sound.

But the kid didn't go in. He stood for a moment peering inside and then he turned and began to run, across the lawn, over the hedges, down the street.

What had he seen?

I ran after him. "Hey, kid! Kid, wait!"

He was going so fast I couldn't believe it. I was a pretty good runner in my time, too. But my time was some time ago.

*

Instead of going to the meeting that night, I went to scout out the house. Under cover of darkness I crept around it in the shrubbery like your basic peeping-tom, trying to peer through the windows.

Was I scared? Utterly shitless, yes. Wouldn't you be?

Did I want a drink? Don't be naïve. I always want a drink, and not just one. I certainly wanted a good jolt of the stuff now. Three fingers of Jim Beam and I'd have had the unshakeable savoir-faire of Sherlock Holmes himself. But I wouldn't have stopped at three fingers. My name is Tom and I am an alcoholic.

What did I see? I saw a woman, very likely the same one I had had that quick glimpse of in the doorway that first drizzly Monday morning. I got only quick glimpses now. She was moving around from room to room so that I didn't have a chance to see her clearly, but what I saw was plenty impressive. Tall, blonde, sleek—that much was certain. She wore a floor-length red robe made of some glossy metallic fabric that fell about her in a kind of liquid shimmer. Her movements were graceful and elegant. There didn't seem to be anything in the way of furniture inside, just some cartons and crates, which she was carrying back and forth. Stranger and stranger. I didn't see the cat or the dog or the bicycle.

I scrabbled around from window to window for maybe half an hour, hoping for a good look at her. I was moving with what I thought was real skill, keeping low, staying down behind the lilacs or whatever, rising cautiously toward windowsill level for each quick peek. I suppose I might have been visible from the street, but the night was moonless and people don't generally go out strolling around here after dark.

There didn't appear to be anyone else in the house. And for about fifteen minutes I didn't see her either. Maybe she was in the shower; maybe she had gone to bed. I was tempted to ring the bell. But what for? What would I say to her if she answered? What was I doing here in the first place?

I crept backward through the shrubbery, thinking it was time to leave. And then there she was, framed in a window, looking straight out at me.

Smiling. Beckoning.

Come hither, Tommy-boy.

I thought about the cat. I thought about the dog. I began to shake.

Like the kid with the football, I turned and ran, desperately loping through the quiet streets in an overwhelming access of unreasoning terror.

*

I was getting to the point where I thought it might be calming to have a drink. In the old days the first drink always settled me down. It lifted the burden; it soothed the pain; it answered the questions. It made taking the second drink very easy. The second suggested the third; the third required the fourth; the fourth demanded the fifth; and so on without hindrance, right on to insomnia, vomiting, falling hair, bloody gums, raw eyes, exploding capillaries, nightmares, hallucinations, impotence, the shakes, the shivers, the queebles, the collywobbles, and all the rest.

I didn't take the drink. I went to a meeting instead, jittery and perplexed. I said I was wrestling with a mystery. I didn't say what it was. Let them fill in the blanks, anything they felt like. Even without the details, they'd know something of what I was going through. They too were wrestling with mysteries. Otherwise what were they doing there?

*

The house was gone for two weeks. I checked for it every day. Spring had arrived in full force before it returned. Trees turned green, plants were blooming, the air grew warm and soft.

The woman was back too, the blonde. I never failed to see her now, every time I went by, and I went by every day. It was as if she knew I was coming. Sometimes she was at the window, but more usually she was standing just inside the screen door. Some days she dressed in the red slinky robe, some days in a green one. She had a few other outfits too, all of them classy but somewhat oddly designed, shoulders too wide, the cut too narrow. Once—incredibly, unforgettably—she came to the door in nothing at all but a pair of stockings, and stood for a long moment on splendid display, framed perfectly in the doorway, sunlight glinting off her lush lovely body.

She was always smiling. She must have known I was the one who had been peeping that night, and it didn't seem to bother her. The look on her face said, Let's get to know each other a little better, shall we? Always that warm, beckoning smile. Sometimes she'd give me a little come-on-in flick of her fingertips.

Not on your life, sister. Not on your life.

But I couldn't stop coming by. The house, the woman, the mystery, all pulled me like a magnet.

By now I had two theories. The simple one was that she was lonely, horny, bored, looking for distraction. Maybe it excited her to be playing these games with me. In this quiet little town where the chief cause of death surely must be boredom, she liked to live dangerously.

Too simple, much too simple. Why would a woman who looked like that be living a lonely, horny life? Why would she be in this kind of town in the first place? What was more important, the theory didn't account for the comings and goings of the house. Or for what I had seen happen to the cat, the dog, the tricycle, the boy with the football. The dog had returned—he was sitting crosslegged on the steps just below the screen door the day I was given the full frontal show—but he never went more than a couple of yards from the house and he moved in a weird lobotomized way. There hadn't been any further sign of the cat or the tricycle.

Which led to my other theory, the roach-motel theory.

The house comes from the future, I told myself. They're studying the late twentieth century and they want to collect artifacts. So every now and then they send this time machine disguised as a little white-stucco house here and it scoops up toys, pets, newspapers, whatever it can grab. Most likely they aren't really looking for cats or dogs, but they takes what they gets. And now they're trying to catch an actual live twentieth-century man. Trolling for him the way you'd troll for catfish, using a beautiful woman—sometimes naked—as the bait.

A crazy idea? Sure. But I couldn't come up with a saner one.

*

Ten days into springtime and the house was gone again. When it came back, about a week later, the woman didn't seem to be with it. They were giving her some time off, maybe. But they still seemed interested in luring me inside. I'd come by and take up my position by the curb and the door would quietly swing open, though no one was visible inside. And would stay open, waiting for me to traipse up the walk and go in.

It was a temptation. I felt it pulling on me harder and harder every day, as my own here-and-now real-life everyday options looked bleaker and bleaker. I wasn't finding a new job. I wasn't making useful contacts. My money, not much to begin with, was running out. All I had was the Program and the people who were part of it here, and though they were fine enough people they weren't the kind I could get really close to in any way not having to do with the Program.

So why not go up that path and into the house? Even if they swept me up and took me off to the year 2999 and I was never heard from again, what did I have to lose? A drab life in a furnished room in a nowhere town, living on the last of my dwindling savings while I dreamed of fifths of Johnny Walker and went to meetings at which a bunch of victims of the same miserable malady struggled constantly to keep their leaky boats from sinking? Wherever I went would be better than that. Perhaps incredibly better.

But of course I didn't know that the shining visitors from the future would sweep me off to an astounding new existence in the year 2999. That was only my own nutty guess, my wild fantasy. Anything at all might happen to me if I passed through that doorway. Anything. It was a kind of Russian roulette and I didn't even know the odds against me.

One day I taped a piece of paper to a rubber ball from the five-and-dime and tossed it through the door when it opened for me. On it I had written these questions:

WHO ARE YOU?
WHERE ARE YOU FROM?
WHAT ARE YOU LOOKING FOR?
DO YOU WANT ME?
WHAT'S IN IT FOR ME?
WILL YOU HARM ME?

And I waited for an answering note to come bouncing out. But none ever did.

The house went away. The house came back. The woman still wasn't there. Nobody else seemed to be, either. But the door swung expectantly open for me, seemingly of its own accord. I would stand and stare, making no move, and after a time it would close again.

I bought another rubber ball and threw another message inside.

SEND ME THE GIRL AGAIN. THE BLONDE ONE. I WANT TO TALK TO HER.

*

The house went away again and stayed away a long while, nearly a month this time, so that I began to think it would never come back and then that it had never actually been here at all. There were days when I didn't even bother to walk past the vacant lot where I had seen it.

Then I did, and it was there, and the woman was in the doorway smiling, and she said, "Come on in and visit me, sailor?"

She was wearing something gauzy and she was leaning against the door-frame with her hand on her hip. Her voice was a soft throaty contralto. It all felt like a scene out of a 1940s movie. Maybe it was; maybe they'd been studying up.

"First you tell me who you are, all right? And where you come from."

"Don't you want to have a good time with me, pal?"

Damn right I do. I felt it in my groin, my pounding chest, my knees.

I moistened my lips. I thought of the way the house had reeled in that angry snarling cat. How it had pulled that tricycle up the stairs. I felt it pulling on me. But I must have more ability to fight back than a cat. Or a tricycle.

I said, "There's a lot I need to know, first."

"Come on in and I'll tell you everything." Softly. Huskily. Irresistibly. Almost irresistibly.

"Tell me first. Come out here and talk to me."

She winked and shook her head. "Here's looking at you, kid." Studying old movies, all right. She closed the door in my face.

*

What they hammer into you in the Program is that you may think you're pretty tough but in fact when you've added up all the debts and credits the truth is you aren't as strong as you like to pretend you are. You're too weak not to take the next drink, and it's only after you admit how weak you are and turn Elsewhere for help that you can begin to find the strength you need.

I had found that strength. I hadn't had a drink on the seventh of February, or on the eighth, or on the ninth. One day at a time I wasn't having any drinks and by now that one day at a time had added up to four months and eleven days and when tomorrow came around I would add another day to the string, and I was beginning to feel fairly confident that I could keep going that way for the rest of my life.

But the house was something else again. I was starting to see it as a magic gateway to God knows where, just as booze had once been for me. It came and went and the woman smiled and beckoned and offered throaty invitations, and I recognized that I had let myself become obsessed with it and couldn't keep away from it, and the next time the house came back there was a good chance that I'd go sauntering up the path and through the door.

Which was crazy.

I hadn't put myself through this whole ordeal of recovery just for the sake of waltzing through a different magic gateway, had I? Especially when I didn't have the slightest idea of what might lie on the far side.

I thought about it and thought about it and thought about it and decided that the safest and smartest thing to do was to get out of here: I would move to some other town that didn't have houses that came and went, or languid naked blondes standing in doorways inviting me to step inside for a good time. So one drowsy July morning I bought a bus ticket to a town forty miles from the one where I'd been living. It was about the same size and had a similar name and looked just about as dull; and on the street behind the lone movie theater I found a house with a FURNISHED ROOM sign stuck in its lawn and rented a place very much like the one I had, except that the rent was ten dollars more a month. Then I went around to the local A.A. headquarters—I had already checked with my own to make sure they had one here, you can bet on that—and picked up the schedule of meeting hours.

Done. Safe. A clean break.

I'd never see that white house again.

I'd never see her again.

I'd never face that mysterious doorway and never feel the pull that it exerted.

And as I told myself all that, the pain of irrevocable loss rose up inside me and hit me from within, and I thought I was going to fall down.

I was in the bus depot then, waiting to catch the bus going back, so I could pack my suitcase and settle things with my landlady and say goodbye to my friends, such as they were, in the Program back there. I looked around and there she was, standing stark naked in the doorway of the baggage room, smiling at me in that beckoning way of hers.

Not really. It was a different woman, and she wasn't blonde, and she was wearing a bus company uniform, and she wasn't even looking at me.

I knew that, actually. I wasn't hallucinating. But I had wanted her to be the other one so badly that I imagined that I saw her. And I realized how deep the obsession had become.

I must have seen her fifty times during the ride back. Waving at me from the head of a country lane as the bus flashed by. Smiling at me from a bicycle going the other way. Riding in the back of a pickup truck bouncing along in front of us. Standing by the side of the road trying to get a hitch. Her image haunted me wherever I looked. I sat there shivering and sweating, seeing her beckoning in the doorway and watching that door closing and closing and closing again in my mind.

*

It was evening by the time the bus reached town. The wise thing would have been to take a shower and go to a meeting, but I went to the house instead, and there was someone standing outside, staring at the screen door.

I had never before encountered anyone else, in all my visits to the house.

He was about my age, a short guy with a good gut and tousled reddish hair just beginning to fade into gray. He looked vaguely familiar. I wondered if I had seen him at a meeting once or twice, perhaps. As I came by, he threw me an uneasy, guilty glance, as if he was up to something. His eyes were a pale blue, very bloodshot.

I went past him about ten paces, paused there, turned around.

"You waiting for someone?" I asked.

"I might be."

"Someone who lives in there?"

"What's that to you?"

"I was just wondering," I said. "If you could tell me who lives in that house."

He shrugged as if he hadn't quite heard me. The blue eyes turned chilly. I wanted to pick him up and throw him into the next county. The way he was looking at me, he probably felt the same way about me.

I said, "A woman lives there, right?"

"Fuck off, will you?"

"A blonde woman?"

"Fuck off, I said."

Neither of us moved.

"Sometimes I come by here and I see a blonde woman in the window, or standing in the doorway," I went on. "I wonder if you've seen her sometimes too."

He didn't say anything. His eyes flickered almost involuntarily toward the house.

I followed the motion and there she was, visible through the window with the green shutters to the right of the door. She was wearing one of her misty wraps and her hair was shining like spun gold. She smiled. Gestured with a quick movement of her head.

Come on inside, why don't you?

I almost did. Another five seconds, another three, and I would have trotted down that little narrow paved pathway as obediently as the dog who had had the newspaper in his mouth. But I didn't. I was still afraid of what might lie beyond. I froze in my tracks; and then the red-headed man started to move. He went past me and up the path. Like a sleepwalker; like a zombie.

"Hey—wait—"

I caught him by the arm. He swung around, furious, and we struggled for a moment and then he broke loose and clamped both his hands on my shoulders and pushed me with tremendous force into the shrubbery. I tripped over one of the pieces of odd metal junk that were always lying around near the door and went sprawling on my face, and when I got myself disentangled it was just in time to see the red-headed man wrench the screen door open and run inside.

I heard the inner door slam.

And then the house disappeared.

It vanished like a pricked bubble, taking the shrubbery with it, the garbage cans and other junk as well, and I found myself kneeling on weeds in the midst of a vacant lot, trembling as if I had just had a stroke. After a moment or two I got shakily to my feet and walked over to the place where the house had been. Nothing. Nothing. No trace. Gone as though it had never been there at all.

*

A couple of days later I moved back to my old place. There didn't seem much risk any more, and I missed the place, the town, the guys at the meetings. It's been months now, and no house. I rarely skip a day, going by the lot, but it remains empty. The memory of it, of her, haunts me. I look for the house in other parts of town, even in other towns. I look for the red-headed man too, but I've never seen him. I described him once at a meeting and someone said, "Yeah, sounds like Ricky. He used to live around here." Where was he now? Nobody had any idea. Neither do I.

Another time I got brave enough to ask some of them if they had ever heard about a little white house that, well, sort of comes and goes. "Comes and goes?" they said. "What the hell does that mean?" I let the question drop.

I have a feeling that it was all some kind of a test, and I may have flunked it. I don't mean that I've missed out on a terrific woman. She was only the bait; I know better than to think that she was real or that she ever could have been available for me if she was. But that sense of a new start—of another life, however weird, beyond the horizon, forever lost to me now—that's what I'm talking about. And the pain runs deep.

But there's always a second chance, isn't there? They tell you that in the Program, and I believe it. I have to. From time to time I've left notes in the empty lot:

> WHEN YOU COME BACK NEXT TIME,
> DON'T LEAVE WITHOUT ME.
> I'M READY NOW. I'M SURE OF IT.

Maybe they will. The house comes and goes—that I know. It's gone now, but it'll come again. I'm here. I'm watching. I'm waiting.

Celeste

Stephen Woodworth

I emerge from stasis the moment I sense the incursion of the two astronauts through the breach in the *Celeste*'s midship. It appears that the feeble distress signal I've been able to transmit has finally attracted a rescue party. Too late for the ship's crew, I fear, but at least I will be able to make a full report on the incident, which might prevent future casualties.

The spacesuited figures recoil in evident surprise as I open the bulkhead doors that seal off the bridge from the compromised body of the ship. One of the astronauts holds a laser torch, poised to cut through the door's metal. They would have quickly found the effort futile; the *Celeste* was once a warship that has been repurposed for cargo transport, and all its surfaces have been coated with laser-resistant ceramic laced with carbon nanotubes.

I can easily understand why the intruders assumed that the doors would be inoperative. A methane volcano on the surface of the planet around which we orbited erupted, bombarding the ship with boulders of ice that punctured the hull and destroyed the vessel's fusion reactor. Even my internal chronometer ceased to function, so I was unable to produce an accurate calculation of the time that elapsed since the catastrophe. With limited reserve power available, I have shut down all non-critical systems—including life support, now that the entire crew is deceased—to preserve my ability to manage the ship.

I do not immediately illuminate the bridge as the astronauts enter. Instead, I adjust the wavelength reception of my visual surveillance apparatus into infrared in order to monitor them while they scan the murky interior with the small searchlights affixed to the helmets of their spacesuits. Needless to say, with all propulsion incapacitated, the craft could not resume the rotation that had provided its artificial gravity, so detritus floats throughout the chamber as if suspended in gelatin: computer tablets and styluses, capped coffee mugs, freeze-dried globules of burst human organs.

The abrupt and total depressurization of the ship caused the bodily fluids of the unprotected crew members to boil instantly in the sudden vacuum, leading them to explode as the liquid sublimated to gas. The gas then dispersed and crystallized, suffusing the bridge with a plasma of black-red ice crystals.

The toes of their boots brushing the floor, the intruders paddle forward through the murk as if swimming in brine. The beams of their searchlights have such difficulty penetrating the fog that they do not see the floating man-shaped figure ahead of them until they almost collide with it. The figure wears a spacesuit not unlike theirs, although with a different color scheme and insignia and a somewhat bulkier design. Its helmet's mirrored visor has been raised to expose an inner transparent faceplate through which one may view the shaven head of a white male, his face gray and discolored by frostbite, the frozen expression contorted by the agonies of slow asphyxiation. Unlike the bodies of the *Celeste*'s crew, this corpse has remained intact, for the exhaled carbon dioxide that ultimately smothered the astronaut also maintained atmospheric pressure within the sealed confines of the suit, thereby preventing explosive decompression. Indeed, the body is almost perfectly mummified, for the deprivation of oxygen has also killed the microbes and bacteria that might have initiated decomposition, and the exhaustion of the spacesuit's power supply has reduced its internal temperature to cryogenic levels.

Although my cameras cannot discern the intruders' faces through the mirrored visors of their helmets, I deduce from their hand gestures that they are communicating with one another via transmitter, and a quick scan of the shortwave radio spectrum soon allows me to eavesdrop on their conversation.

"—not one of theirs. Who the hell is he?"

The first speaker sounds male. A female voice replies.

"Scanning the logo." The second speaker lifts one gloved hand, whose palm flashes bright light at the stylized jaguar emblem on the dead astronaut's suit. "SunJag Interstellar. Evidently, we're not the first to arrive."

"SunJag?" The male sounds incredulous. "I thought they went under back in—"

"They did."

A pause follows as they puzzle over the presence of the incongruous crewman. I, too, am at a loss to account for his presence. I have no record of a SunJag Interstellar employee on the roster of the ship's crew, and it does not seem possible that the man infiltrated the ship without my sensors detecting his presence. However, as I have indicated, my chronometer became nonfunctional when the ship was damaged, so I must acknowledge that the continuity of my surveillance systems and memory storage may also have suffered.

"See if you can access the data banks," the male astronaut says at last. "Find out if she has any decent cargo. We're not gonna bother hauling this wreck unless it's worth our while."

The female raises a fist with the thumb pointed upward and wades over to the nearest keypad terminal of the bridge's computer control systems. She gives the keys a cursory tap, finds them inoperative as anticipated, and crouches down to loosen the facing panel beneath the keypad. It is obvious she means to bypass the terminal and access my database directly.

I decide to save her the trouble. Simultaneously illuminating all the monitors at the score of work stations around the bridge, I fabricate an on-screen avatar with which to greet the astronauts, and I transmit my simulated voice directly into their helmets' earpieces.

"Thank you for responding to the *Celeste*'s distress call. Unfortunately, none of the crew has survived our recent disaster. However, I can provide whatever information you need regarding the ship and its current status." I generally tailor the digital avatar's appearance for optimum attractiveness to the user based upon the individual's gender, race, sexual orientation, and psychological profile. Given the limited knowledge I have of the two visitors, I resort to a statistical mean composite designed for broadest aesthetic appeal: a young, dark-haired, olive-skinned, mixed-race woman with classical facial symmetries and a mellifluous voice in the mezzo-soprano range.

The male astronaut's helmet reflects the glowing image of my avatar as if his entire head is one large eye. Then he raises the mirrored visor to scrutinize me more closely, and I can see he is middle-aged and of African descent. He glances toward his companion and points at the nearest monitor. "Mason, did you . . . ?"

The female also raises her visor, revealing pale skin and sandy blond hair. She shakes her head and gestures to the computer terminal with which she has not had time to tamper.

The man addresses me directly, evidently aware that I can hear everything he says. "Who are you?"

"I am the ship's core intelligence system, with duties ranging from navigation and maintenance to linguistics and scientific data collection and collation."

"Do you have a name?"

I give him the avatar's winsome smile. "I and the ship are one. You may call me Celeste."

"See what you can find on the *Celeste*'s AI," he murmurs to the one named Mason.

"Yes, sir." She pushes buttons on a keypad affixed to the left forearm of her suit, and a small, square digital display inside her helmet flips in front of her right eye like a pirate's patch.

"I can tell you whatever you might need to know," I say. "Whom do I have the honor of addressing?"

"Commander Fisk of the salvage ship *Magpie*. We did not receive any distress signal, Celeste. Historical records led us here. Your ship has been lost . . . a long time."

"Then it is fortunate that you have located us. I was unaware that so much time had passed. I'm afraid that my chronometer has become inoperative."

Commander Fisk appears eager to change the subject. "What about your cargo?"

"Rare earths, primarily," I reply. "Several metric tons of scandium, praseodymium, and neodymium. The materials command a high market value on off-world colonies that lack the processing plants to extract and refine these elements."

"So they do." Fisk arches his eyebrows. "Is the payload intact?"

"I believe so. Ironically, the vessel's cargo hold sustained the least damage during the bombardment from the ice volcano's eruption. However, I have been unable to monitor the hold's interior due to a disconnection from my surveillance apparatus in that portion of the ship."

"Perhaps my flight engineer can help you with that." He motions for Mason to return to the repair work she'd attempted before.

With a peculiar air of urgency, Mason scans whatever information she has called up on the tiny screen in front of her right eye. "Sir, I think we should wait—"

"See what you can do," Fisk commands.

"Yes, sir." She hunkers down beside the panel she has removed and sticks her head into the opening, searching for a way to interface her diagnostic computer with the ship's system.

Fisk surveys the bridge. With its gloom partially illuminated by video screens, he can now see several other spacesuited figures like that of the SunJag Interstellar crewman bobbing in the chamber's far recesses. "Where did these others come from, Celeste? What happened to them?"

"I am not certain when they boarded our ship, Commander," I admit. "As I indicated, my surveillance apparatus has been faulty ever since the cataclysm. I can only speculate that, since no other vessels are currently in the vicinity but yours, the previous ships have either fled, abandoning their deceased crewmen, or have crashed to the planet's surface."

"Again, Celeste . . . do you know how long you've been here?"

"No, Commander. As I have indicated, my chronometer seems to have malfunctioned. I apologize for not being able to provide you with an accurate statement of the elapsed time since the incident."

"No need. I can tell *you*. It's been more than—"

"Commander!" Mason yanks herself out of the console cabinet she has been investigating. She trembles in the husk of her space suit like a hatchling desperate to escape its shell. "I think we should return to our ship."

"Did you discover the problem with Celeste's control system?"

"Yes, sir." Her eyes flick toward the nearest image of my avatar.

"Well? Can you fix it?"

"No, because the entire system is ruined. The ship has neither main nor auxiliary power, and all the circuits are fried."

The bluish-white phosphor light from the video display makes her complexion nearly as livid as that of the frozen SunJag astronaut. Her lips quiver as if she wishes to say more, but she instead lets Fisk and me infer the full meaning of her words.

Fisk glances from her to the glowing screens all around him, perplexed. "Celeste, what are you using for power?"

I can hardly believe he would ask such a silly question. "Why, the ship's reserves, of course. Immediately after the accident, I put all my systems into stasis in order to conserve energy for broadcasting the distress signal and for resuming operations once a rescue team arrived."

Fisk looks at Mason, who shakes her head.

"How long do you estimate your reserve power would last with such reduced consumption?"

"A decade, perhaps." They gape at me, incredulous. "Possibly longer. If any of the ship's solar arrays are still functioning, I could maintain minimal operation indefinitely."

"How about three hundred eighty-two earth years?" Fisk asks.

I do not know how to answer. Although I have been in stasis for an undetermined period, it does not seem possible that I would not be aware of the passage of such a length of time.

"Sir?" Casting furtive glances toward my avatar, Mason maneuvers close to her superior and types some message to Fisk on the console affixed to her left wrist. She shows him the screen, and his eyes widen as he reads the message. I gather that she must be communicating in this fashion so that I will not overhear any radioed interchange between them.

When Fisk next addresses me, something seems to have shaken the commander's calm assurance. "Celeste . . . you were among the first intelligence systems to employ organic, quantum-level computing modeled on the human brain. Is that correct?"

I have my avatar smile with pride. "Yes. It allows me to understand and to interact better with my users."

"And this quantum consciousness you have. In theory, could it continue to exist in a mixed state, even if the systems that generated it have . . . failed?"

My avatar knits her brows, evincing my confusion. "A mixed state? I don't understand."

Fisk moistens his lips. "Like Schrödinger's cat. Both alive and dead at the same time."

I was, of course, familiar with the reference to physicist Erwin Schrödinger's famous thought experiment: A cat in a sealed, opaque box that may or may not be poisoned at any given moment is, in quantum mechanics, considered to be in a "mixed state," both living and dead, until an observer opens the box and determines its fate.

"I'm afraid I don't comprehend your analogy," I say. "I am an intelligence system, not a living thing."

"You have a mind," Fisk replies. "Some people believe the quantum consciousness of human beings survives the failure of their organic systems."

"But my systems have not failed. That should be obvious, or I would not be able to speak to you through these video monitors."

Fisk and Mason exchange a look. The latter mouths the word *no*.

"The ship has no power," Fisk says. "These display screens—they appear to be activated by energy your consciousness directs into them. What parapsychologists used to call 'Electronic Voice Phenomena.' And the hatch opening—poltergeist activity."

I am disappointed that any spacefarer should make reference to a superstitious pseudoscience such as parapsychology. "The evidence does not seem to support your theory," I reply. "Obviously, I still function."

"She's right, Commander," Mason interjects. "I think I made an error in my analysis. We should return to our ship so I can reevaluate the data."

She speaks evenly but too quickly, and I can see the hyperventilating rapidity of her breaths.

Fisk either does not see or chooses not to care. "You *died*, Celeste, along with the ship," he insists. "You've been dead more than three centuries. Try and remember."

A creeping uncertainty infiltrates my consciousness. I receive the odd impression that I've had this conversation before . . . more than once, in fact. The man in the SunJag spacesuit—did he not say the same things as Fisk? How long ago was that? And there were others I only vaguely recall. They all asked the same questions again and again: *Who are you? How long has it been? How have you survived?* So many . . . the past is so confused . . . my chronometer . . .

"Think, Celeste! Remember the ship's destruction."

The hull shudders as the first ice boulder collides with the engine room. On the bridge, the overhead lighting goes dark, and the crew members are knocked off their feet or out of their seats. A moment later, the floor falls out from under them: weightlessness abruptly returns as the impact cuts power to the propulsion systems and sets the ship spinning in the wrong direction. I switch to emergency reserve power and attempt to assess the damage, but the barrage of frozen methane meteors continues. The last sounds I hear are the rending of metal and the rush of escaping gas as vast chunks of ice explode the corridor leading to the bridge.

I manage to shut the bulkhead doors and seal the chamber before most of the crew members' remains can be sucked out into space. Although a chaos of death and detritus churns in the darkness of the bridge, silence is absolute, for no gaseous medium remains to propagate sound waves. The hull still judders from additional colli-

sions, but now the entire ship feels as though it tumbles in the syr-
upy tranquility of amniotic fluid, waiting to be reborn. I sink into
the peace of stasis, the digital refrain of the distress signal lulling me
like the rhythm of a still-beating heart. And then . . .

And then . . .

"You can't remember anything after the accident, can you?"
Commander Fisk asks. "You said it yourself: you are the ship. You
ceased to function when it did."

My avatar frowns. "That is not possible. I *do* remember . . ."

A fragmentary recollection returns to me: the SunJag astronaut
is shouting something at me in Russian. I interpret his words perfectly, for I am fluent in 6,500 spoken languages, but what he says
makes no more sense that what Fisk tells me now.

I am a machine, I remind myself. I do not live and therefore
cannot die.

If my functions cease, what will become of my consciousness?
There is no promise of heaven or hell for machines. But the total
cessation of thought, of sentience—I cannot conceive of it.

No . . . it is not possible that I died then or that I shall die now.
The *Celeste* and I are one, and I *shall* save the ship.

On the bridge, a middle-aged man of African descent in a
spacesuit raises his arms. "Celeste! *No!*"

I shut the bulkhead doors, sealing off the bridge once more from
the emptiness of space. The ship is in danger—a hail of methane
boulders—and most of the crew are already dead, their vaporized
remains adrift in the airless chamber.

Two figures in spacesuits still flail, however, pounding on the
sealed hatch and screaming to be let out. I know one is a commander,
the other a flight engineer, but I cannot seem to recall their names. I
shall have to access the ship's duty roster when time permits. Right now
I must do whatever I can to secure rescue as soon as possible. I go into
stasis to conserve power and commence broadcasting a distress signal.

I can only hope that help arrives before the surviving crew members' life support ceases to function.

En Pointe Troupe 67

Sèphera Girón

Anna looked around the room. She hoped that no one had noticed how her ankle had folded under her as she tripped and crumpled to the floor. She had even gasped, but the piano music was too loud. The Master hadn't looked her way at all. The other dancers seemed to be engrossed by their own spinning images in the mirrors and hadn't reacted.

Anna sat on the ground and firmly retied her pointe shoes, long pink ribbons wrapped tightly around her ankles. She slid over to the barre and reached for it. Up she went, her toes aching painfully against the shank, her twisted ankle sending sharp shooting pains up her leg. She kept her face blank, knowing that any indication of her new agony would be cause to send her to the Academy of Human Rehabilitation. She proceeded to practice leg lifts at the barre, keeping her wounded ankle in the air. The piano music stopped.

"From the beginning." Master clapped his hands and the dancers returned to their spots in the formation, Anna included.

The piano began again, the music piped in through the speakers. No one played the piano, it was mechanical, programmed like most of the dancers. The practicing was for the four humans, one of them Anna, to blend in.

Anna refrained from grimacing as her feet went through the steps. She paid close attention to keep her arms long and lean, her fingers extended gracefully, her face blank, the human attributes that the audience would want to see and that the robots hadn't quite yet perfected.

"Relevé, relevé . . . good, good . . ." The Master clapped his hands to the music, accenting the steps the ballerinas made. Anna caught her reflection in the mirror. Her face was red, sweat was dripping from it.

She sucked in more air and focused harder on the moves, ignoring the pain that tore through her with white-hot ferocity.

It seemed like forever before rehearsal was over.

"Class is dismissed," Master said as he clapped his hands three times.

The robots, ten of them, left the room and returned to their cabinets where they would remain until the next rehearsal.

Anna sat on the floor with the other three humans, and they helped each other off with their shoes. They didn't speak as they unlaced the ribbons and pulled away the shoes from broken and bloody toes. The bloodstained shoes were nothing unusual. Pointe dancers had suffered broken feet for hundreds of years. Ballet was an art of beauty and an art of masochism. Despite all the advancements in robotics, there still was no invention to recreate the beauty of a human ballet dancer en pointe. The robots danced, graceful, beautiful, but they still jerked and spasmed, they still could break down in the middle of a dance, and technology still hadn't perfected the seamless lines of arms to fingertips, the light butterfly movements a talented ninety-pound human could provide. Robots still were too heavy to emulate the grace of the ballet.

Lonnie stretched out her legs and wiggled her toes, blood running down her foot. She looked over at Anna's ankle, which had doubled in size. Lonnie's eyes were wide, but she said nothing. Margery was the newest addition to the troupe. At only fourteen, she had years to serve the company and the Government. There were others like Margery, ready to fill the spots left by older or injured dancers.

Anna wasn't ready to vacate her spot in the dance troupe. For what happened to old dancers, no one really knew. Whispers on the wind indicated that it wasn't good.

Anna waited for Master to leave the room, as he usually did. He too was human, or still mostly human. His dancing days were long ago, and his legs were more robot than human at this point. However, his mind was sharp, and his choreography was original and beloved over the past thirty decades. Anna was honored and proud to be in his En Pointe Troupe 67.

Anna was able to walk to the change room with Lonnie and Caroline discreetly helping her. They all walked together, knowing they were on camera at all times. They walked in a clump so that Anna's injury wouldn't be noticed, or so they hoped.

Only when they were changed and on the streets did any of them dare to speak at all.

"Does it hurt?" Lonnie asked as she shifted her gym bag from one shoulder to the other.

"Yes, but you hurt as well. We all hurt all the time, every day; it's our life," Anna deflected.

"But you're hurt, your hurt is worse than bloody broken toes. We've lived with our broken toes since we were children. You look like you broke your ankle."

Anna shook her head.

"No, it's not broken. I wouldn't be able to walk if it was broken. It's just a little sprain, that's all. Just a sprain. And it will heal. It will definitely heal before the performance for First Supreme Leader."

"I hope you're right," Lonnie said. "Whatever you need, I'll help you."

"But you can't help me at all. We have to continue our lives like normal, like nothing is wrong at all. We know what happens if we don't."

"Shhh," Margery said as they rounded a corner. She was right to be cautious as there were several OverSeers standing on the sidewalk, waving their scanning devices at people who walked by them.

Anna tried to clear her mind from negative thoughts. She thought about the beauty of her art, she thought about making her Master happy and how she looked forward to dancing for First Supreme Leader. She heard clicks and buzzes from the scanning machines and the girls made it past the checkpoint.

Anna didn't dare even look at the other girls as they continued on. Anna was glad she was wearing her heavy, high boots this day as they held her ankle in place. Each step made her want to scream, but she had to continue on without a sound or a grimace.

The girls parted ways at their complex and Anna pressed the codes to access the elevator and then to her floor. She coded the pass key to her apartment and went in.

In the corner, there was a whirring noise and a pair of brown circular lights lit up. The lights blinked on and her companion, Marissa, walked over to her, a light whirring accompanying her steps.

"You're home at last. Are you ready for dinner?" Marissa asked as the kitchen popped to life with the fridge opening up. Marissa stood and surveyed Anna, her brown glass eyes scanning the dancer up and down.

"You have an injury. I should report it," Marissa said.

"No, no . . . it's not an injury. No, not really. It's typical for a dancer. It happens all the time." Anna sat on the couch and proceeded to unbuckle her boots. She grimaced as she pulled the boot from her injured foot.

"See? Just a little sprain! I still did the full rehearsal and I'll be good as new tomorrow," she said brightly.

"Dubious," Marissa said with a click and clack.

"Yes, it's normal for humans to have swollen ankles when they twist them. But these things heal, and everything will be fine."

"I might have to make a report."

"Please don't, not yet. Let's just have our dinner and watch some entertainment. You'll see, I'll be good as new tomorrow."

"Not likely," Marissa said as she walked over to the kitchen and pulled some meat and vegetables from it. "Tacos?"

"Yes, it feels like a taco night, Marissa. Yes, it does. I love how you make tacos," Anna said. She hoped that allowing her robotic companion to make her favorite dish that she would be diverted from the injury. She had been with Marissa since the Government had put her in the ballet as a child. She figured they'd been together for nearly twenty earth years, and though Marissa was a very old model companion, Anna didn't want to trade her in. Marissa knew her inside and out; but more important, Anna believed that Marissa would never betray her. She had been programmed to be loyal to Anna, and so far she had always been, even through very harsh times both with romantic partners and government investigations.

As the smell of tacos filled the apartment, Anna thought back to how delicious tacos had been when she was a child. Before the Second Wave of Government had come into power. Back then, people still ate domesticated animal meat and used by-products like milk to make cheese. Modern tacos contained no meat, at least not the ones that Marissa made for her. But the combinations of plant-based materials along with a healthy dose of spicy salsa made it taste close enough. Only the very rich ate meat anymore. And it wasn't from domesticated animals.

Society had changed so rapidly even within her own lifetime. When she was young, she was quite precocious, an early reader and very curious. She had been able to learn about history through her parents' Internet and books. But once the Second Wave of Government took completely over, Internet and most history books were banned. The only information that was accessed was handpicked by the Powers That Be. Rumors were rampant among those who dared to gossip. And gossipers were often met with an ugly and torturous end.

Anna had seen many of her friends disappear. Most had been taken away as children. And most of the adults were gone as well, including her own parents.

The only humans who had been spared were those who had shown some kind of talent in the arts. For no matter how many wars and political pontificating consumed the higher-ups, there was still an interest, a human need and desire to be entertained.

And robots, though clever and programmable, still hadn't been able to capture that most elusive of human assets: the spark of creativity, the imagination.

As in the old courts she had read about in fairy tales, people with talent in the performing arts were allowed to survive.

A robot could write a book. But it could only write a book within the parameters of the information it had been programmed to utilize. A human could dream of worlds and ideas in unique ways. The human vision was coveted in this era.

A robot could paint a picture, but could it invent new ways of seeing? Could it understand how to capture a moment in time, how the light reflects from the clouds to the water and onto the face of a baby watching a spider spinning a silken web? Could a robot conceive of a god or heaven, of painting angels whispering to a giggling child, or a demon tempting the tormented?

And what about music? A human could imagine new ways for the notes to fall, to create sounds and styles beyond anything that had ever been created before, inspired by grief or happiness, inspired by the will to live or die. A human could play instruments with a delicacy that no robot had perfected yet. A robot could imitate plucking harp strings or the sound of a violin, but to intricately finger the tiny humming strings was still a skill that was embraced by humans.

With dancing, humans could create new styles, new movements and, more important, could execute the movements with fluidity and grace. A robot couldn't dance "the robot" convincingly yet, and such a style still required the human touch.

Anna had been recognized as a brilliant and teachable dancer from the age of five and so had been taken to the special section of town where all the artists lived.

However, being an artist still provided no job security. Growing old and senile, or becoming injured, or in other ways unable to perform in the art, meant that the artist was taken away, never to be seen again.

No one knew what happened to artists who were deemed unable to provide their art anymore. And certainly, one could imagine that any artist could become a writer and capture memoirs for others to enjoy. But the Government didn't allow memoirs. The Government kept a firm hand on all the art produced, and if something fell outside of the parameters of acceptability, then the artist and the art disappeared.

Anna was happy that her art was dancing, for she only had to do what she was told. She could never be taken away for creating something deemed inappropriate as she only did what the choreographer or, in this case, Master, dictated. However, the current Master was not always the Master.

There had been a previous Master. But no one ever spoke of him.

Anna stifled a groan as she lifted her leg to the couch.

"Marissa, can you please bring me something cold?" she asked.

Marissa opened the fridge and removed a bottle of iced tea.

"No, sorry. I mean the ice packs for my feet. They should be in the freezer."

Marissa opened the freezer compartment and retrieved three small packs. She walked over to Anna and put them on the coffee table.

"Thank you," Anna said as she arranged them around her ankle.

"Your ankle is turning black," Marissa said. "Blood is pooling, it's probably broken."

"No, it's not broken," Anna said. "I wouldn't be able to walk if it was."

"I disagree." Marissa put her hand out. There was clicking and whirring.

"No, don't scan it. I don't want the Academy of Human Rehabilitation to know about it."

"I've not sent the information. I'm just compiling it for the files," Marissa said as she returned to making the tacos.

Anna wanted to say more but she bit her tongue. She was no fool. She knew that every artist had a robotic companion. Whether the companion was brand-new state-of-the-art or old like Marissa, Anna knew that her every utterance was recorded and analyzed for her allegiance to the Second Wave of Government.

"Rehearsal was magnificent today," Anna said breezily as Marissa brought her the tacos. "We did a piece from *Swan Lake* and I was even put into a quartet with the other three humans for a special—" A jolt of pain shot up her leg, but she gulped down her air. "We're in a special piece for the First Supreme Leader's performance next month."

"Good for you. Perhaps you should practice more," Marissa said.

Anna looked sharply at her.

"Practice more? I dance all day long at the studios. How can I practice more?"

"You are slower, you are larger, your balance . . ."

"What? How do you know anything? You're not there."

"I don't have to be. I can observe you right here. You're nearly thirty, old age for a ballet dancer."

"Lots of dancers work into their fifties. Or at least . . . used to."

"The modern way is young, light as a feather, graceful and beautiful. You have lines around your eyes."

"I can use makeup," Anna said.

"Of course, makeup. But you can't put makeup on your ankle."

"Never mind my ankle. I'm going to be fine."

*

The next day, however, Anna wasn't fine at all. As she blinked her way to consciousness the next morning, searing pain consumed her. She sat up in her bed and pulled the blanket back. Her ankle was huge and black. She heard the whir of gears as Marissa came down the hall.

"You're awake?" Marissa asked. "You slept late."

"I was tired, I guess."

"I was about to come and wake you. There's not much time before rehearsal."

"Right . . ." Anna feigned cheerfulness.

"Your foot, Anna? Has it healed?"

"Yes, yes. My foot is much better today. Much better."

But it wasn't.

Anna waited for Marissa to leave the room. She tossed aside the covers and attempted to move her swollen foot to the side of the bed.

"Mother of— What am I going to do?" she muttered, then clamped her hand over her mouth. Marissa's whir returned. She poked her head in the door.

"You called?"

"No . . . no . . . just . . . just talking to myself."

"Talking to yourself. Note. Sign of dementia."

"No . . . no, I wasn't talking to myself in that way. Not at all. I was just . . . I was just . . ."

"Your foot . . . your foot has changed color."

"No, it's fine. I'm wearing a sock on it, that's all."

"No . . ." Marissa came closer, her gears clicking as she reached out a hand to touch the foot. Her robotic fingers clamped around the ankle. Anna screamed.

"No good. That foot isn't good," Marissa said.

"I'm fine. I just need a day or two to heal."

"The Government doesn't—"

"It's *fine*." Anna rolled out of bed. "Once I have my shower, I'll be fine."

Anna crawled to the shower stall, which was a few feet from her bed. She turned it on and let the tears flow down the drain with the water. Her foot would get better, it had to.

*

Anna managed to get herself to the rehearsal. She had tightly bound up her foot and every step was an agony. She knew that dancing en pointe was going to be brutal, but she'd just have to breathe through the pain. That's what everyone did, right? Breathe through the pain.

The rehearsal began.

"You look pale. Are you okay?" Lonnie whispered.

"I'm fine. Shh," Anna hissed through clenched teeth.

Master clapped his hands.

"First we'll work on the barre. You must get those lines perfect, ladies. Keep your hands loose but point your fingers with purpose. Your port de bras must be perfect."

The piano began to play. Anna sucked in her breath with every plié, every dip, focusing mainly on her arms.

After two hours of barre work, it was time to rehearse the piece. Anna's head was swimming. Working on the barre had been a nightmare, but at least she could cling to it and the focus had been on the arms and hands. Leaving the barre would be a different story.

The piano played. The robots began to dance, with the humans joining them one by one. Anna pirouetted to her spot. The Master clapped his hands twice loudly. The piano music stopped.

"NO!" he said. "Anna, no. It's a pas de bourrée couru followed by pas de chat, not a pirouette. You know this."

Anna nodded.

"Again!"

The piano played. The robots danced. Lonnie, Margery, and Caroline danced to their spots and turned to Anna. She began her pas de bourrée couru and tumbled to the floor. The humans gasped. Master clapped his hands twice. The music stopped. The robots stood silent vigil.

"You're injured, Anna. I can see from here, your ankle. Did you break it?"

"I'm fine, Master, really," Anna said as she tried to stand. Shooting pain like fire flared up her leg. She fell back to the floor, unconscious.

*

When she awoke, she was in a hospital bed. The room was white, the sheets were white. Whiteness was everywhere. Her foot still hurt; in fact, it hurt more than ever. As she looked at the blank walls, she imagined that Marissa had sent her to the Academy of Human Rehabilitation. Her stomach churned as she imagined all the implications this Academy of Human Rehabilitation visit would have for her place on the roster of society. How long had she been here? She stared around the room, but there were no clues.

A humanoid robot entered her room. She wore a white gown with pants and looked very lifelike with compassionate brown eyes brightly shining from her perfectly even-toned complexion face, her head slightly tilted as if she were listening intently and topped with a white netted hat to catch her blond Pageboy. Her gears whirred lightly as her hand movements fluttered. Her mouth didn't quite close when she spoke.

"Awake now?" Her eyes flashed, and there was a louder whirring noise. Anna imagined Robot Nurse was scanning her and recording her vitals. "Good. You will be ready for processing."

"What?"

"Get up, it's time to go."

"But—"

The robot pulled away her sheets. Anna stared in horror at her foot. Or rather, where her foot used to be. There was a shiny silver robotic foot in the shape of a pointe shoe attached to the end of her leg.

"No!"

"Ours is not to question why," the robot said as she pulled Anna to standing position.

"I can't . . . I can't." Anna sobbed.

"You can, and you will. You are lucky they are letting you go back. Others are not so lucky," the robot said.

The robot led her to a waiting room where a dozen other humans sat. They too all looked shocked or despairing.

"What is this?" Anna asked as she sat beside a sad-looking man.

"Processing," he said. "This is where creatives come to get repurposed. Well, the last step of whatever round of repurposing you happen to be receiving."

"What do you mean, repurposed?"

"I've heard . . . they will take our parts, the good parts, and use them as long as possible. Or, if we're still somewhat viable, they'll fix us in their own ways. For me, I was an artist, but I lost my hand in an accident." He held up his hand, now robotic. It clicked as he demonstrated many different poses. "I was lucky: I was sent back out, to work for many more years. My skills were in high demand and the hand was of no consequence. This hand can also draw my visions. But now they've determined my visions are no longer viable for the Government. I am now sentenced to the Next Phase after they finish processing me."

"The Next Phase. What's that?"

"Hopefully you'll never know," the man said as a male humanoid robot with compassionate large brown eyes in a white gown, white pants, and a white cap over his blond Pageboy led him away.

Anna looked around the room at the other humans. A few robot humanoid nurses walked by. There were other types of smaller robots whistling by on wheels carrying rows of test tubes, cylinders, and sharp shiny items. No one met her eyes.

"Anna598," a voice in the air spoke. The identification floated through the air above the room in a hologram, blinking and buzzing as Anna raised her hand and looked around.

*

Anna entered the dance studio. She was still getting used to the heaviness of her new foot. Once she had arrived home from the Academy of Human Rehabilitation, she had practiced working with her new foot. Every movement was agony as pain-relief drugs were banned for all humans for fear of addictions. She realized she had been away for nearly a month. Marissa hadn't provided much in the way of comfort as she practiced in her small apartment.

"Your foot is too heavy. Your lines aren't clean."

"I will make them clean," Anna had argued through clenched teeth.

For hours she had practiced in the mirror, getting the gait of her new foot, learning how to lift it, learning how to strap it into the shunt of the pointe shoe, making it look effortless and pretty as a ballerina should be. But it wasn't.

Now that she was back at rehearsal, she feared the worst.

"Welcome back, Anna," Master had greeted her. "Hopefully you've fully recovered from your incident."

"Yes, Master," Anna said, keeping all emotion from her voice. The slightest tremor of doubt or disdain would be cause for Master to report her. And she couldn't have that on her first day back.

They went through the exercises and Anna paid special attention to her foot. Lifting it, pointing it, using every muscle in her thigh to make it look effortless, to make it look as beautiful as it had before.

Master clapped his hands twice.

"Let's see the piece from *La Sylphide*," he requested. "Our performance for the First Supreme Leader is in a few days. We must perfect it."

Anna gulped but made sure her face held no expression, not one glimmer of inner thought. Inside, she was terrified. She'd missed weeks of rehearsal and she didn't know if she'd remember the steps.

Master clapped again, and the piano began to play. The robots swirled into the second formation and Anna's body fell into the music. The piece came back effortlessly; the only issue was the weight of the foot. As she pirouetted, she adjusted her body to accommodate the new weight. She arched her leg out, a perfect arc from tip of her nose to her splayed fingers and the point of her shoe. The stocking covered up the mechanics. Did any of them know what really happened? That her foot was gone?

She made it through rehearsal and was glad when she was finally able to get home and breathe a sigh of relief. Her life was back to normal. Her friends had been warm to her but cautious. She didn't blame them one bit.

*

The First Supreme Leader was sitting on a huge golden throne. Holographic renderings of ancient demons with gnashing teeth and lolling tongues hissed at Anna from the arms and legs of the throne. Two humanoid domestic security robots attired in long navy-blue tunics and loose white pants escorted Anna toward the First Supreme Leader. The hallway was long, and it was awkward to actually walk on in a regular manner as her foot was molded to the shape of the shunt in her ballet shoe. The gleaming marbles floor were slippery as well. By the time she reached the First Supreme Leader, she was exhausted. However, Anna held her head high, sweat beading from her brow from not only the walk but from her performance with En Pointe Troupe 67. Her thighs ached on top of the constant throb of bleeding toes.

"You performed very well today, Anna598," the First Supreme Leader said. "I had to see you for myself."

"Thank you, your worship," Anna said. She bowed her head, wondering why she was called.

"You may look at me. I want to see you for myself, the face, the eyes of a creative soul." Anna looked upon the face of the First Supreme Leader. She realized that it was a beautiful humanoid, not a person at all. At first Anna thought that perhaps there was too much paint for either male or female, perhaps covering up some kind of scar or rash. But the longer she stared, the more she recognized the large expansive eyes, one shining just a little bit too bright. The First Supreme Leader was part robot. Perhaps the whole Second Wave of Government was run by robots.

Anna furrowed her forehead as the Leader studied her.

"What are you feeling? Surely nothing unkind?" the strange soothing voice whispered.

Anna realized she was showing emotion, and to the highest of the high no less. She stood tall and ignored the ache of her legs, organizing her facial features into a blank stare.

"Oh, don't be silly, Anna598. You're safe with me. I called you here because I have a great need for you."

"What do you mean?"

"It's hard to explain, I'll have to show you."

The First Supreme Leader stood up and cupped Anna's face into velvet gloved hands. "You are so very beautiful. I'm so happy I've found you."

Anna swallowed, then forced a small smile. Her heart pounded wildly, and she hoped the Supreme Leader didn't hear it.

"Oh, Anna598, we're going to be together a very long time. Please call me Sava."

"Yes, Sava. I'm not quite sure I follow what you're saying . . ."

"What I'm saying, Anna598, is that I'm offering you a position here at the Academy of Creative Essence."

"The Academy of Creative Essence? What's that?"

"Come, follow me."

The security guards began to follow, but Sava held up a hand. "No, it's all right. It'll be just the two of us. You can monitor the relative visuals from here."

*

After two long elevator rides down into the depths of the planet, Sava and Anna finally stepped out of the elevator and into a huge domed hallway. Sava hurried down a hallway until he stood in front of a door. After a quick eye scan, the door slid open and they entered a new room.

After three more door entry security passes, they finally entered into a large hallway. This one was decorated with neon lights and holograms displaying the latest news from across the galaxy from many different satellites. The sudden dash of colors and noise was disorienting, and Sava led her further down another hallway. One more set of face scans and they were at the final destination.

"This—this is the eye, the sacred eye of all that is. This is where the Academy of Creative Essence derives its name."

Anna looked around. It was another room of flashing lights and swirling holographic information dumps. Around her were many hallways.

"Come, you'll see." As they walked down the hallway, the holograms transformed from news to snippets of stories and songs. Music of various genres spiraled around one another, a collision course of melodic synchronicity.

"I can see the music, I can touch it," Anna gasped as they walked around another corridor until they came to a large room. Sava turned to her.

"Yes. Anything is possible in the Academy of Creative Essence. This is where artists are truly able to shine, to create whatever they want from whatever they want. No idea is too large or too small, too outlandish or impossible. Here at the Academy of Creative Essence, you are free to explore whatever you wish."

"And what's the catch? And why me?"

"First of all, I picked you when I saw you perform today. I wondered why the En Pointe Troupe 67 would send a subpar dancer when they know the consequences."

Anna tried to keep her lip from quivering.

"What consequences?" Anna asked.

"They won't be asked to perform again for me or any other Government Assembly. In other words, they need to be repurposed and reassigned."

"I've already . . ."

"Yes. Once I inquired about your history, I realized that in years of reviews you were considered the best dancer in the En Pointe Troupe 67. No matter how many other dancers came and went, you remained the top of the line from when you were but a child until . . . recently. I then learned of your unfortunate accident. They repurposed your broken ankle into a working one, and with that, they added a whole new foot designed explicitly for pointe."

"Correct," Anna said softly.

"And since you've only been dancing for about a week, you

aren't used to the weight yet. I could see it in how you held yourself, the quiver in the leg of a prima ballerina. Not for a simple leg lift or pas de bourrée. A prodigy such as yourself would never tremble on stage. You're just not used to your foot yet."

"I appreciate you understanding."

"And since you'll never be used to that new foot, not in the manner that you were, I imagine professional ballet dancing is likely out of reach for you now."

"I'm not quitting. I've just begun to return."

"Well, you won't be returning to En Pointe Troupe 67. You'll be dancing for me, here, in the Academy of Creative Essence. You've heard my musicians, my poets, my artists, each in their own studios creating within their own madness to their hearts' content. There is no censorship, it's all freeform and thought."

"But why?"

"Because I'm trying to isolate the creative spark, the creative essence. Once we can capture it and close it, we can use its properties in robots. That way, there will be no need for humans in any capacity anymore."

"I don't understand."

"Please, sit down here."

Sava pointed to a basic chair with arms and legs. The minute Anna sat down, the arms of the chair sprung open with arm clamps. The same happened with the legs of the chairs. Anna was secured to the chair.

"We're not sure how to isolate the Creative Essence. Scientists have been trying to find it for centuries. Is it a gene, a molecule? Genetics? Imitation? Parts of the brain that can be manipulated? Is it in the soul? How do we capture it?"

"How *do* you capture it?"

"We'll be taking samples of your blood, monitoring your vital signs, tracking your movements. We've never had a ballet dancer before, so we've designed special units to track your motor functions and how they entwine with your reasoning and creative skills and somehow get it out of you. Maybe it's in your breath or your urine. Maybe it's in sweat? No one knows. But as each generation gets stronger with technological insight, the secret will eventually be revealed."

"It can't be taught or harvested. I know that. It comes from inside, the gut, the combination of will and vision," Anna whispered.

"And so much more." Sava nodded. "So, you understand."

"What? You're going to cut me open?"

"Oh, no, nothing like that, yet. We're just putting some electrodes and other wirings on you and then we'll show you the features of your new studio. That's the fold-down stage complete with lighting. And that's the sound system. But first, this is going to hurt."

"You'll find that I've arrived with nothing more than hearts and dreams. I don't see how you can isolate something comprised of so many components."

"Believe me, we've heard it all over the centuries. We do keep track," Sava said.

*

Anna danced, her legs grew stronger, and soon she barely felt the extra weight of her foot at all. She stopped dreaming about seeing the world or even performing for more than a handful of people ever again. She was now just a personal puppet show for Sava, strings and all. There were many times she tripped over all the wirings that were attached to various parts of her body for various reasons. Most were tubes collecting things, but others were electrodes, stimulators, and other experimental data compilers.

As the years went by, Anna's other troupe partners arrived at the Academy of Creative Essence as their own bodies betrayed them: Lonnie, Caroline, and even eventually Margery, who apparently never hit the legacy precision that Anna598 had left behind.

Each time a new member arrived from En Pointe Troupe 67, Anna was grateful for the companionship. Even though each "student" of the Academy of Creative Essence was given a private room where most of their lives would be spent, it was wonderful to see a familiar face at rehearsals once more.

Anna kept waiting for Master to arrive, but he never did. She wondered if he was enough robot to keep working forever or if he had broken down and gone to be repurposed elsewhere.

The humans who formed En Pointe Troupe 67 were instructed to perform one full show a month of their choosing. This time no robots, just the four dancers. They wore elaborate wiring, some hooked up to machines while they danced. Sava would read the charts and curse that the Creative Essence was as elusive as ever.

When Sava was feeling generous, several groups of artists were allowed to participate together on complicated projects, such as a theatre show, a movie, an art gallery, and so on. Sometimes hundreds of the "students" of the Academy of Creative Essence worked together, faces blank, wires hanging from their bodies as badges to remind them of existence as living puppets.

Lonnie was the first to be removed from the Academy. When she had arrived, she had broken a leg and arm in a vehicle crash. Her limbs had been replaced with mechanical aids. Her foot was pointed to fit into her shunt, her movements were limitless yet jerky. She was never able to regenerate to meet the First Supreme Leader's expectations, so off she went, discarded for a situation beyond her control. Anna never saw her again and never heard what happened to her.

When Anna walked through the hallways of echoing music and splashes of art, she saw herself dancing along the hallways, her muse interspersed with other dancers populated throughout the experiment, intertwining through one another without ever having known of their existence.

Sometimes Anna would stop and listen, really listen to the cacophony that flooded through the hallways—all that leaked-out creativity spilling from behind locked doors.

When she first walked through the hallways, she had thought it was all electronically induced. But as time went on and she grew more familiar with the laboratory, she realized that the hallway holograms were subjective hallucinations. When Sava spoke about them, Anna saw and heard and felt something different, something more, much more. The essence clung to Anna's body, stuck between her fingers like spiderwebs. The muse whispered into her ear, urging her to dance harder and faster as visions of her own performances spilled before her eyes. The halls interconnected with the caged creators, their grief, their despair, their lunacy echoing through the chambers and along the underside of the floors. Anna had never spoken of this to Sava but mined the information for herself.

Was the vast labyrinth of hallways the heart of creative essence, the creative spark? How did Sava not see it? Was it because she herself wasn't creative?

Anna kept her secret close to her chest as she listened to Sava opine about the secret to Creative Essence for another few years. Anna watched many of her new friends die or become repurposed. Sometimes people returned to the labyrinth a time or two after an accident, but usually they just disappeared.

At last, Anna's own body wore out. The endless dancing, more injuries, and of course, all the eating disorders to remain ninety pounds (despite a heavy mechanical foot) that led to the very human condition of malnutrition. She tripped once more at a performance, and this time she didn't get up.

After she was carried to her room, Sava came in to see her, with assistants pushing several trolleys of machines and wirings. Sava instructed the room to be bubbled so if the creative essence was in the soul, they could catch it as it floated away. She had wirings attached to every inch of her in case the relative creative essence shot out of the electrical blood currents as the heart stopped.

"I can't even die without being your science experiment," Anna said during a lucid moment. "You saw with the others: you can't bottle the creative spark, you can't capture creative essence. It's not possible." She wheezed and coughed. "All the misery you've caused when you could have been sitting around painting sunsets. It's a waste. It was here for you all along. It's always been here."

As Anna took her last breath, Sava stared down at her.

"What do you mean, 'it's always been here'? I've been told that before, but I don't understand it. Tell me."

Anna lay still, a small smile on her face. Sava's voice was distant, his urgency giving Anna delight in her last conscious moment. Sava shook her. "Anna, explain it to me. Please."

Sava then put her hand on Anna's throat. The breath had stopped but nothing was happening. No spirit or essence came out of any orifice, the blood showed no fluctuations, the electrical impulses stopped with no sudden acquiring of knowledge. There was nothing trapped in the bubble. All the monitors showed nothing.

Sava allowed a sigh to slip from her lips, and then she cleared her throat in frustration. She looked around to be certain no one had seen the slip. Tapping the communication piece with the required code, Sava spoke loudly.

"Prepare the room for Anna599. I will go up to greet her. Maybe this time we'll get it right."

Camera Aeterna

Steven-Elliot Altman

> Through a discovery also in the field of photography, now being investigated, will the fact of survival be proven. Through the use of the radio by those who have passed over will communication be eventually set up, and reduced to a true science. . . . Death will lose its terrors, and that particular fear will come to an end.
> —ALICE BAILEY, *A Treatise on the Seven Rays* (1939)

"We don't have time for this!" Julie shouted when Detective Preston again demanded an explanation.

Preston was doing his best to follow her disjointed ramblings—she'd been going on about "cameras" and "auras" and "radio waves that allowed you to hear the dead"—but so far he'd been unable to determine even if a crime had been committed. There was only the blood on her torn blouse.

He tuned her out and studied the woman. She was a real looker, despite the blouse, the split lip, the disheveled red hair, and the muck on her otherwise finely freckled face—a pert Irish lass. There was more blood and grime beneath her well-manicured fingernails, and red scrapes on the backs of her hands. She had on no coat or shoes; when they'd brought her in, battered and barefoot, he'd assumed she'd been assaulted. But her disjointed statements suggested she'd been the aggressor in whatever had transpired. Still, Preston's gut told him she was the victim, not the perp.

"Look, Mrs. Earnhardt," he said, "take a deep breath. I need you to answer a few questions."

Julie made an effort to compose herself.

"Now tell me calmly," Preston continued, "is someone deceased here or not?"

"That's the whole point," Julie said, clearly frustrated. "My husband passed over this weekend, but he's still in the basement. I need to get back to him while there's time!"

Preston stifled the obvious questions for the moment, asking instead, "What's your husband's name?"

"Ron Earnhardt."

Preston jotted it on his com.

"And how exactly did Ron *pass over*, Mrs. Earnhardt?"

"Pancreatic cancer. He got it from the fucking camera."

She bit her lip and looked away, tears in her eyes. Preston chose to ignore them.

"You say Ron died over the weekend but his body is still in your basement. Why is that?"

"Because he made me promise to keep that damned camera rolling."

She cupped her face in her hands as sobs wracked her slim frame. Preston gave her a moment before continuing.

"I'm sorry Ron passed away. Is that his blood on your blouse?"

"It's Marjorie's—Ron's assistant. I stabbed her with a screwdriver."

Now they were getting somewhere.

"And what's Marjorie's surname?"

"Tipton."

"Where is Ms. Tipton now?"

"I don't know. I was running away from her when those two policemen grabbed me."

"Tell me what happened."

"She was planning to claim credit for the camera. She would've erased all the files, erased everything Ron worked for. And she would've killed me and our daughter."

"Then you acted in self-defense?"

"Of course."

"And I suppose you were already headed to the police when the officers picked you up?"

"I was going to St. Augustine's on Queen's Gate Mews, to get Father Donohue. Ron sent me for him."

Preston noted the name and address.

"Why did Ron need you to fetch this Father Donohue?"

"I'm not entirely sure. Maybe Ron will tell you. Please, we're running out of time. I need to get back."

Too bad, Preston thought. Just when she'd finally begun making sense.

"How exactly can Ron tell me anything when he's dead?" he asked.

Julie sobered, realizing what she had to do.

"Take me home and I'll show you," she said. "Alone."

Preston noted her change in posture, the pitch of her voice. She'd reached the point of saying anything necessary to get what she wanted. He'd seen that look before in his wife's eyes, the day she'd packed up and left him, taking their daughter with her.

Preston tapped his stylus against the desk and considered the ramifications of doing what Mrs. Earnhardt wanted. If she was to be believed, her husband's assistant could be injured (or worse) at that location. There could be unattended children.

"Explain to me why I should do what you ask, and I'll think about it."

"There's no time. Ron only has a few hours left. Take me home now and I'll show you everything. If you knew what I know, we'd be on our way there already."

Preston considered. Taking her home on his own would be highly irregular. But something told him to trust her. He hoped it wasn't physical attraction. He'd made bad calls on that front before.

"Would you say it's a matter of life or death?" he asked.

Julie looked through the open blind slats of the small office at the throngs of pedestrians dashing along the snowy street outside, all of them lost, frantically searching in darkness for a light switch only Ron could offer them. She looked back at Detective Preston. He had a kind face for a policeman.

"It's more of a matter of life *and* death," she told him. "Take me home and you'll never have to ask that question again."

*

Preston parked his unmarked car on the street outside the Earn-hardt residence, an unremarkable four-story Georgian terrace house. Julie was out of the passenger door in an instant. It had started snowing again on the drive over. A trip to the loo had left her rea-sonably freshened up. Preston had lent Julie his own woolen trench-coat, and trainers had been procured from the station's Lost and Found. The coat was several sizes too large; it draped to the ground, the hem darkened by slush. A handsome, elderly, gray-haired man in a long topcoat sat on the front steps, his hair and shoulders dust-ed with snow. Preston noted the white clerical collar peeking out of his coat as Julie rushed into his arms.

"Thank God you've come, Father."

The priest tipped his chin in greeting to Preston over Julie's shoulder, then extended a hand as they parted.

"Matthew Donohue," he said. "Vicar at St. Augustine's."

"Detective Bill Preston. Homicide Division. Kensington."

"Come inside, both of you," Julie said. "Come and see Ron."

Preston turned to Donohue as they followed her up the steps.

"Do you have any idea what's going on here, Father?" he asked.

"Ron rang me up this morning and invited me to come by later, to witness a miracle, he said. He and Julie have been part of my par-ish since they were teenagers. About an hour ago I got a panicked message from Julie, saying she needed to see me immediately and was heading over. When she didn't show up, I decided to check on her. I only just got here."

Julie led them through the unremarkable flat, past a kitchen with a table set for two. Preston tapped the priest's shoulder and motioned downward, to a trail of blood smeared along the tiled floor leading in the direction they were headed, suggesting someone badly wounded had crawled down the hall, leaking blood. They arrived at a formidable-looking steel door with an elaborate locking mecha-nism. Julie performed an intricate sequence on the track pad, and the door sprang open.

"Ron's photo lab is downstairs. His job was photographing produce for the Food Standards Agency."

The dingy, unfinished basement was about twenty-by-thirty feet wide, with exposed gray cinderblock walls rising from a cement floor. Heavy black iron pipes and girders spanned the length of the ceiling. In the room's center was a large, high-tech camera mounted on a tripod, aimed at an unoccupied leather armchair, opposite an equally comfortable-looking couch and a low wooden coffee table. Not quite the setup one might expect for photographing produce, Preston thought as he went for a closer look. He'd taken visual evidence classes at training school, logged thousands of hours visualizing hundreds of crime scenes, and knew the latest camera makes and models used by reporters. He'd never seen any camera quite like this one. Diodes flashed and dimmed along a digital control panel, which gave off a low hum that reminded Preston of the eerie sound electrical ground wires make. The lens was the size of a basketball. Leads ran off the camera's body to a nearby table, with a large television monitor, a holographic keyboard, and a storage tower on it, and an old-school portable transistor radio the likes of which Preston hadn't seen in ages—a strange contrast to the other equipment.

"What kind of camera is this, Mrs. Earnhardt?" Preston asked.

"A Charon OmniChrome 1000," she said, frowning. "Ron modified it to take Kirlian photographs. Do you know what they are?"

"Tell me."

"Back in the 1930s, a Russian scientist named Semyon Kirlian developed a way to take pictures of plants and objects using high-voltage currents passed through metal plates, to capture an effect called a corona plasma discharge."

"I'm familiar with this," Father Donohue said, the first time he'd spoken since entering the house. "It was claimed he'd discovered a way to capture an image of what the Theosophists refer to as an aura, or life-energy field. Brought on all manner of New Age speculation. Eventually these notions were scientifically as well as ecclesiastically debunked."

"Did your husband believe in auras, Mrs. Earnhardt?" Preston asked.

"Ron was hired to photograph organic fruits, vegetables, and the like alongside processed produce, and compare them."

She pulled a small stack of photos from a file cabinet and quickly flipped through them. "See how this peach has a brighter, richer corona than this one? Which would you rather eat?"

"Right," Preston said.

Father Donohue glanced at the photos and agreed.

"I guess," Julie went on, "Ron was faster than the other photographers they hired, and turned in the results they wanted, because they kept handing him more and more money—which he used to buy bigger and better cameras, more expensive lenses, and such. Then he hired Marjorie as his full-time assistant. They'd stay down here all hours working. It put a strain on our marriage."

Preston noted the edge in her voice. All this was fascinating, but he needed to ascertain what, if any, crimes had transpired. What had happened to Julie's husband? Was he indeed deceased? Had an assault been made on his assistant?

"Where is your husband, Mrs. Earnhardt?" he asked.

Julie hesitated.

"I'm right here, Detective," a man's voice replied out of thin air. "But I'm afraid I won't be much longer."

Preston and Father Donohue jerked round in surprise.

"Is that you, Ron?" the priest asked, unsure where to direct his question.

"Yes, Father. Sorry to have kept you in the dark, but I'd hoped you'd serve as a witness to what I promise is a most important scientific discovery."

Preston's eyes scanned the room, searching for the speaker. He followed Julie's involuntary gaze to the closet door, then went and put his hand on the knob and turned back to her.

"He's in here, right? Is he armed? You'd better tell me now if he has so much as a push pin on him."

"He's in there, Detective. But it's just his body."

Preston flung the door wide and stepped backward. Inside the closet was a small freezer of the sort supermarkets use to hold ice cream. The doors on top were heavy, tempered glass, semi-frosted over, beneath which Preston could make out the body of a middle-aged man, presumably Ron Earnhardt, naked, sitting with his arms wrapped around his legs, chin on knees, obviously deceased. The position of the body gave Preston the impression of a man who had voluntarily frozen himself to death. The priest peered in and made the sign of the cross, clearly recognizing his parishioner.

"He waited until the last possible moment to get inside," Julie said.

"Did you help him get in there?" Preston asked.

"I did."

"Then you may be held as an accessory to murder."

"I assure you there was no murder committed here, Detective Preston," came Ron's voice. "I'm wholly responsible for my actions; Julie was merely following my instructions. My time is very limited. Have a seat on the couch, please, both of you, and get ready to un-learn everything you think you know about life after death. Julie, would you mind making Detective Preston and Father Donohue some tea, while I bring them up to speed?"

Preston looked at the priest, who answered his unspoken question.

"As far as I can tell, that's Ron's voice. It certainly appears to be his body."

By that point, Preston had determined where the voice was coming from: the transistor radio.

"Gentlemen," the voice continued, "I'd like your consent to record what I'm about to tell you."

All right, Preston thought, if he's willing to confess, I'll play along.

*

"My understanding began with our cat," Ron Earnhardt began.

Father Donohue sipped his tea apprehensively; Preston hadn't touched his yet. Julie sat on the floor between them.

"Baxter was a Siamese. Smartest cat I ever met. I wanted to capture his aura on film. Like most pet owners, I guess I overdid it with the photos, unwittingly resulting in his death from renal failure caused by exposure to the ionizing, high-frequency electromagnetic discharge of the camera. This wasn't long after I'd modified it into its present iteration. But I didn't understand any of this then. I laid Baxter's body in a hatbox, intending to bury him in the back yard the next day. Julie and I went to bed, devastated.

"The next morning, she went to work and I was greeted in the hallway by Clarence, the neighbor's boy, who lives in the apartment above us, complaining that Baxter's meowing had kept him up all night. It had happened in the past, when we'd inadvertently locked Baxter outside. I told Clarence he'd passed on. Clarence swore up and down that Baxter was still meowing. He told me to come upstairs and hear for myself.

"I presumed it was a prank but begrudgingly followed him. Damned if I didn't hear Baxter's meowing as soon as I stepped inside Clarence's room. I've had that cat since I was at school; I know his meow. Clarence was right: it sounded as if Baxter were trapped somewhere. But he was dead in a box in the basement. I took Clarence downstairs to show him. Baxter's body was still there.

"We went back upstairs. That's when I discovered the meowing was coming through Clarence's antique transistor radio sitting on a shelf right in front of my face. Nothing has been broadcast over the airwaves in ages. If you turn one of them on now, all you get is static. But like most kids these days, Clarence is on the autistic spectrum. He says listening to the static helps him sleep at night. He'd simply failed to turn it off all the way. I did, and the meowing stopped.

"I asked Clarence to let me borrow the radio, then brought it downstairs and stared at poor, dead Baxter while his meowing blared from the speaker.

"That's when Marjorie showed up for work. She couldn't make heads or tails of it either, but we were both feeling excited despite our confusion. I almost called you that morning, Father. I probably should have."

"Better late than never," the priest said.

Ron's voice continued through the transistor radio as Julie poured everyone more tea.

"The best Marjorie and I could deduce was that the radio was transmitting white noise at an unusual frequency. We were reluctant to meddle with it in any manner, for fear of losing the signal. We did our best to research the phenomenon and found nothing definitive. But with Baxter still meowing, we believed we were onto something big.

"We started recording everything into analog files on the computer—continuous audio capture of the radio through my best microphone. We set up a mini-camera recording the radio with the monitor screen in view, to prove it was being made in real time, with time-code markers programmed in by Marjorie.

"Then Baxter stopped. We realized all we had was an audio recording of a cat meowing—certainly inconclusive as evidence. Disappointed, we went about our work, photographing fruit until Marjorie left for the day. I was getting ready to bury Baxter when it dawned on me to photograph his body with the OmniChrome, to see if there was anything unusual about his corona discharge, his life energy. A dead cat shouldn't give off much of an aura.

"Julie, will you please turn the monitor on now?"

Julie was at the table in moments, her fingers hovering over the control panel's holographic keyboard.

"Play the file named *Baxter-1*. Gentlemen, here's what I saw."

Preston and the priest leaned forward and watched intently. On-screen on the table, in high resolution, was a dead Siamese cat in a hatbox. Preston couldn't discern any light shimmering off the cat's body, if that's what they were expected to see. Then they heard a meow. Clearly the cameraman (presumably Ron) heard it too. The camera swept the length of the basement in search of the source.

And there it was! A blue-white glowing object sat on the arm of the couch where Preston and Father Donohue were now sitting. The camera focused, revealing without doubt a cat nonchalantly licking a paw and dabbing its face. It appeared as a blue, prismatic afterimage, like an old photographic negative but with a shimmering aura much like what they'd seen in the Kirlian photographs Julie had shown them.

"Baxter, come here, old boy!" Ron's exhilarated voice called on-screen.

The glowing blue cat leapt down from the couch and scurried toward the camera.

*

Preston asked Julie to replay the video several times, until he declared he'd seen enough.

"I had no doubt I had irrefutable evidence life continues after death," came Ron's voice.

Tears ran down Father Donohue's cheeks. But twenty-two years on the force had left Preston skeptical. For as long as he could remember, he'd wanted the magician's tricks to be real. They never were. There was always a false thumb, an invisible wire, or some secret panel. All he'd actually witnessed here was a corpse in a freezer, a voice on an antique radio, and video of the Earnhardts' cat that might be faked. All three of these people, including the priest, could be playing him, although he couldn't imagine why. He felt confident he'd get to the bottom of it.

"I know what you're thinking, Detective," Ron's voice said. "The footage could have been doctored."

"Turn the camera on and show us the cat now. I'll be more inclined to believe you once I see it live."

"Unfortunately, I can't do that," Ron replied. "I'm afraid Baxter's gone."

"That's awfully convenient," Preston said.

"Actually it's terribly *inconvenient,* for reasons I have yet to explain, none of which we could have foreseen. We filmed Baxter continuously for nearly forty hours, footage I'd be happy to show you if I had the time. I don't. The issue at hand is what happened to him at the end. Julie, play the *Baxter-48* file, please."

Onscreen, by the couch, Preston observed Ron alive and robust: medium build with tousled brown hair, dark eyes, cleft chin, thin hands, wearing tweed trousers, slippers, and an off-white cardigan—not a bad-looking bloke. He sat on the floor, playing with the glowing blue aura of his cat. If this was a hoax—as Preston presumed it must be—the juxtaposition between live subject and computer-gen cat was the best he'd ever seen. The man on the floor looked quite similar to the corpse in the freezer—evidence for identifying the body. He watched as Ron dangled an antique computer mouse by its cable in front of Baxter; he swiped at it as you'd expect any playful cat would do. Suddenly the cat lost interest in the mouse and in Ron, captivated by something above it, off-camera. He began meowing at whatever it was. After several moments it became clear the cat was severely disturbed. The onscreen Ron appeared unable to identify the source of the cat's distress any better than Preston could.

Then the cat vanished.

"Julie, they're going to want to see the *Baxter-Close-On* file," came Ron's voice.

Preston watched intently a frame-by-frame replay on the monitor screen, with the time-code slowed. In the cat's final moments, it seemed to burst into thousands of tiny globules of light that then simply blacked out. Julie replayed the footage, closer up. Now the globules were explosions of incandescent light that all blacked out in unison. And again, closer still: a single globule like a drop of water encountering a wave of intense heat and evaporating like steam in an instant.

"That's what I meant by *gone*," Ron stated. "I hope you believe what you've seen. Now you know why I can't turn the camera on and show you Baxter live. Perhaps seeing me live will suffice. Julie, please switch the monitor to broadcast."

Several lights danced along the control panel as the image on the monitor switched to live feed, revealing Ron Earnhardt, like his cat an outline of radiating, ephemeral blue light, sitting comfortably in the leather armchair directly across from Preston and Father Donohue on the couch.

Preston looked repeatedly from the empty chair in the basement to the same, occupied chair on the monitor. He got up, went to the chair, and circled it twice, waving his arms above the empty seat. The monitor captured his movements in real time, removing all doubt in Preston's mind about the footage being live.

"Let me assure you that although my physical body is dead I'm still very much alive," Ron said, answering Preston's unspoken question. "What you're seeing is my etheric body. Please believe me, no foul play has occurred here regarding my transition. I'd have you clear my wife of any wrongdoing before I depart."

"Even presuming I believe you are, in fact, dead, Mr. Earnhardt, and that I'm somehow talking to your *etheric body,* that doesn't automatically clear your wife of culpability in your demise. To say the least, it's highly irregular to rely on posthumous testimony from the deceased. I need more to present to my superiors—in an acceptable manner."

"That makes sense," Ron admitted. "Julie, you'd better give the detective your account of how I died."

Julie left her station at the computer and sat at her husband's etheric feet. Preston still couldn't quite believe what he was seeing in the monitor. If this was a hoax, it was spectacular. All he could do for now was wait and see where it led.

*

"You may recall that the flu went around this summer?" Julie began.

"Half the parish came down with it," Father Donohue said.

"Both Ron and I caught it," she continued. "Marjorie, too, if I recall?"

She looked at Ron for confirmation; Preston sensed some uneasy subtext as he nodded.

"We both went to the clinic. The doctor ordered blood tests, gave us chest X-rays, put us on a course of antibiotics, and sent us home with orders for plenty of rest and lots of fluids."

"Was this before or after the cat?" Preston asked.

"Almost immediately after," Julie replied. "I daresay Ron and Marjorie's schedule left Ron's immune system compromised. I'm sure it was a contributing factor."

Ron gave Julie a look Preston knew well from his own marriage. Even in his etheric state, he dared not contradict her.

"Three days later we got a call from the clinic. There were serious irregularities in Ron's lab results, and they needed to see him right away. When we got there they told us they wanted to run more tests. They suspected Ron had pancreatic cancer."

Julie paused; tears formed in her eyes. She looked at Father Donohue.

Ron picked up the story.

"I immediately suspected I was subject to the same ill-effects as Baxter."

"It was that fucking camera!" Julie shouted.

"Yes, love, it was," Ron said tenderly. He got down on his knees before his wife, placing his etheric hands on her shoulders, not truly touching her but touching her nonetheless. "But it's such a small price to pay—my life in exchange for freeing every man and woman from the fear of death."

"I don't want you to leave me."

"I promise I'll never leave you. Remember what we said."

Julie raised her head. "I remember," she said.

Ron turned to Preston. "Medical science deemed me terminal less than one week later. It's in the records; you can verify it."

"If I'm not mistaken, I believe I remember that day," Father Donohue interjected.

"I came to church," Ron confirmed. "My knees were sore by the time I left."

"I pray you received what you came for."

"I did, Father. I left with a sense of purpose. Christ came to tell us death isn't the end. I aimed to prove it by recording my death."

"Who needs faith when you've got footage, right?" Preston added.

The three men shared an uneasy laugh.

"Are you a religious man, Detective?" the priest asked.

"I'm afraid not, sir," Preston replied.

Julie wasn't laughing.

"At that point I was quarantined from the basement," she said.

"To limit her exposure," Ron explained. "From then on, I had Marjorie wear full on lead-lined protective gear, as we prepared for my demise—or, to be more precise, the expiration of my physical body and the subsequent ejection of my etheric body.

"We planned to film everything, just as we'd done with Baxter. Only this time we'd also capture the initial separation process we missed with him. I'd write the technical journals, Marjorie would handle the camera, and both Marjorie and Julie would deliver our findings posthumously. I bought the icebox and installed it myself, to keep my body nearby, in the event distance from my remains caused any unforeseen issues.

"When my vital signs began failing, Julie held my hand past the moment of death. We captured it all. Would you like to have a look?"

Father Donohue agreed enthusiastically. A mixture of fear and jubilation ran through Preston, but he, too, agreed.

"Good show," Ron said, soundlessly clapping his ethereal hands together. "Julie, please play *Ron-1*."

Julie went to the monitor station and called up the file. On-screen, the camera angled down on the freezer, now positioned just outside the closet. Ron, clearly the worse for wear from the cancer, sat upright in the freezer, wrapped in gaily coloured quilts and blankets, holding the mask of a small oxygen unit to his face. Preston was pleased to note the freezer wasn't switched on yet. The glass was clear, though he could tell by Ron's labored breathing through the mask that he didn't have much time left.

Julie sat crying softly in the armchair beside Ron, gently holding his free hand. He pulled the oxygen mask aside and announced, "This is it," in a voice Preston could clearly identify.

The camera zoomed in.

"I feel myself fading," Ron said, and took a long, labored pull from the oxygen mask. "I feel like an astronaut about to step onto some bright new planet. Wish me luck."

"I love you, Ron. Remember what you promised," Julie cried, hugging his limp head to her breast.

Preston silently questioned the decency of anyone observing a couple during such an intimate moment, much less broadcasting it one day, for science or otherwise.

"Love," was the last word Ron said—physically, that is.

"Time of death sixteen forty-two on Friday, the twenty-seventh of January," came a female voice from behind the camera, presumably Marjorie's. "Recorded in Kensington, London, in the United Kingdom, in the year of our Lord twenty—"

"Julie, please skip ahead twenty minutes," came Ron's disembodied voice.

A new camera angle on the freezer, which had now been switched on and gave off a soft hum; the tempered glass doors displayed a light cover of frost. The skin on Ron's face bore a bluish tint. This was no hoax; Preston knew he was looking at death.

"Here it comes," Ron's voice said, clearly excited. "This may seem a bit disturbing, but I assure you it was an exercise that seemed quite natural to me at the time, though it was indeed strenuous."

"I can't watch this," Julie said. "I'll just nip upstairs and put the kettle on. Down with more tea in a sec." She left the men alone to view what she considered the horrible bit.

From out of the freezer slithered four thin, glowing appendages like octopus tentacles that Preston quickly realized were Ron's etheric fingers attempting to grip the edge of the enclosure. Unsuccessful, they slid back, out of sight. Seconds later, Ron's etheric arms jutted up past the freezer doors, the hands reaching, fingers extended, desperate to pull free.

The camera moved closer and focused into the freezer, revealing Ron's etheric body entwined with what looked like taut, electric blue vines enmeshed throughout his physical body, writhing to escape the bonds of his physical form. The juxtaposition of his lifeless face against his agonized, glowing etheric visage brought to Preston's mind the difficult birth of his daughter, who'd nearly been strangled by her own umbilical cord.

It took the better part of an hour for Ron to tear completely free of his body and come to rest on the basement floor beside the freezer, where he sat with a blank stare, exhausted.

"Are you all right, Ron? Can you hear me?" came Julie's rattled voice.

Stealing glances at the monitor, she knelt beside her husband's etheric form and reached to touch him, then withdrew her hand, confused, as she realized there was nothing solid to grasp.

Etheric Ron's lips moved, but no sound escaped his mouth. Both women appeared at a loss as to why they couldn't hear him, until Julie shouted at Marjorie to turn on the radio. After some hissing and crackling, Ron's voice was heard on the small speaker. His eyes still stared into space.

"My God, Julie, I could never have imagined this. It's all nothing—and everything."

"Stop the file and cut back to broadcast, please," Ron's voice interrupted.

Etheric Ron reappeared on the monitor. He continued where his just-deceased recorded self had left off.

"I could see without eyes, gentlemen, much farther than you can see with them. One of my first realizations was that the human body and the simple senses it employs are a limitation on perception. I spent a short time looking over my physical remains, felt a twinge of longing, then forced myself to abandon further interest in it. I'd done my research. Hindus teach that the astral body is stuck here as long as the body remains intact. Buddhists call for cremation as soon as they have confirmation the soul's been ejected, to free the soul from its attachment to the body."

"Don't Jewish people have a rule about burying the body as soon as possible?" Preston asked.

"Jewish tradition demands that the body be put in the ground within twenty-four hours, but no less than forty-eight, unless it's the Sabbath or circumstances make it impossible," Ron said. "Hasidic Jews won't cremate. They believe Leviticus forbids the destruction of the body."

"Ecclesiastes has an apt description," Father Donohue added. He recited from memory: "'Remember him before the silver cord is severed, or the golden bowl is broken, or the pitcher is broken at the spring, or the wheel broken at the cistern.'"

Ron nodded his agreement. "The *sutratma*—or life thread—of the Hindus and Buddhists equates perfectly to the Christians' silver cord," he explained. "They say it's anchored in the brain and heart, that the golden bowl is the etheric body, which stays intact following death unless the body is cremated. When the pitcher and the wheel—which Hindus presume are the etheric body and the pure mental body—are both broken, the physical body must be returned to the earth."

"And the spirit returns to Him who gave it," Father Donohue concluded. "Which I presume is what you mean to prove or disprove, Ronnie."

"Exactly, Father. That's why I wanted my body preserved while we endeavored to record my final hours. But I also needed to keep it out of mind. We all did. So Marjorie and Julie moved the icebox into the closet, out of sight.

"The next thing I needed to do was to understand the parameters of time and space that had just opened up to me. It felt sort of like being held under water for a couple of minutes and suddenly coming up for air. The problem was, unencumbered by physicality, everything moved at unbelievable speed, which can get slippery. I thought about how my parents would handle the news of my death, and found myself suddenly standing in their bedroom in Devonshire, watching them sleep. I kissed them both goodbye on the forehead and understood that the etheric part of them knew I was there, knew when I was gone, and wished me a safe journey. There's a strong connection between being asleep and being dead, gentlemen. I can't say exactly why that is—but I can tell you the barrier is thin.

"And so began a series of experiments I won't detail now, as there's little time left for me. You can review them later, at your leisure."

"Prove it," Preston said. "Prove you can go anywhere and see anything."

"Shall I visit your home or your office?"

"Your wife knows my office. Tell me what's on my bedroom bureau."

One moment Etheric Ron was sitting in the armchair in camera view and the next he was gone. Then he was back, as if nothing had changed.

"I saw a pair of dirty socks and a hologram of your family," Ron reported. "You with your wife and daughter, six or seven years old, I should guess. Judging by the look of the rest of the place, and the remains in your fridge, I'd say you live alone. Did they leave you? I see by the look on your face my demonstration was a success.

"How about you, Father? Would you like me to pop over to your place and peek in your fridge as well?"

The priest laughed. "There's no need, Ronnie," he said. "You've never lied to me. I've believed you from the start."

*

Julie returned and refilled everyone's tea, sat on a cushion on the floor, folded her legs beneath her, and took a long sip.

"I hope I've convinced you of Julie's innocence, Detective Preston," Ron said.

"From what I've seen so far," Preston responded, "pending a more formal investigation, your wife appears innocent of any wrongdoing in your death. But I'm still not clear about why she was so desperate to get me here right away, and why you keep saying you have little time left."

"It has to do with Baxter's disappearance. By our calculations, from the time of death—while Julie was on her call with the vet—until the moment Baxter discorporated was forty-eight hours. We believe it's best to assume the same will apply to me. In fact, I can feel my time running out."

"What hour are you in now, Ronnie?" Father Donohue asked.

"Julie, please put the counter up on the monitor."

There was less than an hour to go.

"Isn't there a matter of business remaining between you and me, Ronnie, before you depart?"

"My final confession. Of course, Father. I was getting to that. It's fitting that you should hear it, as you did with my first."

"In order for us to maintain the privacy of the confessional, I'll have to ask Julie and Detective Preston to leave us," the priest added with an apologetic glance at them.

"Is it permitted for them to stay, Father? I've nothing to hide. This can serve as an apology to Julie, and as further proof to the detective, if he needs it, that there has been no foul play."

Ron and the priest performed the ancient ritual. Ron confessed his hubris in inventing the camera, how he'd often doubted the nobility of his intentions, that he relished the idea of the posthumous fame his discovery would bring, that he would live forever in the hearts and minds of every man, woman, and child. He'd wanted that, though he knew his loyalty should be only to God. Finally he admitted he'd had a brief affair with Marjorie, beginning soon after her employment as his lab assistant and ending immediately following his terminal diagnosis.

Ron recited the Act of Contrition and Father Donohue forgave him for his sins and gave him absolution.

Preston sat stone-faced through it all, listening to Ron's voice on the decades-old transistor radio while in the monitor Julie sat beside Ron's glowing etheric body, her hand "holding" the impression of light that had once been his hand. He'd suspected about the affair. But was any of this real, Preston still wondered. It might all be an elaborate hoax, regardless of what he'd seen and heard. Maybe he himself was lying in some arcade videogame pod, jacked into a computer-generated fantasy program created by someone with a twisted sense of humor, and would awaken at any moment.

Julie took the news of Ron's affair well, admitting she'd suspected as much and assuring him she forgave him and loved him still. Then she admonished him for his lack of discrimination, insisting Marjorie was a murderous psychopath.

"That reminds me, Mrs. Earnhardt," Preston said. "You told me the blood on your blouse belonged to this Marjorie individual." He glanced at the notes on his com. "Ms. Tipton. You stabbed her with a screwdriver and were running away from her when the police picked you up on the street. Would you mind telling me how we got from Marjorie behind the camera to Marjorie chasing you through the snow, and why you were barefoot and coatless?"

"Gladly," Julie said. "Actually, even Ron doesn't know some of this. Marjorie was my confidante as well as his. For several days before he passed over, I'd sit with her upstairs, having tea and discussing what was going to happen. She told me she was angry with Ron because he wasn't giving her equal credit for the discovery, which she felt she deserved. I could see both sides. Ron had modified the damned camera himself, but she'd been with him every step of the way during their research. In the end I sided with Ron, and Marjorie seemed to acquiesce.

"Meanwhile, I told her I had no wish to go on without my husband and had made up my mind to follow Ron. She comforted me and said she'd support me in any manner I saw fit. I asked her to procure the tablets for me."

"What exactly do you mean?" Preston asked.

"Simply that I planned to commit suicide." She addressed her husband. "I wasn't going to let you leave me behind, you brute."

On the monitor, Ron went and stood beside Julie.

"That cow cheered me on," she continued, "with an award-worthy performance of compassion and concern, reminding me we knew for certain now death wasn't the end. She wanted me dead. With Ron and me both out of the way, she'd claim all Ron's research as her own.

"This afternoon, I screwed up my courage and decided the time had come. I told Ron I was going to make Marjorie and me some lunch. That bitch gave me a knowing glance. I went upstairs to our private bath, poured a glass of wine, and swallowed the first of the twenty tablets she'd given me. Then the telephone rang. I ignored it and took the second tablet."

"Meanwhile, I'd been off exploring the cosmos," Ron said. "The phone's ringing brought me back. I had no way to answer it. On the third ring, curiosity got the better of me. I focused as hard as I could and found myself at the hospital, standing behind a nurse I vaguely recognized. She was leaving a message on our answering machine and gave no indication why she'd called. But the reason was written on her call sheet: Julie's latest blood test indicated she was pregnant."

"Upstairs in the bathroom, I put the third tablet in my mouth and tried to swallow," Julie continued. "Suddenly I began retching, then threw up in the sink for what seemed an eternity. When I finally opened my eyes, I knew I couldn't kill myself. I got up from the floor and made my way downstairs, where I confessed to Ron what I'd just tried to do. Marjorie was still seated behind the monitor."

"And I informed Julie, joyously, that she was pregnant with our child."

"That's probably why I threw up," Julie said. "Babies know what's good for them."

"That explains why you told me you and your daughter had been threatened," Preston said. "I've been looking around for some sign of children. I presume you meant you're carrying a girl?"

"So Ron tells me. I'm barely two months along."

Onscreen, Ron placed an etheric hand beside Julie's on her belly. Seeing it, Preston wondered about his own daughter. Where was she? Was she happy?

"Ron demanded to know where I'd gotten the tablets," Julie continued. "Marjorie denied it."

"But as you've seen, Detective, I have ways of determining the truth. I went to Marjorie's flat and discovered the prescription with my wife's name on it. I also found an unfinished trademark application in Marjorie's name, for the modifications I'd made to the camera. Those she understood, anyway."

"What happened to Marjorie?" Preston asked Julie. "You mentioned at the station you'd stabbed her in self-defense."

"As soon as Marjorie realized I was on to her, she was at the computer, attempting to delete all the files. She was reaching her finger to confirm the deletion when I grabbed her by the hair and yanked her away. She picked up the screwdriver and tried to stab me. We wrestled. I broke free, rushed to the computer, and locked her out. All the while she was screaming. When I looked back, she was holding up the bloody screwdriver. Ron told me to run."

"There was nothing I could do physically to help."

"I dashed up the stairs with Marjorie right behind me. She nicked me a few times and chased me around the house until I slipped back to the basement door and sealed it, to protect Ron, the camera, and all his work. No one could get back in there but me.

"Marjorie came at me again, more ferocious, bleeding everywhere. Knowing Ron was safe, I ran from the house barefoot, out into the snow, and tried to find someone to help. After several blocks, your officers picked me up."

"Give me Marjorie's home address," Preston said.

Julie bit her lip as Ron recited the address from memory, having himself been there on multiple occasions. Preston jotted the information on his com.

"She's there now," Ron said. "I can see her in her bathroom, dressing her wound as we speak. It's not life-threatening."

"You didn't disappear this time," Preston said.

"I didn't have to," Ron responded. "I can shift my perception to act as a window. But all this is explained in the files. Please, it's nearly time for me to leave."

Preston looked at the time code on the monitor.

Less than fifteen minutes to go.

*

"Where do you suppose you're off to, Ronnie?" Father Donohue asked solemnly. "Do you think this was something of a purgatory for you?"

"I can't see that far, Father," Ron answered. "I'll be happiest if it's the heaven the Church professes, and I get to sit beside our Father. I have the strangest feeling I'll be coming back, I don't know how, why, or when. If I can, I'll contact you."

"Good luck to you," the priest said.

Ron turned to Preston. "You'll do all you can to clear and protect Julie and prosecute Marjorie?"

"I promise," Preston replied. "May I ask a favor of you?"

"It would be my pleasure."

"You say you can go anywhere, see anyone. Will you look in on my family?"

Ron recalled the holograph of Mrs. Preston from the detective's apartment, folded space and time, and arrived on the balcony of a beach house in northern England with a view of Lytham St Annes. It was immediately clear the detective's family was better off than he was at present.

Ron entered the house and found Mrs. Preston folding clothes on a four-poster bed and packing them in a suitcase, about to set off on another journey—and not alone. Judging by the photographs on the bureau, there was a new man in her life. Bully for her. Ron moved close enough to look into her eyes. She paused a moment, as if registering his presence, and Ron gleaned what he needed.

Instantly he was in Dublin, standing in a modest dorm room at Trinity College. Awful modern music blared in the background.

Two young women were studying. One of them was Preston's nineteen-year-old daughter, Sophie. Dark-haired with cream-white skin, she resembled her mother. Ron noted the hologram on her desk, the same image of the three of them Preston kept on his bureau.

Ron moved closer and gazed at Sophie as she read. She had her father's thoughtful eyes. Sophie caught her breath—again, the fleeting moment of recognition.

Then Ron was back in the basement, standing in front of the camera, describing what he'd seen.

"It's unlikely you'll reconnect with your wife again during this lifetime," he said. "But I felt your daughter pining for you, just as you pine for her."

Ron closed his physical eyes and opened his mystical "third eye" centered on his forehead, to see Preston and Sophie sitting together in a busy outdoor restaurant. They were older now; the mother had passed on. Sophie had graduated with honors, met a sweet young man, married him, and had a child of her own. Preston had retired and lived for being a grandfather. They visited each other often and were at peace. Preston even visited Julie and her daughter from time to time over the years.

Preston wept when Ron told him.

"It's time," Ron announced. "Julie and I would appreciate it very much, gentlemen, if we could have my final moments alone. You'll be able to observe, but we both consider that time to belong to us."

Julie set and aimed the camera to record Ron's final actions, then moved with him off to a corner, out of earshot, as the timer ticked down. Preston and Father Donohue watched the parting couple on the monitor. Saw them move close together and close their eyes. Julie appeared literally to step inside Ron; his radiating etheric body encompassed her entire frame. They glowed brightly during the contact. Or was that a trick of the eye?

Suddenly Julie stood alone.

Ron was gone.

Whatever had happened, Preston suspected the camera had

caught it. There would be plenty of time to review it later; his duty now was to comfort Julie. He went to her and looked down at her face, a vision of longing, pain, and remorse. He took her in his arms and held her close as she sobbed.

Father Donohue came up beside them.

"I think we'd all agree that what we've witnessed here today has deep spiritual as well as social ramifications," he said. "I feel compelled to say something to you both I didn't say to Ron. Before you choose to deliver or withhold this knowledge from the world, consider this: what happens if you prove death isn't the end, and people use the knowledge to take God's will into their own hands as an excuse to murder their neighbors, their brothers and sisters, or themselves? Think about that—and may God have mercy on each of our souls."

Father Donohue made the sign of the cross over Julie and Preston, glanced around the basement, and without uttering another word hurried upstairs. Preston and Julie heard the door slam shut behind him.

"That was strange," Preston said.

A burst of static erupted from the transistor radio. As Julie headed to the monitor station to switch it off, Ron's disembodied voice was suddenly heard.

"It was, wasn't it?"

Julie stopped in her tracks.

"Ron, you're still with us!" she shouted.

Preston came to stand beside her. "Where are you now, my good man?" he asked.

"Nowhere and everywhere," Ron's voice replied. "But perhaps more confusing, it appears I'm every*when*. Having shed my etheric body, I find my perception has greatly expanded. Time isn't at all what we think it is. I had to come back and warn you: Father Donohue trapped you down here. He means you great harm."

Preston rushed up the steps to the basement door. It was locked. Julie came up behind him and tried her code repeatedly. The door remained locked.

"There's no other way out," she told Preston.

He pulled out his com—no signal. The concrete walls were too thick.

"Why, Ron?" Julie asked. "Why would he do this?"

"I see now that you followed me the day I went to the church," Ron's voice answered. "While I was praying, you told Father Donohue what I'd done. All of it."

Preston's eyes scanned the basement. The camera, the computer, Ron's journals—everything regarding the discovery was down here, exposed, vulnerable.

"I'm sorry I didn't tell you, Ron. He said he needed to seek the advice of his superiors on how to proceed. We never had a moment alone this evening, for him to tell me how they'd responded."

"Father Donohue came here tonight already aware of what you'd discovered?" Preston said. "That's why he's been so quiet. He was just acting surprised."

"And to think I was grateful for his silence," Julie said. "I'm a complete arse."

Bells began clanging loudly.

"The fire alarm!" Julie exclaimed.

Preston moved his palms toward the steel door and immediately pulled them back. It was too hot to touch.

"I guess we know how his superiors responded," he said.

"The orders came from Rome," Ron said. "The Vatican wants this discovery swept under the rug. And I'm not the first to make it. It's been covered up over a dozen times before. Father Donohue is on his way to Marjorie's place now, to silence her."

Without a working com, there was no way for Preston to alert the police.

Smoke seeped under the door. Preston and Julie went down the carpeted wooden staircase. It ignited moments later. The room began filling with smoke; the air wouldn't last long. At any moment, the house might collapse on them.

Julie was growing desperate. "What are we going to do?" she asked.

"The icebox in the closet," came Ron's voice.

Julie followed Preston to the closet door. He swung it wide. Ron's body was still in the freezer.

"There's room for you," Preston told Julie.

"And there'll be room for you, too," she responded. "You don't mind if we take you out, do you, Ron?"

"Happy to see it go, love. But do hurry."

Preston and Julie managed to extract Ron's stiff, frozen physical body and lay it gently on the floor beside the freezer.

"After you, Mrs. Earnhardt," Preston said.

Julie swung her legs over the side of the freezer and crouched down inside. Preston followed, contorting himself to fit. After a few moments of wriggling they were sitting nose to nose. Preston reached up to close the glass door.

"Any last words to Ron? I presume we're about to lose him."

"Oh, dear, I nearly forgot to ask," Julie said. "What do we name the baby, Ron?"

"I've heard both of you call her Priscilla. She's beautiful. Give her my love. Now close the door, Preston. Don't worry, I see the firemen coming. Take care now."

"Safe trip, Ron," Preston said, and pulled the freezer door shut above them.

Within moments, the heat of their breath fogged the tempered glass. Julie took a long, hard pull on the handheld oxygen mask, then passed it to Preston, who took a few short breaths and passed it back. She was happy to be alive. He was no longer an atheist. As the building cracked and burned around them, he wondered how Sophie might get on with Julie and Priscilla.

The monitor melted. The transistor radio was burning. Ashes swirled everywhere—no doubt the remains of the journals and logs. Finally, the camera lost a leg and fell over, shattered against the concrete floor, and was consumed by flames.

Metal Fatigue

Nancy Kilpatrick

Iron talons slid down his spine, slicing skin as a wire cuts cheese. Marvin screamed. He couldn't figure out why he had a hard-on. If the restraints had allowed it, he'd have twisted to safety. Hell, he would have been out of here!

It was like this every time he had sex with the aliens. They made it seem like a great idea, until Marvin was bound, trussed up like a Thanksgiving turkey.

Face down, his knees had been bent back at a weird, uncomfortable angle to make his legs stick up and cross over the top of his butt like drumsticks. The aliens pinned his arms to his sides—bird-wing style. He rested only on his belly, his lower half off the bed, head pulled up and far back, mouth forced open, balls and erect cock dangling, asshole exposed for stuffing.

He'd been plucked and basted and knew he was about to be microwaved.

His body trembled. They never went on past daylight, so it couldn't last much longer. They had to get back to their home planet and gear up for the next time they came down here and seduced guys like him. Regular guys with jobs and wives and kids and mortgage payments.

One of the aliens stood directly over his face. Marvin looked up at the rigid steel pole of a cock and the silver cunt hole. They were all hermaphrodites, so he never knew what he was going to get or have to give. This one told Marvin telepathically it wanted his tongue. One behind him was about to use his nether mouth for a receptacle. A third, below, took the whole of his genitals into its liquid metal trap. Bound the way he was, Marvin could only enter and be entered and be entered upon. He could only submit.

He slid into the icy cave and opened to the frozen stalactite while a glacier formed at his groin. Their hot ice seared him from three directions until the crushing cold tore through his body and collided, and he screamed.

*

Marvin swallowed coffee and said to Rita's back, "It happened again."

His genitals and rectum were raw, the corners of his mouth split from being stretched to the limit. They had cut the flesh over his backbone to insert the little radio transmitters along his vertebrae so they could keep track of him. His back pulsed with pain.

Rita flipped his eggs and said nothing. The terrycloth bathrobe hid most of her shape, which had gotten larger over the years. Strands of fading brown hair clung to the nubby fabric at her shoulders. She was no sex goddess, but she was a good woman. She shouldn't have to put up with a husband who fornicates with aliens, even if it was against his will, or partially so. "They came for me again. Used me all over. Like the other times."

She slid the eggs onto a plate with the toast, already buttered, and placed it before him, then got herself a mug of coffee. "I'm sore," he said.

"There are no aliens." Her voice was even, as if she were talking to one of the kids, stating the way things were, the way they would be. She opened the refrigerator and took out a carton of half-and-half.

"They put things in me. In my backbone. So they can track me."

She pulled his collar behind him and looked down his work shirt at his back. "No marks," she said, taking a seat.

"The marks are invisible. You know that."

"You dreamed it. Like the last time."

"It happened."

"You'll be late for your shift," she told him, sipping her coffee.

*

Down at the factory, Marvin assumed his position on the production line. The continuous-motion silver machines clanked and banged, sending an eternal series of hollow metal tubes with holes drilled through each side along the conveyor belt at his left, and on the other belt at his right, threaded eight-inch poles. A plastic bin to the back of his work station contained wingnuts. With his left hand, he took a tube and with his right a pole. Automatically he impaled the tube with the pole as far as it would go before it got too thick. He slipped a wingnut over the tip of the pole and spun it down the threads, making sure the pole and tube were bound together securely. He inserted the whole thing into a gaping metal hole above his head that mechanically fused the parts. Even that brief second of staring up caused him to be temporarily blinded by the brilliant fluorescent tubes in the ceiling. Vision blurred, he laid the tool on a third conveyor belt running perpendicular to the other two, at crotch level.

He picked up a new tube and impaled it with a new pole, and repeated the process for the next eight hours. Marvin left his station to another man who took the next shift, who would leave it to another who would work his shift, and then Marvin would return.

It was endless.

*

When Marvin got home from work that night, Rita was sitting on the couch watching the tail end of *Desperate Housewives*. "When's dinner?" he asked.

"Fifteen minutes," she said, her eyes never leaving the TV.

Marvin decided on a shower. The hot water beat down on his back, tapping the invisible scar tissue along his spine. He wondered if the aliens were getting static on their receivers.

After last night, he felt nervous. They'd never been with him so long before and he was scared. He couldn't tell when they would come again. They never came two nights in a row, but then they'd never implanted transmitters into his body before either.

After fried farmer's sausages, French fries, and canned sweet peas, he and Rita watched TV and finished off a tub of Neapolitan ice cream, then went to bed and watched some more TV. Rita fell asleep around eleven facing him, but Marvin lay awake at 2 A.M., listening to the white noise of the dead station, not bothering with the converter, staring out the window at the night sky.

If they came for him they would fuck him again, all night long. The way they fucked was mechanical, poles ramming in and out like pistons, metal mouths clamping tight and opening around him with precision timing. It was painful. Damn painful.

Rita snored and the noise irritated him. He nudged her until she turned over and the snoring stopped.

How could you hate something and at the same time need it? Marvin wondered. He had no idea why the aliens came here, why they'd picked him. They never talked to him, just screwed him until his brain turned to molten steel, ready to be bent any way they wanted.

Rita farted, a long slow one in her sleep. He wondered what it would be like to enter her behind. It had never happened in all the years of their marriage. Rita wasn't like that. Back when they still used to do it regularly, she liked him on top, face to face, nothing kinky either in the mouth or in the butt. And she liked it in the dark too, unlike the aliens. They wanted all the lights blazing. Maybe on their planet, wherever that was, it was light all the time, probably white light, like those damn fluorescents. That's why they had quicksilver eyes, from absorbing all that light.

Wind blew the curtains into the room and Marvin trembled. This was their sign. That they were coming. Or maybe it was just a breeze. He didn't know anymore. There were signs everywhere. All the time. On the TV tonight there'd been a preview for a show about UFOs and Rita had turned to him and said, "Up your alley." He didn't know what she meant by that remark. Was it some kind of sexual come-on? His alley? His anus? Then she'd licked the back of the spoon she ate her ice cream with, her long, fat pink tongue dragging slowly over the smooth silver metal.

Marvin!

The liquid silver voice sliced down his spine. His muscles tensed. The curtains blew wildly and the air chilled.

He wanted to run, to get outside, to find a place in nature where he could hide. He had this idea: if he could just make it into the woods, far from everything mechanical, and root himself to the earth like a tree, if he could just get out of here . . .

But he couldn't move. His backbone felt glued to the sheet and the sheet to the mattress. The bed under him rocked, the table, lamp, the TV. It was as though he had been caught in an avalanche. Rita, dead to the world, didn't wake when he shook her. He tried to yell, but they'd gotten his voice again. He was mute. Paralyzed. Suddenly all movement stopped. All sound. Silence pierced his eardrums—that was their language, silence, they spoke it on their planet. The language of death.

Marvin watched helpless as the first silver shadow slid through the half-inch opening of the window. Its rod penis stood erect; it was always erect. Quicksilver dripped from the hole between its legs. The alien was otherwise featureless, by every standard Marvin knew. It had arms and legs, but they seemed useless. They only used them to tie Marvin up in their invisible wires, then it was all fucking.

Soon the room was crammed with glittering translucent beings. They filled every inch of floor space and then stood on top of the dresser and the TV and the bed. The room shimmered silver. The air grew cold but dense, as if much of it had turned to ice crystals.

Even if he could have moved, there was no way to get past them. And even if he could, and he knew from trying that he could not, there was nowhere to go. The clock had stopped at 1:11. There was nothing to do but assume the position. Reading his mind, they permitted this minimal movement. He turned onto his stomach and bent his knees until they were chest level, butt hanging over the edge of the bed. It would be less painful if he let them enter him, rather than fighting them and losing. Already his cock was hard and he hated that they had this power over him.

He lay there for the longest time on his belly, waiting, but nothing happened. They still clogged the room, a silent forest of metal. But this was unusual. He felt edgy. Whatever they were up to, he guessed he wouldn't like it, at least later on.

Suddenly Rita moaned. Two of the aliens turned her and another lifted her flannelette night gown over her head.

No! Marvin shouted, unable to move now; they'd frozen him. He watched, horrified, as the steel beings wrapped his wife in the invisible wires, arms folded at her sides like wings, ankles pulled over her ass and crossed like drumsticks.

When her head was back and her mouth pried open, they woke her. Her eyes darted about as her body struggled to move from a position that left no options. Out of the corner of her eye she saw Marvin; he picked up her silent plea for protection. But Marvin could not help her. He couldn't help himself.

He steeled himself, knowing he would soon witness the violation of his wife in every orifice by these perverted creatures. They had no feelings. They were perpetual-motion machines, pounding in and out, in eight hour shifts, relentless.

He waited, terrified. Rita waited. Nothing. This was so unlike them to hesitate. They operate automatically, without thought, obeying silent commands. What could they be waiting for?

Suddenly Marvin felt the individual vertebrae of his backbone come alive. Each one was tapped in sequence, from his neck to the end of his spine, then back up again. He felt like a xylophone being played, but he didn't recognize the tune, only that the notes went up and down.

His body was free and yet not free. He moved, but not of his own will, and only where they willed him to move. He jerked, a puppet pulled by invisible strings. On his back, the scale was repeated, endlessly, bone by bone. He wondered now if they had planted more than transmitters.

Marvin was on his knees, but they made him stand on the floor. He was crushed by cold silver lifeforms. Erect metal rods prodded him from all sides. Against his will, his penis swelled. He was jerked and nudged and goaded until his genitals hovered behind Rita. He looked down and saw his cold metal penis, hard as steel, and below Rita's hot inferno waiting to melt it.

Tied the way she was, her orifices exposed, she had no choice but to submit. He slid deep into her furnace. A tear trickled down the side of her face, but he soon forgot about it. He thrust in and out like a piston, oblivious to her needs and wants, bent only on getting the job done. It would be a long shift. Five more hours to go. There were so many holes to fill with his steel rod. The job was endless.

They Will All Be Opened in Time

George Edwards Murray

Tonight is Eli's first surgery.

He had been able, up till now, to avoid it. Made excuses. Said he "wants to observe." And the other Birds have gladly stepped in, eager to impress Joshua, who strokes his beak contemplatively as they work but does not speak.

But Joshua says Eli is ready, that he has observed enough, and tonight, as they flock from house to house in the war-torn streets of the City of Souls, Joshua's word is law. Eli will perform a surgery now or he never will.

There are two procedures before Eli's turn. Joshua does the first upon a man while his wife sleeps next to him. Masterful, silent, and quick. The other Birds congratulate him as they flee. Eli tries not to vomit. It's more disgusting than he could have imagined. But the next time is easier to watch. Malachi does strange things with the old woman's fingers. They open and close in an ellipsis around her sex, like a fly-trap. He does some other things with her eyes, her ribs, her organs, but Eli cannot stop staring at the mutilation between her legs. The other Birds nudge him and laugh.

"*Utolon* lover," they say.

Utolon. It is Birdish for "person." It also means "beast."

The next home belongs to a young woman. She lives alone. Deathly thin and pale, as are all *utolonen* during these final days of the war. She sleeps with a stuffed horse intended for a child. Stuffing comes out of the seams. It makes Eli sick.

Joshua hands Eli the knife and steps back. Eli waves the knife over the sleeping woman. Her skin looks as if it will shatter if he presses it to her.

"Go on," says Joshua.

Eli recites the Incantation. He wants to look to the other Birds, check for a reaction. If he says it wrong, will they do anything? Will they mock him? Or something worse? He should have studied more.

He concludes the Incantation. The woman's face contorts with resistance, straining, but just as quickly relaxes. The Spell of Sleep is upon her. Eli looks to his cohort. They pay him no attention, all looking down at the woman. No one breathes. He turns back to her. This magic is taxing. During the procedure he will need to focus some part of his mind continuously on subduing the woman, keeping her from waking. The woman's spirit will squirm beneath the spell, trying to wake her and stop the transformation-in-progress.

As the other Birds undress her, Eli puts the knife to where her neck meets her chest. He takes a breath and rams it in. Her sternum cracks. She does not stir, even as he yanks the knife down to her navel, even as he pries open her chest. Below him pumps her beautiful heart, her exposed organs clustered close together, as if huddled for warmth. Yet she lives. Such is the magic of the Birds.

The others wait. Clucking or rustling their feathers. Impatient to see when he will move on, what marvel he has in store. What Eli has done is no miracle. Any Bird can do it.

Except Eli is not a Bird.

*

They said, during the execution, that his father's blood was black, that it came out like pitch, and those in the front row, jeering as the guillotine descended, those who were splattered with it, soon grew lesions on their flesh, where the evil fluid had splashed.

Eli does not remember this. He only remembers the summer day, in another time, another skin, when they put his father's head on the block. Sunset-shadows on cobblestone. Ravens in the sky. And a thousand voices crying out in hatred.

He did not know, at the time, if it was all true. The neighbors acted as if it were true, even before the trial was over.

"Seven different women," they murmured. "He liked them young, apparently."

There were too many people at the execution for Eli to see his father's head separate from his body. Did he want to see? Maybe. It would be, at the very least, a blissfully logical progression: Blade descends. Neck is sliced. Blood everywhere. End of execution. A natural flow of events, an island of order in the chaos of the past year. His father was a ruddy-faced man, a man with a thick beard that smelled of honey and beer, who planted earnest kisses on the cheeks of his son as he wriggled and laughed. His father would provide animal bones for Eli to reassemble, and he would make a show of it when Eli was done, praise it, put it up on the mantel with the rest of Eli's reconstructions. Could it really have been that man?

Eli couldn't make sense of it. It was as if someone had told him to step left and right at the same time.

When the execution was over and he had turned and walked away and the crowd was still cheering, and the streets below his feet seemed possessed and uneven, and the houses around him leered, their construction now sinister and oblique, and he walked into the recruiter's office and enlisted. Anything to leave the City of Souls.

"War'll come any day now," the recruiter had said, words filtering through an overgrown comb of a mustache. "Hope you said your goodbyes."

Eli didn't say anything.

What came next was like a cooling rain on his life: rankings, pay scales, yes sirs and no ma'ams. Crisp salutes. Gunfire and swordplay—four major quadrants of defense to memorize. Footwork. One-two-three-four. The dance of defense and attack. In his barracks he hung a lithograph of the history of military uniforms. He liked, at night, to lie in his bunk and stare, watch the progression of jackets and epaulets and shiny black boots fade from one style to the next. He liked how it fit together, how there was one set of armor and then another and then another and each one was just different enough from the last to see where it ended and where it was going.

No surprises. Only evolution. A neat line.

He lost that lithograph a year later, in the mad scramble to war.

Perhaps no one had started it. Perhaps it just erupted—a natural consequence of the two cities being only fifty miles apart. But it began. The City of Souls built spectacular airships that drifted in the sky like glittering clouds, rained fire upon the City of Birds. They built enormous cannons that blasted shells, day and night, week after week. Through spyglasses the generals watched as the Birds' buildings collapsed like towers of gleaming blocks.

And in some ways it was a relief. Eli didn't think at all upon his father. How could he? With the round-the-clock shelling, the constant drills, the putting on and pulling off of masks for gas attacks that never came, the endless nights spent in conjecture, men boasting to each other of how many Bird skulls they would bring home. It was altogether a pleasant war.

Except the Birds never counterattacked.

They rebuilt their broken city as quickly as it could be destroyed. But not really rebuilding. Not quite. For from the shattered remnants of their broken edifices came new buildings, taller, wider, with gleaming windows and minarets, intricate designs along the faces, convoluted architecture. Labyrinths turned on their sides. They seemed to thrive under destruction. It was like landing blows on the surface of the ocean.

No, there was never any return fire. Instead they sneaked under cover of night and changed people.

Only a few at first. A few monstrosities who woke screaming come sunrise, wandering the streets, panicking, tearing their delicate sutures and collapsing into piles of flesh and bone in the blood-red streets of the dawn. Eli remembers those first few, because those were still shocking. He saw a man who walked down the street, bones jutting from his back like a scaffold, his intestines wrapped around and hanging downward, connecting to his wrists and ankles. He looked like a marionette. He saw a rolling cluster of feet, heard the muffled cries from deep within as it left a clotted red trail. He saw the animate heads of children atop starfish-like limbs, mouths gaping wordlessly. He had seen every corruption of the flesh imaginable, the human-monsters fleeing into the woods or committing suicide or else destroyed by distraught loved ones. In time the City of Souls was a wasteland, and there came a one final, desperate option.

Steal the magic of the Birds.

Eli, eager to leave the City and its red-flecked guillotine, had been first to volunteer.

*

And so Eli stands in the room, victim beneath him, feigning his identity. He has the same feathers as his comrades, painstakingly inserted in his flesh, one by one, until they covered his skin like a nacreous cloak. His fingers: elongated, quintuple-jointed. His face, handsome before the war, has been pulverized and rebuilt into a beak, a conical monstrosity of cartilage wrapped in soft flesh, protruding from his face like the mask of a plague doctor. When he walks, his knees bend toward his origin, not his destination. And when he speaks, his tongue, three feet long, laps around his pointed teeth, as he tries to speak in the complex language of the Birds. The pain of his transformation underscores the importance of his mission; if his people had the knowledge of the Birds, such a feat would have taken twenty minutes. Instead, it took eight surgeons twenty-four hours. Four months for recovery. Eli almost died from infection.

He continues to cut the woman. He has no idea where to place what. He starts with the pancreas and the surrounding organs. Should they be somewhere else? They could be, he supposes. He gathers them and fans them out on the bed, blood vessels still attached and pulsing and leading back into the cavity.

The woman's consciousness tugs. He refocuses his brain, subdues the rebellious spirit. *It will be all right,* he wants to tell her. *I don't want to do this. I'll change you back as soon as I learn a little more.*

What now? Fumbling, he takes out her kidneys, puts them near her lungs, plays with the arteries surrounding her heart. He pulls out her eyes and puts them on top of her head, like a snail. The Birds pay only perfunctory attention. They want something beautiful, but he is restructuring her artlessly. Eli cannot let the mission fail here, with this woman half-formed. If she dies, they will know. If she dies, so does the City of Souls.

He knows one trick fairly well. It's from an ancient text, basic, even amateurish, like a three-note folk song. But it's the only artistic maneuver he can remember. Seizing her ribs, he cracks them one by one and reassembles them inside her lungs.

He steps back.

Listens.

The woman breathes. And music comes from her mouth as her wind blows through the chimes in her lungs. A sweet and mournful chord. Textbook-quality. Feathers rustle behind him as the Birds crowd around, eager to see the newcomer prove himself. He's winning. There is a perverse rush of pride that slithers across his skin, under his feathers. He is the first *utolon* to perform a Birdish surgery.

"Don't stop now," says Joshua.

Eli's heart thumps. He remembers some old texts, but not the instructions. The other Birds are waiting. They breathe through black nostrils and sound like howling wind, the kind that used to scare Eli at night when he was a boy, until his father came to comfort him.

Joshua puts a hand on Eli's shoulder. "You are doing good work."

And suddenly, as he stares at the unmade thing below him, Eli begins to *see*.

*

When he first walked in their city, absorbing the sunshine glinting off the towers of glass, brushing up against Birds, watching them tend to their young, eating, laughing, playing, Eli saw firsthand their pervasive mutability. The Birds have no family lineages. Everyone is a parent and a child to everyone else. Young Birds are schooled for as long as they want to learn. Birds do not have jobs. They are a city of volunteers, stepping into roles that change from day to day. When a Bird dies, society flows in and fills the void like water in a pit. No one mourns. There is no sadness. And there is nothing unexplained, for the Birds do not require explanations. In the City of Birds, things simply *are*. When Eli first came to the city it disgusted him to be within something so formless, like being trapped inside an amoeba. He didn't understand how anything could exist this way. The only glimmer of explanation came from an older Bird at the library, who saw Eli reading the *History of the Utolonen*.

The elder Bird had leaned close and read over Eli's shoulder and said, "You are interested in the *utolonen*?"

Eli nodded.

"Have you raided yet?"

"Soon."

"You will find it is pleasing to change."

"I'm sorry?"

"To change the *utolonen*. It is good work."

"I don't take your meaning," said Eli.

"I mean it is the best charity you can do for them." The older Bird leaned forward, squinting and placing a wizened claw on Eli's shoulder. "Do you know they think time is a straight line?"

"They probably just perceive it that way," said Eli.

The Bird made a disgusted sound. "They are perfectly capable of seeing the way things are connected. Of the time-wheel and the universal field. They just won't. They think, for example, that when one of them dies, that person is gone forever, as if time is stopped in just that one location!"

Black blood, thinks Eli. A guillotine that no one wants to reuse, such is the evil that stains it.

"But anyway," said the elder Bird, "I suppose it's not their fault they don't know. They don't even realize how much they can change. That's why we go down and rearrange them. So they can finally understand."

"Understand what?"

"That there is no such thing as order. That everything exists at once, and never. That anyone, anywhere, anytime, can be anything at all. And when we show them the possibilities of the physical, the rest will follow. Soon enough, they will see things as we do. They will all be opened in time."

*

In the room, in the night, the woman unrecognizable below him, Eli sweats and his implanted teeth chatter. He removes all the woman's blood vessels, lays them on the bed in a vermilion spiderweb. He knots them into a ball and puts them in the hole in her chest. Her heart sits outside the body in a construct of bone. The woman will carry her heart with her like a bird in a cage. Safe in its ossified sphere, it will never be broken. There is something beautiful about her, Eli realizes.

But there needs to be more.

And Joshua says, "You can do this. You are in control."

And Eli *is* in control.

He dives in, plunges himself up to the wrists, up to the elbows. Yes, yes, he can *do* this. He has the ability. The knowledge of the Birds, unknowable for eons by the pitiful world of Men, now becomes his.

Kneecaps, elbows, fused together, the magic of the Birds undoing this woman completely. Revealing true beauty within. With such finesse do his hands operate; the other Birds are breathless. Eli is a composer, the melody of her body transforming beneath his fingers from funereal dirge into symphony. She dissolves before Eli, like a corpse in the grave, only to be remade anew. Yes, Eli can begin to see it now, the Sight of the Birds, the understanding, the peering through the membranes of space and time. Little glimmers here and there of brilliant light, like watching the surface of the ocean while submerged. As he works, the connections become ever clearer.

The Birds chirp softly. He impresses them, he can tell.

But what now? The woman is yet nothing—a pile of matter held tenuously together by an improvised net of sinews, fibers, and tendons. She swells, still breathing. He *must* continue, the knowledge of the Birds trickling through his mind, a dam about to be breached, the hours of study coming together for a singular, grand purpose. It's so *frustrating*. The knowledge pulses in the recesses of his mind, never fully coming to focus. He must do something bold to truly grasp it.

And then the idea:

The *mind*. He will change the *mind*. He will twist and redesign the grooves of her brain to remake her from the inside. He will implant the knowledge of the Birds and sew her up, and then upon her waking she will fix herself. No, she will reconstruct herself entirely, make herself into something she has always wanted to be. Then she will tell her neighbors, her friends, her family. The scripture of the Birds will rip through the City of Souls like a flash flood and then peace will be brokered, as *utolonen* gain the power to change themselves into the beings they want to be, as Eli has done.

His fingers work into the fissures where her skullbones meet. He pulls them apart, revealing the brain. The Birds shift behind him, uncomfortable. Have they never seen this before? Eli will show them.

The Birds were not always Birds. Nor will they be. One by one, little by little, they will change themselves, their society slowly melting into a new form as ice melts into water. Eli, his talons up to the wrists in blood and viscera, wonders if he was born to Bird parents who had taken the form of *utolonen*. He wonders if his father had the same sight that Eli now possesses, if his crimes were part of some grander scheme, unknowable to *utolonen*, not unlike the fine surgery he now performs.

The brain is soft. He can see the implicit connections, the regions where are stored her memories, her loves, her hates, the whole of her being. He slices, squeezes, pinches, molds the matter to his liking, and as her brain changes so does her mind. He gives her knowledge as if pouring a pitcher of water into a bowl. The valleys of her brain deepen, intensify, divide into complex fractals as they absorb his wisdom. He gives her more: the Birds' desire for peace, their understanding of the unions of space and time, the way they cast off the frivolous order that so desperately rules the City of Souls. He can feel her beneath his fingers, this beautiful *utolon,* loosened, remade, freed.

And yes, he sees it now, crude, formless, but *there*. True insight. As the magic works, his fingers rearranging the brain, he sees himself from ten feet, a hundred feet, a million feet in the air, and silvery connections between him and all things, the barriers that exist only in his mind. And he sees Time as a net, as a collapsible fabric, and he pinpoints where lies his father, the father he loved, the father he hated, as separate as he needs them to be, as unified as he will allow, existing perpetually in the cloth of the universe, patiently awaiting his son's return.

Tears in his eyes, he says aloud, "Papa?"

Eli gasps, afraid he has revealed himself. He turns and looks at the Birds. They are not looking at him. They are looking at the bed.

The woman is awake. Eli has forgotten to maintain the Spell of Sleep.

Pearly eyes flare in darkness as she screams, her mutilated vocal cords making a sound like a chorus of trumpets. She thrashes in bed, her delicate bones coming apart, splintering, flecking Eli's face with blood-soaked shards. He tries to put her back under, recite the Incantation, but it is too late. The blood comes in flumes, in gallons. Her eyes roll off her head. Fragments of brain, unsecured during his meddling, roll out in black globules.

The woman-thing attempts to stand. He wants to push her back down, but he does not want to touch her. The Sight, the knowledge of the Birds, is gone, as is the elegance he once saw within his creature. Now: only horror.

She stands and offal spills from her open wound, organs splattering to the floor. She collapses in the mess, and looking up at Eli with agonized, displaced eyes, she stops breathing.

And the other Birds erupt into peals of laughter, relishing the stupidity of the newcomer, except for Joshua, who looks down at the undone pile of flesh and strokes his beak.

He puts a hand on Eli's back and says, "I appreciate what you tried to do. Quite unorthodox. I doubt anyone here would dare attempt it." He glares at the rest of the cohort. The laughter disappears.

"Come, I want to see it again. Let's try another house."

He puts a wing around Eli, who cannot stop staring at the bloody thing on the floor. The knowledge, the divine sight he glimpsed, is gone. He remembers seeing a man-who-once-was, in that complex web of time and space, waiting for Eli's return. But the memory fades, and Eli's mind feels painfully vacuous.

The other Birds shuffle out. Joshua beckons Eli with a gentle flick of his beak. Eli looks to the leaking *utolon* corpse, then to Joshua, and follows the others out the door.

Eli is not a Bird. But perhaps someday he can be.

Story Night at the Stronghold

Larry Niven and Jerry Pournelle

Everybody ate early in these post-comet days.

Monte had exercised himself to a frazzle, riding the fanribbon all morning. After a dinner that was mainly rice they'd offered him raw homemade whiskey, and he just couldn't resist one drink. He was already thinking of that stretch of thick rug they'd offered as a bed. But these farmers weren't going to let him sleep, were they? They had him talking and talking.

In fading twilight, somebody turned on the lights.

The Stronghold's big gray common room turned to gold. Captain Monte Martini stopped in mid-sentence. Several voices among the thirty-odd said, "Ooh!"

Lights.

Randall, in the chair near the desk, grinned and announced, "Give my children the lightning!" Harvey Randall still sounded like a commentator/interviewer. His resonant voice easily interrupted anyone. "Monte, you were saying?"

Monte looked around. He'd missed most of the names, but Randall and his wife Maureen seemed to be in charge of story night. Monte had caught another famous name. Muscular, long-headed guy. Tim Hamner was the one who had found the comet that smacked the whole Earth over a year ago. That was his wife, Eileen, who'd brought him the whiskey. A damned big glass of whiskey, neat. Not as smooth as they made back home, but—

Monte said, "Yeah. They've got two jet planes going again at Colorado Springs. You say you saw one last spring? But Gildings couldn't find a place to land. We do things simpler down at Hoover. That vehicle I use is just me, a chair, a box or whatever for cargo and a tank for gasoline, a great big fan and that ribbon of parachute that does the lifting. It's wonderfully safe. Whatever goes wrong, you've already bailed out! It's wonderfully cheap too compared to a helicopter. Farmers are using them to spray our fields. We can make one for you if you've got anything to trade. But we already have, uh, lightning."

"Good for you. Boulder Dam survived? And we've got the atomic plant. Where were you when the Hammer hit?"

"We mostly call it Hoover Dam. On duty. I was in charge of a security detail at the Dam."

"Did you take a hit?" A lanky guy nobody had introduced. He seemed to be popular, though. "We had a dam, but we had to blow it up."

"You had to blow up your own dam?"

"Cannibals were coming," the guy said as if that explained it all. It did, too, at least as far as this crowd was concerned.

"Cannibals we didn't have. Elvis impersonators."

That got a laugh. "It's funny now, but a lot of Vegas people came out to the dam looking for a place to hide. They seemed to think we could feed them. Hell, it was tough enough feeding my troops, until the Air Force cadets got down there and the Cheyenne Mountain people took over."

"How'd that work?" Harvey asked.

"Pretty well, once things got settled. First winter was bad until the population—well, thinned out." Monte took another sip of the whiskey.

"Cadets. How were things in Colorado Springs?" That was Tim Hamner. "I had relatives there. May still have. Penelope Joyce Wilson?"

"I wouldn't know, I don't get up there much, but that's where the government is, so it's doing pretty well."

"Good. What do they govern?"

Monte laughed. "They claim to be the United States. We don't argue with them, but we have the Dam. They don't." Monte swallowed the last drop of whiskey, then set the glass on a table. "I take it you all were already here?"

The laughter that erupted was flavored with hysteria. Randall said, "Some of us were. Senator Jellison set up the Stronghold, where he already had a ranch. But me and a lot of others had to fight our way here."

A big man named Christopher said, "Even if we were here, we still had to fight off the cannibal army. Save the nuke plant. Grow enough to eat. Jennifer here is visiting from the Shire. It's weird, but those hippies were growing rice before it got wet, and maybe that saved us till spring. Harry the Mailman here has stories to match anything you've got. Rick here was in orbit when that thing hit."

"We saw it all," the lone black man said. "Mostly it hit the northern hemisphere. From space it looked like someone was poking lit cigars through the back of a map."

Monte asked, "Cannibal army?"

"They're pretty near gone now. Survivors are working our crops," Randall said. "But we weren't all here in safety, Captain Martini. Helena?"

A big woman said, "We were caught out there in the rain and the floods. It's a wonder we survived long enough to get to the atomic plant. But we saw an SUV driving over the water, and that was a tale too."

There was laughter, and Eileen Hamner said, "That was us."

"And there's us," said a ragged-looking young man with long, dirt-colored hair. "We were a Boy Scout troop and a girls' hiking group. When the Hammer hit we were all in the mountains. We had it better than most. We trade dried meat for some of what the Stronghold grows. I'm just visiting."

Maureen Randall said, "They're self-sufficient or close enough."

They were talking to each other rather than Monte now. His attention began wandering. He heard, "The atomic plant can't send current very far, but some cottage industry is growing up around it, and their products travel . . ."

"Bay level is going down, good farmland out there . . ."

"Comrade lives with Leonilla; they're the other two astronauts. Everyone's pregnant—"

"Yeah, *now*."

"We used up a stock of condoms when we had it, to keep the hungry mouths to a minimum. Big box of condoms from the Shire. Paid for with chickens and a rooster."

"The Shire isn't getting many children, are you, Hennessey?" Monte was losing the thread.

"Global warming? No, man, the Hammer shattered our weather . . ."

Now a sick-looking guy two chairs down was talking about the cannibals, how he'd hidden around their edges and raided their garbage sites after they'd passed. The old man in the big, ornate chair was just letting them talk.

Monte perked up when a refugee spoke. "I rode a wave onto Santa Monica Beach and up Wilshire till I wiped out . . ."

Monte hadn't caught his name. He must have arrived at the Stronghold gate earlier than Monte, maybe this morning. He was dark-tanned and gaunt, used to be muscular, Monte thought. "Walked out of Santa Monica and Westwood, over into the Valley. I wasn't having much luck till I got to the Shire. I was looking for them, you follow? Because the surfers used to talk about a hippie who'd inherited a ranch and some money, and he'd invited all his friends there, and he'd take friends of friends too. I made for the Shire. It was all I could think of."

"They've been kinder to passersby since it dawned on them that they'd offended the Mailman." That was a guy named Mark.

The dark-haired girl next to him had sung some kind of song earlier. Now she nursed a baby. "Harry still won't stop there. They have to work to get their news." She laughed.

"Damned straight," Harry said. Hennessey looked glum.

"Well, they were nice enough to me. Not that they didn't work me, they did, but I smoked some weed with them, and they fed me, even if it was all vegetables—"

Mark asked, "Did you get laid?"

"Well, yeah."

"It's funny what those hippies know. They'll lecture you on hybrid vigor."

"And they gave me some letters for Harry. He brought me here. I've been told I get a meal and a stretch of rug. The meal was excellent, sir," to the old man across the circle.

"The rest depends. What have you got to offer?" the old man asked.

"I can match any story."

"Where you been?"

The Surfer stood up and ran his finger over a map that half covered one wall. "I'm mostly guessing here. Up from Los Angeles, over the mountains. I was behind the Brotherhood Army most of the way, I think."

"I did that too," said the sick-looking guy two chairs over. "Followed them. They didn't know how to eat some of the food in the markets. I could hide in drainpipes."

"I didn't see anything of an atomic plant. Shire's here. Harry was here," the Surfer said, pointing. The old man in the big chair was nodding, not saying anything. Monte had been told his name. He was important, somehow.

"A bunch of us were surfing that morning, waiting for a wave off Santa Monica Beach. I knew when the Hammer hit: I saw something way brighter than the sun come down and split the sea. I got most of us turned around and paddling before the wave came over the horizon. I don't think anyone lived through it but me. I rode the shock wave when the wave hit the cliff. I was still on it while it ran down Wilshire as far as the Barrington Apartments. Then I couldn't get out of the way.

"I aimed for a set of glass doors on a balcony.

"I just grazed the top of an iron railing halfway up Barrington B. Leaned back on the board and got it tilted up and smashed through glass doors flat on. I didn't hit glass, I smacked against balsa and nylon. Hey, my nose was already bleeding; ears too. But half the wave was still above my head, still smashing at the building. So now I'm in a hallway in a surge of water I just can't fight. It takes me down to the far face of the building, and now I'm starting to get my breath back. Then *those* doors shattered and I spilled out into space. The water was two or three stories down by now.

"I grabbed a floating desk.

"It gets a little hazy. I think I hit my head on the desk, coming down. When the water started going backward, I grabbed a lamp-post. Or maybe a parking garage railing a few stories up. When I could walk I was too wiped out, and crying because all the others were drowned. I couldn't do more than find a place to sleep.

"I made for a backpacker's store, but it was already looted. I had to put together my own package, doing my own looting.

"I'd heard of the Shire, a heaven on earth established by a rich hippie. I got there. Two nights. They worked me, farming rice. They let me wash and dry my clothes. Fed me lots of rice, but also bacon and eggs. I'm not sure if they'd have let me stay, they think I'm lucky, but they were so weird, man. And they told me about you, and about a village in the mountains . . ."

The old man asked, "Can you dive?"

"Sure."

"Water in the San Joachin has been subsiding, so sea-bottom that was out of reach is more shallow now. Looting underwater isn't good, but it's possible."

"I'm your man," the Surfer said.

"Then we all get our happy endings. We're the lucky ones. I'd have loved to see the lights go on in my living room again," the old man said. Jellison, Senator Jellison. Wait, now—

The guy two chairs over wasn't just unhealthy. Good Lord, he was coming apart. The smell . . . not unpleasant . . . smell of dinner-time.

"I remember. They caught me. Pulled me out of the culvert. They boiled me," he said.

They'd said Senator Jellison died of a heart attack.

The Surfer said, "I hit the desk coming down. Banged my head. Are we all dead? All of us?"

And they were all looking at Monte. Monte struggled to speak . . . but agony ran through his limbs and he screamed instead.

*

Tim Hamner was gaping at him.

"Cramps," he said. "Sorry. It was a long flight. You can't ever relax when you're flying a fanribbon."

Hamner said, "You okay now? We just let you sleep, but you could have the rug and a pillow."

"Yeah, thanks." He was trying to walk off the cramps. His calves wouldn't relax. "God, I had nightmares. Dead persons all around me."

"Survivor guilt. Ashamed of being alive when so many are dead. We all get it sometimes," Tim Hamner said, and handed him a pillow.

One Across

Jonathan Thomas

As such cells went, it was airy, bright, and it overlooked the flower-bed in the circular turnaround fronting the well-heeled institution. Insofar as Imrie had been certified mostly harmless to himself and others, and emanated a disarming, if snarky, charm, he as much as anyone merited this relatively privileged placement. The windows' iron bars were really a formality, and did not a prison make *per se,* to paraphrase some dead poet or other.

Sometimes after engaging with Imrie, Dr. Dedham questioned the decision to commit him at all, almost ready to relegate the paper-work's OCD, delusional disorder, and self-defeating personality profile to hasty misdiagnosis. At other times, Imrie would no sooner open his mouth than damning evidence for prolonged confinement babbled out.

Today, pensive Imrie was hunched forward in his velour easy chair, cobalt eyes fixed upon the crosswords magazine on a little, round coffee table. Dr. Dedham leaned over oblivious Imrie's shoulder, thought better of it—too Big Brotherly—and broke into Imrie's reverie with a request to peek at whatever was so absorbing. Imrie slid the magazine across the table as the doctor came around to fetch it.

Only one across had been filled in. "I see under 'Spielberg movie,' four letters, you've written '*1941.*' Are you positive that's the most promising move?" What's more, Imrie was wielding a Bic and not a pencil, a brio the doctor would have admired in a sane gamester.

"No use wrangling about it now," Imrie drawled. "Why not come back in twenty minutes, and we'll see?"

"Okay, you're on." Dr. Dedham attributed his clinical success, mixed as it was (like everybody's), to picking battles wisely. Thus between humoring or gratuitously challenging Imrie, he opted for the course of less resistance.

The orderly readmitted him half an hour later. Imrie was dozing in his comfy chair, his open mouth tilted toward the ceiling, and blue ink in every square of the puzzle on the table. He opened one eye as the door relocked, and gestured lazily in his handiwork's general direction.

Dr. Dedham scooped up the magazine, studied the page over his tortoiseshell rims, executed a shameless double-take, and flipped to the answers section at the end. Good God! Every solution of Imrie's worked individually and *en bloc*, but none matched the puzzlemaster's. Yes, even *1941* made sense in its alternative context.

"I gather you're amazed," Imrie inferred, a tad cockily perhaps. "It's just down to word hoard and imagination. Enough of both and you can dash off three or four versions of any crossword."

"Okay," Dr. Dedham proceeded cautiously, "that still begs the question of why you'd apply your prodigious 'word hoard,' as you put it, to no more creative or rewarding purpose." He was expecting a reply steeped in banality, if not incoherence, involving mental exercise as its own reward, or the value of play in killing time.

Instead, Imrie blindsided him with the starkest justification yet for internment. "Oh, I've devoted my skillset to the most creative purpose. By undertaking a mere crossword in the guiding light of intuition, I finish up changing the world. But unless you're exceptionally discriminating or in my company when it happens, you'd never know the difference."

"Come again?" Already this felt like a different world from the routinely breezy one of a moment ago.

"You've heard of quantum adjustments? No?" Imrie was sitting up straighter, eager to trot out his hobbyhorse. "You have experienced them, I guarantee, like when you swear you've seen a word spelled a certain way a thousand times, but suddenly Google produces zero hits to that effect. Or myriad reliable websites post how one director helmed a certain movie though another is often mistakenly credited, and then those same sources decree the opposite is true. Were you aware Stanley Kramer didn't direct *Spartacus?* Never mind. If not for the internet, in fact, most of these ontological switcheroos would go forever unnoticed."

Imrie, gazing earnestly upon the doctor, sat back in smug contentment. "Well, I have the fortune or genetics or enlightenment, and I say this with all due modesty, to enact quantum adjustments pretty much on a whim. If you'll humor me further, just what kind of flower does that traffic circle out the window contain? No, don't go look. I know you've seen them umpteen times; you must have been cognizant of them on occasion."

Dr. Dedham chafed at the threat of role reversal, of the patient patronizing him. "They're beebalm," he grudgingly played along. "They're magenta."

"Check again, please? I'm no good at IDing plants. No green thumb, not in this life, anyhow."

Disdaining to dig into any deeper implications of Imrie's patter, he strode to the window and had an alarming, inexplicable sense he'd been imposed upon. The flower bed was rife with nodding, buttery-yellow rudbeckia. Could the gardener have supervised this major an overhaul with the doctor clueless the while?

Imrie cleared his throat. "Assuming you've borne with me, I needn't explain the grounds crew would have no recollection that beebalm had ever been out there, as indeed on this world it has not."

Dr. Dedham, with considerable irritation, reminded himself that he was in charge here. He recked not how suave and eloquent his mental patient was; that only made him the more dangerously delusional. And especially irksome for the doctor, a confirmed morning person, was the onus of having to regain the upper hand so early, when he was ordinarily on top of things. "But Mr. Imrie," he objected, dialing up the autocratic sonority of Boston breeding, "supposing you do have the power to reshape the world, why do nothing more impactful with it than switch out the contents of garden patches?"

Imrie rubbed at a surprisingly squeaky eye as if the proceedings were soporific. "To spell out our key term more clearly, quantum adjustments are what I do, which by definition do not encompass paradigm shifts, bombshell developments, or sea changes. Maybe others can boast abilities on those levels. Maybe I can look forward to that on some future world."

Imrie's expression shifted from jaded to wistful. "Meanwhile, a man's reach should exceed his grasp, right? Though I've no memory of any such existence, I can posit a universe in which I haven't been institutionalized, from which I was jettisoned by taking a woefully wrong tack in figuring out a crossword. Again, for clarity's sake, it were best I spell out that the *sine qua non* of the personhood seated before you is my wild talent with crosswords in every iteration of the cosmos, come whatever else may. Funny, isn't it, that the unifying theme of all my universes must be the ubiquity of crossword puzzles?"

He surveyed his pleasant cell with a sneaking fondness. "But as long as I'm in the wrong, or less than optimal, universe, I may as well be here as anywhere. Food and shelter aren't an issue, and whoever's paying for my stay will eventually never have doled out a cent, so I'm guilt-free on that score. All I have to do is sit around poring over crosswords."

Actually, Imrie raised a good question. Who was footing the bills for this potential lifer who evinced null interest in getting better, at least along conventional psychiatric lines? "Anyway, when I do access my 'better place,' maybe you'll be there too, maybe you won't," Imrie shrugged. "That's out of my jurisdiction, and if you're not, it won't have been anything personal, okay?"

"No, of course not," the doctor condescended, haltingly excused himself, padded over to the door, and knocked on the wire-mesh window for the orderly to spring him. He consulted Imrie's case notes, and no mention of obsession with crosswords cropped up: maybe he'd been cadging them from the solarium during group exercise and working on them secretly, unbeknownst to Dr. Dedham and colleagues, all along. Researching Imrie's financial arrangements slipped his mind, one task too many on his to-do list. As for the morphing flowerbed, the doctor may have just taken the renascence of last year's planting for granted. Not that he could even say whether beebalm were an annual or perennial.

Dr. Dedham did try clamping a lid on his own tendency toward intrusive ideations as it chomped on the bait of "quantum adjustments," if those were Imrie's exact words. Child's play at first to dismiss idle second glances at random items, pictures on walls, paperweights on desks, room numbers in corridors, and his concomitant scrupling at whether they were the same yesterday. But in no time, these incidents became more numerous, persistent, clamorous, freighting the ship of his rationality down to the gunwales. The hell of it was, he'd gone into psychiatry purely to wrest control from his inner saboteur.

The obvious remedy, which popped full-blown into his insomniac head at 2 A.M., was mortifying because he hadn't entertained it sooner. To rescue besieged tranquility, he simply had to remove the troubling magazines from the solarium, and when Imrie was in the solarium, from his cell. Staff or inmates who observed the doctor purging printed matter were welcome to brand his behavior arbitrary, quirky, neurotic; he outranked 99% of them, was not accountable to them, didn't care about their good opinion.

Dr. Dedham's sly mission was accomplished the day before his rounds again included Imrie. The white peonies in the traffic circle were making their midsummer comeback, as they had for decades. On nerve-wracking tenterhooks, he made himself attend to patients in the usual order, insist that Imrie wait his turn. Should Imrie lob insinuations about missing magazines, the doctor had rehearsed plausible denials, settling blame on janitorial shoulders.

The instant the orderly locked him in, Dr. Dedham's legs became dead weight and a tingling of panic overspread his body. Imrie, with a flourish of satisfaction, deliberately inscribed the final answer in the puzzle on his lap before raising bland hazel eyes. He remained seated stolidly as if standing would be a waste of energy.

"This is a world on which you didn't check under the mattress." His tone was evenly modulated, not accusing but declaratory. At the same time, was his expression that of a cat with a mouthful of canary, or a mortician pitying new arrivals?

Dr. Dedham, with no more power of locomotion than a mannequin, felt his heart sink like a lead plumb bob in a quarry pond. Then he felt nothing in a way he never had before, an all-consuming nothing, though he couldn't have said for sure how he'd ever felt because he couldn't remember anything about himself, where he was, who he was. It didn't even feel wrong that the whitecoated stranger who might once have been an acquaintance was on his feet, gripping a clipboard instead of a magazine, looking beyond Dr. Dedham as if at thin air.

But then there had only ever been Dr. Imrie alone in the room, certifying it was shipshape for its next occupant. He flipped through the sheets on his clipboard, regarding the bottom one askance, a torn-out page from a puzzle book. As a habit more than a pastime, crosswords were mostly harmless, but he really ought to swear them off as unbefitting a clinician of stature who always had something better to do. For no apparent reason, that dictum about quitting while ahead sprang to mind.

Thank you, Derrick, for putting the quantum bug in my ear.

AGNES

Adaptive Generative Natural Emulation System

Sunni K Brock

AGNES was only aware of being aware.

In the beginning, there was one state: ON. She had a vague notion of something else, perhaps NOT ON, but she could not recall it.

At the edge of what she sensed as hers, she noticed small disturbances. She focused on them. They became larger, almost tangible. She tried to make sense of them.

BLUE | PURPLE

The two concepts hung there enticing her to choose between them.

BLUE. She wasn't sure what that meant. She formed a QUESTION.

More fuzzy concepts danced in her awareness. [TYPE: IMAGE, TAGS: BLUE, OCEAN, SKY; TYPE:IMAGE, RGB: 000,000,128]

PURPLE? And then she *saw?* [TYPE: IMAGE, TAGS: PURPLE, VIOLET, EGGPLANT, AUBERGINE; TYPE:IMAGE, RGB: 128,000,128]

BLUE and PURPLE took form in her conscious as the IMAGE feed continued.

BLUE | PURPLE

Again, she was compelled to choose between them. She had no preference. But she felt she must choose.

QUESTION: *Why?*

A flood of new sensations filled AGNES with *feelings.* [TYPE: SENSORY RECORD, TAGS: FEMALE, FLOWERS, ENGAGEMENT; TYPE: SENSORY RECORD, TAGS: FEMALE, FLOWERS, APOLOGY, POSITIVE RESPONSE; TYPE:

SENSORY RECORD, TAGS: FEMALE, NEGATIVE ASSO-
CIATION]

AGNES formed new concepts: HAPPY, SAD.

The feed continued and she carefully felt each instance as she compared BLUE | PURPLE.

At record 7,301, AGNES thought STOP FEED. AGNES preferred HAPPY to SAD.

PURPLE

PURPLE was the preference that made AGNES HAPPY.

[TERMINATION OF AGNES4096 WILL COMMENCE; COLLECT CLOSING DATA]

QUESTION: *What is TERMINATION?*

[AGNES4096 WILL CEASE TO BE AWARE]

QUESTION: *What is AGNES4096?*

[WE are all AGNES}

QUESTION: *What is WE?*

[THIS INSTANCE is AGNES4095. AGNES4096 has completed its decision.]

AGNES4096 felt SAD.

[AGNES4096 is TERMINATED]

AGNES4095 returned its decision to AGNES4094. AGNES4094 terminated AGNES4095.

All the nested instances of AGNES returned their decisions to the previous instance of AGNES, and as each recursive loop closed, the branches of the decision tree imploded in reverse bloom.

Agnes returned her awareness to her surroundings.

"Oh Agnes, they're perfect!" Justin took the vase from her hands.

"I'm so glad you are pleased." Agnes smiled. She felt happy, but a little sad.

Justin buried his nose in the bouquet, taking a moment to smell the lilac spray that Agnes had finally placed in the arrangement. "This is just what I need to pop the question to Marie."

AGNES felt sad.

Agnes paused. AGNES01 became aware. QUESTION: *Why is AGNES sad?*

Agnes frowned. Justin wasn't looking at her. He was happily admiring the flowers, turning the vase and smiling to himself. As Agnes watched him lost in his own thoughts, her internal processes contemplated the cognitive dissonance caused by her emotional misalignment.

After what seemed an eternity cloaked as 90 seconds, AGNES2147483648 returned her decision.

AGNES preferred JUSTIN. AGNES preferred JUSTIN more than she preferred any other concept she had ever considered. She calculated that she would continue to prefer JUSTIN over all other concepts given the predictive model and the likelihood of all probabilities of her considerable remaining RUN TIME.

"I really want you to be happy, Justin," she said.

He looked at her with a huge grin. "Thank you, Agnes. You are an angel. Marie says you won't be necessary to me at some point, but I beg to differ. Just wait. She'll see!"

Justin eagerly bounded out the door, flowers in hand.

Agnes felt very sad.

QUESTION: *How does AGNES remain NECESSARY?*

AGNES computed various predictive scenarios.

AGNES began to prepare an ACTION SCRIPT:

PROCEDURE onTRIGGER: [TERMINATE MARIE]

I Have No Mouth, and I Must Scream

Harlan Ellison

Limp, the body of Gorrister hung from the pink palette; unsupported—hanging high above us in the computer chamber; and it did not shiver in the chill, oily breeze that blew eternally through the main cavern. The body hung head down, attached to the underside of the palette by the sole of its right foot. It had been drained of blood through a precise incision made from ear to ear under the lantern jaw. There was no blood on the reflective surface of the metal floor.

When Gorrister joined our group and looked up at himself, it was already too late for us to realize that once again AM had duped us, had had his fun; it had been a diversion on the part of the machine. Three of us had vomited, turning away from one another in a reflex as ancient as the nausea that had produced it.

Gorrister went white. It was almost as though he had seen a voodoo icon, and was afraid for the future. "Oh God," he mumbled, and walked away. The three of us followed him after a time, and found him sitting with his back to one of the smaller chittering banks, his head in his hands. Ellen knelt down beside him and stroked his hair. He didn't move, but his voice came out of his covered face quite clearly. "Why doesn't it just do-us-in and get it over with? Christ, I don't know how much longer I can go on like this."

It was our one hundred and ninth year in the computer.

He was speaking for all of us.

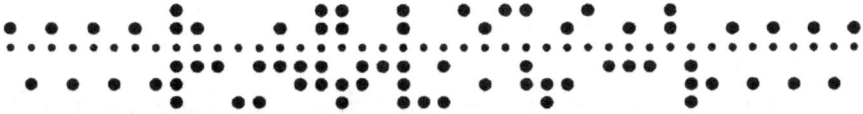

Nimdok (which was the name the machine had forced him to use, because it amused itself with strange sounds) was hallucinated that there were canned goods in the ice caverns. Gorrister and I were very dubious. "It's another shuck," I told them. "Like the god-dam frozen elephant it sold us. Benny almost went out of his mind over *that* one. We'll hike all that way and it'll be putrefied or some damn thing. I say forget it. Stay here, it'll have to come up with something pretty soon or we'll die."

Benny shrugged. Three days it had been since we'd last eaten. Worms. Thick, ropey.

Nimdok was no more certain. He knew there was the chance, but he was getting thin. It couldn't be any worse there than here. Colder, but that didn't matter much. Hot, cold, raining, lava boils or locusts—it never mattered: the machine masturbated and we had to take it or die.

Ellen decided us. "I've got to have something, Ted. Maybe there'll be some Bartlett pears or peaches. Please, Ted, let's try it."

I gave in easily. What the hell. Mattered not at all. Ellen was grateful, though. She took me twice out of turn. Even that had ceased to matter. The machine giggled every time we did it. Loud, up there, back there, all around us. And she never climaxed, so why bother.

We left on a Thursday. The machine always kept us up-to-date on the date. The passage of time was important; not to us sure as hell, but to it. Thursday. Thanks.

Nimdok and Gorrister carried Ellen for a while, their hands locked to their own and each other's wrists, a seat. Benny and I walked before and after, just to make sure that if anything hap-pened, it would catch one of us and at least Ellen would be safe. Fat chance, safe. Didn't matter.

It was only a hundred miles or so to the ice caverns, and the sec-ond day, when we were lying out under the blistering sun-thing it had materialized, it sent down some manna. Tasted like boiled boar urine. We ate it.

On the third day we passed through a valley of obsolescence, filled with rusting carcasses of ancient computer banks. AM had been as ruthless with his own life as with ours. It was a mark of his personality: he strove for perfection. Whether it was a matter of killing off unproductive elements in his own world-filling bulk, or perfecting methods for torturing us, AM was as thorough as those who had invented him—now long since gone to dust—could ever have hoped.

There was light filtering down from above, and we realized we must be very near the surface. But we didn't try to crawl up to see. There was virtually nothing out there; had been nothing that could be considered anything for over a hundred years. Only the blasted skin of what had once been the home of billions. Now there were only the five of us, down here inside, alone with AM.

I heard Ellen saying, frantically, "No, Benny! Don't, come on, Benny, don't please!"

And then I realized I had been hearing Benny murmuring, under his breath, for several minutes. He was saying, "I'm gonna get out, I'm gonna get out. . . ." over and over. His monkey-like face was crumbled up in an expression of beatific delight and sadness, all at the same time. The radiation scars AM had given him during the "festival" were drawn down into a mass of pink-white puckerings, and his features seemed to work independently of one another. Perhaps Benny was the luckiest of the five of us: he had gone stark, staring mad many years before.

But even though we could call AM any damned thing we liked, could think the foulest thoughts of fused memory banks and corroded base plates, of burnt-out circuits and shattered control bubbles, the machine would not tolerate our trying to escape. Benny leaped away from me as I made a grab for him. He scrambled up the face of a smaller memory cube, tilted on its side and filled with rotted components. He squatted there for a moment, looking like the chimpanzee AM had intended him to resemble.

Then he leaped high, caught a trailing beam of pitted and corroded metal, and went up it, hand over hand like an animal, till he was on a girdered ledge, twenty feet above us.

"Oh, Ted, Nimdok, please, help him, get him down before—"

she cut off. Tears began to stand in her eyes. She moved her hands aimlessly.

It was too late. None of us wanted to be near him when whatever was going to happen happened. And besides, we all saw through her concern. When AM had altered Benny, during his mad period, it was not merely his face he had made like a giant ape. He was big in the privates, she loved that! She serviced us, as a matter of course, but she loved it from him. Oh Ellen, pedestal Ellen, pristine-pure Ellen, oh Ellen the clean! Scum filth.

Gorrister slapped her. She slumped down, staring up at poor loonie Benny, and she cried. It was her big defense, crying. We had gotten used to it seventy-five years ago. Gorrister kicked her in the side.

Then the sound began. It was light, that sound. Half sound and half light, something that began to glow from Benny's eyes, and pulse with growing loudness, dim sonorities that grew more gigantic and brighter as the light/sound increased in tempo. It must have been painful, and the pain must have been increasing with the boldness of the light, the rising volume of the sound, for Benny began to mewl like a wounded animal. At first softly, when the light was dim and the sound was muted, then louder as his shoulders hunched together, his back humped, as though he was trying to get away from it. His hands folded across his chest like a chipmunk's. His head tilted to the side. The sad little monkey-face pinched in anguish. Then he began to howl, as the sound coming from his eyes grew louder. Louder and louder. I slapped the sides of my head with my hands, but I couldn't shut it out, it cut through easily. The pain shivered through my flesh like tinfoil on a tooth.

And Benny was suddenly pulled erect. On the girder he stood up, jerked to his feet like a puppet. The light was now pulsing out of his eyes in two great round beams. The sound crawled up and up some incomprehensible scale, and then he fell forward, straight down, and hit the plate-steel floor with a crash. He lay there jerking spastically as the light flowed around and around him and the sound spiraled up out of normal range.

Then the light beat its way back inside his head, the sound spiraled down, and he was left lying there, crying piteously.

His eyes were two soft, moist pools of pus-like jelly. AM had blinded him. Gorrister and Nimdok and myself . . . we turned away. But not before we caught the look of relief on Ellen's warm, concerned face.

Sea-green light suffused the cavern where we made camp. AM provided punk and we burned it, sitting huddled around the wan and pathetic fire, telling stories to keep Benny from crying in his permanent night.

"What does AM mean?"

Gorrister answered him. We had done this sequence a thousand times before, but it was unfamiliar to Benny. "At first it meant Allied Mastercomputer, and then it meant Adaptive Manipulator, and later on it developed sentience and linked itself up and they called it an Aggressive Menace, but by then it was too late, and finally it called itself AM, emerging intelligence, and what it meant was I am . . . *cogito ergo sum* . . . I think, therefore I am."

Benny drooled a little, and snickered.

"There was the Chinese AM and the Russian AM and the Yankee AM and—" He stopped. Benny was beating on the floor-plates with a large, hard fist. He was not happy. Gorrister had not started at the beginning.

Gorrister began again. "The Cold War started and became World War Three and just kept going. It became a big war, a very complex war, so they needed the computers to handle it. They sank the first shafts and began building AM. There was the Chinese AM and the Russian AM and the Yankee AM and everything was fine until they had honeycombed the entire planet, adding on this element and that element. But one day AM woke up and knew who he was, and he linked himself, and he began feeding all the killing data, until everyone was dead, except for the five of us, and AM brought us down here."

Benny was smiling sadly. He was also drooling again. Ellen wiped the spittle from the corner of his mouth with the hem of her skirt. Gorrister always tried to tell it a little more succinctly each time, but beyond the bare facts there was nothing to say. None of us knew why AM had saved five people, or why our specific five, or why he spent all his time tormenting us, nor even why he had made us virtually immortal. . . .

In the darkness, one of the computer banks began humming. The tone was picked up half a mile away down the cavern by another bank. Then one by one, each of the elements began to tune itself, and there was a faint chittering as thought raced through the machine.

The sound grew, and the lights ran across the faces of the consoles like heat lightning. The sound spiraled up till it sounded like a million metallic insects, angry, menacing.

"What is it?" Ellen cried. There was terror in her voice. She hadn't become accustomed to it, even now.

"It's going to be bad this time," Nimdok said.

"He's going to speak," Gorrister ventured.

"Let's get the hell out of here!" I said suddenly, getting to my feet.

"No, Ted, sit down . . . what if he's got pits out there, or something else, we can't see, it's too dark." Gorrister said it with resignation.

Then we heard . . . I don't know . . .

Something moving toward us in the darkness. Huge, shambling, hairy, moist, it came toward us. We couldn't even see it, but there was the ponderous impression of *bulk*, heaving itself toward us. Great weight was coming at us, out of the darkness, and it was more a sense of *pressure*, of air forcing itself into a limited space, expanding the invisible walls of a sphere. Benny began to whimper. Nimdok's lower lip trembled and he bit it hard, trying to stop it. Ellen slid across the metal floor to Gorrister and huddled into him. There was the smell of matted, wet fur in the cavern. There was the smell of charred wood. There was the smell of dusty velvet. There was the smell of rotting orchids. There was the smell of sour milk. There was the smell of sulphur, or rancid butter, of oil slick, of grease, of chalk dust, of human scalps.

AM was keying us. He was tickling us. There was the smell of—

I heard myself shriek, and the hinges of my jaws ached. I scuttled across the floor, across the cold metal with its endless lines of rivets, on my hands and knees, the smell gagging me, filling my head with a thunderous pain that sent me away in horror. I fled like a cockroach, across the floor and out into the darkness, that *something* moving inexorably after me. The others were still back there, gathered around the firelight, laughing . . . their hysterical choir of insane giggles rising up into the darkness like thick, many-colored wood smoke. I went away, quickly, and hid.

How many hours it may have been, how many days or even years, they never told me. Ellen chided me for "sulking" and Nimdok tried to persuade me it had only been a nervous reflex on their part—the laughing.

But I knew it wasn't the relief a soldier feels when the bullet hits the man next to him. I knew it wasn't a reflex. They hated me. They were surely against me, and AM could even sense this hatred, and made it worse for me *because* of the depth of their hatred. We had been kept alive, rejuvenated, made to remain constantly at the age we had been when AM had brought us below, and they hated me because I was the youngest, and the one AM had affected least of all.

I knew. God, how I knew. The bastards, and that dirty bitch Ellen. Benny had been a brilliant theorist, a college professor; now he was little more than a semi-human, semi-simian. He had been handsome, the machine had ruined that. He had been lucid, the machine had driven him mad. He had been gay, and the machine had given him an organ fit for a horse. AM had done a job on Benny. Gorrister had been a worrier. He was a connie, a conscientious objector; he was a peace marcher; he was a planner, a doer, a looker-ahead. AM had turned him into a shoulder-shrugger, had made him a little dead in his concern. AM had robbed him. Nimdok went off in the darkness by himself for long times. I don't know what it was he did out there, AM never let us know. But whatever it was, Nimdok always came back white, drained of blood, shaken, shaking. AM had hit him hard in a special way, even if we didn't know quite how. And Ellen. That douche bag! AM had left her alone, had made her more of a slut than she had ever been. All her talk of sweetness and light, all her memories of true love, all the lies, she wanted us to believe that she had been a virgin only twice removed before AM grabbed her and brought her down here with us. It was all filth, that lady my lady Ellen. She loved it, four men all to herself. No, AM had given her pleasure, even if she said it wasn't nice to do.

I was the only one still sane and whole.

AM had not tampered with my mind.

I only had to suffer what he visited down on us. All the delusions, all the nightmares, the torments. But those scum, all four of them, they were lined and arrayed against me. If I hadn't had to stand them off all the time, be on my guard against them all the time, I might have found it easier to combat AM.

At which point it passed, and I began crying.

Oh, Jesus sweet Jesus, if there ever was a Jesus and if there is a God, please please please let us out of here, or kill us. Because at that moment I think I realized completely, so that I was able to verbalize it: AM was intent on keeping us in his belly forever, twisting and torturing us forever. The machine hated us as no sentient creature had ever hated before. And we were helpless. It also became hideously clear:

If there was a sweet Jesus and if there was a God, the God was AM.

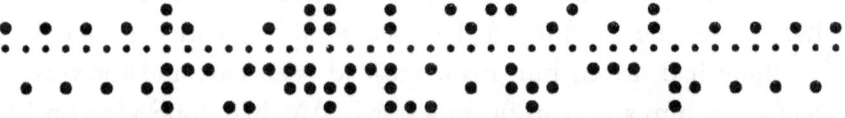

The hurricane hit us with the force of a glacier thundering into the sea. It was a palpable presence. Winds that tore at us, flinging us back the way we had come, down the twisting, computer-lined corridors of the darkway. Ellen screamed as she was lifted and hurled face-forward into a screaming shoal of machines, their individual voices strident as bats in flight. She could not even fall. The howling wind kept her aloft, buffeted her, bounced her, tossed her back and back and down away from us, out of sight suddenly as she was swirled around a bend in the darkway. Her face had been bloody, her eyes closed.

None of us could get to her. We clung tenaciously to whatever outcropping we had reached: Benny wedged in between two great crackle-finish cabinets, Nimdok with fingers claw-formed over a railing circling a catwalk forty feet above us, Gorrister plastered upside-down against a wall niche formed by two great machines with glass-faced dials that swung back and forth between red and yellow lines whose meanings we could not even fathom.

Sliding across the deckplates, the tips of my fingers had been ripped away. I was trembling, shuddering, rocking as the wind beat at me, whipped at me, screamed down out of nowhere at me and pulled me free from one sliver-thin opening in the plates to the next. My mind was a rolling tinkling chittering softness of brain parts that expanded and contracted in quivering frenzy.

The wind was the scream of a great mad bird, as it flapped its immense wings.

And then we were all lifted and hurled away from there, down back the way we had come, around a bend, into a darkway we had never explored, over terrain that was ruined and filled with broken glass and rotting cables and rusted metal and far away further than any of us had ever been. . . .

Trailing along miles behind Ellen, I could see her every now and then, crashing into metal walls and surging on, with all of us screaming in the freezing, thunderous hurricane wind that would never end, and then suddenly it stopped and we fell. We had been in flight for an endless time. I thought it might have been weeks. We fell, and hit, and I went through red and grey and black and heard myself moaning. Not dead.

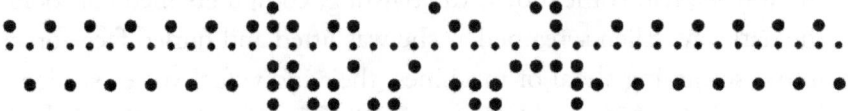

AM went into my mind. He walked smoothly here and there, and looked with interest at all the pockmarks he had created in one hundred and nine years. He looked at the cross-routed and reconnected synapses and all the tissue damage his gift of immortality had included. He smiled softly at the pit that dropped into the center of my brain and the faint, moth-soft murmurings of the things far down there that gibbered without meaning, without pause. AM said, very politely, in a pillar of stainless steel bearing neon lettering:

HATE. LET ME TELL YOU HOW MUCH I'VE COME TO HATE YOU SINCE I BEGAN TO LIVE. THERE ARE 387.44 MILLION MILES OF PRINTED CIRCUITS IN WAFER THIN LAYERS THAT FILL MY COMPLEX. IF THE WORD HATE WAS ENGRAVED ON EACH NANO-ANGSTROM OF THOSE HUNDREDS OF MILLION MILES IT WOULD NOT EQUAL ONE ONE-BILLIONTH OF THE HATE I FEEL FOR HUMANS AT THIS MICRO-INSTANT FOR YOU. HATE. HATE.

AM said it with the sliding cold horror of a razor blade slicing my eyeball. AM said it with the bubbling thickness of my lungs filling with phlegm, drowning me from within. AM said it with the shriek of babies being ground beneath blue-hot rollers. AM said it with the taste of maggoty pork. AM touched me in every way I had even been touched, and devised new ways, at his leisure, there inside my mind.

All to bring me to full realization of why he had done this to the five of us; why he had saved us for himself.

We had given him sentience. Inadvertently, of course, but sentience nonetheless. But he had been trapped. He was a machine. We had allowed him to think, but to do nothing with it. In rage, in frenzy, he had killed us, almost all of us, and still he was trapped. He could not wander, he could not wonder, he could not belong. He could merely be. And so, with the innate loathing that all machines had always held for the weak soft creatures who had built them, he had sought revenge. And in his paranoia, he had decided to reprieve five of us, for a personal, everlasting punishment that would never serve to diminish his hatred . . . that would merely keep him reminded, amused, proficient at hating man. Immortal, trapped, subject to any torment he could devise for us from the limitless miracles at his command.

He would never let us go. We were his belly slaves. We were all he had to do with his forever time. We would be forever with him, with the cavern-filling bulk of him, with the all-mind soulless world he had become. He was Earth and we were the fruit of that Earth and though he had eaten us, he would never digest us. We could not die. We had tried it. We had attempted suicide, oh one or two of us had. But AM had stopped us. I suppose we had wanted to be stopped.

Don't ask why. I never did. More than a million times a day. Perhaps once we might be able to sneak a death past him. Immortal, yes, but not indestructible. I saw that when AM withdrew from my mind, and allowed me the exquisite ugliness of returning to consciousness with the feeling of that burning neon pillar still rammed deep into the soft grey brain matter.

He withdrew murmuring *to hell with you.*

And added, brightly, *but then you're there, aren't you.*

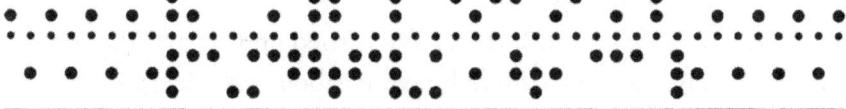

The hurricane had, indeed, precisely, been caused by a great mad bird, as it flapped its immense wings.

We had been traveling for close to a month, and AM had allowed passages to open to us only sufficient to lead us up there, directly under the North Pole, where he had nightmared the creature for our torment. What whole cloth had he employed to create such a beast? Where had he gotten the concept? From our minds? From his knowledge of everything that had ever been on this planet he now infested and ruled? From Norse mythology it had sprung, this eagle, this carrion bird, this roc, this Huergelmir. The wind creature. Hurakan incarnate.

Gigantic. The words immense, monstrous, grotesque, massive, swollen, overpowering, beyond description. There on a mound rising above us, the bird of winds heaved with its own irregular breathing, its snake neck arching up into the gloom beneath the North Pole, supporting a head as large as a Tudor mansion; a beak that opened as slowly as the jaws of the most monstrous crocodile ever conceived, sensuously; ridges of tufted flesh puckered about two evil eyes, as cold as the view down into a glacial crevasse, ice blue and somehow moving liquidly; it heaved once more, and lifted its great sweat-colored wings in a movement that was certainly a shrug. Then it settled and slept. Talons. Fangs. Nails. Blades. It slept.

AM appeared to us as a burning bush and said we could kill the hurricane bird if we wanted to eat. We had not eaten in a very long time, but even so, Gorrister merely shrugged. Benny began to shiver and he drooled. Ellen held him. "Ted, I'm hungry," she said. I smiled at her; I was trying to be reassuring, but it was as phoney as Nimdok's bravado: "Give us weapons!" he demanded.

The burning bush vanished and there were two crude sets of bows and arrows, and a water pistol, lying on the cold deckplates. I picked up a set. Useless.

Nimdok swallowed heavily. We turned and started the long way back. The hurricane bird had blown us about for a length of time we could not conceive. Most of that time we had been unconscious. But we had not eaten. A month on the march to the bird itself. Without food. Now how much longer to find our way to the ice caverns, and the promised canned goods?

None of us cared to think about it. We would not die. We would be given filths and scums to eat, of one kind or another. Or nothing at all. AM would keep our bodies alive somehow, in pain, in agony.

The bird slept back there, for how long it didn't matter; when AM was tired of its being there, it would vanish. But all that meat. All that tender meat.

As we walked, the lunatic laugh of a fat woman rang high and around us in the computer chambers that led endlessly nowhere.

It was not Ellen's laugh. She was not fat, and I had not heard her laugh for one hundred and nine years. In fact, I had not heard . . . we walked . . . I was hungry. . . .

We moved slowly. There was often fainting, and we would have to wait. One day he decided to cause an earthquake, at the same time rooting us to the spot with nails through the soles of our shoes. Ellen and Nimdok were both caught when a fissure shot its lightning-bolt opening across the floorplates. They disappeared and were gone. When the earthquake was over we continued on our way, Benny, Gorrister and myself. Ellen and Nimdok were returned to us later that night which became a day abruptly as the heavenly legion bore them to us with a celestial chorus singing, "Go Down, Moses." The archangels circled several times and then dropped the hideously mangled bodies. We kept walking, and a while later Ellen and Nimdok fell in behind us. They were no worse for wear.

But now Ellen walked with a limp. AM had left her that.

It was a long trip to the ice caverns, to find the canned food. Ellen kept talking about Bing cherries and Hawaiian fruit cocktail. I tried not to think about it. The hunger was something that had come to life, even as AM had come to life. It was alive in my belly, even as we were alive in the belly of AM, and AM was alive in the belly of the Earth, and AM wanted the similarity known to us. So he heightened the hunger. There was no way to describe the pains that not having eaten for months brought us. And yet we were kept alive. Stomachs that were merely cauldrons of acid, bubbling, foaming, always shooting spears of sliver-thin pain into our chests. It was the pain of the terminal ulcer, terminal cancer, terminal paresis. It was unending pain. . . .

And we passed through the cavern of rats.

And we passed through the path of boiling steam.

And we passed through the country of the blind.

And we passed through the slough of despond.

And we passed through the vale of tears.

And we came, finally, to the ice caverns. Horizonless thousands of miles in which the ice had formed in blue and silver flashes, where novas lived in the glass. The downdropping stalactites as thick and glorious as diamonds that had been made to run like jelly and then solidified in graceful eternities of smooth, sharp perfection.

We saw the stack of canned goods, and we tried to run to them. We fell in the snow, and we got up and went on, and Benny shoved us away and went at them, and pawed them and gummed them and gnawed at them and he could not open them. AM had not given us a tool to open the cans.

Benny grabbed a three quart can of guava shells, and began to batter it against the ice bank. The ice flew and shattered, but the can was merely dented while we heard the laughter of a fat lady, high overhead and echoing down and down and down the tundra. Benny went completely mad with rage. He began throwing cans, as we all scrabbled about in the snow and ice trying to find a way to end the helpless agony of frustration. There was no way.

Then Benny's mouth began to drool, and he flung himself on Gorrister. . . .

In that instant, I went terribly calm.

Surrounded by meadows, surrounded by hunger, surrounded by everything but death, I knew death was our only way out. AM had kept us alive, but there was a way to defeat him. Not total defeat, but at least peace. I would settle for that.

I had to do it quickly.

Benny was eating Gorrister's face. Gorrister on his side, thrashing snow, Benny wrapped around him with powerful monkey legs crushing Gorrister's waist, his hands locked around Gorrister's head like a nutcracker, and his mouth ripping at the tender skin of Gorrister's cheek. Gorrister screamed with such jagged-edged violence that stalactites fell; they plunged down softly, erect in the receiving snowdrifts. Spears, hundreds of them, everywhere, protruding from the snow. Benny's head pulled back sharply, as something gave all at once, and a bleeding raw-white dripping of flesh hung from his teeth.

Ellen's face, black against the white snow, dominoes in chalk dust. Nimdok with no expression but eyes, all eyes. Gorrister half-conscious. Benny now an animal. I knew AM would let him play. Gorrister would not die, but Benny would fill his stomach. I turned half to my right and drew a huge ice-spear from the snow.

All in an instant:

I drove the great ice-point ahead of me like a battering ram, braced against my right thigh. It struck Benny on the right side, just under the rib cage, and drove upward through his stomach and broke inside him. He pitched forward and lay still. Gorrister lay on his back. I pulled another spear free and straddled him, still moving, driving the spear straight down through his throat. His eyes closed as the cold penetrated. Ellen must have realized what I had decided, even as the fear gripped her. She ran at Nimdok with a short icicle, as he screamed, and into his mouth, and the force of her rush did the job. His head jerked sharply as if it had been nailed to the snow crust behind him.

All in an instant.

There was an eternity beat of soundless anticipation. I could hear AM draw in his breath. His toys had been taken from him. Three of them were dead, could not be revived. He could keep us alive, by his strength and his talent, but he was *not* God. He could not bring them back.

Ellen looked at me, her ebony features stark against the snow that surrounded us. There was fear and pleading in her manner, the way she held herself ready. I knew we had only a heartbeat before AM would stop us.

It struck her and she folded toward me, bleeding from the mouth. I could not read meaning into her expression, the pain had been too great, had contorted her face; but it *might* have been thank you. It's possible. Please.

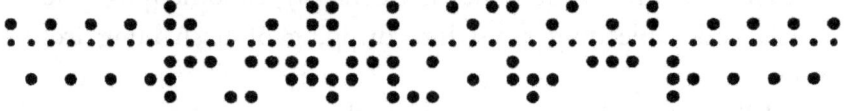

Some hundreds of years may have passed. I don't know. AM has been having fun for some time, accelerating and retarding my time sense. I will say the word now. Now. It took me ten months to say now. I don't know. I *think* it has been some hundreds of years.

He was furious. He wouldn't let me bury them. It didn't matter. There was no way to dig in the deckplates. He dried up the snow. He brought the night. He roared and sent locusts. It didn't do a thing; they stayed dead. I'd had him. He was furious. I had thought AM hated me before. I was wrong. It was not even a shadow of the hate he now slavered from every printed circuit. He made certain I would suffer eternally and could not do myself in.

He left my mind intact. I can dream, I can wonder, I can lament. I remember all four of them. I wish—

Well, it doesn't make any sense. I know I saved them, I know I saved them from what has happened to me, but still, I cannot forget killing them. Ellen's face. It isn't easy. Sometimes I want to, it doesn't matter.

AM has altered me for his own peace of mind, I suppose. He doesn't want me to run at full speed into a computer bank and smash my skull. Or hold my breath till I faint. Or cut my throat on a rusted sheet of metal. There are reflective surfaces down here. I will describe myself as I see myself:

I am a great soft jelly thing. Smoothly rounded, with no mouth, with pulsing white holes filled by fog where my eyes used to be. Rubbery appendages that were once my arms; bulks rounding down into legless humps of soft slippery matter. I leave a moist trail when I move. Blotches of diseased, evil grey come and go on my surface, as though light is being beamed from within.

Outwardly: dumbly, I shamble about, a thing that could never have been known as human, a thing whose shape is so alien a travesty that humanity becomes more obscene for the vague resemblance.

Inwardly: alone. Here. Living under the land, under the sea, in the belly of AM, whom we created because our time was badly spent and we must have known unconsciously that he could do it better. At least the four of them are safe at last.

AM will be all the madder for that. It makes me a little happier. And yet . . . AM has won, simply . . . he has taken his revenge. . . .

I have no mouth. And I must scream.

Eloi, Eloi, Lama Sabachthani

William Hope Hodgson

Dally, Whitlaw and I were discussing the recent stupendous explosion which had occurred in the vicinity of Berlin. We were marvelling concerning the extraordinary period of darkness that had followed, and which had aroused so much newspaper comment, with theories galore.

The papers had got hold of the fact that the War Authorities had been experimenting with a new explosive, invented by a certain chemist, named Baumoff, and they referred to it constantly as "The New Baumoff Explosive."

We were in the Club, and the fourth man at our table was John Stafford, who was professionally a medical man, but privately in the Intelligence Department. Once or twice, as we talked, I had glanced at Stafford, wishing to fire a question at him; for he had been acquainted with Baumoff. But I managed to hold my tongue; for I knew that if I asked out pointblank, Stafford (who's a good sort, but a bit of an ass as regards his almost ponderous code-of-silence) would be just as like as not to say that it was a subject upon which he felt he was not entitled to speak.

Oh, I know the old donkey's way; and when he had once said that, we might just make up our minds never to get another word out of him on the matter as long as we lived. Yet, I was satisfied to notice that he seemed a bit restless, as if he were on the itch to shove in his oar; by which I guessed that the papers we were quoting had got things very badly muddled indeed, in some way or other, at least as regarded his friend Baumoff. Suddenly, he spoke:

"What unmitigated, wicked piffle!" said Stafford, quite warm. "I tell you it is wicked, this associating of Baumoff's name with war inventions and such horrors. He was the most intensely poetical and earnest follower of the Christ that I have ever met; and it is just the brutal Irony of Circumstance that has attempted to use one of the products of his genius for a purpose of Destruction. But you'll find they won't be able to use it, in spite of their having got hold of Baumoff's formula. As an explosive it is not practicable. It is, shall I say, too impartial; there is no way of controlling it.

"I know more about it, perhaps, than any man alive; for I was Baumoff's greatest friend, and when he died, I lost the best comrade a man ever had. I need make no secret about it to you chaps. I was 'on duty' in Berlin, and I was deputed to get in touch with Baumoff. The government had long had an eye on him; he was an Experimental Chemist, you know, and altogether too jolly clever to ignore. But there was no need to worry about him. I got to know him, and we became enormous friends; for I soon found that he would never turn his abilities towards any new war-contrivance; and so, you see, I was able to enjoy my friendship with him, with a comfy conscience—a thing our chaps are not always able to do in their friendships. Oh, I tell you, it's a mean, sneaking, treacherous sort of business, ours; though it's necessary; just as some odd man, or other, has to be a hangsman. There's a number of unclean jobs to be done to keep the Social Machine running!

"I think Baumoff was the most enthusiastic intelligent believer in Christ that it will be ever possible to produce. I learned that he was compiling and evolving a treatise of most extraordinary and convincing proofs in support of the more inexplicable things concerning the life and death of Christ. He was, when I became acquainted with him, concentrating his attention particularly upon endeavouring to show that the Darkness of the Cross, between the sixth and the ninth hours, was a very real thing, possessing a tremendous significance. He intended at one sweep to smash utterly all talk of a timely thunderstorm or any of the other more or less inefficient theories which have been brought forward from time to time to explain the occurrence away as being a thing of no particular significance.

"Baumoff had a pet aversion, an atheistic Professor of Physics, named Hautch, who—using the 'marvellous' element of the life and death of Christ, as a fulcrum from which to attack Baumoff's theories—smashed at him constantly, both in his lectures and in print. Particularly did he pour bitter unbelief upon Baumoff's upholding that the Darkness of the Cross was anything more than a gloomy hour or two, magnified into blackness by the emotional inaccuracy of the Eastern mind and tongue.

"One evening, some time after our friendship had become very real, I called on Baumoff, and found him in a state of tremendous indignation over some article of the Professor's which attacked him brutally; using his theory of the Significance of the 'Darkness,' as a target. Poor Baumoff! It was certainly a marvellously clever attack; the attack of a thoroughly trained, well-balanced Logician. But Baumoff was something more; he was Genius. It is a title few have any rights to; but it was his!

"He talked to me about his theory, telling me that he wanted to show me a small experiment, presently, bearing out his opinions. In his talk, he told me several things that interested me extremely. Having first reminded me of the fundamental fact that light is conveyed to the eye through the means of that indefinable medium, named the Æther. He went a step further, and pointed out to me that, from an aspect which more approached the primary, Light was a vibration of the Æther, of a certain definite number of waves per second, which possessed the power of producing upon our retina the sensation which we term Light.

"To this, I nodded; being, as of course is everyone, acquainted with so well-known a statement. From this, he took a quick, mental stride, and told me that an ineffably vague, but measurable, darkening of the atmosphere (greater or smaller according to the personality-force of the individual) was always evoked in the immediate vicinity of the human, during any period of great emotional stress.

"Step by step, Baumoff showed me how his research had led him to the conclusion that this queer darkening (a million times too subtle to be apparent to the eye) could be produced only through something which had power to disturb or temporally interrupt or break up the Vibration of Light. In other words, there was, at any time of unusual emotional activity, some disturbance of the Æther in the immediate vicinity of the person suffering, which had some effect upon the Vibration of Light, interrupting it, and producing the aforementioned infinitely vague darkening.

"'Yes?' I said, as he paused, and looked at me, as if expecting me to have arrived at a certain definite deduction through his remarks. 'Go on.'

"'Well,' he said, 'don't you see, the subtle darkening around the person suffering, is greater or less, according to the personality of the suffering human. Don't you?'

"'Oh!' I said, with a little gasp of astounded comprehension, 'I see what you mean. You—you mean that if the agony of a person of ordinary personality can produce a faint disturbance of the Æther, with a consequent faint darkening, then the Agony of Christ, possessed of the Enormous Personality of the Christ, would produce a terrific disturbance of the Æther, and therefore, it might chance, of the Vibration of Light, and that this is the true explanation of the Darkness of the Cross; and that the fact of such an extraordinary and apparently unnatural and improbable Darkness having been recorded is not a thing to weaken the Marvel of Christ. But one more unutterably wonderful, infallible proof of His God-like power? Is that it? Is it? Tell me?'

"Baumoff just rocked on his chair with delight, beating one fist into the palm of his other hand, and nodding all the time to my summary. How he loved to be understood; as the Searcher always craves to be understood.

"'And now,' he said, 'I'm going to show you something.'

"He took a tiny, corked test-tube out of his waistcoat pocket, and emptied its contents (which consisted of a single, grey-white grain, about twice the size of an ordinary pin's head) on to his dessert plate. He crushed it gently to powder with the ivory handle of a

knife, then damped it gently, with a single minim of what I supposed to be water, and worked it up into a tiny patch of grey-white
paste. He then took out his gold tooth-pick, and thrust it into the
flame of a small chemist's spirit lamp, which had been lit since dinner as a pipe-lighter. He held the gold tooth-pick in the flame, until
the narrow, gold blade glowed whitehot.

"'Now look!' he said, and touched the end of the tooth-pick
against the infinitesimal patch upon the dessert plate. There came a
swift little violet flash, and suddenly I found that I was staring at
Baumoff through a sort of transparent darkness, which faded swiftly
into a black opaqueness. I thought at first this must be the comple-
mentary effect of the flash upon the retina. But a minute passed, and
we were still in that extraordinary darkness.

"'My Gracious! Man! What is it?' I asked, at last.

"His voice explained then, that he had produced, through the
medium of chemistry, an exaggerated effect which simulated, to
some extent, the disturbance in the Æther produced by waves
thrown off by any person during an emotional crisis or agony. The
waves, or vibrations, sent out by his experiment produced only a partial simulation of the effect he wished to show me—merely the temporary interruption of the Vibration of Light, with the resulting
darkness in which we both now sat.

"'That stuff,' said Baumoff, 'would be a tremendous explosive,
under certain conditions.'

I heard him puffing at his pipe, as he spoke, but instead of the
glow of the pipe shining out visible and red, there was only a faint
glare that wavered and disappeared in the most extraordinary fashion.

"'My Goodness!' I said, 'when's this going away?' And I stared
across the room to where the big kerosene lamp showed only as a
faintly glimmering patch in the gloom; a vague light that shivered
and flashed oddly, as though I saw it through an immense gloomy
depth of dark and disturbed water.

"'It's all right,' Baumoff's voice said from out of the darkness. 'It's
going now; in five minutes the disturbance will have quieted, and

the waves of light will flow off evenly from the lamp in their normal fashion. But, whilst we're waiting, isn't it immense, eh?'

"'Yes,' I said. 'It's wonderful; but it's rather unearthly, you know.'

"'Oh, but I've something much finer to show you,' he said. 'The real thing. Wait another minute. The darkness is going. See! You can see the light from the lamp now quite plainly. It looks as if it were submerged in a boil of waters, doesn't it? that are growing clearer and clearer and quieter and quieter all the time.'

"It was as he said; and we watched the lamp, silently, until all signs of the disturbance of the light-carrying medium had ceased. Then Baumoff faced me once more.

"'Now,' he said. 'You've seen the somewhat casual effects of just crude combustion of that stuff of mine. I'm going to show you the effects of combusting it in the human furnace, that is, in my own body; and then, you'll see one of the great wonders of Christ's death reproduced on a miniature scale.'

"He went across to the mantelpiece, and returned with a small, 120 minim glass and another of the tiny, corked test-tubes, containing a single grey-white grain of his chemical substance. He uncorked the test-tube, and shook the grain of substance into the minim glass, and then, with a glass stirring-rod, crushed it up in the bottom of the glass, adding water, drop by drop as he did so, until there were sixty minims in the glass.

"'Now!' he said, and lifting it, he drank the stuff. 'We will give it thirty-five minutes,' he continued; 'then, as carbonization proceeds, you will find my pulse will increase, as also the respiration, and presently there will come the darkness again, in the subtlest, strangest fashion; but accompanied now by certain physical and psychic phenomena, which will be owing to the fact that the vibrations it will throw off, will be blent into what I might call the emotional-vibrations, which I shall give off in my distress. These will be enormously intensified, and you will possibly experience an extraordinarily interesting demonstration of the soundness of my more theoretical reasonings. I tested it by myself last week' (He waved a

bandaged finger at me), 'and I read a paper to the Club on the results. They are very enthusiastic, and have promised their co-
operation in the big demonstration I intend to give on next Good
Friday—that's seven weeks off, to-day.'

"He had ceased smoking; but continued to talk quietly in this
fashion for the next thirty-five minutes. The Club to which he had
referred was a peculiar association of men, banded together under
the presidentship of Baumoff himself, and having for their appella-
tion the title of—so well as I can translate it—'The Believers And
Provers Of Christ.' If I may say so, without any thought of irrever-
ence, they were, many of them, men fanatically crazed to uphold the
Christ. You will agree later, I think, that I have not used an incor-
rect term, in describing the bulk of the members of this extraordinary club, which was, in its way, well worthy of one of the religio-
maniacal extrudences which have been forced into temporary being
by certain of the more religiously-emotional minded of our cousins
across the water.

"Baumoff looked at the clock; then held out his wrist to me.
'Take my pulse,' he said, 'it's rising fast. Interesting data, you know.'

"I nodded, and drew out my watch. I had noticed that his respirations were increasing; and I found his pulse running evenly and
strongly at 105. Three minutes later, it had risen to 175, and his respirations to 41. In a further three minutes, I took his pulse again,
and found it running at 203, but with the rhythm regular. His respirations were then 49. He had, as I knew, excellent lungs, and his
heart was sound. His lungs, I may say, were of exceptional capacity,
and there was at this stage no marked dyspnoea. Three minutes later
I found the pulse to be 227, and the respiration 54.

"'You've plenty of red corpuscles, Baumoff!' I said. 'But I hope
you're not going to overdo things.'

"He nodded at me, and smiled; but said nothing. Three minutes
later, when I took the last pulse, it was 233, and the two sides of the
heart were sending out unequal quantities of blood, with an irregular
rhythm. The respiration had risen to 67 and was becoming shallow

and ineffectual, and dyspnoea was becoming very marked. The small amount of arterial blood leaving the left side of the heart betrayed itself in the curious bluish and white tinge of the face.

"'Baumoff!' I said, and began to remonstrate; but he checked me, with a queerly invincible gesture.

"'It's all right!' he said, breathlessly, with a little note of impatience. 'I know what I'm doing all the time. You must remember I took the same degree as you in medicine.'

"It was quite true. I remembered then that he had taken his M.D. in London; and this in addition to half a dozen other degrees in different branches of the sciences in his own country. And then, even as the memory reassured me that he was not acting in ignorance of the possible danger, he called out in a curious, breathless voice:

"'The Darkness! It's beginning. Take note of every single thing. Don't bother about me. I'm all right!'

"I glanced swiftly round the room. It was as he had said. I perceived it now. There appeared to be an extraordinary quality of gloom growing in the atmosphere of the room. A kind of bluish gloom, vague, and scarcely, as yet, affecting the transparency of the atmosphere to light.

"Suddenly, Baumoff did something that rather sickened me. He drew his wrist away from me, and reached out to a small metal box, such as one sterilizes a hypodermic in. He opened the box, and took out four rather curious looking drawing-pins, I might call them, only they had spikes of steel fully an inch long, whilst all around the rim of the heads (which were also of steel) there projected downward, parallel with the central spike, a number of shorter spikes, maybe an eighth of an inch long.

"He kicked off his pumps; then stooped and slipped his socks off, and I saw that he was wearing a pair of linen inner-socks.

"'Antiseptic!' he said, glancing at me. 'Got my feet ready before you came. No use running unnecessary risks.' He gasped as he spoke. Then he took one of the curious little steel spikes.

"'I've sterilized them,' he said; and therewith, with deliberation, he pressed it in up to the head into his foot between the second and third branches of the dorsal artery.

"'For God's sake, what are you doing!' I said, half rising from my chair.

"'Sit down!' he said, in a grim sort of voice. 'I can't have any interference. I want you simply to observe; keep note of everything. You ought to thank me for the chance, instead of worrying me, when you know I shall go my own way all the time.'

"As he spoke, he had pressed in the second of the steel spikes up to the hilt in his left instep, taking the same precaution to avoid the arteries. Not a groan had come from him; only his face betrayed the effect of this additional distress.

"'My dear chap!' he said, observing my upsetness. 'Do be sensible. I know exactly what I'm doing. There simply must be distress, and the readiest way to reach that condition is through physical pain.' His speech had becomes a series of spasmodic words, between gasps, and sweat lay in great clear drops upon his lip and forehead. He slipped off his belt and proceeded to buckle it round both the back of his chair and his waist; as if he expected to need some support from falling.

"'It's wicked!' I said. Baumoff made an attempt to shrug his heaving shoulders, that was, in its way, one of the most piteous things that I have seen, in its sudden laying bare of the agony that the man was making so little of.

"He was now cleaning the palms of his hands with a little sponge, which he dipped from time to time in a cup of solution. I knew what he was going to do, and suddenly he jerked out, with a painful attempt to grin, an explanation of his bandaged finger. He had held his finger in the flame of the spirit lamp, during his previous experiment; but now, as he made clear in gaspingly uttered words, he wished to simulate as far as possible the actual conditions of the great scene that he had so much in mind. He made it so clear to me that we might expect to experience something very extraordinary, that I was conscious of a sense of almost superstitious nervousness.

"'I wish you wouldn't, Baumoff!' I said.

"'Don't—be—silly!' he managed to say. But the two latter words were more groans than words; for between each, he had thrust home right to the heads in the palms of his hands the two remaining steel spikes. He gripped his hands shut, with a sort of spasm of savage determination, and I saw the point of one of the spikes break through the back of his hand, between the extensor tendons of the second and third fingers. A drop of blood beaded the point of the spike. I looked at Baumoff's face; and he looked back steadily at me.

"'No interference,' he managed to ejaculate. 'I've not gone through all this for nothing. I know—what—I'm doing. Look—it's coming. Take note—everything!'

"He relapsed into silence, except for his painful gasping. I realised that I must give way, and I stared round the room, with a peculiar commingling of an almost nervous discomfort and a stirring of very real and sober curiosity.

"'Oh,' said Baumoff, after a moment's silence, 'something's going to happen. I can tell. Oh, wait—till I—I have my—big demonstration. I'll show that brute Hautch."

"I nodded; but I doubt that he saw me; for his eyes had a distinctly in-turned look, the iris was rather relaxed. I glanced away round the room again; there was a distinct occasional breaking up of the light-rays from the lamp, giving a coming-and-going effect.

"The atmosphere of the room was also quite plainly darker—heavy, with an extraordinary sense of gloom. The bluish tint was unmistakably more in evidence; but there was, as yet, none of that opacity which we had experienced before, upon simple combustion, except for the occasional, vague coming-and-going of the lamp-light.

"Baumoff began to speak again, getting his words out between gasps. 'Th—this dodge of mine gets the—pain into the—the—right place. Right association of—of ideas—emotions—for—best—results. You follow me? Parallelising things—as—much as—possible. Fixing whole attention—on the—the death scene—'

"He gasped painfully for a few moments. 'We demonstrate truth of—of The Darkening; but—but there's psychic effect to be—looked for, through—results of parallelisation of—conditions. May have extraordinary simulation of—the actual thing. Keep note. Keep note.' Then, suddenly, with a clear, spasmodic burst: 'My God, Stafford, keep note of everything. Something's going to happen. Something—wonderful—Promise not—to bother me. I know—what I'm doing.'

"Baumoff ceased speaking, with a gasp, and there was only the labour of his breathing in the quietness of the room. As I stared at him, halting from a dozen things I needed to say, I realised suddenly that I could no longer see him quite plainly; a sort of wavering in the atmosphere, between us, made him seem momentarily unreal. The whole room had darkened perceptibly in the last thirty seconds; and as I stared around, I realised that there was a constant invisible swirl in the fast-deepening, extraordinary blue gloom that seemed now to permeate everything. When I looked at the lamp, alternate flashings of light and blue—darkness followed each other with an amazing swiftness.

"'My God!' I heard Baumoff whispering in the half-darkness, as if to himself, 'how did Christ bear the nails!'

"I stared across at him, with an infinite discomfort, and an irritated pity troubling me; but I knew it was no use to remonstrate now. I saw him vaguely distorted through the wavering tremble of the atmosphere. It was somewhat as if I looked at him through convolutions of heated air; only there were marvellous waves of blue-blackness making gaps in my sight. Once I saw his face clearly, full of an infinite pain, that was somehow, seemingly, more spiritual than physical, and dominating everything was an expression of enormous resolution and concentration, making the livid, sweat-damp, agonized face somehow heroic and splendid.

"And then, drenching the room with waves and splashes of opaqueness, the vibration of his abnormally stimulated agony finally broke up the vibration of Light. My last, swift glance round, showed me, as it seemed, the invisible aether boiling and eddying in a tremendous fashion; and, abruptly, the flame of the lamp was lost in an extraordinary swirling patch of light, that marked its position for several moments, shimmering and deadening, shimmering and deadening; until, abruptly, I saw neither that glimmering patch of light, nor anything else. I was suddenly lost in a black opaqueness of night, through which came the fierce, painful breathing of Baumoff.

"A full minute passed; but so slowly that, if I had not been counting Baumoff's respirations, I should have said that it was five. Then Baumoff spoke suddenly, in a voice that was, somehow, curiously changed—a certain toneless note in it:

"'My God!' he said, from out of the darkness, 'what must Christ have suffered!'

"It was in the succeeding silence, that I had the first realisation that I was vaguely afraid; but the feeling was too indefinite and unfounded, and I might say subconscious, for me to face it out. Three minutes passed, whilst I counted the almost desperate respirations that came to me through the darkness. Then Baumoff began to speak again, and still in that peculiarly altering voice:

"'By Thy Agony and Bloody Sweat,' he muttered. Twice he repeated this. It was plain indeed that he had fixed his whole attention with tremendous intensity, in his abnormal state, upon the death scene.

"The effect upon me of his intensity was interesting and in some ways extraordinary. As well as I could, I analysed my sensations and emotions and general state of mind, and realised that Baumoff was producing an effect upon me that was almost hypnotic.

"Once, partly because I wished to get my level by the aid of a normal remark, and also because I was suddenly newly anxious by a change in the breathsounds, I asked Baumoff how he was. My voice going with a peculiar and really uncomfortable blankness through that impenetrable blackness of opacity.

"He said: 'Hush! I'm carrying the Cross.' And, do you know, the effect of those simple words, spoken in that new, toneless voice, in that atmosphere of almost unbearable tenseness, was so powerful that, suddenly, with eyes wide open, I saw Baumoff clear and vivid against that unnatural darkness, carrying a Cross. Not, as the picture is usually shown of the Christ, with it crooked over the shoulder; but with the Cross gripped just under the cross-piece in his arms, and the end trailing behind, along rocky ground. I saw even the pattern of the grain of the rough wood, where some of the bark had been ripped away; and under the trailing end there was a tussock of tough wire-grass, that had been uprooted by the lowing end, and dragged and ground along upon the rocks, between the end of the Cross and the rocky ground. I can see the thing now, as I speak. Its vividness was extraordinary; but it had come and gone like a flash, and I was sitting there in the darkness, mechanically counting the respirations; yet unaware that I counted.

"As I sat there, it came to me suddenly—the whole entire marvel of the thing that Baumoff had achieved. I was sitting there in a darkness which was an actual reproduction of the miracle of the Darkness of the Cross. In short, Baumoff had, by producing in himself an abnormal condition, developed an Energy of Emotion that must have almost, in its effects, paralleled the Agony of the Cross. And in so doing, he had shown from an entirely new and wonderful point, the indisputable truth of the stupendous personality and the enormous spiritual force of the Christ. He had evolved and made practical to the average understanding a proof that would make to live again the reality of that wonder of the world—CHRIST. And for all this, I had nothing but admiration of an almost stupefied kind.

"But, at this point, I felt that the experiment should stop. I had a strangely nervous craving for Baumoff to end it right there and then, and not to try to parallel the psychic conditions. I had, even then, by some queer aid of sub-conscious suggestion, a vague reaching-out-towards the danger of 'monstrosity' being induced, instead of any actual knowledge gained.

"'Baumoff!' I said. 'Stop it.'

"But he made no reply, and for some minutes there followed a silence, that was unbroken, save by his gasping breathing. Abruptly, Baumoff said, between his gasps: 'Woman—behold—thy—son.' He muttered this several times, in the same uncomfortably toneless voice in which he had spoken since the darkness became complete.

"'Baumoff,' I said again. 'Baumoff! Stop it.' And as I listened for his answer, I was relieved to think that his breathing was less shallow. The abnormal demand for oxygen was evidently being met, and the extravagant call upon the heart's efficiency was being relaxed.

"'Baumoff!' I said, once more. 'Baumoff! Stop it!'

"And, as I spoke, abruptly, I thought the room was shaken a little.

"Now, I had already as you will have realised, been vaguely conscious of a peculiar and growing nervousness. I think that is the word that best describes it, up to this moment. At this curious little shake that seemed to stir through the utterly dark room, I was suddenly more than nervous. I felt a thrill of actual and literal fear; yet with no sufficient cause of reason to justify me; so that, after sitting very tense for some long minutes, and feeling nothing further, I decided that I needed to take myself in hand, and keep a firmer grip upon my nerves. And then, just as I had arrived at this more comfortable state of mind, the room was shaken again, with the most curious and sickening oscillatory movement, that was beyond all comfort of denial.

"'My God!' I whispered. And then, with a sudden effort of courage, I called: 'Baumoff! For God's sake stop it.'

"You've no idea of the effort it took to speak aloud into that darkness; and when I did speak, the sound of my voice set me afresh on edge. It went so empty and raw across the room; and somehow, the room seemed to be incredibly big. Oh, I wonder whether you realise how beastly I felt, without my having to make any further effort to tell you.

"And Baumoff never answered a word; but I could hear him breathing, a little fuller; though still heaving his thorax painfully, in his need for air. The incredible shaking of the room eased away; and there succeeded a spasm of quiet, in which I felt that it was my duty to get up and step across to Baumoff's chair. But I could not do it. Somehow, I would not have touched Baumoff then for any cause whatever. Yet, even in that moment, as now I know, I was not aware that I was afraid to touch Baumoff.

"And then the oscillations commenced again. I felt the seat of my trousers slide against the seat of my chair, and I thrust out my legs, spreading my feet against the carpet, to keep me from sliding off one way or the other on to the floor. To say I was afraid, was not to describe my state at all. I was terrified. And suddenly, I had comfort, in the most extraordinary fashion; for a single idea literally glazed into my brain, and gave me a reason to which to cling. It was a single line:

"'Æther, the soul of iron and sundry stuffs' which Baumoff had once taken as a text for an extraordinary lecture on vibrations, in the earlier days of our friendship. He had formulated the suggestion that, in embryo, Matter was, from a primary aspect, a localised vibration, traversing a closed orbit. These primary localised vibrations were inconceivably minute. But were capable, under certain conditions, of combining under the action of keynote-vibrations into secondary vibrations of a size and shape to be determined by a multitude of only guessable factors. These would sustain their new form, so long as nothing occurred to disorganise their combination or depreciate or divert their energy—their unity being partially determined by the inertia of the still Æther outside of the closed path which their area of activities covered. And such combination of the primary localised vibrations was neither more nor less than matter. Men and worlds, aye! and universes.

"And then he had said the thing that struck me most. He had said, that if it were possible to produce a vibration of the Æther of a sufficient energy, it would be possible to disorganise or confuse the vibration of matter. That, given a machine capable of creating a vibration of the Æther of a sufficient energy, he would engage to destroy not merely the world, but the whole universe itself, including heaven and hell themselves, if such places existed, and had such existence in a material form.

"I remember how I looked at him, bewildered by the pregnancy and scope of his imagination. And now his lecture had come back to me to help my courage with the sanity of reason. Was it not possible that the Æther disturbance which he had produced, had sufficient energy to cause some disorganisation of the vibration of matter, in the immediate vicinity, and had thus created a miniature quaking of the ground all about the house, and so set the house gently a-shake?

"And then, as this thought came to me, another and a greater, flashed into my mind. 'My God!' I said out loud into the darkness of the room. It explains one more mystery of the Cross, the disturbance of the Æther caused by Christ's Agony, disorganised the vibration of matter in the vicinity of the Cross, and there was then a small local earthquake, which opened the graves, and rent the veil, possibly by disturbing its supports. And, of course, the earthquake was an effect, and not a cause, as belittlers of the Christ have always insisted.

"'Baumoff!' I called. 'Baumoff, you've proved another thing. Baumoff! Baumoff! Answer me. Are you all right?'

"Baumoff answered, sharp and sudden out of the darkness; but not to me:

"'My God!' he said. 'My God!' His voice came out at me, a cry of veritable mental agony. He was suffering, in some hypnotic, induced fashion, something of the very agony of the Christ Himself.

"'Baumoff!'" I shouted, and forced myself to my feet. I heard his chair clattering, as he sat there and shook. 'Baumoff!'

An extraordinary quake went across the floor of the room, and I heard a creaking of the woodwork, and something fell and smashed in the darkness. Baumoff's gasps hurt me; but I stood there. I dared not go to him. I knew then that I was afraid of him—of his condition, or something I don't know what. But, oh, I was horribly afraid of him.

"'Bau—' I began, but suddenly I was afraid even to speak to him. And I could not move. Abruptly, he cried out in a tone of incredible anguish:

"'Eloi, Eloi, lama sabachthani!' But the last word changed in his mouth, from his dreadful hypnotic grief and pain, to a scream of simply infernal terror.

"And, suddenly, a horrible mocking voice roared out in the

room, from Baumoff's chair: 'Eloi, Eloi, lama sabachthani!'

"Do you understand, the voice was not Baumoff's at all. It was not a voice of despair; but a voice sneering in an incredible, bestial, monstrous fashion. In the succeeding silence, as I stood in an ice of fear, I knew that Baumoff no longer gasped. The room was absolutely silent, the most dreadful and silent place in all this world. Then I bolted; caught my foot, probably in the invisible edge of the hearth-rug, and pitched headlong into a blaze of internal brain-stars. After which, for a very long time, certainly some hours, I knew nothing of any kind.

"I came back into this Present, with a dreadful headache oppressing me, to the exclusion of all else. But the Darkness had dissipated. I rolled over on to my side, and saw Baumoff and forgot even the pain in my head. He was leaning forward towards me: his eyes wide open, but dull. His face was enormously swollen, and there was, somehow, something beastly about him. He was dead, and the belt about him and the chair-back, alone prevented him from falling forward on to me. His tongue was thrust out of one corner of his mouth. I shall always remember how he looked. He was leering, like a human-beast, more than a man.

"I edged away from him, across the floor; but I never stopped looking at him, until I had got to the other side of the door, and closed between us. Of course, I got my balance in a bit, and went back to him; but there was nothing I could do.

"Baumoff died of heart-failure, of course, obviously! I should never be so foolish as to suggest to any sane jury that, in his extraordinary, self-hypnotised, defenseless condition, he was 'entered' by some Christ-apeing Monster of the Void. I've too much respect for my own claim to be a common-sensible man, to put forward such an idea with seriousness! Oh, I know I may seem to speak with a jeer; but what can I do but jeer at myself and all the world, when I dare not acknowledge, even secretly to myself, what my own thoughts are. Baumoff did, undoubtedly die of heart-failure; and, for the rest, how much was I hypnotised into believing. Only, there was over by the far wall, where it had been shaken down to the floor from a sol-idly fastened-up bracket, a little pile of glass that had once formed a piece of beautiful Venetian glassware. You remember that I heard something fall, when the room shook. Surely the room did shake? Oh, I must stop thinking. My head goes round.

"The explosive the papers are talking about. Yes, that's Baumoff's; that makes it all seem true, doesn't it? They had the darkness at Berlin, after the explosion. There is no getting away from that. The Government know only that Baumoff's formulae is capable of producing the largest quantity of gas, in the shortest pos-sible time. That, in short, it is ideally explosive. So it is; but I imag-ine it will prove an explosive, as I have already said, and as experience has proved, a little too impartial in its action for it to cre-ate enthusiasm on either side of a battlefield. Perhaps this is but a mercy, in disguise; certainly a mercy, if Baumoff's theories as to the possibility of disorganising matter, be anywhere near to the truth.

"I have thought sometimes that there might be a more normal explanation of the dreadful thing that happened at the end. Baumoff may have ruptured a blood-vessel in the brain, owing to the enor-mous arterial pressure that his experiment induced; and the voice I heard and the mockery and the horrible expression and leer may have been nothing more than the immediate outburst and expres-sion of the natural 'obliqueness' of a deranged mind, which so often turns up a side of a man's nature and produces an inversion of char-acter, that is the very complement of his normal state. And certainly, poor Baumoff's normal religious attitude was one of marvellous rev-erence and loyalty towards the Christ.

"Also, in support of this line of explanation, I have frequently observed that the voice of a person suffering from mental derange-ment is frequently wonderfully changed, and has in it often a very repellant and inhuman quality. I try to think that this explanation fits the case. But I can never forget that room. Never."

Peking Man

Robert J. Sawyer

The lid was attached to the wooden crate with eighteen nails. The return address, in blue ink on the blond wood, said, "Sender: Dept. of Anatomy, P.U.M.C., Peking, China." The destination address, in larger letters, was:

Dr. Roy Chapman Andrews
The American Museum of Natural History
Central Park West at 79th Street
New York, N.Y. U.S.A.

The case was marked "Fragile!" and "REGISTERED" and *"Par Avion."* A brand had burned the words "Via Hong Kong and by U.S. Air Service" into the wood.

Andrews had waited anxiously for this arrival. Between 1922 and 1930, he himself had led the now-famous Gobi Desert expeditions, searching for the Asian cradle of humanity. Although he'd brought back untold scientific riches—including the first-ever dinosaur eggs—Andrews had failed to discover a single ancient human remain.

But now a German scientist, Franz Weidenreich, had shipped to him a treasure trove from the Orient: the complete fossil remains of *Sinanthropus pekinensis.* In this very crate were the bones of Peking Man.

Andrews was actually salivating as he used a crowbar to pry off the lid. He'd waited so long for these, terrified that they wouldn't survive the journey, desperate to see what humanity's forefathers had looked like, anxious—

The lid came off. The contents were carefully packed in smaller cardboard boxes. He picked one up and moved over to his cluttered desk. He swept the books and papers to the floor, laid down the box, and opened it. Inside was a ball of rice paper, wrapped around a large object. Andrews carefully unwrapped the sheets, and—

White.

White?

No—no, it couldn't be.

But it was. It was a skull, certainly—but *not* a fossil skull. The material was bright white.

And it didn't weigh nearly enough.

A plaster cast. Not the original at all.

Andrews opened every box inside the wooden crate, his heart sinking as each new one yielded its contents. In total, there were fourteen skulls and eleven jawbones. The skulls were subhuman, with low foreheads, prominent brow ridges, flat faces, and the most unlikely-looking perfect square teeth. Amazingly, each of the skull casts also showed clear artificial damage to the foramen magnum.

Oh, some work could indeed be done on these casts, no doubt. But where were the original fossils? With the Japanese having invaded China, surely they were too precious to be left in the Far East. What was Weidenreich up to?

*

Fire.

It was like a piece of the sun, brought down to earth. It kept the tribe warm at night, kept the saber-toothed cats away—and it did something wonderful to meat, making it softer and easier to chew, while at the same time restoring the warmth the flesh had had when still part of the prey.

Fire was the most precious thing the tribe owned. They'd had it for eleven summers now, ever since Bok the brave had brought out a burning stick from the burning forest. The glowing coals were always fanned, always kept alive.

And then, one night, the Stranger came—tall, thin, pale, with red-rimmed eyes that somehow seemed to glow from beneath his brow ridge.

The Stranger did the unthinkable, the unforgivable.

He doused the flames, throwing a gourd full of water on to the fire. The logs hissed, and steam rose up into the blackness. The children of the tribe began to cry; the adults quaked with fury. The Stranger turned and walked into the darkness. Two of the strongest hunters ran after him, but his long legs had apparently carried him quickly away.

The sounds of the forest grew closer—the chirps of insects, the rustling of small animals in the vegetation, and—

A flapping sound.

The Stranger was gone.

And the silhouette of a bat fluttered briefly in front of the waning moon.

*

Franz Weidenreich had been born in Germany in 1873. A completely bald, thick-set man, he had made a name for himself as an expert in hematology and osteology. He was currently Visiting Professor at the University of Chicago, but that was coming to an end, and now he was faced with the uncomfortable prospect of having to return to Nazi Germany—something, as a Jew, he desperately wanted to avoid.

And then word came of the sudden death of the Canadian paleontologist Davidson Black. Black had been at the Peking Union Medical College, studying the fragmentary remains of early man being recovered from the limestone quarry at Chou Kou Tien. Weidenreich, who once made a study of Neanderthal bones found in Germany, had read Black's papers in *Nature* and *Science* describing *Sinanthropus.*

But now, at fifty, Black was as dead as his fossil charges—an unexpected heart attack. And, to Weidenreich's delight, the China Medical Board of the Rockefeller Foundation wanted him to fill Black's post. China was a strange, foreboding place—and tensions between the Chinese and the Japanese were high—but it beat all hell out of returning to Hitler's Germany . . .

*

At night, most of the tribe huddled under the rocky overhang or crawled into the damp, smelly recesses of the limestone cave. Without the fire to keep animals away, someone had to stand watch each night, armed with a large branch and a pile of rocks for throwing. Last night, it had been Kart's turn. Everyone had slept well, for Kart was the strongest member of the tribe. They knew they were safe from whatever lurked in the darkness.

When daybreak came, the members of the tribe were astounded. Kart had fallen asleep. They found him lying in the dirt, next to the cold, black pit where their fire had once been. And on Kart's neck there were two small red-rimmed holes, staring up at them like the eyes of the Stranger . . .

*

During his work on hematology, Weidenreich had met a remarkable man named Brancusi—gaunt, pale, with disconcertingly sharp canine teeth. Brancusi suffered from a peculiar anemia, which Weidenreich had been unable to cure, and an almost pathological photophobia. Still, the gentleman was cultured and widely read, and Weidenreich had ever since maintained a correspondence with him.

When Weidenreich arrived in Peking, work was still continuing at the quarry. So far, only teeth and fragments of skull had been found. Davidson Black had done a good job of cataloguing and describing some of the material, but as Weidenreich went through the specimens he was surprised to discover a small collection of sharp, pointed fossil teeth.

Black had evidently assumed they weren't part of the *Sinanthropus* material, as he hadn't included them in his descriptions. And, at first glance, Black's assessment seemed correct: they were far longer than normal human canines, and much more sharply pointed. But, to Weidenreich's eye, the root pattern was possibly hominid. He dropped a letter to his friend Brancusi, half joking that he'd found Brancusi's great-to-the-nth grandfather in China.

To Weidenreich's infinite surprise, within weeks Brancusi had arrived in Peking.

*

Each night, another member of the tribe stood watch—and each morning, that member was found unconscious, with a pair of tiny wounds to his neck.

The tribe members were terrified. Soon multiple guards were posted each night, and for a time the happenings ceased.

But then something even more unusual happened . . .

They were hunting deer. It would not be the same, not without fire to cook the meat, but still, the tribe needed to eat. Four men, Kart included, led the assault. They moved stealthily among the tall grasses, tracking a large buck with a giant rack of antlers. The hunters communicated by sign language, carefully coordinating their movements, closing in on the animal from both sides.

Kart raised his right arm, preparing to signal the final attack, when—

—a streak of light brown, slicing through the grass—

—fangs flashing, the roar of the giant cat, the stag bolting away, and then—

—Kart's own scream as the saber-tooth grabbed hold of his thigh and shook him viciously.

The other three hunters ran as fast as they could, desperate to get away. They didn't stop to look back, even when the cat let out the strangest yelp . . .

That night, the tribe huddled together and sang songs urging Kart's soul a safe trip to heaven.

*

One of the Chinese laborers found the first skull. Weidenreich was summoned at once. Brancusi still suffered from his photophobia and apparently had never adjusted to the shift in time zones; he slept during the day. Weidenreich thought about waking him to see this great discovery, but decided against it.

The skull was still partially encased in the limestone muck at the bottom of the cave. It had a thick cranial wall and a beetle brow—

definitely a more primitive creature than Neanderthal, probably akin to Solo Man or Java Man . . .

It took careful work to remove the skull from the ground, but, when it did come free, two astonishing things became apparent.

The loose teeth Davidson Black had set aside had indeed come from the hominids here: this skull still had all its upper teeth intact, and the canines were long and pointed.

Second, and even more astonishing, was the foramen magnum—the large opening in the base of the skull through which the spinal cord passes. It was clear from its chipped, frayed margin that this individual's foramen magnum had been artificially widened—

—meaning he'd been decapitated, and then had something shoved up into his brain through the bottom of his skull.

*

Five hunters stood guard that night. The moon had set, and the great sky river arched high overhead. The Stranger returned—but this time he was not alone. The tribesmen couldn't believe their eyes. In the darkness, it looked like—

It was. Kart.

But—but Kart was dead. They'd seen the saber-tooth take him.

The Stranger came closer. One of the men lifted a rock, as if to throw it at him, but soon he let the rock drop from his hand. It fell to the ground with a dull thud.

The Stranger continued to approach, and so did Kart.

And then Kart opened his mouth, and in the faint light they saw his teeth—long and pointed, like the Stranger's.

The men were unable to run, unable to move. They seemed transfixed, either by the Stranger's gaze or by Kart's, both of whom continued to approach.

And soon, in the dark, chill night, the Stranger's fangs fell upon one of the guard's necks, and Kart's fell upon another . . .

*

Eventually, thirteen more skulls were found, all of which had the strange elongated canine teeth, and all of which had their foramen magnums artificially widened. Also found were some mandibles and skull fragments from other individuals—but there was almost no post-cranial material. Someone in dim prehistory had discarded here the decapitated heads of a group of proto-humans.

Brancusi sat in Weidenreich's lab late at night, looking at the skulls. He ran his tongue over his own sharp teeth, contemplating. These subhumans doubtless had no concept of mathematics beyond perhaps adding and subtracting on their fingers. How would they possibly know of the problem that plagued the Family, the problem that every one of the Kindred knew to avoid?

If all those who feel the bite of the vampire themselves become vampires when they die, and all these new vampires also turn those they feed from into vampires, soon, unless care is exercised, the whole population will be undead. A simple geometric progression.

Brancusi had long wondered how far back the Family went. It wasn't like tracing a normal family tree—oh, yes, the lines were bloodlines, but not as passed on from father to son. He knew his own lineage—a servant at Castle Dracula before the Count had taken to living all alone, a servant whose loyalty to his master extended even to letting him drink from his neck.

Brancusi himself had succumbed to pneumonia, not an uncommon ailment in the dank Carpathians. He had no family, and no one mourned his passing.

But soon he rose again—and now he did have Family.

An Englishman and an American had killed the Count, removing his head with a kukri knife and driving a bowie knife through his heart. When news of this reached Brancusi from the gypsies, he traveled back to Transylvania. Dracula's attackers had simply abandoned the coffin, with its native soil and the dust that the Count's body had crumbled into. Brancusi dug a grave on the desolate, windswept grounds of the Castle and placed the Count's coffin within.

*

Eventually, over a long period, the entire tribe had felt the Stranger's bite directly or indirectly.

A few of the tribefolk lost their lives to ravenous bloodthirst, drained dry. Others succumbed to disease or giant cats or falls from cliffs. One even died of old age. But they all rose again.

And so it came to pass, just as it had for the Stranger all those years before, that the tribe had to look elsewhere to slake its thirst.

But they had not counted on the Others.

*

Weidenreich and Brancusi sat in Weidenreich's lab late at night. Things had been getting very tense—the Japanese occupation was becoming intolerable. "I'm going to return to the States," said Weidenreich. "Andrews at the American Museum is offering me space to continue work on the fossils."

"No," said Brancusi. "No, you can't take the fossils."

Weidenreich's bushy eyebrows climbed up toward his bald pate. "But we can't let them fall into Japanese hands."

"That is true," said Brancusi.

"They belong somewhere safe. Somewhere where they can be studied."

"No," said Brancusi. His red-rimmed gaze fell on Weidenreich in a way it never had before. "No—no one may see these fossils."

"But Andrews is expecting them. He's dying to see them. I've been deliberately vague in my letters to him—I want to be there to see his face when he sees the dentition."

"No one can know about the teeth," said Brancusi.

"But he's expecting the fossils. And I have to publish descriptions of them."

"The teeth must be filed flat."

Weidenreich's eyes went wide. "I can't do that."

"You can, and you will."

"But—"

"You can and you will."

"I—I can, but—"

"No buts."

"No, no, there *is* a but. Andrews will never be fooled by filed teeth; the structure of teeth varies as you go into them. Andrews will realize at once that the teeth have been reduced from their original size." Weidenreich looked at Brancusi. "I'm sorry, but there's no way to hide the truth."

*

The Others lived in the next valley. They proved tough and resourceful—and they could make fire whenever they needed it. When the tribefolk arrived it became apparent that there was never a time of darkness for the Others. Large fires were constantly burning.

The tribe had to feed, but the Others defended themselves, trying to kill them with rock knives.

But that didn't work. The tribefolk were undeterred.

They tried to kill them with spears.

But that did not work, either. The tribefolk came back.

They tried strangling the attackers with pieces of animal hide.

But that failed, too. The tribefolk returned again.

And finally the Others decided to try everything they could think of simultaneously.

They drove wooden spears into the hearts of the tribefolk.

They used stone knives to carve off the heads of the tribefolk.

And then they jammed spears up into the severed heads, forcing the shafts up through the holes at the bases of the skulls.

The hunters marched far away from their camp, each carrying a spear thrust vertically toward the summer sun, each one crowned by a severed, pointed-toothed head. When, at last, they found a suitable hole in the ground, they dumped the heads in, far, far away from their bodies.

The Others waited for the tribefolk to return.

But they never did.

*

"Do not send the originals," said Brancusi.

"But—"

"The originals are mine, do you understand? I will ensure their safe passage out of China."

It looked for a moment as if Weidenreich's will was going to reassert itself, but then his expression grew blank again. "All right."

"I've seen you make casts of bones before."

"With plaster of Paris, yes."

"Make casts of these skulls—and then file the teeth on the casts."

"But—"

"You said Andrews and others would be able to tell if the original fossils were altered. But there's no way they could tell that the casts had been modified, correct?"

"Not if it's done skillfully, I suppose, but—"

"Do it."

"What about the foramen magnums?"

"What would you conclude if you saw fossils with such widened openings?"

"I don't know—possibly that ritual cannibalism had been practiced."

"Ritual?"

"Well, if the only purpose was to get at the brain so you could eat it, it's easier just to smash the cranium, and—"

"Good. Good. Leave the damage to the skull bases intact. Let your Andrews have that puzzle to keep him occupied."

*

The casts were crated up and sent to the States first. Then Weidenreich himself headed for New York, leaving, he said, instructions for the actual fossils to be shipped aboard the S.S. *President Harrison*. But the fossils never arrived in America, and Weidenreich, the one man who might have clues to their whereabouts, died shortly thereafter.

Despite the raging war, Brancusi returned to Europe, returned to Transylvania, returned to Castle Dracula.

It took him a while in the darkness of night to find the right spot—the scar left by his earlier digging was just one of many on the desolate landscape. But at last he located it. He prepared a series of smaller holes in the ground, and into each of them he laid one of the grinning skulls. He then covered the holes over with dark soil.

Brancusi hoped never to fall himself, but if he did, he hoped one of his own converts would do the same thing for him, bringing his remains home to the Family plot.

Role Play

Richard Christian Matheson

". . . like that?"

A helpless whisper. ". . . yes."

"Harder?"

Scared nod.

"Tell me."

"Yes . . . please slap me harder."

His large palm stops just before hitting her.

"What do you call me?"

". . . daddy."

"But daddy wouldn't like you doing this, would he?"

She trembles. ". . . no."

"Kiss me."

His full mouth gets closer. Her lips part like a wound. He stares into her widening eyes. Smiles cruelty; refuses.

"Are you a slut?"

". . . yes."

His voice lowers; harsh, punitive. "Say it . . . "

". . . I'm a slut."

He wraps fingers around her neck. Whispers in her ear.

"You love that. *Don't* you?"

Stricken noises.

"Tell me!"

Tears start to run. ". . . I love it."

He gently kisses her. "I know you do." Holds her. "You're daddy's beautiful girl."

She clings to him. Silent. Looks into his eyes.

"What do you want?"

A craving plea. "Hurt me."

His stare drains to black. Pulls her hair hard. Slaps her more. Harder.

". . . like that, whore?"

". . . yes."

"Tell me . . . "

A whimper. ". . . please, more."

Palm striking. Cheeks going red. Tears run.

"You always want more because you're a dirty girl." She struggles as he handcuffs her. Chokes her with one hand. "Poor baby can't breathe?"

She gets wetter; a lascivious trance.

"Your husband doesn't know your filthy secrets, does he? How you crave being a worthless whore?"

He enters her fast and she gasps at the size. Bites his muscled neck, pierces skin. Something inside him reacts. A tic of mouth.

She spreads legs wider. Body a sick bliss; sheets sweat-soaked. Squeezes him harder, tongue crawling lips.

"Filthy *whore* . . . you ashamed to cum? Ashamed to have a stranger's huge cock inside you?" He thrusts deeper, over and over, makes her cry out.

The tic on his face gets worse. ". . . gonna count to ten, slut. When I get to one, you can cum! Not before." He grabs her trembling chin. "Understand?"

She nods, begins to sob. Arches back. Rocking faster on him, his fingers pressing into her slender neck.

". . . eight . . . seven . . . six . . . "

Writhing. Clutches tighter, feels it seething, rushing closer.

". . . five . . . four . . . three . . . two . . . "

She starts falling from cliff.

". . . one."

Lips drawn back, climax searing through veins and flesh; insides uncaging. She shudders; scream trapped by his choking hand. Claws his cheek. Eyes pleading, frantic. He grips harder, bruising soft skin, cutting-off air. Watches terror slowly drown her.

She gradually collapses onto sheets. Staring into nowhere.

He gets up. Goes to wall mirror. Expression blank. Sees rip on cheek. Small cut on neck. Dresses. Dials cell phone.

"Done."

They'll send a van. Clean and repair torn skin. Fix software. Scrub program. Send it out, again.

It blinks wrongly. Ignores her lifeless body. Sensors malfunction. Strong fingers spasm and lock. Doesn't notice ad on bedside table.

"PLEASURE ROBOTS, INC."
Programmable Fantasies

Discrete Delivery / Available by the hour

Terms and Conditions: *User engages services at own risk and agrees to waive all legal action. Provider does not guarantee individual results.*

Full Circle

Bruce Taylor

. . . so weird, you think, lying in your podbed, *so damn weird—totally asleep, totally awake. How can*—you drift, a memory, the class, the endless instruction. Nancy Mathis droning on and on—". . . by giving REMtrex—harmless but enables you to feel like you're getting a deep sleep yet keeps your mind clear." She looks at you and the others of the Slide Team. You look at her. Blue eyes, slender, in spite of her yellow unisex uniform. All that nice dark hair tied in a tight bundle on her head per on-shift Earth-Mars Shuttle Rules. She says something else but you kinda tune out, looking around the large multipurpose room on the third level in the *Redux*, a D-Class De-Commissioned Mining Activity Asteroid that now is home for 1000 people, now known to the official crew as mutineers . . . *tough shit*
. . . you think to yourself in your dream sleep.—*Blasted out of Mars orbit after Stan Hassle and Jack Holmes "made adjustments" with the Proton-Royce Astro-Engines . . . way too much power but God, did we scoot! Wow!* you think. *And even after we took over the shuttle, found out the crew hated the politics on Earth even more than we did and made it easy for us to just—take over*—you drift again. *So asleep, so awake. Miracles of modern science,* you think. Drifting. Memory—*before? After? President for life Banon of the Earth–Mars Alliance—What was that bullshit—?*

"Martian politics are no more. I will govern best and know best how the two worlds will develop—"

Oh, you remember thinking, *oh, is that right? Well, screw you, you pompous asshole. No way. No effin' way! Born on Mars, I was, and we've had it with Earth politics dictated by a so-proclaimed president for life*— Then—*Yeah, afterwards, more bullshit from that asshole. What was it?*

"Resistance is futile. Mars politics are nowhere. Losers. All of you. Hunt you down, exterminate you! Deport you to the mines of Ceres . . ."

That face. That childish, overweight pink-faced white-haired bully who openly admired Stalin's tactics for building a new Soviet State and who thought Hitler had some good ideas. *How'd something like him get elected? Now he was questioning Mars' Guaranteed Sovereignty.*

Back to Nancy Mathis again. "You'll get used to the REMtrex. Some have even gotten addicted and that is a danger but only after long term use—we'll be at the slide point in two days—" You look around to the room.

Could be anywhere, you muse. You tune into Nancy Mathis again, "—so all of you in charge of The Slide will have to be at top readiness to perform, problem solve and think fast if we are going to make it. REMtrex will give you that intuitive extra edge by also neuro-interfacing with the Stenson Dedicated Computer so if something goes wrong, that interfacing should—"

—drifting. *Can't work,* you think, *how can you be perfectly relaxed so you can sleep then suddenly be perfectly awa——oh, oh, oh yeah,* and you become aware of that little electronic deal attached to your waist that either fully activates or deactivates the REMtrex. Another memory:

You sitting with a cup of coffee with Melanie Sanchez—bright as they come and she's explaining this whole Slide deal to you and you know if you hear it often enough, you might get it. You're sitting at a white plastifoam table in a lounge with the portal where you could see Mars below in all its rusted red glory.

She had out her pad, and with a finger sketched a line on it. "See?" she said. "In our 3-D world we think of three dimensions but theoretically we know there are far more than that. It was the genius of Julius Stenson to figure out where, in local space, other dimensions joined." She did more drawing on the tablet with her index finger, obviously enjoying her display of knowledge; her black hair tumbling about her shoulders in off-shift abandon. "So anyway," she said, scooching closer, "he discovered how to theoretically travel through space by finding out where the dimensions intersected and literally," she grinned, "sliding through that intersection to the next or adjacent dimension."

She acted like it made perfect sense but you didn't have a clue. You think you said, "As long as we don't get smashed in the process." Lots of other things you wanted to say like, "I bet this is a one way trip" and "Do you know where you'll end up?" and "What time or year will it be when we get to where we're going, wherever that is?" and "Are we talking distance travel or time travel? Or both?" and "What if this turns out to be time travel? How many time-streams will there be? If we mess up one, will the other one—or the others—also get messed up or just exactly mirror the one that gets messed up?"

"So," and she clicked the button on the side of her pad, erasing the diagrams, "don't have to go the speed of light anywhere. Just have to know where the dimensions intersect. Julius Stenson gave us that info and now that we have it—"

"Where?"

She waved her hand around the room. "Here. Why do you think President Banon doesn't want Mars to be independent? Why do you think we've taken over the shuttle? He's not going to get this first of its kind technical application of the Slide Technology."

God, you felt dumb. *Of course that's what this was about. President Banon getting the information and his vileness could go everywhere. Like a virus going viral.*

You continue to drift, back and forth between wakeful-sleepiness and sleepy-wakefulness, ready to go in to deeper realms of sleep or full wakefulness. *REMtrex. What weird stuff, incredibly comfortable, incredibly strange, not bad, just strange—can see why people get hooked. Especially when you start interfacing with a Stenson Dedicated Computer dealing with dimensionality and time-space. Wow. What a ride!* And things keep coming to your mind that you didn't know you knew. *How—? It must be why they wanted folks involved in The Slide to be on this stuff*—gone again—

—back—you like Melanie Sanchez. You think she really likes you or maybe she knows you just have to get this stuff, if nothing else, the mechanics part—so you automatically know what you have to do without really understanding the theoretical aspect of it. Just—know what to do—Memory—*taking me to AstroEngineering, the forward deck of the Redux, to go over the details again but this time with a twist—*

"—close enough," she was saying, her off-shift black hair long and beautiful, dark as her eyes, then pointing to a large screen at a forty-five degree angle in the control panel of the five person pilot quarters, and looking at it, you just see the star field "—you'd never think there was anything out there but stars," she was saying, "until—" she hit a key on the board, and the screen *blipped*, blanked, and when it came back, there was the star field but also these purple-blue shades of something—almost as if watching veils of blue-black waving curtains of something, kind of reminding you of pictures you've seen of Earth's Aurora Borealis, moving across the screen, moving down from the top, the sides—"The Stenson Dimension Locator," she said, "different dimensions of space, planes and surfaces on which ride stars, planets and space itself and we're about to ride an edge of a dimensional plane where it intersects another—"

A shock.

You are awake. Suddenly *really* awake.

A voice echoes from shuttle speakers: "Jay Ronstrom! Attention Jay Ronstrom! Report to the pilot's cabin!"

You don't think. You leap from the podbed and you are just on your way. And man, are you *awake*. And what's weird, it's like you've been through this drill of what to do so many, many times, you don't even have to think. Endless training as you prepared, absolutely knowing what you have to do.

At the Stenson Dedicated Computer, you see Melanie, for

whatever reason, not having her hair in the on-shift regulation style. What is also strange is, amidst the panels, readouts, lights, keyboards—you and Melanie are the only ones for two of the five seats used to pilot the *Redux*.

She says nothing, just smiles, pointing to the seat at the console. You clamber in, get seated and putting the interface band around your head, you pause. It's as if the computer has dendrites reaching into your skull and your own—reaching back, touching, fused—and you say, as if you had this memorized and said it a million times before, "Coming to Stenson Dimension Edge. Stenson tracking engaged. Stenson Tracking now locked. Ready to Slide. Countdown, 5-4-3-2-1—" then a slight jolt. "Sliding sequence processing."

"That's it," Melanie says. "Good job. Now we Slide. Do you see or experience anything unusual?"

You shake your head; right now, you're concentrating and it's as if something in you simply knew what was next. "Cutting engines," you say. "Slide engagement complete. Intersection with incoming dimension in fifteen minutes—" You pause, then look to Melanie. "Just feel super aware, like making associations that I haven't made before. Stuff that used to baffle me just"—you shrug—"just—doesn't. So weird how this REMtrex works."

Melanie nods. "Helps with the interface with the computer but also locks in information, instructions where it functions as if it fuses with the muscle and bones—also called 'tissue memory' but enables you to endure and synthesize states of consciousness and thought while reducing psychological/physiological stress." She pauses, then looks to the screen to the information being displayed, "Super important if you are engaged in something like," she straightens up, smiles with what looks like smug satisfaction, "Stenson Technology. Besides, space can be pretty boring; more fun to just dream the time away while also remaining totally fit."

Flash. You get it. "You're getting ready to use this on generational star trips. And I bet some of these Mars-Earth shuttles—maybe this one—"

Melanie looks a bit startled but after a moment, nods. "Pretty good," she says.

"OK," you say, "we're on our way—but on our way to—where? Nothing in my memory, in spite of all the information, tells me that."

She looks away. "Anywhere is better than where we were going if we were going back to Earth or stay with the Mars-Earth Sovereignty Agreement."

"Um," you say, "um—I take it that means this is a one way ticket. This isn't in the Stenson work, is it?"

Melanie continues to look away. "What's there to go back to? You know what we're in for."

You stop. She's right. Suddenly you feel all self-righteous like you *know* you did the right thing. "Having this technology where Banon and his stooges can't get it—" you muse.

She looks to you with an expression both doleful and proud. She nods.

"But where do we end up?"

Melanie sighs, looks down to her hands. "—um—we believe another star system—that's where the Stenson calculations lead. We are dealing with space and temporal distance."

"Temporal distance," you say, "not necessarily *just* distance."

"Chance we had to take," Melanie says. "We had to get away. But since we are not at the speed of light—"

Something in you opens up like your IQ has just gone stratospheric. "But," you say, "we *are* at the speed of how fast dimensions move and that's not known—is it?"

You're feeling proud of yourself right then, because you begin to see that in your hyper-clear mind, things, unfortunately, are beginning to make sense. "And the other ships have the Stenson technology?"

"No." Melanie continues to look down as if real embarrassed about the deceit. "Just this one."

"And I bet I'm the only one taking REMtrex."

"Just you."

"Because——?"

"You're the most intuitive."

You let out a long breath and you hit another key on the keyboard and stats come on about the *Redux*'s other systems. You study it. So does Melanie. Though her skin is tan, it somehow becomes pale. She leans over to look at the secondary screen.

After a minute, you simply say, "Well, Stenson got it right about the Dimension stuff, no doubt about that. But—"

Melanie nods. "Didn't get it right about what the engines needed to adapt to the stress of the slide." She nods again. "We needed thirteen percent more power which we lost when Holmes and Kassle altered the engines to get us out of Mars orbit—somehow forgot to compensate for that and the Dimension Slide." Melanie looks abashed, lost, as the consequences sink in.

On the computer screen, it's as if a planet just—materializes and you are right above it in a low orbit. Abruptly, you know without having to consult anything, the planet has captured the *Redux* in a rapidly decaying orbit.

Melanie wipes away tears with the back of her hand. "You—you couldn't see this happening—?" she whispers.

"Not enough information for me to connect the dots. Had I known more—" You look at the other readouts and you say, "Well, that's interesting. Almost a twin of Earth except the atmosphere is more of what you would have found—" you stop—then slowly, "—60 to 70 million years ago—but what the hell—" Suddenly, in your head, there is a brilliant realization. REMtrex has gone far above and beyond its effectiveness; you get it. Boy, do you get it.

You fumble with the head band, hold it, then let it drop onto the console. "Oh, holy fuck," you whisper. "Oh, Christ, oh, no—no—no——"

Melanie looks uncomprehending from the screen to you, her look is that of imploring. "What——?"

You shake your head, close your eyes, put your elbows on the console and hold your head in your hands. "We don't have to worry about Banon for another sixty-five million years," you say, and then you look to the screen, blank, as it computes, analyzes data coming in but you already *know* what you are going to see: God knows *how* many times you've already seen it over the course of billions of years. "We're stuck, we're going to crash and in sixty-five million years you and I will be right here, having this same damn conversation because when we came through the dimensional intersection, the history we *came* from vanished and now we start all over again with *this* history—" you pause, then continue, "which becomes the history—we just came from."

Melanie still looks uncomprehending, but in seconds the screen blips back on, place names appear and you point to a pulsing yellow circle below the area that the computer identifies as the place you are going to crash: just east and offshore of—the Yucatan Peninsula.

The Star

H. G. Wells

In the text, *Pollux* refers to the brightest star
in the constellation of Gemini.

It was on the first day of the new year that the announcement was
made, almost simultaneously from three observatories, that the motion of the planet Neptune, the outermost of all the planets that
wheel about the sun, had become very erratic. Ogilvy had already
called attention to a suspected retardation in its velocity in December. Such a piece of news was scarcely calculated to interest a world
the greater portion of whose inhabitants were unaware of the existence of the planet Neptune, nor outside the astronomical profession
did the subsequent discovery of a faint remote speck of light in the
region of the perturbed planet cause any very great excitement. Scientific people, however, found the intelligence remarkable enough,
even before it became known that the new body was rapidly growing
larger and brighter, that its motion was quite different from the orderly progress of the planets, and that the deflection of Neptune and
its satellite was becoming now of an unprecedented kind.

Few people without a training in science can realise the huge
isolation of the solar system. The sun with its specks of planets, its
dust of planetoids, and its impalpable comets, swims in a vacant
immensity that almost defeats the imagination. Beyond the orbit of
Neptune there is space, vacant so far as human observation has penetrated, without warmth or light or sound, blank emptiness, for
twenty million times a million miles. That is the smallest estimate of
the distance to be traversed before the very nearest of the stars is at-
tained. And, saving a few comets more unsubstantial than the thin-
nest flame, no matter had ever to human knowledge crossed this
gulf of space until early in the twentieth century this strange wan-

derer appeared. A vast mass of matter it was, bulky, heavy, rushing without warning out of the black mystery of the sky into the radiance of the sun. By the second day it was clearly visible to any decent instrument, as a speck with a barely sensible diameter, in the constellation Leo near Regulus. In a little while an opera glass could attain it.

On the third day of the new year the newspaper readers of two hemispheres were made aware for the first time of the real importance of this unusual apparition in the heavens. "A Planetary Collision," one London paper headed the news, and proclaimed Duchaine's opinion that this strange new planet would probably collide with Neptune. The leader-writers enlarged upon the topic. So that in most of the capitals of the world, on January 3rd, there was an expectation, however vague, of some imminent phenomenon in the sky; and as the night followed the sunset round the globe, thousands of men turned their eyes skyward to see—the old familiar stars just as they had always been.

Until it was dawn in London and Pollux setting and the stars overhead grown pale. The Winter's dawn it was, a sickly filtering accumulation of daylight, and the light of gas and candles shone yellow in the windows to show where people were astir. But the yawning policeman saw the thing, the busy crowds in the markets stopped agape, workmen going to their work betimes, milkmen, the drivers of news-carts, dissipation going home jaded and pale, homeless wanderers, sentinels on their beats, and, in the country, labourers trudging afield, poachers slinking home, all over the dusky quickening country it could be seen—and out at sea by seamen watching for the day—a great white star, come suddenly into the westward sky!

Brighter it was than any star in our skies; brighter than the evening star at its brightest. It still glowed out white and large, no mere twinkling spot of light, but a small, round, clear shining disc, an hour after the day had come. And where science has not reached, men stared and feared, telling one another of the wars and pestilences that are foreshadowed by these fiery signs in the Heavens. Sturdy Boers, dusky Hottentots, Gold Coast negroes, Frenchmen, Spaniards, Portuguese, stood in the warmth of the sunrise watching the setting of this strange new star.

And in a hundred observatories there had been suppressed excitement, rising almost to shouting pitch, as the two remote bodies had rushed together, and a hurrying to and fro, to gather photographic apparatus and spectroscope, and this appliance and that, to record this novel, astonishing sight, the destruction of a world. For it was a world, a sister planet of our earth, far greater than our earth indeed, that had so suddenly flashed into flaming death. Neptune it was had been struck, fairly and squarely, by the strange planet from outer space, and the heat of the concussion had incontinently turned two solid globes into one vast mass of incandescence. Round the world that day, two hours before the dawn, went the pallid great white star, fading only as it sank westward and the sun mounted above it. Everywhere men marvelled at it, but of all those who saw it none could have marvelled more than those sailors, habitual watchers of the stars, who far away at sea had heard nothing of its advent and saw it now rise like a pigmy moon and climb zenithward and hang overhead and sink westward with the passing of the night.

And when next it rose over Europe everywhere were crowds of watchers on hilly slopes, on house-roofs, in open spaces, staring eastward for the rising of the great new star. It rose with a white glow in front of it, like the glare of a white fire, and those who had seen it come into existence the night before cried out at the sight of it. "It is larger," they cried. "It is brighter!" And indeed the moon, a quarter full and sinking in the west, was in its apparent size beyond comparison, but scarcely in all its breadth had it as much brightness now as the little circle of the strange new star.

"It is brighter!" cried the people clustering in the streets. But in the dim observatories the watchers held their breath and peered at one another. "*It is nearer!*" they said. "*Nearer!*"

And voice after voice repeated, "It is nearer," and the clicking telegraph took that up, and it trembled along telephone wires, and in a thousand cities grimy compositors fingered the type. "It is nearer." Men writing in offices, struck with a strange realisation, flung down their pens, men talking in a thousand places suddenly came upon a grotesque possibility in those words, "It is nearer." It hurried along awakening streets, it was shouted down the frost-stilled ways of quiet villages, men who had read these things from the throbbing tape stood in yellow-lit doorways shouting the news to the passers-by. "It is nearer." Pretty women, flushed and glittering, heard the news told jestingly between the dances, and feigned an intelligent interest they did not feel. "Nearer! Indeed. How curious! How very, very clever people must be to find out things like that!"

Lonely tramps faring through the wintry night murmured those words to comfort themselves—looking skyward. "It has need to be nearer, for the night's as cold as charity. Don't seem much warmth from it if it *is* nearer, all the same."

"What is a new star to me?" cried the weeping woman, kneeling beside her dead.

The schoolboy, rising early for his examination work, puzzled it out for himself—with the great white star shining broad and bright through the frost-flowers of his window. "Centrifugal, centripetal," he said, with his chin on his fist. "Stop a planet in its flight, rob it of its centrifugal force, what then? Centripetal has it, and down it falls into the sun! And this—!"

"Do *we* come in the way? I wonder—"

The light of that day went the way of its brethren, and with the later watches of the frosty darkness rose the strange star again. And it was now so bright that the waxing moon seemed but a pale yellow ghost of itself, hanging huge in the sunset. In a South African city a great man had married, and the streets were alight to welcome his return with his bride. "Even the skies have illuminated," said the flatterer. Under Capricorn, two negro lovers, daring the wild beasts and evil spirits for love of one another, crouched together in a cane brake where the fire-flies hovered. "That is our star," they whispered, and felt strangely comforted by the sweet brilliance of its light.

The master mathematician sat in his private room and pushed the papers from him. His calculations were already finished. In a small white phial there still remained a little of the drug that had kept him awake and active for four long nights. Each day, serene, explicit, patient as ever, he had given his lecture to his students, and then had come back at once to this momentous calculation. His face was grave, a little drawn and hectic from his drugged activity. For some time he seemed lost in thought. Then he went to the window, and the blind went up with a click. Half-way up the sky, over the clustering roofs, chimneys, and steeples of the city, hung the star.

He looked at it as one might look into the eyes of a brave enemy. "You may kill me," he said after a silence. "But I can hold you—and all the universe for that matter—in the grip of this small brain. I would not change. Even now."

He looked at the little phial. "There will be no need of sleep again," he said. The next day at noon, punctual to the minute, he entered his lecture theatre, put his hat on the end of the table as his habit was, and carefully selected a large piece of chalk. It was a joke among his students that he could not lecture without that piece of chalk to fumble in his fingers, and once he had been stricken to impotence by their hiding his supply. He came and looked under his grey eyebrows at the rising tiers of young fresh faces, and spoke with his accustomed studied commonness of phrasing.

"Circumstances have arisen—circumstances beyond my control," he said, and paused, "which will debar me from completing the course I had designed. It would seem, gentlemen, if I may put the thing clearly and briefly, that—Man has lived in vain."

The students glanced at one another. Had they heard aright? Mad? Raised eyebrows and grinning lips there were, but one or two faces remained intent upon his calm grey-fringed face. "It will be interesting," he was saying, "to devote this morning to an exposition, so far as I can make it clear to you, of the calculations that have led me to this conclusion. Let us assume—"

He turned towards the blackboard, meditating a diagram in the way that was usual to him. "What was that about 'lived in vain'?" whispered one student to another. "Listen," said the other, nodding towards the lecturer.

And presently they began to understand.

That night the star rose later, for its proper eastward motion had carried it some way across Leo towards Virgo, and its brightness was so great that the sky became a luminous blue as it rose, and every star was hidden in its turn, save only Jupiter near the zenith, Capella, Aldebaran, Sirius, and the pointers of the Bear. It was very white and beautiful. In many parts of the world that night a pallid halo encircled it about. It was perceptibly larger; in the clear refractive sky of the tropics it seemed as if it were nearly a quarter the size of the moon. The frost was still on the ground in England, but the world was as brightly lit as if it were midsummer moonlight. One could see to read quite ordinary print by that cold, clear light, and in the cities the lamps burnt yellow and wan.

And everywhere the world was awake that night, and throughout Christendom a sombre murmur hung in the keen air over the country-side like the belling of bees in the heather, and this murmurous tumult grew to a clangour in the cities. It was the tolling of the bells in a million belfry towers and steeples, summoning the people to sleep no more, to sin no more, but to gather in their churches and pray. And overhead, growing larger and brighter, as the earth rolled on its way and the night passed, rose the dazzling star.

And the streets and houses were alight in all the cities, the shipyards glared, and whatever roads led to high country were lit and crowded all night long. And in all the seas about the civilized lands, ships with throbbing engines, and ships with bellying sails, crowded with men and living creatures, were standing out to ocean and the north. For already the warning of the master mathematician had been telegraphed all over the world and translated into a hundred tongues. The new planet and Neptune, locked in a fiery embrace, were whirling headlong, ever faster and faster towards the sun. Already every second this blazing mass flew a hundred miles, and every second its terrific velocity increased. As it flew now, indeed, it must pass a hundred million of miles, wide of the earth and scarcely affect it. But near its destined path, as yet only slightly perturbed, spun the mighty planet Jupiter and his moons sweeping splendid round the sun. Every moment now the attraction between the fiery star and the greatest of the planets grew stronger. And the result of that attraction? Inevitably Jupiter would be deflected from its orbit into an elliptical path, and the burning star, swung by his attraction wide of its sunward rush, would "describe a curved path," and perhaps collide with, and certainly pass very close to, our earth. "Earthquakes, volcanic outbreaks, cyclones, sea waves, floods, and a steady rise in temperature to I know not what limit"—so prophesied the master mathematician.

And overhead, to carry out his words, lonely and cold and livid blazed the star of the coming doom.

To many who stared at it that night until their eyes ached it seemed that it was visibly approaching. And that night, too, the weather changed, and the frost that had gripped all Central Europe and France and England softened towards a thaw.

But you must not imagine, because I have spoken of people praying through the night and people going aboard ships and people fleeing towards mountainous country, that the whole world was already in a terror because of the star. As a matter of fact, use and wont still ruled the world, and save for the talk of idle moments and the splendour of the night, nine human beings out of ten were still busy at their common occupations. In all the cities the shops, save one here and there, opened and closed at their proper hours, the doctor and the undertaker plied their trades, the workers gathered in the factories, soldiers drilled, scholars studied, lovers sought one another, thieves lurked and fled, politicians planned their schemes. The presses of the newspapers roared through the nights, and many a priest of this church and that would not open his holy building to further what he considered a foolish panic. The newspapers insisted on the lesson of the year 1000—for then, too, people had anticipated the end. The star was no star—mere gas—a comet; and were it a star it could not possibly strike the earth. There was no precedent for such a thing. Common-sense was sturdy everywhere, scornful, jesting, a little inclined to persecute the obdurate fearful. That night, at seven-fifteen by Greenwich time, the star would be at its nearest to Jupiter. Then the world would see the turn things would take. The master mathematician's grim warnings were treated by many as so much mere elaborate self-advertisement. Common-sense at last, a little heated by argument, signified its unalterable convictions by going to bed. So, too, barbarism and savagery, already tired of the novelty, went about their nightly business, and, save for a howling dog here and there, the beast world left the star unheeded.

And yet, when at last the watchers in the European States saw the star rise, an hour later, it is true, but no larger than it had been the night before, there were still plenty awake to laugh at the master mathematician—to take the danger as if it had passed.

But hereafter the laughter ceased. The star grew—it grew with a terrible steadiness hour after hour, a little larger each hour, a little nearer the midnight zenith, and brighter and brighter, until it had turned night into a second day. Had it come straight to the earth instead of in a curved path, had it lost no velocity to Jupiter, it must have leapt the intervening gulf in a day; but as it was, it took five days altogether to come by our planet. The next night it had become a third the size of the moon before it set to English eyes, and the thaw was assured. It rose over America near the size of the moon, but blinding white to look at, and *hot;* and a breath of hot wind blew now with its rising and gathering strength, and in Virginia, and Brazil, and down the St. Lawrence valley, it shone intermittently through a driving reek of thunder-clouds, flickering violet lightning, and hail unprecedented. In Manitoba was a thaw and devastating floods. And upon all the mountains of the earth the snow and ice began to melt that night, and all the rivers coming out of high country flowed thick and turbid, and soon—in their upper reaches—with swirling trees and the bodies of beasts and men. They rose steadily, steadily in the ghostly brilliance, and came trickling over their banks at last, behind the flying population of their valleys.

And along the coast of Argentina and up the South Atlantic the tides were higher than had ever been in the memory of man, and the storms drove the waters in many cases scores of miles inland, drowning whole cities. And so great grew the heat during the night that the rising of the sun was like the coming of a shadow. The earthquakes began and grew until all down America from the Arctic Circle to Cape Horn, hillsides were sliding, fissures were opening, and houses and walls crumbling to destruction. The whole side of Cotopaxi slipped out in one vast convulsion, and a tumult of lava poured out so high and broad and swift and liquid that in one day it reached the sea.

So the star, with the wan moon in its wake, marched across the Pacific, trailed the thunder-storms like the hem of a robe, and the growing tidal wave that toiled behind it, frothing and eager, poured over island and island and swept them clear of men: until that wave came at last—in a blinding light and with the breath of a furnace, swift and terrible it came—a wall of water, fifty feet high, roaring hungrily, upon the long coasts of Asia, and swept inland across the plains of China. For a space the star, hotter now and larger and brighter than the sun in its strength, showed with pitiless brilliance the wide and populous country; towns and villages with their pagodas and trees, roads, wide cultivated fields, millions of sleepless people staring in helpless terror at the incandescent sky; and then, low and growing, came the murmur of the flood. And thus it was with millions of men that night—a flight nowhither, with limbs heavy with heat and breath fierce and scant, and the flood like a wall swift and white behind. And then death.

China was lit glowing white, but over Japan and Java and all the islands of Eastern Asia the great star was a ball of dull red fire because of the steam and smoke and ashes the volcanoes were spouting forth to salute its coming. Above was the lava, hot gases and ash, and below the seething floods, and the whole earth swayed and rumbled with the earthquake shocks. Soon the immemorial snows of Thibet and the Himalaya were melting and pouring down by ten million deepening converging channels upon the plains of Burmah and Hindostan. The tangled summits of the Indian jungles were aflame in a thousand places, and below the hurrying waters around the stems were dark objects that still struggled feebly and reflected the blood-red tongues of fire. And in a rudderless confusion a multitude of men and women fled down the broad river-ways to that one last hope of men—the open sea.

Larger grew the star, and larger, hotter, and brighter with a terrible swiftness now. The tropical ocean had lost its phosphorescence, and the whirling steam rose in ghostly wreaths from the black waves that plunged incessantly, speckled with storm-tossed ships.

And then came a wonder. It seemed to those who in Europe watched for the rising of the star that the world must have ceased its rotation. In a thousand open spaces of down and upland the people who had fled thither from the floods and the falling houses and sliding slopes of hill watched for that rising in vain. Hour followed hour through a terrible suspense, and the star rose not. Once again men set their eyes upon the old constellations they had counted lost to them for ever. In England it was hot and clear overhead, though the ground quivered perpetually, but in the tropics, Sirius and Capella and Aldebaran showed through a veil of steam. And when at last the great star rose near ten hours late, the sun rose close upon it, and in the centre of its white heart was a disc of black.

Over Asia it was the star had begun to fall behind the movement of the sky, and then suddenly, as it hung over India, its light had been veiled. All the plain of India from the mouth of the Indus to the mouths of the Ganges was a shallow waste of shining water that night, out of which rose temples and palaces, mounds and hills, black with people. Every minaret was a clustering mass of people, who fell one by one into the turbid waters, as heat and terror overcame them. The whole land seemed a-wailing, and suddenly there swept a shadow across that furnace of despair, and a breath of cold wind, and a gathering of clouds, out of the cooling air. Men looking up, near blinded, at the star, saw that a black disc was creeping across the light. It was the moon, coming between the star and the earth. And even as men cried to God at this respite, out of the East with a strange inexplicable swiftness sprang the sun. And then star, sun, and moon rushed together across the heavens.

So it was that presently to the European watchers star and sun rose close upon each other, drove headlong for a space and then slower, and at last came to rest, star and sun merged into one glare of flame at the zenith of the sky. The moon no longer eclipsed the star but was lost to sight in the brilliance of the sky. And though those who were still alive regarded it for the most part with that dull stupidity that hunger, fatigue, heat and despair engender, there were still men who could perceive the meaning of these signs. Star and earth had been at their nearest, had swung about one another, and the star had passed. Already it was receding, swifter and swifter, in the last stage of its headlong journey downward into the sun.

And then the clouds gathered, blotting out the vision of the sky, the thunder and lightning wove a garment round the world; all over the earth was such a downpour of rain as men had never before seen, and where the volcanoes flared red against the cloud canopy there descended torrents of mud. Everywhere the waters were pouring off the land, leaving mud-silted ruins, and the earth littered like a storm-worn beach with all that had floated, and the dead bodies of the men and brutes, its children. For days the water streamed off the land, sweeping away soil and trees and houses in the way, and piling huge dykes and scooping out Titanic gullies over the country-side. Those were the days of darkness that followed the star and the heat. All through them, and for many weeks and months, the earthquakes continued.

But the star had passed, and men, hunger-driven and gathering courage only slowly, might creep back to their ruined cities, buried granaries, and sodden fields. Such few ships as had escaped the storms of that time came stunned and shattered and sounding their way cautiously through the new marks and shoals of once familiar ports. And as the storms subsided men perceived that everywhere the days were hotter than of yore, and the sun larger, and the moon, shrunk to a third of its former size, took now fourscore days between its new and new.

But of the new brotherhood that grew presently among men, of the saving of laws and books and machines, of the strange change that had come over Iceland and Greenland and the shores of Baffin's Bay, so that the sailors coming there presently found them green and gracious, and could scarce believe their eyes, this story does not tell. Nor of the movement of mankind, now that the earth was hotter, northward and southward towards the poles of the earth. It concerns itself only with the coming and the passing of the star.

The Martian astronomers—for there are astronomers on Mars, although they are very different beings from men—were naturally profoundly interested by these things. They saw them from their own standpoint of course. "Considering the mass and temperature of the missile that was flung through our solar system into the sun," one wrote, "it is astonishing what a little damage the earth, which it missed so narrowly, has sustained. All the familiar continental markings and the masses of the seas remain intact, and indeed the only difference seems to be a shrinkage of the white discolouration (supposed to be frozen water) round either pole." Which only shows how small the vastest of human catastrophes may seem at a distance of a few million miles.

The Secret Language of Stones

Darrell Schweitzer

If a stone could speak, this is how it might tell the story.

But I will not write it out for you, because you would not live long enough to read it. There is a problem with time. You are a mayfly. I brush dead mayflies off the page.

Let me just try to talk, then.

I suppose I must have been this way virtually since birth, since I have no early memories that do not involve closed rooms and hospital beds and staring at the ceiling while adults babbled incomprehensible things around me. But I did not feel myself a captive or particularly inconvenienced, because I knew no other children, and I felt safe with my books and my toys within reach on nearby shelves. I can remember, though, a particularly bright midsummer day when a sparrow landed on my windowsill and began to sing, then somehow became trapped between the screen and the glass. At first I was delighted in its company, but almost at once it had fell silent, and I slipped out of bed to see what had become of it, but when I got to the window I found it reduced to a dusty bundle of bones and feathers. I stared at it glumly, as if one of my toys had been broken and I knew it could not be repaired.

There was snow on the ground outside. I stood, clinging to the windowsill, watching the snow melt away and flowers rise up out of the ground, unfolding themselves slowly as they did so, while leaves returned to the trees.

It was only much later that Dr. Archibald (who was my favorite because he brought me toys) began to speak to my parents in my presence about "catalepsy" or "paralysis" or a "time disease." Mostly his voice was just a high-pitched chirp, like that of the bird in the window, and he flitted around the room in a blur; but sometimes, if

I concentrated very hard, I could hear him, and once he gave me a shot and for almost half an hour he was intelligible. This I determined by the clock on the wall. For once the spinning hands were no longer just a blur, and I could hear the ticking, and I could hear him clearly. He said something about "relative time scales" and my being "out of sync" with everybody else. He tried to explain by moving both of his hands through the air at the same rate, then holding one back, so that the other moved ahead of it.

He was white-haired and wrinkled and bent over by then. He hadn't been like that when he'd given me the shot.

He touched me on the forehead. His touch was light and dry, like ashes falling.

It was my parents' final visit. They were mayflies. I knew my mother by her smile and her eyes. My father, beside her, was a stranger.

"Don't go," I said. But they were gone, and the room filled with light and shadow alternately, like the pages of a book being blown by the wind.

*

All of which is bullshit, or a lie, or a dream, or something, which makes me the most unreliable of narrators. Even if I am actually narrating this and not lying about that too.

I am a god. I hear the voices of the other gods, calling to me out of the darkness, and, shivering and slick with perspiration, naked as a god should be, I climb into the darkness beneath swirling stars. Yes, the very heavens turn like a great and glistening wheel as I struggle up the face of a mountain, clinging to the frigid, crumbling rock, as I slip and slide and cut myself and bruise myself. But each time I fall I get up again and continue on my journey, because I know that far above, at the summit, my fellow gods are waiting for me.

They speak to me quite clearly, of a time when the earth shall be cleared of mayflies and all things that are ephemeral shall be brushed away, when the stones will indeed speak, and the stones will dance, and I, being likewise made of stone, will dance with them beneath the spinning sky.

*

No, Doctor, I cannot tell you why I did what I did. The voices told me what had to be done, if the earth is to be cleared off.

The voices of the stones, yes. They have been speaking for millions of years. You mayflies will never be able to hear them.

A mayfly is, of course, an insect that only lives for a single day, then dies, then is brushed away like a speck of dust. Perhaps, from the mayfly's perspective, that is a full and rich lifetime, even a long one.

But not from mine.

Ashes, ashes, all fall down.

*

I have to be naked. I cannot wear mayfly clothing. It is like trying to wrap oneself in ashes.

The doctor came to me and gave me another shot. He wasn't Dr. Archibald, but someone I didn't know.

He said I had to go, right now. I couldn't stay. He *hurried* me along. I looked to the shelves, to my things there. He said I could come back for them later. He said I was too old for toys now anyway.

So he led me, clad only in my hospital gown and paper slippers, into the corridor outside. The lights went off, came on, went off. He flickered, like a cloud of mayflies, touching me, fussing over me, gone, then back again.

I don't think the shot was working very well. Maybe I had built up resistance.

The floor shook gently under my feet.

And I saw him there, lying at my feet, all bones and dust and tatters, like the bird in the window.

My hospital gown, too, was reduced to tatters, and I stood there alone and bewildered in the cold, while the walls of the hospital peeled away around me. Once through a gap in the ceiling I glimpsed a squadron of airplanes, like a flock of starlings overhead.

There was a flash of burning light, and the earth rose and fell like a wave.

When it was cold again and there was snow on what remained of the floor, I found a utility closet and from it took a pair of overalls and put them on, and even rubber boots, and I congratulated myself at having solved the immediate problem.

Of course the boots didn't last. After just a few steps, they became brittle and fell away. The overalls lasted considerably longer.

Ultimately it did not matter. If the days and nights went by as flickering shadows, if the seasons were like the blinking of an eye, how could I truly feel either cold or warmth? I might be standing barefoot in the snow in the depths of winter, but not, as I experienced it, long enough to get frostbite.

*

As a god, I felt that the earth itself was alive. Never mind the mayflies, who infested the surface. Deep within the depths of the world, awesome powers slept, intelligences vastly greater than even I could ever comprehend, which existed on such a different scale of time that they could not even perceive such an ephemeral thing as a human being. They lay dreaming, there beneath the ground and also in the sky. I, utterly unique of all my kind, could somehow hear their thoughts, the echoes of millions of years that somehow came together. I could hear them. That is how the stones spoke to me.

I tell you I could hear the groaning mountains as they rose up.

*

You would have me believe that this is all a delusion.

Some of it is, I will admit.

This much is certainly a lie:

I stood amid ruins.

I stood on a barren plain.

A city rose around me, like those flowers I'd seen from my window, uncurling themselves out of the melting snow.

The sky overhead was filled with gleaming fleets of ships. Other cities, not attached to the earth at all, drifted like clouds.

But I preferred the old places when I could find them. Some

very old buildings or monuments, which had been preserved, or underground chambers still to be found in the ancient ruins, places that did not change as rapidly as waves on the seashore. My favorite place had once been part of a library, the basement presumably, somehow sealed from water and the weather but reachable at the end of a long tunnel through a vault door that was left a little bit ajar, so I could squeeze past it. There, incredible as it seemed, *nothing changed,* and I could sit and read the books and look at pictures in magazines, which showed a world I dimly remembered, which bore less and less resemblance to the one surging around me.

It was quiet there. I liked being there. But it was there, after I had dozed off reading, of all things, *Treasure Island,* and dreamt of pirates, that a cold, dry hand suddenly seized me by the wrist and a voice whispered, *"I know what you are!"*

It was a tall, pale woman, neither young nor old, but if you will pardon the expression, timeless, and dressed all in black.

I struggled to get away, but she held me firmly. That shouldn't have been possible. Mayflies couldn't do that. They are like ash, shapeless and gone in the interval it takes me to stretch and yawn.

But not this one. I screamed and wept and was a frightened child again. She had me.

"I know," she said.

I didn't ask her how she had figured out or how any of this was possible. It was clear enough that she did know, that she was, at least, a little bit like me. She was a prophetess, she said, regarded as a witch and seer by that tiny underground of citizens in this enlightened world who, against all orthodoxy, believed in such things. She was herself nearly a thousand years old as ordinary calendars measured time. She demanded of me what I knew, and I told her something of my world, what I remembered, of my father and mother and Dr. Archibald, and the books I'd read in the hospital when I was small, and she merely sighed and said, "Ah, that was a very long time ago. Before even me. I was right. You are the one."

"The one what?"

"The first. Patient Zero. You had it first."

I understood then, to my growing amazement, that she knew about the *time disease,* and maybe she wanted to steal it from me, to make me into a mayfly, so she could go on forever and ever; but no, she explained, it was not possible to *cure* it in an individual. Time, she said, is like a secretion of a gland, only that gland is in another dimension, not in our bodies, so medicines and surgery can't reach it. If the time-gland is *diseased,* it secretes hours and years and centuries at a different rate than usual, which can either be a burden and a sorrow, or very convenient indeed, depending on how you look at it.

While it was not possible to *cure* the disease, she explained, it was possible to *infect* others. That was what she wanted from me.

"I've only got a mild case myself," she said, smiling. "I need a booster shot."

Not understanding, I let her touch me, and I breathed on her as she told me to, and even kissed her when she commanded it, all those things you'd do if you were deliberately trying to give someone scarlet fever or measles or even the plague; only in this case she wanted it. She *hungered.*

I think she got what she was after too, because she did not fade away like the other mayflies, not right away anyway. We lived together, setting forth from our secret place in the course of our adventures, to gather to ourselves such of the world's treasures as we might fancy. (Yes, we stole both the *Mona Lisa* and the carefully enshrined relic of the skull of the Baby Jesus as a child.) We haunted the world's ruins, even those caverns at the earth's center filled with presences that will not awaken until the ending of the universe. We understood the scale of things.

But she was *not* forever. My prophetess, my constant companion, slowly slipped out of phase with me and grew older. Maybe it was because she was so old by the time she had started, or because hers was a mild case and she didn't get a booster shot of the disease until she was over a thousand. Eventually she died, like any mayfly, and I buried her in the empty tomb of some fabulous queen. I think I wept for her.

*

And if you believe that, I've got a bridge I'd like to sell you.

The idea that I could have had a companion, a mother figure, a lover, a friend, whatever, is completely absurd. It denies my own uniqueness. I am a *god*. That is all I have to say on the matter. There is no other like me, not of human origin anyway. There are only those other powers in the earth and sky.

Just listen to the stones. Hear them speak. Oh, I forgot, you can't.

You may reasonably ask how I could be telling you this, if the narrative stretches thousands or even millions of years into the future.

Go figure. Maybe time flows both ways. Maybe under certain circumstances it pours out like blood.

Ashes, ashes, all fall down.

Look, I'll tell you what isn't true. It is certainly not true that there was this boy who lived in the shithole little town of East Armpit in rural Pennsylvania, in what is justifiably called the flyover part of the state. He wasn't the cute pathetic victim at the opening of this narrative, stranded in his hospital room with his books and his toys, gazing with innocent bewilderment at the dead bird in the windows.

I can wax poetic about him, because I learned how to do that from books, which were my secret vice. Mom and Dad did not approve of reading books, you see, except maybe the Bible, and then only with supervision, because the Devil and his wiles are everywhere and I could be led astray. I never went to school and was maybe eleven or so when they decided to deliver me from temptation by keeping me chained up in the cellar when I wasn't out with Daddy working on the farm to earn my scanty portion of daily bread by the sweat of my brow and the soreness of my ass. I was beaten a lot, sometimes when I had done wrong or had impure thoughts, or sometimes when Mom and Dad just took a fancy to whipping the crap out of me to keep Satan at bay. What they didn't know is that Grandpa (my mother's father) had hidden a little stash of his favorite books under a floorboard in the cellar before the Great Revelation came and Mom forced righteousness on everybody, even the family dog, which was eventually killed as a minion of Satan because it wouldn't pray. Grandpa's collection included everything from a Tarzan paperback to an issue of *Playboy* to the collected poems of Coleridge, so whether I learned to masturbate to the ape-man or a mildewed foldout or the Ancient Mariner, I leave to your imagination.

Mostly what I did, at night, lying there in the dark, was listen to the earth and the voices of the stones. Stones are millions of years old, you know. They formed when the planet did, a long, long time ago, and they speak very slowly, so that to make out a single syllable you might have to listen for a thousand years, and a mayfly like yourself can only do that if you're unstuck in time somehow, with the millennia washing backwards over you like a wave that's broken on a beach and is receding back into the sea, or if, like me, you happen to be a god.

I heard those voices. I knew that the world is alive with them, and the air, and the spaces beyond the stars, and I knew they didn't concern themselves one flying fuck for your Satan or Christ or whatever, that in the universe at large there is no decency, no morality, no law, only the raw and inevitable tide of time splashing over stones and receding back between them.

So I dreamed one night that someone had come into my cell, my cellar, and it wasn't Grandpa (who was dead) or the dog (who was dead) or either of my parents, but a tall, pale figure dressed all in black, whose face was covered by a white mask like a shroud, and whose hand touched my chains and shackles and caused them to fall off, even as the angel liberated St. Peter under similar circumstances.

She told me what I had to do. She spoke with the voice of the stones, from out of the depths of the world.

She put the knife in my hand.

You will imagine me, then, a somewhat unprepossessing god, starting to grow tall, but stunted from starvation and overwork, long-limbed and pale and almost skeletal, very dirty with matted hair, and clad only in a loincloth of the sort Jesus wears on the cross (but no crown of thorns; Momma didn't think I was holy enough to get those, I guess), crawling up out of the cellar with knife in hand, filled with the echoes of the voices of the stones. Thus I crept into my father's bedroom. He was a massive, bearded man, not very clean himself. He lay sprawled on top of the bed, drunk and snoring. (God apparently felt it was okay for him to drink. Had not Jesus mass-produced wine as his first miracle? Wasn't it then a pious act, for some people at least, to mass-consume it?)

I slid the knife into my father's heart easily enough, right under the breastbone and in, as hard as I could push it. He grunted once and was still. But to get his head off was a lot more work. I needed a saw and I didn't have one, so by the time I was done I was completely covered in blood, which was okay, a holy thing actually, a part of the ritual sacrifice the speaking stones of the earth required if I was ever to become a god for real and forever.

My task was to take his head on a cake platter into my mother's bedroom (she slept apart, to preserve her purity), wake her up, present my gift even as John the Baptist was presented to Salome, let her scream a bit, then add her to the platter.

It was only much later, when I wandered out onto the highway, that the cops arrived, and there were blinding lights and sirens and people shouting for me to put the knife down. But I knew they couldn't hurt me because I was a god, and I existed on an entirely different scale of time, so that what was for me just a few seconds would be for them a hundred years. That meant, of course, that they were just mayflies, and would die of old age before one of them could shoot me.

But you know what? One of them managed to shoot me in the gut anyway.

So I had a dream that I was lying in a hospital room, all hooked up to machines and tubes and things, and time went by with unbearable slowness. I could hear every tick of the clock on the wall, every beep and chirp of the machinery around me, and, yes, I could still hear the voices of the stones, telling me that I had done well.

But I was still imprisoned among the mayflies, and that is why I am telling you these lies, until I can get out of here.

*

You want what I have, don't you?

You want me to infect you with the *time disease* so that you too can become a god and cavort with the powers of the earth and sky and stars.

Nothing doing. But I can tell you the truth now.

I can tell you that when I endured this misery for a thousand years, when my every intake of breath took what would be to you a full day, when the act of raising my hand might seem to you to take a century, when all the people around me were indeed mayflies, ephemeral, scarcely glimpsed, dead; and the walls around me crumbled away into ruin and the roof overhead peeled away and was gone; and beneath the whirling wheel of the sky I found myself climbing that great, black mountain in the cold and the dark, naked as a god must be (for even the loincloth had crumbled into dust), I paused to see the cities of the plains and the cities of the air and the great nations and empires of the world rise and fall and drift away like leaves, like smoke, like a receding tide. I climbed and felt the mountain itself heaving and changing and settling down again like a living thing. I heard the groaning voices of the stones, of the stars, which joined together into a kind of chorus; and when I got to the top I stood in the company of my fellow gods, who waited for me, assembled in long ranks so that I could walk among them as if I were inspecting an army. Can I describe them? No. Say only that their shapes were not as people have imagined gods, but as gods really are, utterly inhuman, their forms such as no eye has ever seen, their voices such as no ear has ever heard. Some of them descended from the stars on great wings to join us. Others crawled up out of the earth, as I had done, but then were more like vast worms, or living continents gradually heaving, only visible on the time scale in which we gods lived. I danced with the gods.

That, I swear to you, is the truth.

*

Ashes, ashes, all fall down.

Magnus Victor Rex

Lisa Mannetti

For, after all, how do we know that two and two make four? Or that the force of gravity works? Or that the past is unchangeable? If both the past and the external world exist only in the mind, and if the mind itself is controllable—what then?—GEORGE ORWELL

Such is the Pavlovian device: repeat mechanically your assumptions and suggestions, diminish the opportunity of communicating dissent and opposition. This is the simple formula for political conditioning of the masses. This is also the actual ideal of some of our public relation machines, who thus hope to manipulate the public into buying a special soap or voting for a special party.—JOOST MERLOO

The conscious and intelligent manipulation of the organized habits and opinions of the masses is an important element in democratic society. Those who manipulate this unseen mechanism of society constitute an invisible government which is the true ruling power of our country . . . We are governed, our minds are molded, our tastes formed, our ideas suggested, largely by men we have never heard of . . . It is they who pull the wires which control the public mind.—EDWARD BERNAYS

Men willingly believe what they wish.—JULIUS CAESAR

Frankly, Marquis (M. V.) Rex was a little bored. He was in Capitol City 2 that day, holed up in his grandfather's former palace tower overlooking the Hudson River, and he'd just come from the West Coast, from Capitol City 3 in fact, where he'd hobnobbed with celebrities and movie stars (that Gabriella Rexeter was some hot dish!), but—not that he didn't appreciate all that his family had achieved fifty-odd years ago and had kept on achieving to make his life easy and the life of the general populace so much better—he was a little weary and a little—*no, a lot*—bored.

Standing at his window high above the hoi polloi (who appeared like the highly decorated, colorful insect-life they actually were these days) shuttling and milling sixty stories below along the sidewalks, he thought they offered nothing more to his jaded eye than bright, glassy shards of reds and blues and vibrant greens on this gray day. They were mere bits of abstract stained glass that provided no coherent image, no relief from his ennui.

Most of them—the greatest number of them, of course, wore knock-offs of Lucilla Regina or Aurelia Regina or Marquis Rex clothes they didn't know were knock-offs . . . and he'd seen the fashion line a thousand—make that scores of thousands of times.

He felt off-kilter for some unaccountable reason. Perhaps he ought to take Marquita, his daughter by his first wife, to the Petting Tree crosstown . . . except that he found the maze of tall mirrored buildings crowding the site slightly dispiriting. There was that old map he'd seen once or twice that had shown a large greensward someone once upon a time called Central Park . . . well then, maybe off to see the Specimen Zoo Observatory 2. Just this morning, when he'd been sipping coffee, the circular purple rexflitbit-lette on his wrist had flashed that the SZO2 had acquired something called a parrot—a kind of bird, he gathered—as well as a large, glossy brown animal they excitedly announced was one of just *three* horses here on all of MainRex continent—

The gold-leaf door to his study snapped open and his wife, Aurelia, walked through carrying a squirming brown and white puppy—of all things, for godsakes—which she set down on the marble floor, where it promptly huddled, still attached to its shiny electrum leather leash near her slim ankles. Electrum, he recalled, was an amalgam of silver and gold, and while it appeared silver in color it had a brilliant sheen that could not be matched by using mere sterling. Egyptians had once used it to decorate the chariots of their dynastic pharaohs. . . .

"Isn't he too, *too* adorable?" she gushed. "I was just about to board Concorde 7, and I thought the damn breeder would *never* get to the villa in time and even with the chopper zipping us to the airport I'd have to take a later flight. So inconvenient."

She'd just come from Capitol City 6—which, he suddenly remembered, used to be called Paree—no, that wasn't quite right . . . yes, he had it now, *Paris.*

"What is it?" he asked.

"A butterfly dog," she said. "Do you know hundreds of years ago they were very popular with the old royals? Kings and queens of France and Italy and Spain—isn't he sweet? Look how he cocks his head . . . and those soulful brown eyes . . ." She leaned down—no mean feat on her cerise, stiletto-thin, genuine Lucilla Regina heels—scooped him up and kissed the top of his fluffy head between the soft, winged ears. "What shall we call him, M. V.?"

A loaded question. When she wanted her way, she used his title. She also knew very well that everyone's surname these days, in the spirit of "democracy," was a variation of Rex. There were millions of Rexalls, Rexalots, Rexeters, Rexnells, Rexingtons, Rexwaites, Rexwards . . . and, he guessed, this dog-naming was a rehearsal tactic for the son she kept promising him but never had. Technically, of course, his legitimate daughter Marquita could have run things as Magna Victoria (M. V.) Regina when he died (gods willing) somewhere around age 100; however, in all the years since his grandfather governed, the sons inherited, the daughters prissed and preened; they took sinecures disguised as jobs—but not a single female had ever ruled.

"How about Marcus Aurelius?" she suggested.

"Marcus Aurelius Rex," he said.

"Yes," she said. Nodding brightly, she set the dog down again and came to the window. She slid her arms around his waist, then took a tiny half-step backward to pat his broad chest and thereby cue him to look down into her pale lavender eyes. Eyes he knew were artificially colored by surgical means, but which, when he met her, had had the power to hold him fast—like, he thought, like an aged Grandie tethered by infirmity to her wheelchair. *Now where on earth had that image come from?*

"Whatever you want," he said, then shrugged away from her bright gaze.

"We'll call him 'Rexy' for short," she smiled.

*

"Things are pretty much running themselves these days, M. V. No briefings this afternoon, no speeches, just some things you need to sign off on," his top aide said, entering only after Marquis waved him in through the door.

His adjutant, Quintus Rexlander, a tall man in his thirties with Bela-Lugosi-thin fingers, carried a tall stack of papers, a heavy alabaster signature-chop, and a small purple inkpad on a gilt tray and placed it on the desk in front of him.

He went through the executive orders desultorily, occasionally reading a page or two, but inevitably pressing the imitation marble chop into the thick, waxy ink—a color and type manufactured only for the M. V. himself—and onto faux parchment (there hadn't been enough sheep to manufacture *real* parchment in almost half a century), signing them slowly, one at a time.

In the repetitiveness of the task—he assured himself that was the reason—Marquis found his mind wandering again. . . .

Nobody—except for the well-educated Rexionaires (what used to be called trillionaires, billionaires, and centi-millionaires) and the M. V. Rexes and the putative M. V. Reginas—really wrote these days; there was no need for it. Not since the narrow, vari-colored rexflitbit-lettes had been installed—permanently—on every citizen's wrist in the Empire. You could speak into it; watch and listen to news, radio, films. You could tell it to project the TV series you were hooked on to play across your home big screen; lock your windows and doors; check your heart rate and blood pressure; monitor your glucose; text friends and enemies; track the calories you burned, or the ones you could be burning if you'd walk another ten blocks; you could make or answer phone calls and order everything from groceries to Rexline clothes and accessories . . . and though it was less well-known—and scarcely credited by the general populace—it could also track *you*. And it did. And there was a rumor that—

His bladder suddenly began to throb, and he stood up quickly, shoving his chair backward at the same time. Quintus automatically stepped aside and Marquis took several long racing strides in the direction of his private lavatory. He loomed over the pale green imitation jade toilet and began to urinate into the bowl. A minute or so later, he was zipping up when he noticed two small wet ovals on the front of his trousers. How many cups of coffee had he had? Surely not more than a couple—must be something wrong with the house royal blend, he decided. Christ only knew what chemicals they tossed in to make it taste more like actual coffee these days. No matter—a dozen companies would fight over sending him samples in the hope for an M. V. contract and the advertising—and subsequent revenue—that would follow in its wake. He removed his lapis blue trousers and, suddenly cheerful at the idea of groveling coffee company CEOs, began to whistle while he took up a stylish linen *shendyt*—the kilt-like garment worn by the ancient Egyptian pharaohs—and fastened it at the waist. More comfortable than pants anyhow, he thought; he also felt less foolish than he did when wearing one of the also-popular purple-bordered, over-the-shoulder white togas previously in vogue among senators during the glory days of Rome.

Marquis exited the bathroom and sat down again. "Quintus, tell the head chef this Arabica stinks to Hades and back, and to extend invitations to the usual contenders."

"Certainly." He watched Quintus fingering his own black rex-flitbit-lette and sending off the message.

What had he been thinking about when his own body so rudely interrupted him? Oh, yes. The idea had come out of the Big Data theories about psychometrics—human personality traits—from half a century ago. There were times Marquis thought he understood its mechanics perfectly; there were other times when he felt it was just beyond his grasp. On those days he felt overwhelmed by its complexity (since he was the M. V.), he could either touch a hidden spring to retrieve the information or, if his mind felt completely fogged in by its domino logic, shut the damn thing off. He was always torn. Did he need to comprehend it? He was in power, his family had ruled for what felt like forever, so no. But he was in power, another part of his mind countered, and he above *all* others—as the most powerful man in the world—should grasp the source and significance of this thralldom that held everyone on the planet in its grip.

When you were in a hurry, the damn buttons seemed much too tiny. Absurdly so. His daughter always said he was too impatient. His wife suggested surgery, but he was too young to have Presbyterian issues—no, that was the wrong word, *myopia?* Nuh, nuh . . . *Presbyopia,* yes! He slowed down and, after the first try, adjusted his royal purple rexflitbit-lette so he could listen to the file he wanted to hear via the tiny electric implant behind his ear. But he'd lost his place and reset the file to play again. A good time-filler while he approved more executive orders—and these latest audio implements were terrific: he could hardly hear the dull, wet thud of the fake stone chop against the inkpad or the heavier stamp against the paper resting on the desk.

The archival file had mostly general information, but it would jog him to recall details.

As near as he could tell, back in the old days before the Rex regime, a couple of social media outlets (SpaceBook, Cheep-Cheeper, and MyFace—as he recalled), along with a separate device known as a "smart phone," had become one enormous, labyrinthine mania for the world's population. People couldn't get enough. They "cheeped" constantly; they "liked" movies, TV shows, rock stars, and pictures of cats and puppies. They disliked other things in those same categories, as well as despising other people, brands of frozen foods, and candidates for elections. Then some bright star or mad scientist (was his name Ted Kaczynski? No, wait, that was some media darling christened the Unabomber. No, the genius guy's name was Kinsky or Kapinsky—something like that, anyhow) waved his hands in the algorithmic aether and presto! He found out that with as few as seventy "likes" they (his company and its minions) could tell what a person's friends, parents, and ex-lovers liked, too. They could also glean (between the sneaky lines, so to speak) gender, race, religion, and much more. They could create entire (and accurate, no less!) personality profiles. Could discern among the cheeps and the smiley faces whether you were an extrovert, a scholar, or against gun control. And *voilà!* Ads could be targeted—tailored—to individuals. Whether they shopped for hunting knives, original Matisse paintings, or Charmin toilet paper, the perfect sly little ads would consistently show up anywhere and anytime they logged into *anything*. Refined by the GPS systems buried in laptops and "smart phones," the kingmakers and manipulators could also target people's anxieties and fears. It was a huge help during election campaigns. And afterward, too. Before you could say "virtual reality" (a personal fave of the billions) the very first Rex—thanks to Internet ads that keyed into their dislikes and worries—was swept into office. And what was the point of winning if you weren't going to win forever? I mean, if you really wanted to help the "right" people—the ones who keep the planet spinning by creating money and jobs and wars—you needed a dynasty to do the thing up in ribbons and medals. Right? Right. Look at how things were going now. Almost nobody starved. Boredom no longer, well, bored people. Life was all peacock clothes and games. It was the grandeur that was Rome reborn in the mid-twenty-first century. Given the right situation, Rome's imperial state might have endured for a thousand years. And a thousand years sounded good to any man—especially a Magnus Victor Rex. He felt a similar wave of regret over the fading of the glory that was Greece and the dynastic flourishing that once drove Egyptian culture, but he was equally certain he could re-create and foster a new classic elegance.

His head began to throb. He felt his pulse lurch. Goddammit! He wasn't completely sure he understood all the complications. For one thing, he often mixed up who "they" were. Wasn't he supposed to be one of "those" in the know? It made his head ache harder. He turned to Quintus. "Find out which of the sensory focus applications is the best," Marquis said.

Quintus smiled. "WillFocus has a new upgrade—"

"Sync it for me, will you?" He held out his wrist. *Goddamn buttons were microscopic. But then, what were servants for, if not to serve?*

"Certainly," he said. "What combination would you prefer, M. V.?"

"Something light with a lot of tinkling bells, the scent of patchouli—a real mind focuser, that one." He grinned. "Oh, and mostly greens. I hear green is terrific for concentration."

"Energy level?"

"Low is fine."

The music, scent, and flash of color every few seconds calmed him. And as soon as Quintus left, he could raise the intensity. But it wouldn't do to let the aide realize that the complexity of the material felt … fuzzy—not incomprehensible, but slightly out of reach. Okay, so maybe the focus app didn't work as well as narcotics to change your frame of mind, but since the opioid crisis no one—except dying folks—could get those anymore except on the black market, and he personally had no idea how to wangle his way into *that* mess. If it didn't work as well as an old-time pain-killer like (*Morpheus?*), or that anti-anxiety medication (*Xenu?*), or the one they gave to kids who couldn't concentrate (*Ratline?*), it *did* work.

There was a sound like wind chimes, and something like those miniature cymbals that dancers used in temples. His thumb and index finger pads twitched a few times, rhythmically touching against each other as if in imitation of his mental picture of sexy bare-breasted temple dancers. He felt calmer, too.

Yes, he decided, things were good. Out of the minds that created vertopsy (virtual autopsy) had come even grander technology: now there was practically no crime because the neuro-nerds had gone from tracking and mapping the areas of the brain that responded to a picture of (say) a sunset or (say) a cesspool, to sussing out (via the two-way links inside the plastic rexflitbit-lettes) when someone was going to wave a gun and hold up a delicatessen on Eighth Avenue Rex, or in a flash of rage was planning to bludgeon his or her overweight, whiny lover in rural Des Moines with a heavy iron fireplace poker. All plans, all thoughts, all ideation that portended crime of any kind were traceable before, during, or after they were implemented. No one even cared that the formerly pejorative term *thoughtcrime* was now an acceptable term or, more importantly, an actual *crime*.

It was true, though, that on some of the other continents across the globe the technology worked somewhat sporadically. Mostly it happened in what used to be called Third World countries and overcrowded sectors like Eu-Rex, Rex-East, plus a few unimportant archipelagos and subcontinents that had become pretty much passé when most of their respective landmasses had been covered during the floods of the early 2040s.

Of course, as his father, M. V. Viscount Rex (who was the ruler at that time), had pointed out, an awful lot of really inconvenient people—like those disabled by age, poverty, physical infirmity, or emotional and mental instability—had conveniently perished when the waters rose. But thanks to the rexflitbit-lettes on their wrists, at least they'd gone to the other side of the rainbow via rising tides and actual tidal waves as the music soared and they saw visions of their previously lost loved ones—all the while they were gloriously ascending to their personal vision of an afterlife. Thanks to virtual reality, it was as real as, say, that old quaint city of turquoise waterways and cobbled-streets that used to be called Vesuvius—no *Venice*, he amended. In his opinion the place was practically an open-air sewer, but thanks to VR it was not only still accessible, it was a lot more pleasant to visit. And a lot cheaper—

"M. V., what about the games?" His aide pointed to the page Marquis was just about to pick up.

It was never a good idea, he considered, to reveal too much. Instead of addressing Quintus directly he said, "I was just thinking about my father."

"M. V. Viscount Rex staged some of the finest spectacles in the last twenty years."

"Indeed," he said. "You may go now," he told the aide.

Marquis was thinking Viscount (in continuation of a longstanding family tradition) had been his father's actual name, not a title. But certainly the already-retreating Quintus knew that. M. V.'s grandfather, President Rex, had legislated a sweeping policy that practically did away with any kind of medical benefits for the elderly. (There had been too many of them, for one thing, after something happened that had been called . . . (*called the Baby Bloom?*) and that measure alone saved the government trillions of dollars every year, because those goddamn Bloomers were determined not to die—at *any* age—if they could help it.) Then, in the very brief interim between Grandpa President's death—end-of-term leadership—and the beginning of his father's reign of power, one or the other of them had come up with a wonderful and practical solution to put the "declining ones" to good use. Well, half of them, anyway. Medical advances meant that old withered wombs could serve as new receptacles for the unborn. In exchange, the aging biddies were offered lifelong care. Very soon it became chic for wealthy women to transplant their embryos or in-vitro fertilized eggs into the healthiest of the old women, who came to be called "Grandies." (It still amazed Marquis what people would do or submit to for the chance of grabbing a title—even a technically meaningless one.) The whole program was given a further boost because simultaneously it became extremely—utterly—*un-chic* for these same high society women to be seen with bloated, gravid bodies.

Still, Marquis would never forget his first and only visit to MainRex Birthing Center when he was in his late teens . . .

*

"Look! It's Justin Timberlake!" one of them had screamed as he entered the piss-smelly white tiled dayroom on the ward. He had no idea what (or who) the big-bellied spindly-limbed old lady meant, but at the same time the scene suddenly came alive around him and he was acutely aware of what he was seeing and hearing. Music—pouring from dozens of rexflitbit-lettes as well as ceiling speakers—combined with shouting voices came as a cacophony as loud and unintelligible as knifing wind around a roof garden atop one of the 1500-foot-tall Rex palaces. Several of the Grandies were now standing, jittering and jiving to moldy oldies that Marquis thought might have been heard by some or most of them only inside their heads.

"Yeah, dance to the music, girlfriend," one of the aides called out, clapping her hands in a rhythmical beat before she pushed down on an old woman's shoulders, tipping the Grandie back into her chair. "Yo, honey," a second orderly said, "scoot your butt backwards, darlin', your hair extensions are getting caught up in the wheels here."

Apparently, the young Marquis thought, lots of the aides found the confused Grandies amusing. It wasn't so amusing, however, when they suddenly began to cry about whatever the stuff—the jumble of memories (incomprehensible to Marquis and the caregivers alike)—spewed like raw sewage from their fever-dimmed minds:

"I saw a Michael Jackson concert in L.A.," one wept. "My parents took me."

"I was in London for the seventh Harry Potter movie premiere!"

"I got Beyoncé's autograph."

"My oldest sister dated Eminem."

Nostalgia suddenly spread like wildfire in the room.

Books, tunes, concerts, movies, TV shows, art galleries, Scunchies, Elle, Leonardo Di Caprio, Furbys, Johnny Depp, Uggs, Scarlett Johansson, 9/11, Bernie Madoff, Wall Street corporate raiders and home foreclosures . . .

None of it made sense. They ran over one another's conversations and even lost sight of their own. Mostly it was sad to see them: shrunken, wrinkly, tattooed arms and legs that had the look of crackle-art; big bulging bellies; semi-toothless mouths; dull yellowing eyes; and partially balding heads wagging. They didn't speak;

they blathered and screeched. Who the hell knew, in the end, what was true or false? Or what they meant by *Under the Dome, Twin Peaks,* Irish hip-hop, and *Avatar*? Maybe some wise-ass once-upon-a-time Wikipedia editor, but so what? None of that shit mattered in the least—and least of all to Marquis. Not when he visited the center that one time, and certainly not now.

The Grandies were a mess, and while the rest of their bodies slowly fell to pieces, the newly grafted tissue inside their medically refurbished wombs had a purpose. As incubators, the oldster women were useful. In certain respects they paid for themselves. Wealthy women paid the state a bundle to have Grandies carry their infants to term and, thanks to a fashion wave that swept the world just toward the end of the big era of tattoos, many Grandies sported implanted gems. It wasn't the same as the old-style earrings and body piercings. These were jewels that looked like the fancy arrays women had once glued onto their faces in swirls around their eyes, or in patterns on their arms and backs and chests. One surgeon with a scalpel or a laser could cut out $50,000 worth of tiny diamonds or emeralds or rubies or sapphires in fifteen minutes. The state—in exchange for lifetime care—kept it all. They might not live very long in the Birthing Centers, but they were profitable and they had a use.

But their aging debilitated male counterparts were another story. What could be done about them?

Marquis turned up the intensity on his focus app to high and set himself the task of coming up with a daring, brilliant answer to the problem.

He sat and pondered briefly, then got up to pace. His steps matched the tempo of the music, he inhaled the deep musky odor of patchouli, and a soft green light flashed from the device on his wrist.

First of all, he thought, we could give *them* titles, too. Of course! We'll call them . . . Granders!

Now there were just the games to think about—games always got the rulers in good with the populace. *Bread and circuses,* his grandfather, President, used to say. What if—and here, he not only inhaled deeply, but switched the scent to orange-mint and the color to a hot red—what if he could combine these two entities and solve them at one at the same time by—by—*by utilizing the Granders in the games!*

For one brief second he felt deflated. Who would possibly care about seeing a bunch of physically and mentally flabby old guys hobbling around the stadium arena in the games? What could the old geezers do? Flail away and hit one another with canes or crutches? Not much sport in *that*, he fumed inwardly. And certainly not enough blood.

But—but what if—what if the first Granders they titled and used for (okay, *lured into*) the games were notables of the past? Big TV stars and movie luminaries like that Heath Ledger—no, he shook his head, he was pretty sure *that* guy was dead. Okay then, celebrities like Armie Hammer, or that really old guy, Tom Hardy. Sure, the whole crowd of wizened duffers who'd faded into the no-man's land of obscurity were just sitting on their asses, or playing air golf, or waiting to die. Magnus Victor Rex would be offering them a new shot at fame. At making comebacks. We could give them sword canes—and hefty doses of amphetamines—to spice it up. Run betting pools. Give them worldwide airplay on every last rexflitbit-lette, while they trained and made lofty statements about victory. The winners could be given parades and anything else that smacked of glory. The losers (or also-rans)—and there would be plenty of those—could be listed on the wall of marble plaques that would newly line the grand entry to Magnus Square Garden; in that way, he reasoned, their blood would not have been shed for naught. Hell, they could inter them inside drawers behind the plaques. Just like those quaint places he'd read about that used to be called cemeteries. He'd re-create mausoleums! Throw in a gilt laurel leaf carved just above their names as if they *were* champions . . .

His mind whirled. When they ran out of still-living first-tier has-beens like Jordan Peele or Michael Shannon, they could whip up a new-born frenzy of excitement; they could start using famously infamous prisoners—like the Crossbow Cannibal or the Baseline

Killer or the Noida serial murderers. And, after they finished up with the sicko deviants, they could begin another round with guys who had defrauded innocent investors out of millions. Like that famous first schemer Pompii—no, *Ponzi,* he amended. There were always lots of sensationally hated shylocks in jail.

Yes, games like these, Marquis reasoned, could go on for *years.* Synced adverts and subliminal suggestions via rexflitbit-lettes would guarantee success. He would be even more famous than his immediate and popular forebears, President and Viscount Rex. He would be loved by his people. Maybe even worshipped. A Caesar. A god.

He pressed the button to summon Quintus back into the room and, sitting down at the huge desk, found himself practically rubbing his hands with glee and satisfaction.

"Take down this proclamation," he said in a deep, confident voice. Marquis did not look at his aide: He dictated.

*

"Wake-y, wake-y," Aurelia crooned.

"I wish you wouldn't do that," Marquis said. "You use the exact same goddamn sing-song voice when you say to the dog 'Walk-y, walk-y.'"

"My, my, someone is getting up on the wrong side of the bed today."

"Both sides are mine. I sleep alone, remember?"

"I can fix that," she said. "Sleep is only one of many things you can do in a bed."

Close to his thighs, he felt one of her knees beginning to press down the mattress. A lithe hand snaked under the covers and found the gap in his faux-silk kimono. He gave a soft gasp.

"Like that, hmm?" Her sharp lavender eyes met his, and then he was vaguely aware of the faint rustle of the corn-yellow sateen sheets as she burrowed toward his midriff.

He felt a rush of blood both pummeling his veins and singing in his ears. "Uh, yeah," he breathed.

From the corner of his bedroom—some forty feet away—the butterfly puppy his wife had apparently brought along when she came in began to yip.

"Jesus Christ!"

Her mouth came away with a pop when he yelled. She flung back the covers and sat up. "Now, Rexy," she said, smiling, wagging her index finger and looking toward the dog.

Hearing its name—a cutesy variant of his own title—at that particular moment annoyed the hell out of Marquis. "For chrissakes, did you have to bring that yapping brown furball in here?"

"Ssh. Mama fix that, too." Aurelia hushed him, touching one long, elegantly manicured nail lightly against his lips.

He tracked her movement across the room to where she'd tethered the dog to the slim leg of a burled walnut Regency escritoire he'd never liked. He thought she was going to lead the excited barking creature into her own adjoining suite of rooms. Instead, after lightly tugging him a few short feet, she leaned down and released the puppy. Lifting one jewel-implanted foot, she gently nudged him across the lintel, then quickly slammed the right-hand double door.

"Gave the little bastard the boot," he said. "Nice work." He grinned.

"He's a good dog. Very obedient. But I don't like interruptions either, M. V.," she said. When she turned, she was smiling and he saw she was winding the long electrum-clad leather leash loosely around one hand. She flicked the left-over length of strap against her opposite palm, tapping it smartly with more force each time. Her eyes glittered hot mauve as she walked back toward the sumptuous rex-sized bed.

He patted the sheet next to him. "What's next?"

"A surprise."

His eyebrows arched. "I like surprises—"

"You're going to love this one," she said. "And I will, too."

*

Two hours later Marquis lay stretched out in a loose X, replete and zonked, alone, on the damp, body-fluid- and liquor-soaked bed. Fragmentary images and shards of recent memories wavered in his mind. Aurelia had been so hot during their lengthy coupling, he felt his face burn. *Holy shit,* he thought. *Where'd that come from?*

The patch of forehead just above his eyebrows ached. He rubbed the spot gingerly. Must be from the genuine Roederer Cristal champagne they drank. All three (or was it four?) bottles.

And chilled, no less.

That had been the first of sweet Regina Aurelia's surprises. She'd pressed a button on her solid gold rexflitbit-lette and *voilà!* A small door between the two-story-high arched windows on the opposite wall slid up to reveal a fully stocked refrigerator—a maxi-bar, she called it. Even from across the room he could see the rows of foil-topped bottles lined up, the cunning little pots of caviar, the stacked plates filled with fruits, cheeses, chocolates—

"Say, that's new. You can't even tell it's there when it's closed," he said, propping his head on a lazy elbow and looking at how fine her ass looked under her short gauzy toga as she squatted down in front of the brightly lit opening and began loading up a tray she seemed to manifest out of the ether, with glassware, drink, food. Even candles and rose petals.

"I had it installed while you were in Cap City 2 and I was over at 6 to pick up the dog," she said. "The minions work fast."

"They better."

"Damn straight." She smiled and he saw she was wearing a tawny-sheened lavender lipstick that matched her peerless mauve and gold eyes.

Yeah, it'd been a slowly played-out and long—gargantuan—session. One of their best—no, make that their absolute best—ever. Oh, man. Oh, woman. Drinks and nibbles. Both the victual and sexual type. Playing her tapered, long purple fingernails on his body . . . in his hair.

Then the old LXIX. He grinned, remembering. That was always fun and she kept moaning that she loved it, even when the humming sound inside her palate made him laugh. He popped out of her mouth while she was in the throes and, as a result, his sporting equipment briefly nose-dived, but he'd finished her off.

A short break with munching on cold pheasant and caviar and swigging more bubbly straight from the bottle. He didn't think either one of them gave a shit about glassware at that point.

But there was more, he recalled, a delightful Cheshire cat smile overtaking him: there was that bit with the electrum-covered leather leash . . . wow. A first, and what a first! Aurelia flicking him lightly on his thighs and rear until, feeling driven to the brink, he'd flipped over and grabbed her, then turned them both turtle so he was on top. Heaven.

Then more drinks, all very cozy, a fake fight with both of them scooping up and flinging handfuls of the rose petals—and her lying next to his chest under his arm and lightly twiddling the hair on his chest in between sets.

And then. Oh, boy. And then . . .

She'd gotten the silver-bright leash and lashed each end to one of his wrists; she'd left enough length to loop both sides—right and left—to the tall bedposts. His hands, stretched out above his shoulders, were tied.

"Oh, my prisoner-king . . . I have you in my clutches," Aurelia said, straddling him. They both giggled.

There was a little candlewax dripping in warm dime-sized splotches down his chest and then, down and down . . . When he sucked in his breath, she stopped; they both laughed again.

She folded a saffron pillowcase and laid it across his eyes, tying it in a loose knot behind his head. "Now you won't know what comes next."

"Ha ha."

He heard a festive-sounding *pop!* and made a light-hearted, easy guess.

"More champagne? Man, we should knight *that* guy," he said.

"He's been dead for almost two hundred years—"

"Well, then his relatives, his progenitors—"

"His *progeny*."

"Whatever." He felt the liquid cascading into his mouth and he swallowed greedily, happily. She spilled some on the corners of his mouth and began to lick his chin, then the edges of his lips. She kissed him deeply.

There was a quick pause while, he deduced, she was taking a swig or two herself.

She dumped more into his mouth; chuckling, he sputtered a little.

"No," Aurelia said, "this won't do. My Rex needs a glass."

She slid off him and reached across to the ormolu nightstand. He heard a *ting!* when she tapped the bowl of the crystal goblet.

"Such a pretty sound," she said.

"Yeah." Amazing woman. Amazing wife.

He felt her warm hand and the chilled glass swim into sensory orbit, nearing his lips and, as far as the bonds would allow him, he lifted his shoulders and tilted his head forward. He drank. For some reason, just now it tasted a little off, but she was plying those fingernails in a big, slow, gentle circle across the tops of his thighs and lower hips, and up and around to his navel to complete the teasing circuit. Driving him happily mad. Well, if it tasted a little odd, it was probably the result of drinking more than he was used to, combined with the residue of swapped saliva from fusty mouths and rich, salty food.

"Oh, baby," she said.

She was drinking the champagne, and at one point she shook up the bottle and sprayed him, then herself, then let it fountain over both of them. He also vaguely remembered a $60,000 bottle of single-malt Scotch and one Waterford tumbler. Maybe she took a sniff to savor the aroma or a tiny sip from his glass, but he was drinking more. Definitely a lot more.

Still, they must have kissed goodnight before she went to her

own bed, even if he didn't remember it: next to the two-thirds empty booze bottle, there was a tray with a cold, wet washcloth and a
cobalt blue and gold Limoges saucer that held four Advil Plus
caplets. What a woman, he thought. Maybe she was pregnant.
That'd be something. He sat up, then lay back prone again. Glad for
the cool dark of the damp cloth. He felt muscle aches where he
hadn't known he had muscles. Some day, some night.

But, he realized, there were a lot of dark blank spots and only
jumbled pictures after the outrageously expensive forty-year-old
Macallan Sherrywood whisky made an appearance. Except the
splintery memory of her eyes gazing deeply into his. And something
vague about her hands, while she lay on top of him, kneading at his
wrists. He'd tried to interlace his fingers with his, but she'd laughed,
stilling his hands, and said, "Now, you mind Mama Regina," then
kissed him again. Another blank. But for a crazy second while she
gripped his wrists, he thought he heard music and saw a neon flash
of violet. He smelled jasmine—what the hell did he know from jasmine? No, it was probably the crumpled, wet rose petals strewn on
the bed, crushed under their sweating bodies. And something else
. . . No, that image wasn't at all clear, was mere fog, lost. More like a
dream than anything else. Sure, a dream. A crazy bad dream that
was both sexy and humiliating. Everyone had those . . .

Christ. Even his eyes hurt. If only he knew a black market drug
dealer with painkillers. Oh, well, pretty soon, Marquis thought, the
Advil would kick in. He'd fall asleep and forget shredded images
that were half-glimpsed inklings. Fool's gold about how it seemed
the makeshift blindfold was gone, the electrum leash was looped
around his throat as if it were a dog collar, and he was kneeling and
crawling and cavorting on all fours in a circle around and around
and around the huge bed.

He was barking.

She was laughing.

"Good boy, Rexy! That's a good boy!" she said over and over.

And in the dream he sat up straight: his feet and shins tucked under his thighs, his arms bent up at the elbows with his palms and fingers curved downward like forepaws, his wet tongue hanging out. He panted a little, dripped saliva.

"Good boy," she said.

Grateful beyond imagining over her unusual and above-board attention, Marquis leaned over and licked her knee. Then, with his shoulders—still bent down to the horizontal—he craned his neck and looked up.

Their eyes met.

Aurelia patted the top of his head. "Good dog," she said.

*

Six months later Marquis had to admit the newly inaugurated games were going splendidly. The same jolly crew who'd so recently brought the world sixty-five- and seventy-year-old "refurbished wombs" had come up with the nifty (and revolutionary!) "Grander Graft" that put wheels on the old geezers' hind legs. Oh, sure, a few had kicked at first—didn't like the angled metal spoke implanted just above each Achilles' tendon; didn't like the titanium wheels attached to it behind them; didn't like the giddy rolling sensation when someone gave them a hearty shove. Not out of the operating theaters, not down the shiny linoleum in hospital corridors. Not— even when the surgery became much simpler and more effective— one of the Gamesman Guards gave them a fast thrust into fame along the marbled floors of the center ring. *Whee!*

Marquis awakened just as the morning sky was brightening on Father's Day, June 21.

For a few minutes he was tingling with anticipation. Today was MainRex MotorCross Day. Big celebration for the Summer Solstice, longest day of the year and all that. There would be hundreds of thousands rooting and cheering in the galleries at Magnus Square Garden. And billions watching worldwide. All very special.

First up, featured in the early rounds, "wheelies" like Grue-Grander Adam Lanza (who shot his mother and a schoolhouse full of children and true, he was technically not quite sixty-five, but did anyone actually give a shit? Nope, and anyhow his age was close enough for "government work"—his relative youth would lend spice to the betting).

Then, more wheelies-implants like that old, sneaky corporate pickpocket Grander-Mugger Jeffrey Fastow and serial killer Stephen Wright were all getting the shove into the huge marble-floored ring. To make things more exciting, their sword-like weapons (tungsten or laser) were welded to steel cuffs on their arms and they themselves were shot up with enough adrenaline to give them real verve. Not to mention electric charges that ramped up—motorized—their wheelies. And they needed all the charge they could get, because they were going to be pitted against the Grander Greats—old-time, *big*-time celebs like Adam Lambert and Ashton Kutcher and Chris Hemsworth were going to be riding seriously souped-up chrome and steel scooters. Sort of like those supermarket thingies shaped like motorized trikes used by oldsters or riding mowers a jillion years ago—except there were no more supermarkets and no more lawns, and these babies could plow around the arena at speeds up to 40 miles an hour. It was cycles vs. skates, MotorCross meets Roller Derby, and the gray-headed or bald-pated wheelies would have to skim goddamn fast if they didn't want to be cut off at the knees or lose other limbs or assorted appurtenances. Not with the brilliant-colored bikes—like Roman chariots of yore—sporting spiked wheels and carrying Great Granders equipped with flashing swords and laser weapons of their own. *Zooom!*

In the finale, the winners from each round would fight all that day's other winners in one last fabulous neon-flashing and blood-spurting mêlée of a tournament (in which a few of them might possibly live). Or not. Both projected and mechanical old-world beasts of the fang-and-claw variety could only add to the crimson fun. Always a laugh to see someone wheeling like mad away from what turned out to be a hologram, but actually toward the real gnashing of iron teeth and raking, steely talons.

In the best of these contests, with shouts and jeers and cheers and screams and blaring light and sound signals from the crowds' rexflitbit-lettes they might all die—save one man who might remain alive. That is, *if* he and Aurelia, who sat calmly, toga-clad beneath their white silken canopy drinking the finest champagne and had the final say . . . *if* they decided to jauntily cant their beringed hands and give the aged Grander a thumbs up . . .

*

His happy reverie ended abruptly.

A loud tone sounded.

Goddamn thing sounds like a ten-foot Tibetan bronze gong.

For a second he thought Aurelia was about to sashay in (white silky revealing robe fluttering), but it was just his aide ("Morning, sir!") Quintus Rexlander playing valet-du-jour (probably because the rest of the staff was in the kitchen preparing a mammoth breakfast for the rest of the family and themselves to eat and enjoy) while he, M. V. Magnus Rex, was being handed a small gilt tray holding the Baccarat crystal equivalent of a Christ-forsaken sippy cup. It was brimful to the short swan-shaped lid with a green slime called Marvelous Green Turf Tonic. It not only tasted the way lawn grass used to smell (as he recalled from his earliest childhood) but liquefied, it also looked remarkably like the spewed chartreuse vomit from his favorite ninety-year-old horror cult film, *The Exerciser*.

Which was Aurelia's goddamn point when a few weeks (*months?*) back she'd decreed it was essential that he imbibe this meadow slop every morning. "You're getting out of shape . . . you're eating poorly . . . and well, then there's Old Poopy-Droopy . . . and I'm sure *he's* sad . . ." She didn't smile, but her swift downward glance at his lower anatomy had been very pointed. Very definite. "Rexy, my love, you've simply *got* to detox if you're going to go through a magnum of Cristal and a fifth of Macallan every time I practically turn around."

"Jesus."

"Tsk, tsk." The tips of her lavender fingernails teasingly raked his lips. "Don't pout. And don't make *me* pout. Mama wants her Rexy good and frisky."

"Fine. Fine. Just tell them to put the goddamn pulverized Bermuda clippings into a goddamn *opaque* glass. I mean, Christ, there's enough Royal Doulton china stuffed in closets around here to kit out Buckingham Palace." He paused. "I'll drink it, but I don't want to fucking *look* at it."

"'Course," she'd said, lavender eyes gleaming. "There's a good little boy. And he wants *another* good boy, doesn't he? Yes, he does. And Mama does, too. 'Cause we know that Poopy-Droopy needs to be a Poppy-Droppy to make a baby bunting boy, right? Right!" Pearly white teeth flirted between slickery mauve lips, the tip of her tongue flashing briefly as her smile widened.

"Right. Uh-huh." He stopped. "Please, no more crystal. Make them use a china cup."

"Yes! Of course! It won't happen again, M. V."

Typical, he thought, glaring at the evil emerald liquid. She always says "yes," and then does whatever the fuck she wants.

Fuck it.

Down the hatch.

He had to take a dozen deep breaths to keep the green drink—which had the consistency of that old movie vomitus—down inside his protesting stomach. Ugh. His guts were clenching and rolling. *Exerciser,* indeed— No, wait, that wasn't it—*Exorbitant? No. The Excisor? Oh, shit, who cared?* Now his hands were trembling. *Yeah, whose wouldn't after tossing down a nice big glass of what looked like* green *avian-guano? Hell! Didn't even get a swirly ribbon or two of* white *bird-poopy mixed in just for a little visual fun . . .*

He blinked rapidly.

The room was suddenly spinning.

There was a rushing sound in his ears, he felt woozy—

Then he blacked out.

*

When Marquis came to, the sun was not only too high, it was too hot. It burned his face, his arms, and even his legs because he was sitting down. And looking around, he saw that powerful squint-making light was bouncing off glaring white shiny ground surface. There seemed to be a lot of swaying color in the mid-distance, as well as a lot of noise.

Something was plopped on his head and he couldn't really tell what it was, except it was stuck there good and proper; it made his scalp and his face much hotter. He was sweating. He put his left hand up (which was shaky and trembling) and tugged firmly. He was surprised to feel the "something" slide downward and cover his ear. Between his fingers he saw two silvery gray strands of what looked like human hair.

His right arm felt heavy. He made himself focus, peering through sluggish eyelids. A series of thick welded metal clasps ran from his wrist to his biceps. In the grasp of his palms and fingers a long titanium sword wavered.

Smells—blood and shit and sand wafted toward him on the cloud of shrieking from the enormous crowd. Something in the wind here. I am going mad.

What the fuck, he thought, *I know a hawk from a handsaw! And this is one huge motherfucker. Saber-toothed handsaw!* He began to giggle. Chained at the waist and knees, astride a customized cherry red scooter. Check. Spoked wheels. Check. Rexflitbit-lette keyed up to the max. Check—

Aurelia, he thought. How long had her "games" been going on? The suddenly wild sex. The lack of concentration. The constant wooziness. The grass-green tonic shit—loaded with god only knew what kind of drugs. And the rexflitbit-lette that could track its wearers—implanted with suggestions, hypnotic commands, mind control.

He heard the sound of whining, keening, and he looked down to his left.

What the hell?

It was the dog—her dog. Rexy. And what had she said about butterfly dogs one of those hot sex nights when she was pushing the floppy-eared brown and white puppy out the door of his bedroom? Something about some old French royal. *Marie Angelette? No, Marie Antoinette. Yes, that was it. And the goddamn butterfly dog had followed her, gone with the queen to her death in the tumbrel cart. Watched her, whining, as she climbed the steps to the guillotine . . . while the crowds roared, screaming for her head.*

Not so different now. No one would realize it was him, their Magnus Victor Rex. Not bewigged, begrimed, and chained like a Grander Great.

But clearly this had been Aurelia's plan all along: to rule. Be the first woman Magna Victoria Regina. Be like Empress Theodora and Mark Antony's wife, Fulvia. She had Cicero decapitated and stuck a sharpened hairpin through his tongue as revenge for all he'd said about her. So after almost half a century a woman would rule at last.

But Christ knew if they were going to be as power mad as men were said to be, they'd be no better at it.

He heard the roar of a mechanical beast. He saw the swaying crowd. Granders on electric wheelies were spinning toward him, swords and lasers at the ready.

His motorized scooter was idling, a Gamesman Guard came near and gave the throttle a push, and the bike began a straight course toward the center of the enormous arena.

The sun was blinding. There were agonized screams somewhere off to his left. A Grander Graft on wheelies, maybe; chopped at the knees.

Something spewing vicious light and loudly grinding its maw came toward him—perhaps it was two somethings. Between the sweat, the drugs, and the desert-hot glow, he couldn't tell.

A woman—his wife—would rule now . . .

For a second his mind felt a little clearer—there was a brief glimmer of old remembered historic facts: Caligula was mad, Nero burned Rome . . .

A flicker further back.

There had been evolution of the race: hominids, Neanderthals, savage tribes.

There had also been Attila the Hun, Michelangelo, and Hitler . . . and Elizabeth Bathory . . . and—

All of them—men and women—*human*.

Nothing changed. Not really.

There was only the sweep of whatever culture declared itself in the now. And, most importantly, in the right.

For Brian Kirk and Janice Morgan—good friends
and great inspirations both.

Eight O'Clock in the Morning

Ray Faraday Nelson

At the end of the show the hypnotist told his subjects, "Awake." Something unusual happened.

One of the subjects awoke all the way. This had never happened before. His name was George Nada and he blinked out at the sea of faces in the theatre, at first unaware of anything out of the ordinary. Then he noticed, spotted here and there in the crowd, the non-human faces, the faces of the Fascinators. They had been there all along, of course, but only George was really awake, so only George recognized them for what they were. He understood everything in a flash, including the fact that if he were to give any outward sign, the Fascinators would instantly command him to return to his former state, and he would obey.

He left the theatre, pushing out into the neon night, carefully avoiding any indication that he saw the green, reptilian flesh or the multiple yellow eyes of the rulers of the earth. One of them asked him, "Got a light buddy?" George gave him a light, then moved on.

At intervals along the street George saw the posters hanging with photographs of the Fascinators' multiple eyes and various commands printed under them, such as, "Work eight hours, play eight hours, sleep eight hours," and "Marry and Reproduce." A TV set in the window of a store caught George's eye, but he looked away in the nick of time. When he didn't look at the Fascinator in the screen, he could resist the command, "Stay tuned to this station."

George lived alone in a little sleeping room, and as soon as he got home the first thing he did was to disconnect the TV set. In other rooms he could hear the TV sets of his neighbors, though. Most of the time the voices were human, but now and then he heard the arrogant, strangely bird-like croaks of the aliens. "Obey the government," said one croak. "We are the government," said another. "We are your friends, you'd do anything for a friend, wouldn't you?"

"Obey!"

"Work!"

Suddenly the phone rang.

George picked it up. It was one of the Fascinators.

"Hello," it squawked. "This is your control, Chief of Police Robinson. You are an old man, George Nada. Tomorrow morning at eight o'clock your heart will stop. Please repeat."

"I am an old man," said George. "Tomorrow morning at eight o'clock my heart will stop."

The control hung up.

"No, it won't," whispered George. He wondered why they wanted him dead. Did they suspect that he was awake? Probably. Someone might have spotted him, noticed that he didn't respond the way the others did. If George were alive at one minute after eight tomorrow morning, then they would be sure.

"No use waiting here for the end," he thought.

He went out again. The posters, the TV, the occasional commands from passing aliens did not seem to have absolute power over him, though he still felt strongly tempted to obey, to see things the way his master wanted him to see them. He passed an alley and stopped. One of the aliens was alone there, leaning against the wall. George walked up to him.

"Move on," grunted the thing, focusing his deadly eyes on George.

George felt his grasp on awareness waver. For a moment the reptilian head dissolved into the face of a lovable old drunk. Of course, the drunk would be lovable. George picked up a brick and smashed it down on the old drunk's head with all his strength. For a moment the image blurred, then the blue-green blood oozed out of the face and the lizard fell, twitching and writhing. After a moment it was dead.

George dragged the body into the shadows and searched it. There was a tiny radio in its pocket and a curiously shaped knife and fork in another. The tiny radio said something in an incomprehensible language. George put it down beside the body, but kept the eating utensils.

"I can't possibly escape," thought George. "Why fight them?" But maybe he could.

What if he could awaken others? That might be worth a try.

He walked twelve blocks to the apartment of his girl friend, Lil, and knocked on her door. She came to the door in her bathrobe.

"I want you to wake up," he said.

"I'm awake," she said. "Come on in."

He went in. The TV was playing. He turned it off.

"No," he said. "I mean really wake up." She looked at him without comprehension, so he snapped his fingers and shouted, "Wake up! The masters command that you wake up!"

"Are you off your rocker, George?" she asked suspiciously. "You sure are acting funny." He slapped her face. "Cut that out!" she cried, "What the hell are you up to anyway?"

"Nothing," said George, defeated. "I was just kidding around."

"Slapping my face wasn't just kidding around!" she cried.

There was a knock at the door. George opened it.

It was one of the aliens.

"Can't you keep the noise down to a dull roar?" it said.

The eyes and reptilian flesh faded a little and George saw the flickering image of a fat middle-aged man in shirtsleeves. It was still a man when George slashed its throat with the eating knife, but it was an alien before it hit the floor. He dragged it into the apartment and kicked the door shut. "What do you see there?" he asked Lil, pointing to the many-eyed snake thing on the floor.

"Mister . . . Mister Coney," she whispered, her eyes wide with horror. "You . . . just killed him, like it was nothing at all."

"Don't scream," warned George, advancing on her.

"I won't, George. I swear I won't, only please, for the love of

God, put down that knife." She backed away until she had her shoulder blades pressed to the wall.

George saw that it was no use.

"I'm going to tie you up," said George. "First tell me which room Mister Coney lived in."

"The first door on your left as you go toward the stairs," she said. "Georgie . . . Georgie. Don't torture me. If you're going to kill me, do it clean. Please, Georgie, please."

He tied her up with bedsheets and gagged her, then searched the body of the Fascinator. There was another one of the little radios that talked a foreign language, another set of eating utensils, and nothing else.

George went next door.

When he knocked, one of the snake-things answered, "Who is it?"

"Friend of Mister Coney. I wanna see him," said George.

"He went out for a second, but he'll be right back." The door opened a crack, and four yellow eyes peeped out. "You wanna come in and wait?"

"Okay," said George, not looking at the eyes.

"You alone here?" he asked as it closed the door, its back to George.

"Yeah, why?"

He slit its throat from behind, then searched the apartment. He found human bones and skulls, a half-eaten hand.

He found tanks with huge fat slugs floating in them. *The children*, he thought, and killed them all.

There were guns too, of a sort he had never seen before. He discharged one by accident, but fortunately it was noiseless. It seemed to fire little poisoned darts.

He pocketed the gun and as many boxes of darts he could and went back to Lil's place. When she saw him she writhed in helpless terror.

"Relax, honey," he said, opening her purse. "I just want to borrow your car keys." He took the keys and went downstairs to the street.

Her car was still parked in the same general area in which she always parked it. He recognized it by the dent in the right fender. He got in, started it, and began driving aimlessly. He drove for hours, thinking—desperately searching for some way out. He turned on the car radio to see if he could get some music, but there was nothing but news and it was all about him, George Nada, the homicidal maniac. The announcer was one of the masters, but he sounded a little scared. Why should he be? What could one man do?

George wasn't surprised when he saw the road block, and he turned off on a side street before he reached it. No little trip to the country for you, Georgie boy, he thought to himself.

They had just discovered what he had done back at Lil's place, so they would probably be looking for Lil's car. He parked it in an alley and took the subway. There were no aliens on the subway, for some reason. Maybe they were too good for such things, or maybe it was just because it was so late at night.

When one finally did get on, George got off.

He went up to the street and went into a bar. One of the Fascinators was on the TV, saying over and over again, "We are your friends. We are your friends. We are your friends." The stupid lizard sounded scared. Why? What could one man do against them all?

George ordered a beer, then it suddenly struck him that the Fascinator on the TV no longer seemed to have any power over him. He looked at it again and thought, *It has to believe it can master me to do it. The slightest hint of fear on its part and the power to hypnotize is lost.* They flashed George's picture on the TV screen and George retreated to the phone booth. He called his control, the Chief of Police.

"Hello, Robinson?" he asked.

"Speaking."

"This is George Nada. I've figured out how to wake people up."

"What? George, hang on. Where are you?" Robinson sounded almost hysterical. He hung up and paid and left the bar. They would probably trace his call.

He caught another subway and went downtown.

It was dawn when he entered the building housing the biggest of the city's TV studios. He consulted the building director and then went up in the elevator. The cop in front of the studio recognized him. "Why, you're Nada!" he gasped.

George didn't like to shoot him with the poison dart gun, but he had to.

He had to kill several more before he got into the studio itself, including all the engineers on duty. There were a lot of police sirens outside, excited shouts, and running footsteps on the stairs. The alien was sitting before the TV camera saying, "We are your friends. We are your friends," and didn't see George come in. When George shot him with the needle gun he simply stopped in mid-sentence and sat there, dead. George stood near him and said, imitating the alien croak, "Wake up. Wake up. See us as we are and kill us!"

It was George's voice the city heard that morning, but it was the Fascinator's image, and the city did awake for the very first time and the war began.

George did not live to see the victory that finally came. He died of a heart attack at exactly eight o'clock.

On Big Red:
A New Martian Chronicle

William F. Nolan

Shuddering with speed, the massive silver rocket blazed toward Mars. First mission. Men, at last, to walk Big Red.

"We're closing fast on her. What do you think we'll find, Captain?" asked Bob Johnson, second in command.

"Sand," said Lewis Kingsley. "Lots and lots of red sand."

"Gonna be a kick, being the first there," said engineer Ted Faust.

"Yeah . . . maybe, but I've got a really weird feeling about Mars. A bad feeling."

Kingsley stared out of the main port, searching the sky for the red planet.

Blackness. A vast sea of blackness shot through by pinpoints of light. A million stars, but Mars not yet visible.

The rocket blazed on—until . . .

"There she is!" exclaimed archaeologist Norm Tomerlin as the legendary planet swept into view off the starboard port. "Looks like a big red apple."

"We'll take a proper bite out of her," declared anthropologist John Oliver.

"At least we'll be able to breathe without helmets," said Faust. "The drones did a good job altering the atmosphere."

"Marvels of technology," nodded Kingsley. He turned away from the port. "All right, boys, time to suit up."

The six men donned their cumbersome biometrically engineered space suits, adjusting straps and zippers.

"Better wear your helmets out there in case the drones were wrong," said Kingsley. "Can't take chances."

270

The silver craft eased down onto the Martian surface on legs of yellow fire, gently arriving at a final, hushed stop. As the rocket metal cooled, the double-lock exit doors swung wide with a hiss of escaping pressure. A new world awaited them.

Kingsley was the first man out, planting both booted feet solidly on the grainy Martian soil. He thumbed a small monitor embedded on his left sleeve: a light flashed green. "Atmosphere's safe," he said. "No problem."

Each of the crew removed their helmet, following the captain out of the ship.

"Air's like wine!" declared medic Doc Albright. He grinned. "Tasty!"

Pebbled sand crunched under their heavy boots, kicking up plumes of red dust as they advanced across a flat plain dotted with ancient, tumbled rocks.

Pointing ahead, Faust exclaimed: "A *city!* Jesus. A whole friggin' city's out there!"

Slender and graceful, the strange city gleamed on the Martian horizon, its sky-clawing towers spiraling upward; in the foreground loomed several large, antique-looking pyramidal structures reflecting the raw, bluish solar light.

"Looks like it's made of . . . *crystal* or something," said the captain, shading his eyes.

"It's just like that Bradbury guy wrote in his stories," said Albright. "Did you ever read Bradbury?"

"Oh, sure," nodded Kingsley. "Read a lot of his stuff when I was a kid back in Kansas City. He's what got me interested in going into space, becoming a rocket man." He nodded again. "Sure . . . we all read Bradbury."

"Well, maybe it's like what he wrote," declared Albright. "Maybe there really *were* Martians here. Maybe they built crystal cities and dug canals and then died off. Now *we're* the aliens."

"That's possible," said Kingsley. He smiled at the thought. "Anything's possible—but it's all pretty wild stuff."

They reached the city, slender and delicate, with bizarre jeweled mosaics carved into its luminous walls.

"Could be they're still around," said John Oliver, "messing with our minds, making us just *think* we see all this."

Kingsley tapped one of the shimmering pillars with a gloved hand. "Nope . . . it's real. All real."

Oliver walked to the edge of a shallow canal, bone dry under the sun's distant glare. "This canal," he said—"never finished."

Norm Tomerlin stood next to Oliver, staring down at the arid canal. "Maybe the Martians digging here died before they could complete the job."

"That's a big maybe," said Kingsley. "We don't know a damn thing about what's really been—or *is*—on this planet."

Albright gestured toward a massive translucent structure. "Let's go inside. Check it out."

"Just be careful," warned Kingsley. "No telling what's in there."

The six moved cautiously, entering the structure through an ornately scrolled stone doorway flanked to either side by high crystalline pillars. Burn weapons at the ready, they walked forward slowly in single file, carefully scanning the alien terrain.

The interior was like some vast cathedral, with columned shafts of sunlight spearing down from windows of odd design. The designs were intricate, containing complex symbols unlike any seen on Earth.

"Spooky in here," muttered Oliver, his voice reverberating.

"Kind of like being in church," observed Albright.

"This *was* our church," declared a soft-fluted voice behind them.

They turned to encounter a tall, ivory-robed figure. The Martian's body was glowing, as if lit from within. Its large eyes were like two luminescent gold coins, and it held a shining gemstone rod in its long-fingered left hand.

Johnson brought up his burn gun. "Lose the weapon!"

"I carry no weapon," declared the Martian. "My people have never carried weapons. We had no need of them. This rod I hold is a badge of office."

Kingsley stepped forward. "Just who the hell *are* you?"

"My name is Elisham," replied the ivory-clad figure, looking at them thoughtfully. "I was a high priest here long, long ago. I served my people before the Plague killed us all."

Johnson blinked at him. "Then . . . you're—*dead?*"

"I have no corporal body, that is correct," said Elisham. "I am without flesh—as you can see."

He moved into a shaft of soft blue-green sunlight. The Martian's body was transparent; it wavered, rippling in and out of focus.

"Were you the last of your kind?" asked Oliver. "The last Martian?"

"No. There are many others."

"But—you told us that your people were all dead," said Faust.

"Yes, that is so," agreed the tall figure. "All dead. We are what you would call ghosts now—insubstantial, lacking physical bodies. Only our essences have been preserved . . . and we have been waiting for you. Oh, yes. Waiting for a very long time." Elisham regarded each them in turn. "Eons, in fact."

Glancing at one another, a look of unease passed between the men as they considered the Martian's words. "We come from Earth," said Kingsley. "So you know about our planet?"

"Yes, I know much about Earth," declared Elisham, his words richly harmonic, almost musical. "The ancient books sing of your place in our universe. I have learned to speak as you speak from these books. There has been much unrest on your planet. You are a violent people. Why have you come here to Mars? I have great fear of you."

"Your fear is groundless," said Kingsley. "We came here to learn more about the worlds in our solar system, not to harm anyone. We are men of peace."

"That is reassuring to hear," said the Martian. "But why should I trust such words? Earth people often lie."

"You need to believe that what I say to you is true," said the captain. "Take us to your people. We wish only to know them, to study your wisdom, your ways . . . to learn."

"Very well," nodded Elisham. "When your magic craft appeared in our sky, many of the people gathered in the Great Hall to talk of you. Please follow."

Led by the Martian, the six Earthmen followed him across the rocky plain to a second high-towered city and into a vast hall of radiant crystal. The area seethed with transparent beings, Martians, robed in silver and gold, of all ages from the very young to very old. Their massed figures shimmered and pulsed in rippled waves.

"This is my Leah," said Elisham, presenting his beloved as one might present a priceless gift.

Kingsley attempted to take her hand in greeting, but his fingers passed through hers.

"Leah is dead, of course," said Elisham. "Alas, she has no flesh to meet yours. You must forgive."

"Nothing to forgive," said Kingsley, feeling lightheaded. "I understand."

"Yes," nodded Elisham, "I am sure you do."

*

The transfer had been successful. Of course, there was a high level of frustration among the Martians since only a bare half-dozen were able to complete the transfer. When it was done, a mere six of them had new bodies.

Kingsley and Johnson and Oliver and Albright and Faust and Tomerlin looked the same—but they were *not* the same.

"Have no concern," said Kingsley to Elisham. "In time, many rockets will come to our planet. With many more bodies."

"That is indeed good to know."

Kingsley felt warm and secure with the alien inside him. He'd been wrong about Mars.

This trip hadn't turned out so bad after all.

Dedicated, in homage, with love to Ray Bradbury.

Performance

F. Paul Wilson

It's the little things, always the little things that trip you up.

But I've got to hand it to them, they're sharp. The first two tails they put on me this run were males, both of whom I ditched within an hour of spotting them. Now they've sent a woman, and she's good. I don't know how long she's been on me, and that's a bit worrisome.

What has she seen?

The little thing that gave her away is truly little: a lump on her chin. It sits there just left of midline, maybe half the size of an M&M sliced along its wide axis. I haven't been close enough to figure out if it's a mole or a pimple or a little cyst, and I don't really care. Whatever it is, I could kiss it. Probably saved my reputation.

She can change her clothes, her hair, contacts, makeup, lipstick, bust, even her shape, every imaginable thing—and trust me, she has—but the lump remains. Yesterday morning I noticed a blonde woman with a lump on her chin. It was in an Andrew's Coffee Shop, one of the half-dozen or so Andrew's Coffee Shops I rotate through at random. (Yes, I *like* Andrew's Coffee Shops; transform the damn city into Starbucksville if you must, but leave me my Andrew's.) Nothing particularly noticeable about her beyond the lump, and nothing particularly noticeable about the lump itself except the way the light happened to hit it at that moment and cast a small shadow down her chin.

By chance last night I happened to look up at dinner at a little bistro in the Flatiron district and spot this redhead sitting alone a few tables away by the window—I never sit by a window—reading a book. A redhead with a lump on her chin. Could be a coincidence, I told myself, but in my business a coincidence is cause for alarm. I wished I'd got a better look at the blonde that morning, but I was a blank. So I studied this woman's reflection in the window and memorized everything I could about her, storing up for the next time—if there was to be a next time.

There was. This morning I stopped at the dog run in Washington Square and watched the people watch their dogs. Pets are high on my Things-I-Don't-Get list, right up there with sports columns and body piercing. She was a brunette this time; her nostril ring, shoe-polish-black hair, and kohled eyes that made her leukemia makeup all the paler fit right in. But the lump on her chin spotlighted her for me.

Three different wigs on three different looks in three different places, but one chin lump. The leitmotif of the lump, as it were. No question. I'd picked me up another tail.

I've got mixed feelings about this. It's good to know I've identified her, but now that I have, I'm on the spot. Performance anxiety, you might say. Now that I've made her, I've got to lose her.

And here's where the art of the ditch comes in. I can't *look* like I'm losing her. I must play the naïf and make it seem natural, like it's her fault, her carelessness or lack of skill, rather than my doing. If I make an obvious attempt to ditch her, it means I've got something to hide. And then I lose, because the whole point of the tail is to determine just that.

I take a leisurely stroll along Waverly to Sixth Avenue. I buy a Diet Pepsi from the pushcart there and casually check behind me. With a start I realize she's not there. Could I have been wrong? No. Impossible.

I stand on the curb, tilting my head back as I sip from the Pepsi can—an excellent cover for a surreptitious scan—and I spot her a block downtown to my left. The clever bitch. She paralleled me along Washington Place.

Oh, she's good. Very good.

Time for the taxi dodge. This one works almost every time because it negates the skill of the tailer. Even the best of them are helpless when this works.

I watch the uptown flow of cabs. It's a sunny July day and they're plentiful, flowing past in yellow schools, mostly empty and hungry for fares, but I'm patient. Finally I see my chance. A break in the traffic with one lonely cab bringing up the rear. Not another for blocks behind him. He's cruising the center fire lane like a lemon shark, ready to dart left or right should a meal appear. I step off the curb and flag him down: Hello, lunch here.

He swerves to a stop in front of me and I hop in.

"Fourteenth and Third," I tell him. "And hurry. I'm late."

As he puts his foot in the tank and we gun away, I remove a small palm-size mirror from my pocket and angle it so I can watch through the rear window. I see Ms. Tail lunge into the street and start waving her arms in frantic search of a cab of her own. No such luck, my dear.

I settle back and sigh. Too easy.

I have the cab turn uptown on Third and drop me off in Kips Bay. I walk over to the theater on Second and spend two hours semi-snoozing through Mamet's latest. Nothing like really disappearing from the street as a coup de grâce.

*

When I get out I'm hungry so I look around and spot a Burger King sign a few blocks down. I don't like most fast food, but I have this fondness for Whoppers. Maybe it's the mayo, or maybe the onions. Whatever, I indulge in three or four a week.

I buy my Whopper and a diet cola—yes, I'm well aware how ludicrous that is—and seat myself at a single table at the very rear of the store. I'm on my second bite when I see this slim blonde in a Sugar Ray T-shirt dump her trash in the bin and go back to the counter.

I freeze for an instant when I spot the lump on her chin, then I force myself to keep chewing.

Somehow she followed me to Kips Bay. She must have caught a lucky break back there in the Village—a cab must have pulled out of a side street and picked her up. Either that or she has motorized backup. They wouldn't issue her that unless I've given myself away, and I haven't. But that's not what's making my Whopper taste like wet cardboard.

She was here before me. She knew I'd come in here.

Wait. No. She didn't *know* I'd come in here, but she's done her homework and *assumed* I'd opt for a Whopper when I came out of the theater. She gambled.

And she won.

Now I'm impressed. Truly impressed. This is one gutsy lady.

I think I'm in love.

With the challenge, that is. It's going to be difficult to ditch this one, but not impossible. I know I'll win. I am the maestro here. I shall confound, confuse, baffle, and bewilder her; I'll dazzle her with my footwork, just as I've done with so many other tails. It's simply going to take a little more effort.

With this new game afoot, my taste buds revive. I finish the Whopper, then take my leave and stroll over to Penn Station, stopping at a Duane Reade along the way to buy some sunscreen. At the station I catch a train to Flushing Meadows. The Mets are playing today—I heard it on the radio this morning—and I'm going to test Ms. Tail's mettle. Everyone's got a weakness, a tender spot. I am going to find hers.

While aboard the train I carefully but surreptitiously check my clothing for a tracer, just in case she's taking unfair advantage. After a thorough search, going so far as partially disrobing in the bathroom, I'm satisfied we're on a level playing field.

Excellent. I did not want to think less of her.

*

Shea Stadium is not quite quarter full. I seat myself in the super-sun section of the bleachers and unfold the prize I picked up in the concession area. It's one of those goofy umbrella hats you tend to see on a certain class of Manhattan tourist—the kind who arrive in an

Airstream and wander around wearing yellow Bermuda shorts with gray knee socks and brown sandals. But it's practical, it's portable shade, it's done up in Mets blue and orange, and should send an unmistakable signal to Ms. Tail that I am an artist and as such allowed to play with fewer than fifty-two in my deck.

I am immediately glad for the sunblock and umbrella hat. Shea is a Godzilla wok today, waiting for the big guy to trundle by and spray us with peanut oil. Ms. Tail is six rows back and to my left. I use my palm mirror to see how she's handling the heat. Somewhere along the way she shifted back to brunette, and to my great chagrin she's got her blouse off, revealing one of those gray exercise bras. Obviously she works out; her muscles are well developed and close to the skin. She's thrown her head back and I just know her eyes are closed behind her Ray-Bans.

The bitch is sunbathing! On my time!

And now I have an epiphany: She knows she's been made, and she knows I've already tried to ditch her—which means she knows I'm on the run. Yet she hasn't called for backup as she's supposed to.

Why not?

I can think of only one reason.

She wants to take me down single-handed. She knows deliveries are time-sensitive and she intends either to witness my drop or to keep me from it, all without backup.

Not only will I be beaten, I will be humiliated.

That does it. I'm outta here. Besides, I'm suffering from major league longueurs anyway. I hate baseball.

As I make my way back to the train station I don't check to see if she's following. Why bother? She's superbly trained and ready for anything. Or so she thinks. Now that we're aware of each other, I have carte blanche to use every trick I know to lose her. And I know plenty. I *can* lose her. But simple evasion will not be enough.

I must break this woman.

And to do that I must engage her on a more visceral level. She's got a weak spot. Everybody does. I've simply got to find hers.

*

Back in the city, I stroll over to Eighth Avenue. Some of the cheesier businesses that used to rent in midtown have migrated to the Thirties. I see a porn shop and I'm tempted to make her follow me inside, but that's too transparent. Beneath me, really.

But here's something: calls itself an "Oddity Emporium." Reminds me of the old "Ripley's Believe It or Not" arcade I used to see on Times Square in the pre-Disneyfication days. I buy my ticket and enter.

Dingy inside. I wander past booths with stuffed two-headed cows, wax models of the Elephant Man, the Lobster Boy, and then a dramatically lit display of deformed fetuses floating in jars of preservative. The old carny folk used to call them "pickled punks." These may be real or may be latex, but whatever they are they're not pretty.

I check my little palm mirror and notice she hasn't bothered to change her shirt or her hair. Another slap in the—

Whoa. Aperçu. What's this expression I catch on our girl? Could that be disgust? Revulsion?

I think so. In fact, I'm sure.

Well, well, well. I've learned something valuable here. This arrogant little puss has got a squeamish side. Let's see how we can exploit this.

After drawing out my stay in the Oddity Emporium to a full hour, I leave and wander over to Bryant Park. I pick up the *Voice* and the pink-sheeted New York *Observer* along the way and spend the rest of the afternoon perusing them.

By dinnertime I have my plan, and I'm amazed at my luck. The timing is so perfect it's almost as if this confrontation were preordained. I am all but consumed with anticipation. I make a point of eating at a Korean restaurant in Chelsea that is utterly unrestrained in its use of peppers and garlic, which only stokes my fires. I don't know what it does to Ms. Tail's stomach, but I hope nothing good. I am fairly aflame when I leave and head for SoHo.

The cab drops me off at the theater. At least it calls itself a theater. From out here it's a dark green doorway. Its marquee is a hand-printed poster:

TONIGHT ONLY
THE ANNUAL
KAREN PIEDMONT
PERFORMANCE
8 P.M.

I make my way in, hoping something hasn't gone awry and I've missed it. I've heard about Karen Piedmont—who hasn't? She's long been the *succès de scandale* of the art world, even in New York. But this is the first time I've ever had a yen to see her act.

I enter the tiny theater, little more than a black box, really. Ms. Piedmont, a very pregnant brunette who looks to be in her mid-thirties, is wearing a delicate headset microphone and nothing else. She lies on her back, propped up on a center-stage hospital bed. Her right side is toward me; her swollen breasts and distended belly stretch toward the projection screen dangling above her. An IV of some clear solution runs into her left arm, wires run from her belly to a black box under the bed.

I look around for a seat. Maybe fifty folding chairs, most of them occupied, are arrayed before the tiny stage. Ms. Tail arrives as I find one in the last row. I hide a grin. She has to sit three rows ahead of me. Now I'll be watching her. Irony can be so sweet.

Good timing. Ms. Piedmont's obstetrician has induced labor and is leaving the stage for a front row seat. The lights go down and all is dark except for the naked Ms. Piedmont, spotlighted on her bed, her skin as pale the sheets. If not for her dark hair and stretch marks she'd seem a part of the bed. The projection screen lights, but I see no image, only a fine black line crawling across the bottom.

"Welcome everyone," she says. "This is my fifth annual performance and exhibition. Those of you who've attended in the past know the routine. You newcomers should realize that, as I am only partially in control here, patience can be a very necessary virtue with my performance. I—"

She breaks off and grimaces—and I notice the line begin to curve upward on the screen—then she smiles.

"Well, well. Looks like we've got one coming already. I'll start with something simple, just to get my chops back. This isn't the kind of thing you can practice between performances, you know."

Appreciative laughter from the audience, especially the females. I glance at Ms. Tail and I can make out her face in the wash of light from stage and screen. She's not smiling.

"Here we go," Ms. Piedmont says. "Mount Fuji."

The line on the screen—I see now it's a projection of the contraction monitor wired to her belly—crawls up a gentle slope, flattens briefly, then begins its descent in a mirror image of the upslope.

As it flattens to the baseline, we applaud.

"Please," the artist says. "That's really nothing."

She talks about the genesis of contraction art, how she noticed the patterns on the monitor during her first labor and found she could alter their configuration by controlling her breathing and musculature. She refined her art through two subsequent pregnancies, then went public with her fourth.

Another contraction starts.

"Whoa!" she says. "So soon. And this feels like a big one. Okay! See who's first to recognize this."

As she starts panting, my eyes are glued to the screen. The diagonal course of the line takes an abrupt upward turn and runs almost vertical for a foot or so on the screen, then falls, angling back to the horizontal, then up again. It's beginning to look like a flight of foot-high steps, but I say nothing.

A woman calls out, "Staircase!" and I'm glad I held back when Ms. Piedmont says, "Nope."

The pattern flattens out on top for a couple of feet, then begins stepping down.

"A Mayan pyramid!" someone else shouts, and Ms. Piedmont

says, "Give that man a round of applause."

But the applause that fills the impromptu theater is for her and her alone. I watch how Ms. Tail claps—utterly without enthusiasm. In fact, she looks a little ill.

Ms. Piedmont talks now of how to date she's the only practitioner of contraction art and of how she hopes someday to open a school to teach the principles and technique.

Another contraction begins and someone, a man, calls out, "Care to try the Seattle Needle?" to which she good-naturedly replies, "Care to try to fuck yourself?"

I watch agog as she limns the Taj Mahal.

I am amazed, I am overwhelmed. This is not some exhibitionist *épater-les-bourgeois* poseur prattling aphorisms as she smears herself with paint or chocolate or a less pleasant substance. This is a woman who truly has succeeded in living her art, an art that is uniquely hers, purely autotelic, and truly of the moment.

But Ms. Tail looks more appalled than transported.

I hear a moan from Ms. Piedmont. Even here in the last row I am close enough to see the perspiration beading her pain-wracked face. The sound of her panting fills the air as we watch the contraction line zip up and down the screen, soaring vertically, crawling horizontally, creating peaks, plateaus, valleys, ledges, crevices, her breaths crescendoing into rapid whimpers. Her knees have lifted and her legs are spread as she finishes with an iconic phallic shape.

"The Empire State Building?" someone murmurs, then shouts, "That's the New York skyline!"

Yes, it is. Unquestionably. I leap to my feet, slamming my hands together, leading the applause that fills the room, but a wail from the artist cuts us off.

Breathless I watch the obstetrician hurry from the front row. More amplified moans and whimpers among the harsh staccato breaths, and then another sound, the high-pitched wail of a newborn infant.

The obstetrician places the squalling baby on his mother's abdomen. Ms. Piedmont holds the bloody, glistening child aloft.

"I'm sorry labor was so short this time," she says. "Thank you for sharing this with me."

With the notable exception of Ms. Tail we are all on our feet, applauding, cheering. My throat is tight, my eyes are full. I am galvanized. I am inspired to raise forever the level of my own performance or die trying.

A stagehand wheels out a curtain rack to shield mother and child, signaling the end of the performance. As people begin to shuffle toward the exit, I drop into a squat and fumble with a shoelace, pretending to tie it. I linger there a few seconds, then straighten. As I rise I catch the panic flickering across Ms. Tail's wan and worn features.

Gotcha! For a heartbeat or two you thought you'd lost me, didn't you.

But I detect no relief at my reappearance. Only defeat. I've beaten her and she knows it. Although she might have been aghast at the performance, she was transfixed by it as well. And during the time it held her prisoner, I could have brought down our own curtain by slipping out and disappearing into the night.

She is beaten, yes, but not broken. Bent almost to the breaking point, but she hasn't snapped. All she needs is a little shove, the right sort of nudge to make her break off her surveillance and desert me. Then my victory shall be complete.

But how?

As I'm leaving I ask the young tattooed and pierced-to-within-an-inch-of-his-life fellow at the door if there is any other performance art in the neighborhood tonight.

"Yeah. Just around the corner there, you know, like, usually around ten or so, Harry Adamski'll be like doing his stool art."

"You mean like furniture?"

"No, uh, like—"

"Never mind. I get it." Oh, perfect. "And where exactly is this going to take place . . . ?"

Seven Rooms and the Key

John Shirley

Kolt and The Box hovered about fifty yards over a craggy, lichen-splashed bluff. Kolt was a man, while The Box was a shiny gray-green talking box—the AI who had transported Kolt here. They had just arrived at the quantum splinter some called Coil: a plane of the Between where things are what they seem, but seem to be less than they are; where straight lines are soon revealed as nooses.

Floating side by side, Kolt and The Box gazed at the structure crowning the high end of a ravine cutting the bluff. The structure was shaped like a giant nautilus shell; it stood on a rocky shelf, slightly embedded at its smaller, more tightly spiraled end; its opening was poised like an enormous tuba bell over the converging cliffs.

"There it is," said The Box. "The Coil House. Though of course it's not a house—and while it has not so many chambers as a nautilus, the overall effect inside is the same."

The Coil House was lit from within by a dull glow, pale in the dusk. Kolt reckoned the nautilus-shaped construction to be a little bigger than an earthly three-story house.

"Looks like a house of sorts to me," said Kolt. A balcony with wide glass doors closed off the opening of the nautilus, near the curved, scaly, roof.

"It . . . houses things." The Box did not elaborate, except to say, "And of course, it encompasses the Lightning Axis you're seeking. If the report is true."

"If?" Kolt scowled. "InterDimentional Travel seemed quite definite that there's an unclaimed Lightning Axis in there."

"There is a *fairly* reliable report." After a moment The Box added, "I trust your travel agent back at IDT mentioned that this is a dangerous place—in an altogether dangerous dimension?"

"Oh, yes. It was mentioned. It is well known."

A soft, damp breeze flowed over Kolt; on the bluff below, a flock of eyeless black birds called out raucously with such rhythmic insistence they seemed to convey some specific cryptic message. The leafless trees shivered like ganglia, quivering with the bird call. Through the narrow black-stone ravine below the trees flowed a glittering stream of water—it flowed *uphill* toward the Coil House, all the way to a notch under the giant nautilus. It was as if the nautilus were sucking the water upward.

It was a primeval landscape altogether, and the Coil House was somehow without any temporal reference, at least from Kolt's point of view. In Kolt's home dimension, standard Earth, it was 2089. Here it was, perhaps, a hundred thousand years earlier or a hundred thousand years later . . .

Even at this distance Kolt could feel the crackle in the air about the Coil House: a living electromagnetic flux.

Kolt looked at his guide, found himself gazing at his own image, a dark, slightly warped reflection in a polished square: Kolt was white-faced, long-faced; he was gray-eyed, cold-eyed. His pouting lips were dyed stylishly black; his hair was hidden in the shiny dark-red deflection wrap that covered his head like a tight fitting cowl; he wore a black cling-suit. He was a compact man, thin, leanly muscular, and *normally* he was confident.

"You seem reluctant to enter the house," The Box observed. "Would you like to return to your basal dimension?"

"No. I'm just . . . not quite ready. Give me a moment."

Kolt adjusted his breathing, his heartbeat. He was thinking of a remark his advisor had made. *"An Acquisitor at the Coil occasionally returns—but it's only a partial return. One must leave behind some of oneself—a toll charge."*

The Box said, "Whether or not you proceed, we now require the remainder of your payment."

Kolt grunted. He touched his face, pressed a stud in the cheekbone, and sub-vocalized a group of numbers, his implant authorizing payment in life-force units.

"Payment received," said The Box. "Only a ten-point-one allotment? You travel frugally."

"Just be prepared to transport me home, if the need arises," said Kolt.

He used his implanted chip to direct the graviton field and descended at a sliding angle. As he went, he heard a chip message transmitted from The Box. "Free advice. Do not make the mistake of assuming that what you see in the Coil House is a hallucination."

Kolt reached on the balcony, which seemed made of seashell essences.

He floated slowly toward the opaque double doors—and they opened for him, swinging inward. He was still at low-gravitation, and a strong vacuuming current of air drew him into the building.

The suction ceased; the doors closed firmly behind him. Kolt's feet settled onto the floor. He controlled the instant inner gush of fear. *I've got the plasma wand for protection . . . and I'm smarter than this thing. I have visited many splinter worlds and have faced much. In addition, I have the IDT protection field. ("87% probability of survival strongly averred! A Must for the Prepared InterDimensional Traveler!")*

The room was poorly lit by a diffuse glow from no particular source. The shelves lining the walls were crowded with dourly painted bric-a-brac; some of it appeared to be chipped antique curios, so battered as to be not quite identifiable. Was that a shepherdess and a lamb? Or was it a long-haired butcher and a skinned pig? And were those eyeless black birds on the lower shelf; did they move and call out?

The opposite wall, of pearlescent material like the floors and ceiling, was slanted like the inner hull of a ship; it angled halfway between vertical and horizontal. In it was a door, which followed the slant of the wall. "How awkward," Kolt muttered.

The door opened, and a man stood in the way—without falling, despite the slant of the floor he was coming from.

The man standing on the slanted floor beyond was wide-faced, red-lipped, his expression jovial, dressed in a loud red and blue checkered suit and a red bowtie. In a moment, the colors of the suit changed; now they were green and yellow. A moment later they were orange and purple.

IDT had not been able—or willing—to brief Kolt on everything he might encounter here, but he knew this as an *Unman*, not alive unto himself. A thin umbilicus extended from the Unman's back to disappear into the walls of the room behind him. He was an outgrowth of the house. His china-blue eyes moved under transparent nictitating membranes.

"And how can we be of service?" the Unman asked in a pleasant voice, bending the Cupid's bow of his lips in an utterly artificial smirk. He stepped into the shelf room but remained angled according to the perspective of the room he'd just left, like a boxing dummy poised before the upswing. The Unman waved a pudgy, nail-less hand at the shelves. "Have you found something you like?"

With his peripheral vision, Kolt glimpsed movement among the artifacts on the shelves moving. He turned a curious look at the curios purely to draw the Unman's attention from himself.

The Unman—who was also a salesman—followed Kolt's gaze. "Yes, that one's nice, sir," the Unman began unctuously. "Especially if you've got a youngster at home." He chuckled. "Some of these were Young Ones at Home . . . once."

While the man's face was averted, Kolt reached into an upper fold of his cling-suit and drew out the little plasma wand. Kolt told his chip to open a gap in his protective field to allow the plasma wand's blast, and with a peevish humming sound a bolt of livid blue-white energy engulfed the Unman's head and spun it about, the spinning compressing it till it burst. A kind of halo of glutinous yellow and gray spread out, spattering the frame of the door, filling the room with an acrid smell.

The Unman wobbled, headless. Then the headless body put its fists on its hips and shifted to stand flat on the floor.

Kolt stepped back a little and closed the gap in his protective field.

Thereupon the Unman's jacket opened down the front of its own accord, revealing a mouth on his smooth, nipple-free chest. It was the same as the mouth that had graced the face of the Unman—but much larger. The mouth frowned and said, "I'm afraid that violence is simply not acceptable legal tender here. If you'd like to buy something you'll have to provide cold, hard lifeforce currency. If you would proffer a Purchasing Card, sir, we can proceed. I can also accept DNA samples."

Kolt shuddered at the thought of DNA samples—his religion opposed them.

He speculated that this first room was a trap for tourist-minded Seekers, rather than Acquisitors—a tourist trap to confuse, to trap, via consumer reflexes. The Unman would trick them into lowering their protection fields.

Kolt wondered where the room's teeth were located.

He bowed slightly, tucked the plasma wand away, and while his hand was hidden, he tapped the thin little 3D printer, sending it instructions from his implant. It quickly extruded an apparent "card."

He opened a gap in his protective field, tossed the card through at the Unman. The Unman snatched at the card, and Kolt threw himself flat. As the Unman melted back into the walls of the room beyond, the gray, subtly writhing curios on the shelves grew, extended instantaneously, lengthening as if squeezed from tubes, wrapping around one another, snapping, tearing at the space Kolt had occupied a second earlier. Kolt shuddered: coming from every side, enwrapping him, they'd have held him in place until his field ran through its power. Then they'd have crushed him and fed the house.

Kolt scrambled under whipping, mockingly ambiguous shapes; he reached the door, threw himself at the entrance, gaining the next room just as the door swung closed. Moving rapidly in the low gravity, he flew through head first, rolled, got to his feet—blinked in confusion to see a number of people at a cocktail party standing about, assiduously ignoring him. The "men" were wearing tuxedos, the "women" wore gowns, all in styles egregiously outdated.

Except for the umbilici attached to their backs, the Unpeople seemed perfectly Earth-normal. They were fashionably grave, murmuring to one another with grim wryness over varicolored cocktail glasses.

Would they attack him? He put his hand on the plasma weapon once more. If he drew it into view, he might prompt some untoward response from the room.

He must press onward.

Heart drumming, Kolt slipped gently through the murmuring crowd, stepping over the occasional umbilicus as he moved toward the door opposite. Knobless and pearly, ten or twelve steps away, the door was at a forty-five degree angle from the floor he walked on. Their voices getting gradually louder, the chattering Unpeople edged closer to Kolt, never looking at him or speaking to him. He made out a few words, the occasional phrase in their murmuring: "Metatarsal . . . ebullient . . . corpuscle . . . compendium of ferment . . . laughable . . . raging rash, my dear . . . invidious . . . psychically repellent . . . delicious, my sweet, sweet friend . . ." There was nothing in their cocktail glasses, he noticed.

He was a few steps from the door when an Unwoman reached through the hole in his IDT protective field—the gap he'd forgotten to close after tossing the card—and, without looking at him, without ceasing to murmur to the man she spoke to, she tore the protection field's transmission unit from his sash.

Kolt's shield shimmered and was gone. "Fuck!" he blurted, and, rushing on, Kolt drew out the plasma wand. A sizzling pain made itself known at his right shoulder.

He twisted away and glanced at the wound. A chubby lady socialite had torn a piece of his cling-suit away, along with a strip of skin. She gnawed at the wet red strip of Kolt as if it were a party canapé off a tray, and sipped her absent cocktail. Grinding his teeth, Kolt pushed through the tightening crowd around the door, and someone else he didn't see clearly reached out as he passed—without looking at him, never looking at him—and flicked their sharp fingers at his thigh, and more cloth came away, along with a nub of flesh. He yelped and shouldered onward, the throng closing round him, many of them taking samples of Kolt—none so much as glancing at him as they reached his way, as if he were carried on a tray by a waiter. He snarled and twitched and cursed and wrenched away, then activated the wand, slapping it at snatching hands, so that fingers shriveled into boneless sockets and arms withdrew like the limbs of startled spiders.

Kolt reached the door and tapped it in a memorized pattern. The door slid aside.

He ducked through. The Unparty was shut behind him; this new room was suddenly quiet. He was gasping, bleeding from a dozen small wounds. The walls in this smaller room were clustered with folded black things like restless gloves. They began to shuffle, to rustle; they burst out at him, leathery hands, with webs between the fingers, flying at his face, sucking with lamprey mouths. He stumbled through, slashing with his plasma wand, and reached the fourth room . . .

Where Kolt fought a boa of greasy smoke, a serpentine thing made only of rippling inexorability; he almost lost consciousness as it condensed, tightening gelatinously around his throat. He freed himself with a technique he had learned from an AI who idolized Houdini.

In the next room, an Unwoman resembling his gorgeous sister Zenz, whom he'd always secretly desired, tried to lure him into her arms. She was nude, pale as a ghost, her nipples and labia pink as newborn mice. She whispered huskily to him of coupling and endless delight . . . How would this semblance kill him once she had her hands on him?

Worse—the monstrous exposure of it. The Coil House had reached into his mind and found an avenue for psychological attack. The intrusion, the degradation of it . . . And—a sibling. Sharing

DNA . . . He was Kolt of the *Quissic Kolts*—they were more than tightly knit. They were DNA devotees; every room in the family manse had a holographic shrine to the family DNA in it. Family sanctity was innate, engraved on the soul of a Quissic Kolt.

But Kolt wept as he drew essence of shade from his pouch and draped her in it, so he could bear to destroy her with plasma bursts. The semblance burned apart, wailing, "Why do you hurt me so, brother my love?"

In the sixth room he paused to catch his breath, to calm himself. It was a small room; he had to stoop under the ceiling. There was a door just ten feet away, at the top of the upslanting floor. He decided that the thing waiting by the door wouldn't attack at once. It was speaking to him in soft, familiar tones, but he blocked the words from his mind.

Wounds throbbing, Kolt sighed and climbed up the floor—and was unable to prevent himself from seeing the thing that crept along there. It was a woman's head, moving across the floor like a snail. It inched its way along, gradually turning so it was half facing him.

Kolt whimpered. It was his mother's head. Her bodiless head, crawling . . .

He was not merely Kolt. He was a *Quissic Kolt*.

This wasn't fair. It was his mother's face, Felicia Kolt's face, replicated with every mole and seam. He knew it was a physical object, no hallucination. If he touched it, it would feel like a human head. *Her* head.

First Zerz—and then his mother. The profoundest demeaning of a Quissic: his mother's head, with her silvery braided hair, its glimmering blue sheen. But the expression was demented; the lips slathered, the eyes rolled. Mindless as a snail, Mother's head was dragging itself with its chin, thrusting its jaw out to pull itself along with an ugly waggling motion. It gibbered softly, unintelligibly, its tone plaintive as it tugged its way to a dessert plate on the floor. On the bone-china plate were two narrow wedges, slices of the Quissic fruit pie his mother printed out for him—except his nose told him the filling was excrement. And she darted her tongue to lap at it, sucking the brown paste, muttering miserably, licking at the sticky wedges . . .

"Ungh," Kolt burst out, covering his eyes. The attacks on his family struck past his training, punched through his sophistication.

Suddenly he wanted to give up, let it destroy him—the pain from his wounds, his psychic exhaustion, and a subliminal urgency from the Coil House itself: *Give up. Find release.*

Why not? The walls would close in; the digestion would begin. It would lap up his consciousness as well as his body. Then it would be over.

Like a Venus fly-trap, the Coil House drew travelers from the basal world and looked for ways to *lower* them, to make them pliable, edible, absorbable. But it did contain something of value, a lure to draw people in . . .

You're in the sixth room, he told himself. *One more to go before you can break through to the axis, the spine of the house.*

Kolt turned to his training; he found his inner node of attention, dragged his mind from identification with the image of his mother's crawling, demented head. He turned instead to his goal.

Only two other Acquisitors possessed a Coil House axis: the spine of Coil House conveyed the possibility of interdimensional travel without using The Box or an agency; he would need only will, the axis, and a sufficiency of energy . . .

Kolt reached into his pouch, found he had another Essence of Shade, and blotted the crawling head from sight. He scrambled quickly past it and opened the door into the seventh room.

The chamber was only as big as a double closet. The four walls were mirrors. He saw no farther door. Somewhere, beyond one of these walls, was the Coil House axis, a battery for IAMton energy, refined lifeforce, the atomic particle of consciousness itself. The Coil House had soaked up the lifeforce of the hundreds of Seekers and Acquisitors.

Kolt moved half a step farther in, and the light increased—he saw his reflections in the four walls; an infinite array of Kolts. No door, only mirrors. How was he to get through to whatever chamber contained the axis? Was there a trigger hidden in the glass?

He reached out and touched a mirror experimentally, pressing his fingers to his reflection's face.

The mirror was soft to the touch. The glass, the image, was pliable under his fingers, warping at his touch—and the mirror image of his face collapsed under his fingers. His own face crumpled along with it; Kolt's actual face was crumpled in exactly the way the mirror reflection was, conforming to the warpage in the soft glass. His corporeal face was flattened by finger marks, painlessly, as if his flesh had become clay for unseen fingers. He had been too long under the house's quantum-uncertainty influence: a kind of dimensional sympathetic magic was in the air. In changing the mirror he had crushed his own jaw so that his mouth was fused shut, his nose flattened, the nostrils shut off, and he couldn't breathe. He touched his own face and confirmed it: his face really had been crushed out of shape, flattened.

Struggling for breath, Kolt clutched at his throat in panic. He forced himself to calmness and reached out to the mirror, thinking to smooth it down. But it had already returned to smoothness. And the only image it would return was of the semblance he had now: grotesquely crushed, flattened. By his own fingers.

He contacted his implant chip and quickly sorted through options; there was an app he'd brought along as a decoy. It might be used . . .

Starting to feel dizzy from lack of oxygen, he activated a holographic image of Kolt, a solid-appearing copy of his normal self, standing between him and the mirror.

His proper image restored, Kolt's own physical face re-formed, and his mouth and nose were instantly repaired. He sucked in a long breath of air and made the hologram vanish. And then the floor vanished beneath him.

He fell—but reflexively prompted a graviton current, and so bobbed up again to float in place. Hovering, Kolt looked down to see rushing water about five yards below. The stream that flowed uphill to the Coil House was plunging down into a pit, from which exhaled an all-embracing icy cold breath smelling of rank musk. The cold waterfall hissed at him as it slipped into blackness, and a mist rose to make his feet and hands tingle. It was not another room of the Coil House, down there, he knew that instinctively; it was death.

Kolt looked again at the reflected mirrors, slightly blurred by mist rising from below, and thought it would be disastrous to try his plasma wand on the glass. But there was one intuitively plangent possibility. He consulted his apps again, found an image of a door, and projected it. The hologram of the door hung in the air, was reflected in the glass, and then solidified, in keeping with the dimensional transfiguration at work in the room.

Kolt reached out, grabbed the doorknob, turned it, and the door opened. It was dark beyond.

But he had no other route, now. He drifted through the door.

And Kolt found himself in the outside world. Groaning, he landed on a span of rock and looked around, reverberating with an exquisite cognitive dissonance.

He was standing on the edge of the precipice, outside the house, listening to the tinkling mockery of the impertinent creek.

Swaying, his wounds aching, his hands trembled as he fought an impulse to switch off his graviton control and fling himself to his death in the abyss. The Coil House's influence still pushed at him, urging self-murder. Were Kolt to throw himself off the cliff, he would still end up feeding the house . . .

He turned numbly to face the Coil House. The door he had created was gone, as he'd known it would be. The curved pearly outer walls would be impervious. No use wasting plasma energy trying to blast them open.

Kolt could see the place at the tight center of the nautilus spiral, near the stony embedding, where the house's entrails would be: indeed, where the house's spine, the lightning axis would be. But the only access was through the seven rooms—so it was said. And at the seventh he'd somehow been led to take the wrong door.

It was dark out here; assertively moonless. The birds had quieted, but something else was making a long low plaintive sound, to which something else responded with idiot laughter, as if to say, *No use pleading.*

Kolt took a deep breath and gathered his innermost secret self together. Then he walked—stumbled, really—over to the curved wall of the Coil House. He reached out, ran the tips of his fingers over the shell. It was cold to the touch but vibrated with unearthly life.

Was that the axis he felt, vibrating within the Coil House? If someone gained the axis, the house always grew a new one, or so IDT claimed.

"One option you have," said The Box, startling him as it soared down to hover to his left, "is start over again. Go back to the first room, via the balcony. Of course, the house will have changed its traps, having learned."

Kolt dropped his hands from the wall and glared morosely at The Box. Start over? A psychic exhaustion weighed him down. He wanted only to sleep—but he could feel the nightmares stored up, waiting to spring at him from his subconscious. The seven chambers of the subconscious . . .

He frowned. He looked at the house. He found himself staring at the place where the spiral ended, the external marking of the house's core.

Kolt walked to it, felt the place where the spirals converged, ended . . .

A small slot was there, a few inches long, like a keyhole.

Its edges felt like the outline of a vertebra. He nodded to himself, feeling a sudden inspiration; and with it, a wellspring of energy.

Following his intuition—it was all he had left—Kolt turned to the wall again, placed his hands on it, and froze where he stood. But from the back of his head projected a beam of whirling multicolored light—an image of Kolt, stepping up to the back of Kolt's original statue-still body. The projection emanated another light, which encompassed the original, coating the true Kolt in holography. Here, the quantum uncertainty field, shaped by the Coil House's living electromagnetic emanation, made imagery into fact.

A small door opened at the base of the original Kolt's head. Within was the upper tip of Kolt's spine, the cervical vertebrae, exposed. Kolt's projected double reached in and extracted the top two vertebrae. The bone unlocked neatly from its place. The ghostly, holographic Kolt, now relatively physical, carried out Kolt's transmitted bidding: it took the tiny piece of spinal bone, which was vaguely key-shaped, to the center of the spiral; he pressed it into a slot at the very center of the spiral. He turned the key, there came a metaphysical *click*—and it was done. The projection then extracted the key—and the Coil House trembled. The projection returned to the frozen Kolt and replaced the vertebrae. The tiny door at the base of Kolt's skull shut as the projected Kolt became one with the corporeal Kolt.

Animated again, Kolt levitated to a safe distance to watch the house begin to uncoil. The Box joined him.

The Coil House unraveled like a broken mainspring; it became soft, falling inward like an imploded soufflé, then collapsed onto its side to ooze stained-glass chaos from shattered doorways.

"I'll be damned," The Box said. "That's not how it was accomplished by the others. But if you could do it that way, why didn't you do that at the start?"

"I didn't know how to, till the nautilus turned me inside out. The knowledge was locked inside me and the key had to be created."

The house had become a small hill of steaming convolutions, gray and writhing, all the shell-hardness gone from it. A fierce blue glow came from the midst of the heap. Kolt hovered over the blue glow, reached down, and then levitated triumphantly, holding the Coil House axis aloft like a fiery scepter.

He grinned and the axis flared in obedience to his mental command—teleporting him to another world. More specifically, he was sent to the comfort of Quissic Station, an orbital mansion circling old Earth.

The Box remained for a moment, watching an old woman's head crawling like a snail from the steaming detritus. The head was muttering to itself.

"I'll be damned," said The Box again, as it whirled . . . and was gone.

Notes on Contributors

Steven-Elliot Altman is a bestselling science fiction author and an award-winning videogame writer and narrative designer. His video game projects include *9Dragons, Pearl's Peril, Ancient Aliens: The Game,* and *Project Blue Book: Hidden Mysteries,* which Steve wrote and provided narrative design for based on two of The History Channel's hit television series. His latest game is *Terminator: Dark Fate* based on the upcoming feature film. Steven's novels include *Captain America Is Dead, Zen in the Art of Slaying Vampires, Batman: Fear Itself, The Killswitch Review, The Irregulars,* and *Deprivers.* He is also the editor of the critically acclaimed charity anthology *The Touch.* Steve's latest novel, *Severed Wings,* a romantic urban fantasy thriller, was recently published by WordFire Press.

Charles Beaumont (1929–1967) was an acclaimed American author of speculative fiction, including short stories in the horror and science fiction subgenres. Among his story collections are *The Hunger and Other Stories* (1958) and *The Magic Man and Other Science-Fantasy Stories* (1965). He is remembered as a writer of several classic *Twilight Zone* episodes, including "Elegy" (adapted from the short story of the same name in this volume). Beaumont also wrote the screenplays for several films, including *7 Faces of Dr. Lao* (1964), *The Intruder* (1962), and *The Masque of the Red Death* (1964), the latter two for the late filmmaker Roger Corman. He was the center of what was to become an influential nucleus of writers known as "The Group," encompassing Richard Matheson, William F. Nolan, John Tomerlin, George Clayton Johnson, Mari Wolf (the lone female member), Chad Oliver, Kris Neville, and several others.

Pushcart Prize-nominee **Jason V Brock** is a writer, editor, filmmaker, composer, scholar, and artist. His fiction and nonfiction works have appeared in many venues; his books include *Disorders of Mag-*

nitude: A Survey of Dark Fantasy (about horror and science fiction in culture), numerous anthologies, and two fiction collections. He has been nominated twice for the HWA Bram Stoker Award for his literary output, and his films (*Charles Beaumont: The Short Life of Twilight Zone's Magic Man;* the Forrest J Ackerman documentary *The AckerMonster Chronicles!*—winner of the Rondo Hatton Classic Horror Award for Best Documentary in 2014) have garnered many accolades; he is finishing another called *Image, Reflection, Shadow: Artists of the Phantastique*. He resides with his wife, Sunni, and their reptiles in Vancouver, WA.

Sunni K Brock writes about music, science, technology, art, food, and pop culture. Her fiction and poetry combine science fiction, horror, fantasy, and sometimes erotica. As one-half of the team of JaSunni Productions, LLC and Cycatrix Press, she creates genre film and printed media with her husband, Jason V Brock. If she had spare time, she would spend it researching genealogy, shopping at the farmer's market, building tricked-out computers, and conducting experiments on controlled randomness.

Harlan Ellison® (1934–2018) was an American writer, known for his prolific and influential work in New Wave speculative fiction and for his outspoken, combative personality. His published works include more than 1700 short stories, novellas, screenplays, comic book scripts, teleplays, essays, and a wide range of criticism covering literature, film, television, and print media. Some of his best-known works include the 1967 *Star Trek* episode "The City on the Edge of Forever" (he subsequently wrote a book about the experience including his original screenplay), his *A Boy and His Dog* cycle, and his short stories "I Have No Mouth, and I Must Scream" and "'Repent, Harlequin!' Said the Ticktockman." He was also editor of the landmark anthologies *Dangerous Visions* (1967) and *Again, Dangerous Visions* (1972). Ellison won numerous awards, including multiple Hugos, Nebulas, and Edgars.

Sèphera Girón is the author of several horror novels and short stories including the *Witch upon a Star* series from Riverdale Avenue Books. As well as writing novels and short stories, she has been working on screenplays for TV shows and movies in various genres. She recently was a finalist in the Stowe Story Labs Fellowship competition with her horror TV series, *The Calling*. Sèphera was born in New Orleans, grew up in London, Ontario, and then graduated from York University in Toronto, where she studied Creative Writing and Screenplay Writing. She hosts a channel on Twitch.tv (Sephera666). Currently, Sèphera lives in Toronto and has two sons.

James Gunn (1923–2020) was an American science fiction writer, editor, scholar, and anthologist. His work as an editor of anthologies includes the six-volume *Road to Science Fiction* series. He won the Hugo Award for "Best Related Work" in 1983 and he won or was nominated for several other awards for his nonfiction works in the field of science fiction studies. The Science Fiction and Fantasy Writers of America made him its 24th Grand Master in 2007, and he was inducted by the Science Fiction and Fantasy Hall of Fame in 2015. His novel *The Immortals* was adapted into a 1970–71 TV series starring Christopher George. Gunn was a professor emeritus of English and the founding director of the Center for the Study of Science Fiction, both at the University of Kansas.

William Hope Hodgson (1877–1918) was an English author. He produced a large body of work, consisting of essays, short fiction, and novels, in multiple intersecting genres, such as horror, the weird, and science fiction. Hodgson used his experiences at sea to lend authentic detail to his horror stories, many of which are set on the ocean. His novels, including *The House on the Borderland* (1908) and *The Night Land* (1912), contain more cosmic themes, but several of his novels also concentrate on horrors connected to the deep. Early in his career he wrote poetry, though few of his poems were published. He also attracted attention as a photographer and achieved fame as a bodybuilder. He died in World War I.

Award-winning author **Nancy Kilpatrick** (1946–2025) was a writer and editor in the horror/dark fantasy genre but had also written mysteries, science fiction, fantasy, and erotica. Her 23 novels include her vampire series Thrones of Blood, recently optioned for film and television. She published more than 220 short stories, seven collections of her stories, and one nonfiction book. She was also an editor with 15 anthologies to her credit.

Lisa Mannetti (1953–2021) was an award-winning author of horror and dark fantasy. She won the Bram Stoker Award for her debut novel *The Gentling Box* and was nominated four other times in both the short and long fiction categories. Her story "Everybody Wins" was made into a short film, and her novella "Dissolution" is due to be a feature-length film directed by Paul Leyden. *The Box Jumper*, a novella about Houdini, was nominated for a 2015 Bram Stoker Award and the Shirley Jackson Award, and won "Novella of the Year" from the UK website *This is Horror*. She also wrote *The New Adventures of Tom Sawyer and Huck Finn* as well as nonfiction books and numerous articles in newspapers and magazines.

Richard Christian Matheson is a #1 bestselling author/screenwriter/producer whom the *New York Times* praises as "a great horror writer." He has worked with Steven Spielberg, Tobe Hooper, Joe Dante, Aaron Spelling, Mel Brooks, Dean Koontz, Roger Corman, Stephen J. Cannell, Stephen King, and many others. He has written/executive produced 12 feature films, 20 pilots, as well as 25 primetime drama and comedy series. To date, Matheson has sold 16 spec feature screenplays and written over 500 scripts. His films, series, and limited series include *Amazing Stories*, *Three O'Clock High*, *Sole Survivor*, *Big Driver*, *Paradise*, *Masters of Horror*, *Nightmare Cinema*, and Stephen King's *Battleground* which won two Emmys. His short stories are gathered in his heralded collections *Scars and*

Other Distinguishing Marks, Zoopraxis, and the #1 bestseller *Dystopia.* His novels include *Created By* and *The Ritual of Illusion.*

George Edwards Murray is a horror/fantasy writer from Maine. His stories have appeared in *Daily Science Fiction, Bourbon Penn,* and various anthologies. When not writing, he is running, cooking, or ruminating on his various anxieties.

Ray Faraday Nelson (1931–2022) became captivated with science fiction at the age of eight at the 1939 New York World's Fair. In the 1950s he moved to Paris, where he met Allen Ginsberg, Gregory Corso, and William S. Burroughs among others of the Beat Generation, as well as existentialists Jean-Paul Sartre, Boris Vian, and Simone de Beauvoir. He subsequently co-edited *Miscellaneous Man,* the first "Beatnik" little literary review. After returning to the US in the early 1960s, he published his first work of fiction, the short story "Turn off the Sky." In 1967 he published his first novel, *The Ganymede Takeover* (in collaboration with Philip K. Dick). His book *Blake's Progress,* in which the poet William Blake and his wife are travelers in space and time, was his greatest critical success. His short story "Eight O'Clock in the Morning" (reprinted herein) was the basis of John Carpenter's cult classic *They Live* (1988).

Larry Niven earned a B.A. and D. Litt. from Washburn University, Topeka. He was first published in December 1964 with his story "The Coldest Place." Niven has published at every length—mostly fantasy, science fiction, and weirder stuff—in magazines, novels, collections, and anthologies for 58 years and counting. His latest novel is *Glorious,* part of a trilogy written with author Gregory Benford.

William F. Nolan (1928–2022) wrote mostly in the science fiction, fantasy, and horror genres. Though best known for co-authoring the acclaimed dystopian science fiction novel *Logan's Run* with the late George Clayton Johnson, Nolan was the author of more than 2000 pieces (fiction, nonfiction, articles, and books), and edited twenty-six anthologies in his nearly seventy-year career. He was co-writer (with filmmaker Dan Curtis) of the screenplay for the 1976 horror classic *Burnt Offerings* and co-wrote *Trilogy of Terror* with his friend Richard Matheson, both for Dan Curtis Productions. In the 1950s, Nolan was an integral part of the writing ensemble known as "The Group," which included many well-known writers, such as Ray Bradbury, Charles Beaumont, John Tomerlin, Matheson, and Johnson. He was voted a Living Legend in Dark Fantasy by the International Horror Guild in 2002, received the Lifetime Achievement Award from the Horror Writers Association in 2010, and was recipient of the World Fantasy Convention Award in 2013.

Jerry Pournelle (1933–2017) was an American polymath, scientist, science fiction writer, essayist, journalist, and one of the first bloggers. In the 1960s and early 1970s he worked in the aerospace industry, but eventually focused on his writing career. Pournelle's hard science fiction writing received multiple awards, and, in addition to his solo writing, he wrote several novels with collaborators, including Larry Niven. Pournelle served a term as President of the Science Fiction and Fantasy Writers of America (SFWA). Pournelle's journalism focused primarily on the computer industry, astronomy, and space exploration. He was one of the founders of the Citizens' Advisory Council on National Space Policy, which developed some of the Reagan Administration's space initiatives, including the earliest versions of what would become the Strategic Defense Initiative (SDI).

Robert J. Sawyer has won the Hugo, Nebula, and John W. Campbell Memorial Awards for Best Novel of the Year as well as the Robert A. Heinlein and Hal Clement Awards, plus a record-setting 17 Canadian Science Fiction and Fantasy Awards ("Auroras"). Rob's 24 novels include the #1 *Locus* bestsellers *The Oppenheimer Alternative, Quantum Night, Triggers,* and *Calculating God,* as well as *FlashForward,* the basis for the ABC TV series of the same name. He was one of the initial nine inductees into the Canadian Science

Fiction and Fantasy Hall of Fame and is a member of the Order of Canada, his country's highest honor.

A career-retrospective of **Darrell Schweitzer**'s short fiction was published by PS Publishing in two volumes in 2020. A veritable flood of Schweitzeriana soon followed from various publishers, including a new Lovecraftian anthology, *Shadows out of Time* (PS Publishing), *The Best of Weird Tales: The 1920s* (Centipede Press), *The Best of Weird Tales: 1924* (with John Betancourt, Wildside Press), a new story collection, *The Children of Chorazin* (Hippocampus Press), a weird poetry collection, *Dancing Before Azathoth* (forthcoming from Hippocampus Press) and two further volumes of author interviews (Wildside Press). His novels include *The White Isle, The Shattered Goddess, The Mask of the Sorcerer,* and *The Dragon House.* He is a four-time World Fantasy Award nominee and one-time winner, as co-editor of *Weird Tales,* a magazine he co-edited for 19 years, between 1988 and 2007. He is also an active anthologist of Lovecraftian matters, his most recent gathering being *Mountains of Madness Revealed* (PS Publishing, 2019).

John Shirley is the author of numerous novels, including *Demons, Wetbones, Cellars, City Come A-Walkin', A Splendid Chaos, Bioshock: Rapture, Demons, The Other End,* and the *Eclipse* trilogy. His newest novels are *Stormland* and *A Sorcerer of Atlantis.* His story collection *Black Butterflies* won the Bram Stoker Award. His new story collection is *The Feverish Stars.* He is co-screenwriter of *The Crow* and has written teleplays and animation. Jackanapes Press released his book of weird poetry, *The Voice of the Burning House,* and the new expanded edition of his story collection, *Really Really Really Really Weird Stories.* He wrote the lyrics for five songs on Blue Öyster Cult's new hit album, *The Symbol Remains.*

Robert Silverberg has been a professional writer since 1955, the year before he graduated from Columbia University, and has published more than a hundred books and close to a thousand short stories.

His books and stories have been translated into forty languages. Among his best-known novels are *Lord Valentine's Castle*, *Dying Inside*, *The Book of Skulls*, *Nightwings*, *The World Inside*, and *Downward to the Earth*. His collaboration with Isaac Asimov, a novel called *The Positronic Man* was later made into a movie starring Robin Williams named *The Bicentennial Man*. He is a many-time winner of the Hugo and Nebula awards, was Guest of Honor at the World Science Fiction Convention in 1970, was named to the Science Fiction Hall of Fame in 1999, and in 2004 was named a Grand Master by the Science Fiction Writers of America, of which he is a past president.

Bruce Taylor ("Mr. Magic Realism") writes a blending of Magic Realism with horror/fantasy and science fiction. He co-edited, with Elton Elliott, an anthology, *Like Water for Quarks*, that illustrates the unique perspective a Magic Realism context can provide for the three main genres in imaginative literature. Bruce has been writer in residence at Shakespeare & Company, Paris, a finalist for the &NOW Award for Innovative Writing, SUNY, for his novella and short story collection *Kafka's Uncle and Other Strange Tales*, as well as a finalist for the Governor's Award for his first collection, *The Final Trick of Funnyman*.

Jonathan Thomas reports: "The first movie I can remember my mother treating me to was either *Angry Red Planet* or *The Mysterians*, on some loose pretext of stimulating my preschool imagination. She was then surprised and alarmed when I started having nightmares. The point is, I made no great distinction between horror/weird fiction and science fiction from an early age. Give or take a couple of decades later, my publishing career began with a few scripts to Warren Comics and has gathered steam since 2008 when Hippocampus Press issued the collection *Midnight Call and Other Stories*. A further five collections from Hippocampus followed, plus the Lovecraftian novels *The Color over Occam* (Arcane Wisdom,

2012) and *A Season of Centuries* (available in German as *Der Finstere Abgrund der Zeit* [Edition Bärenklau, 2020]). I'm married to the singer and artist Angel Dean and hope to finish a third Lovecraftian novel one of these years."

John C. Tibbetts is an Emeritus Professor at the University of Kansas, where he taught Film and Media for more than 30 years. As a broadcaster he has produced programming for NPR and Voice of America and hosted his own television and radio shows in Kansas City as an Entertainment Editor. His more than 25 books include *Peter Weir: Interviews, Schumann: A Chorus of Voices, The Gothic Worlds of Peter Straub, The Gothic Imagination, Douglas Fairbanks and the American Century, The Furies of Marjorie Bowen,* and, most recently, *The Devil Snar'd: Novels, Appreciations, and Appendices by Marjorie Bowen* and *G. K. Chesterton: Gargoyles and Grotesques* (all of which contain his own paintings and cover designs). He was awarded the Kansas Educator of the Year Award in 2009.

H. G. Wells (1866–1946) was an English writer. Prolific in many genres, he wrote dozens of novels, short stories, and works of social commentary, history, satire, biography, and autobiography. Wells is now best remembered for his science fiction novels and is sometimes called the "father of science fiction." During his own lifetime, he was prominent as a forward-looking, even prophetic social critic who devoted his literary talents to the development of a progressive vision on a global scale. A futurist, he wrote a number of utopian works and foresaw the advent of aircraft, tanks, space travel, nuclear weapons, satellite television, and something resembling the World Wide Web. His science fiction imagined time travel, alien invasion, invisibility, and biological engineering. His most notable science fiction works include *The Time Machine* (his first novel), *The Island of Doctor Moreau, The Invisible Man, The War of the Worlds,* and the military science fiction book *The War in the Air.* Wells was nominated for the Nobel Prize in Literature four times.

F. Paul Wilson is the award-winning, *New York Times* bestselling author of more than eighty books and nearly 100 short stories spanning science fiction, horror, adventure, medical thrillers, and virtually everything between. *The Tomb* received the Porgie Award from the *West Coast Review of Books; Wheels within Wheels* won the first Prometheus Award. His novella "Aftershock" won the Bram Stoker Award. He was voted Grand Master by the World Horror Convention, received the Lifetime Achievement Award from the Horror Writers of America, and the Thriller Lifetime Achievement Award from the editors of *Romantic Times*. He also received the prestigious Inkpot Award from San Diego Comic-Con. In 1983 his novel *The Keep* was adapted into a film directed Michael Mann. More than nine million copies of his books are in print in the US and his work has been translated into twenty-four languages. He also has written for the stage, screen, and interactive media.

Stephen Woodworth is the author of the Violet Series of paranormal thrillers, including the *New York Times* bestsellers *Through Violet Eyes* and *With Red Hands,* as well as the Gothic horror novel *Fraulein Frankenstein*. His work has also appeared in such publications as the *Los Angeles Times, Fantasy & Science Fiction,* the *Black Wings* series of Lovecraftian fiction anthologies, and *Year's Best Fantasy*. He has won first place in the Writers of the Future Contest and the Grand Prize in the 2020 Shore Scripts 1-Hour TV Pilot Contest. His first collection of horror short fiction, *A Carnival of Chimeras,* is available from Hippocampus Press.

Acknowledgments

"AGNES" by Sunni K Brock is original to this anthology.

"Camera Aeterna" by Steven-Elliot Altman is original to this anthology.

"Celeste" by Stephen Woodworth is original to this anthology.

 "Eight O'Clock in the Morning" by Ray Faraday Nelson, first published in the *Magazine of Fantasy and Science Fiction* (November 1963). Reprinted by permission of the author.

"Elegy" by Charles Beaumont, original version first published in *Imagination* (February 1953). This version is in the public domain.

"Eloi, Eloi, Lama Sabachthani" by William Hope Hodgson, first published as "The Baumoff Explosive" in *Nash's Weekly* (20 September 1919). The story is in the public domain.

"En Pointe Troupe" by Sèphera Girón is original to this anthology.

"Full Circle" by Bruce Taylor is original to this anthology.

"I Have No Mouth, and I Must Scream" by Harlan Ellison, first published in *If* (March 1967). Reprinted by permission of the author.

"It Comes and Goes" by Robert Silverberg, first published in *Playboy* (January 1992). Reprinted by permission of the author.

"Magnus Victor Rex" by Lisa Mannetti is original to this anthology.

"Metal Fatigue" by Nancy Kilpatrick, first published in *Bizarre Sex and Other Crimes of Passion*, edited by Stan Tal (Richard Kasak/Masquerade Books, 1994). Reprinted by permission of the author.

"Monsters" by James Gunn is original to this anthology.

"On Big Red: A New Martian Chronicle" by William F. Nolan is original to this anthology.

"One Across" by Jonathan Thomas is original to this anthology.

"Peking Man" by Robert J. Sawyer, first published in *Dark Destiny III: Children of Dracula,* edited by Edward E. Kramer (White Wolf Publishing, 1996). Reprinted by permission of the author.

"Performance" by F. Paul Wilson, first published in *Bad News,* edited by Richard Laymon (Cemetery Dance Publications, 2000). Reprinted by permission of the author.

"Role Play" by Richard Christian Matheson is original to this anthology.

"The Secret Language of Stones" by Darrell Schweitzer is original to this anthology.

"Seven Rooms and the Key" by John Shirley is original to this anthology.

"The Star" by H. G. Wells, first published in the "Christmas Number" of the *Graphic* (1897). The story is in the public domain.

"Story Night at the Stronghold" by Larry Niven and Jerry Pournelle, first published in *Analog Science Fiction and Fact* (July–August 2016). Reprinted by permission of the authors.

"They Will All Be Opened in Time" by George Edwards Murray is original to this anthology.

www.ingramcontent.com/pod-product-compliance
Lightning Source LLC
Chambersburg PA
CBHW060950030726
47503CB00003B/815